FIRST SUN, LAST SUN

by Robert Kline

This is a work of fiction. All events, locations, institutions, themes, persons, characters, and plot are completely fictional. Any resemblance to places or persons, living or dead, are of the invention of the author.

Copyright ©2002 by Robert Kline. All rights reserved. Printed in the United States of America

This book or any portion thereof may not be reproduced in whole or in part in any form or by any means without written permission of the publisher, except by a reviewer who may quote brief passages in a review. For information, or to order copies, contact:

>Galaxy Books, Inc.
>Post Office Box 1421
>Orange Park, FL 32067 or
>www.galaxybooksinc.com or
>Email info@galaxybooksinc.com

First Edition
Publisher: Galaxy Books, Inc., Orange Park, Florida
Cover Design: Graphics Ink Design Studio, St. Augustine, Florida
Cover Photos: Angela Kline

ISBN 0-9652682-4-1

It would be a lesser journey without a family.
Sheree, Angela, Mathew, Maxwell, Ariana —
thanks for your love.

FIRST SUN, LAST SUN
by Robert Kline

CHRISTINA

The first sun brushed the brick of the high keep tower, flowed orange down its sides, and then washed the slate roof below. The mansion awoke with the new day; its servants bustling from room to room, opening windows, laying out silver, or simply checking to be certain everything was in its proper place. The sun cleared the distant tree tops and its light burst upon scores of windows and thousands of panes before it finally settled to the lawn and warmed the tended grass.

It was morning.

Christina, barely seventeen and still in her night dress, stood behind the keep's castellated wall and watched. She was almost fifty feet above the flagstones at the front entry, for the broad tower rose rectangular from the heart of the manor and soared above all but the tallest chimneys. The roofs slanted off beneath the girl. The house spread at her feet.

The gardeners were not about yet but Christina watched the horse carts from the local farms clomp up the long delivery road with fresh milk and cream, eggs and vegetables and meat.

And then something else caught her attention. First one and then another of the carriage house doors yawned slowly outward and Christina saw a small figure leave the last door and dance in the shadows around one of her father's automobiles. It was Rudolph, she was certain, and he would be driving off soon for the rail station to pick up packages.

She no sooner thought these things when a small cloud of smoke tumbled out past the stable doors, followed by a muted rumble. But it was the long touring car, not the Ford, which rolled out and headed toward the mansion.

Papa is going somewhere!

It was business, therefore, and once he departed, Christina and her sisters would enjoy a modicum of freedom, for Mrs. Van Luxall could not enforce his iron discipline. When he was home he was the master of their grand ship, and the girls moved quietly at the periphery of his moody shadow, but in his absence they were no longer conscripts on an unsinkable liner parting the turbulent seas. It was at anchor and vulnerability immediately tormented Mrs. Van Luxall. She wandered the halls, she stayed in her room, she took naps.

Rudolph guided the long auto to the front entry and when he drove off moments later, Christina saw there were only a few leather suitcases strapped to the back.

Pittsburgh or Cleveland.

And with her father and Rudolph away the girls were not the only ones unfettered; the fun would begin at any moment for Stephen, the chauffeur's son.

Christina smiled to herself and watched her father's automobile mutter softly past the gatehouse and out of sight. She immediately ran to the back wall of the keep and peered through one of the slotted gaps. She could see beyond the reflecting pool and into the hidden garden.

"The English Garden" her parents called it, but to the children it was the hidden garden, for from nowhere but where she now stood could anyone see into it; the stone walls too high, the occasional barred window too small.

It was the place for a rendezvous.

Christina moved along the wall, studying each slightly different view afforded by the succession of crenels. She saw a movement to the left, hesitated, and then rolled her eyes when she realized it was a fat duck waddling toward the pond near the forest.

Again and again she covered every shadow and each open way until she thought, *Perhaps I'm wrong. Maybe he'll stay inside and work his mischief there.*

But she didn't really believe that, for the servants and staff were everywhere and just as anxious as she to discover something deliciously clandestine — particularly, if it involved Stephen, the driver's son. He was the manor's devil and its delight. He was handsome and humorous and without fear, relying on fortune to keep him ahead of the grasp of reality. And so far he was very, very lucky.

Christina paced back to the middle and watched both entrances to the garden. As she did she saw a flash of white by the benches and the statue. White — a chambermaid! And she guessed who it would be — little Rosey, the saucy daughter of the linen mistress. Tart and often angry, she was in love with boys and the pleasure she could take from them.

Christina cursed herself for having forgotten the spy glass.

She squinted into the distance and then turned and raced to the trap door. She moved quickly down the narrow stairs, pulling the door closed over her as she descended, then exited the fourth story library, took the spiral stairs to the third floor study and passed into her bedroom.

The size of her bedroom and its proximity to the upper rooms of the keep had been conceived with the notion of their being a portion of the master suite; but Christina's mother had moved to the front when she realized a bedroom at the rear of the house did not afford a view of arriving guests.

That was the only mistake their architect had made, and Christina often heard her father boast that, "It was only one error and not so bad; but if it had happened a few hundred years earlier, on a different continent, he would have lost his head!"

The first time she heard him say that, it had been in the stout little architect's presence, and while the man was renowned, she had seen him flinch and whither. But she had watched many do that when receiving her father's attention. She had done so herself often enough when she was younger.

Not any more.

Christina drew a dark cloak over her sleeping gown and stepped into the tiny elevator beside her dressing room. Her father loved to remind visitors that there were five elevators in their home — more than in all of the buildings downtown, combined.

The apparatus descended smoothly through the interior walls of the house, passing the second and first floors, finally coming to rest in the cavernous basement. The young girl pulled the paneled door quietly to the side and listened. It was still. The smell of mold and coal intermingled and crept into the elevator with her. Hooded lights disappeared in three cool and haunting directions, casting shadows across the vaulted brick ceiling and the smooth, cobbled floor. After she was certain there was nothing to be heard, Christina studied the dark corners nearest her. At last she summoned her courage and hurried past them, rushing headlong into a tunnel which ran under the terrace and the reflecting pool, ending at the hidden garden.

There were other passages, leading to the Carriage House, the Octagon, and the Hexagon — each designed to unobtrusively connect the Main House kitchen with the serving areas in the walled garden and the two pavilions; and in the case of the Carriage House, to provide covered access to the motor vehicles should it be required.

Following the baby's death the hidden garden fell into disuse, and so the only persons who traveled its tunnel did so for reasons other than the service of food. It was the least well lighted of all the passages; but fortunately, it was also the shortest.

Christina hurried through it. She came to the door at its terminus and listened carefully before she swung it inward. The back windows flooded the sitting room with light and the girl hesitated as her eyes adjusted.

There was an adolescent laugh and then a giggle from the garden.

Christina peeked through one of the clear panes in a leaded window. She could not see them, so they weren't standing. She was sure of that.

And the new sounds confirmed it. A spirited and rhythmic moaning echoed softly inside the stone room.

Christina bit her fist to stifle a laugh. She lowered herself slowly to a crouch and reached up and carefully depressed the latch on the thick wooden door. It stuck at first then finally broke loose and raised without a sound.

She slowly pulled the door open an inch and peered out, her auburn hair falling forward as she did.

It was Stephen, alright, she was sure — not that she saw his face or recognized his pale bobbing bottom. It was Stephen, and the flash of red hair confirmed that he was with Rosey.

They lay entangled on one of the stone benches flanking Christina's door, their movements suggesting a complex and many-levered machine. Because of their preoccupation and the way they faced — Rosey toward the sky and Stephen at the ivied wall beside them — neither noticed what Christina was about.

On another bench, the one closer to the open door, was a pile of clothing. The boy had apparently tossed his pants aside first, and on them was a black broadcloth dress and various articles of underclothing. Beside the multicolored mound was a white bib apron, its ties hanging limply to the ground, snaking across Stephen's collarless shirt.

Christina stared and chose.

With a furtive hand she grabbed the garments one by one and dragged them unnoticed through the crack at the portal.

Stephen began to grunt loudly.

Christina's eyes widened when she heard desperation in his voice.

Rosey urged Stephen to continue.

Christina hurriedly bunched the clothes behind her, sneaked another quick look at the couple, and then pushed the door closed as quietly as possible. She jumped when Rosey and then Stephen raised their voices in protest and assent, at first thinking she had been seen.

"NO!"

"YES! YES!"

Christina leaned against the door, concerned for Stephen. It wasn't until she heard them whispering and giggling once more that she continued.

But Christina didn't leave the door as she had found it. Instead, she massaged a wrought iron bar through its guides, locking the door securely. The only return now available to Stephen and his friend was through the gardens and across the lawn.

Christina listened for one more moment, even though she knew that if she dallied much longer she'd be missed. It wouldn't do to be discovered running around in her night clothes.

The cramped elevator seemed to take forever to lift her to her room. Finally, it slowed and then stopped, but Christina hesitated before she opened the door. Someone was in her room.

The elevator door was opened from outside.

Her sisters, dressed for breakfast, stood and gaped at her.

Katherine, darker and almost as tall, stepped to the side. "Christina! Where've you been?"

"Tell us! Tell us!" Abegaile begged. She was the shortest and seemed always on the verge of a sad discovery.

"I tricked Stephen!" Christina exclaimed, "And I caught Rosey, too!" and the three sisters laughed and shrieked as Christina dressed for breakfast and recounted the details.

"You saw his bum!" Katherine gasped and drew her hands to her mouth.

"They were — ", Abegaile couldn't think of a word she could use. She gave up and whispered, " — really?"

"You actually *saw* him?" Katherine pursued. She considered herself the most mature of the three and couldn't believe Christina had just leaped ahead of her in life experiences.

They discussed the encounter for a while longer, until Abegaile pulled away from the story and added somberly, "You're not fair, Chrissy; if Mama finds out she'll surely have Rosey and her mother sent off."

"Mama should!" Christina answered without pause. "Rosey shouldn't be running about the grounds without her clothing. How would it look for Papa? Besides, I didn't undress them. And, if they'd been paying the least bit of attention, they'd never have lost their clothes in the first place." She reached her conclusion with shaky finality, for in spite of her proclamation, she didn't wish either of them to get into real trouble — even though Rosey was too attractive for her own good. So was Stephen, for that matter.

"And what about Stephen?" Abegaile added. "What if he's caught and he and his father have to leave? Papa wouldn't let them stay. What then?"

There was a discreet knock. A subdued voice carried through the door. "You are expected in the breakfast room."

The three girls looked at each other. Christina quickly combed through her hair. Katherine brushed the front of her dress and Abegaile shined the toes of her shoes on the backs of her fresh stockings.

"Dough boys!" Christina whispered.

The girls were all in their late teens, but their isolation and wealth, and the fact that they were never taken seriously, gave them little reason to mature.

They lined up in army seriousness — Christina followed by Katherine, followed by Abegaile — and marched to the door and down the hall. They descended the stairs, still in file. It was not until they reached the wide and open entrance to the breakfast room that they broke ranks and entered, each the picture of the well-behaved and humble child.

"Good morning, Mama," they said, one after the other, and a tired but friendly woman smiled at each of them.

Mrs. Van Luxall loved her children — loved her girls — as she loved her husband. But they, as the rest of the world, exhausted her with their constant demands. Requests, really; most times subtle and often imagined, but regardless, she felt she was bombarded from dawn through dusk.

The girls, chair-straight and correct, ate in silence until their mother spoke.

"Your father will be gone for a week. He asked me to tell you that he expects you to cause no problems, to be kind to one another, and to do as you're told."

As he always did. At least as Mrs. Van Luxall always said he did. The girls doubted he mentioned them at all.

Christina looked across the table at Katherine. Katherine stared back and Abegaile watched them.

It was as if Christina and Katherine were the twins and Abegaile the odd one; when in fact, Katherine and Abegaile had been born minutes apart, Abegaile waiting even then for Katherine to go first. But everything was mixed up now and nothing was right. Especially since each of the girls desperately wished she had been born a boy — born her father's son — as much to be what their father wanted as to provide the peace the others craved.

The one who died — Mrs. Van Luxall's last baby — had been that son.

After breakfast the girls separated, each to take an hour's instruction in music, history, or etiquette, whereupon they traded instructors and continued their lessons for another hour, trading once more, until three hours had passed and their tutors departed.

Afterward, they met in Katherine's room.

Abegaile was unhinged. "This could be dreadful; I think Rosey's been caught!" She ran to one of the back windows and stared in the direction of the walled garden as if she could see it all re-enacted, the bare girl dashing from bush to bush.

"But how could you *know*?" Christina asked. She sat on Katherine's bed and kicked her legs idly. "You've been in lessons, too. Surely, neither Mr. Stittsdom nor Miss Wuthersly nor Miss Hagemann would have heard anything. And they wouldn't pass it on to any of us if they had — they wouldn't dare."

Abegaile dropped her head and walked to her twin's bed. She threw herself onto it with resignation. Christina felt sorry for her. She hadn't intended to hurt her feelings; it just didn't make sense that she could know anything about Rosey.

"But how do you *know*, Abbie?" Katherine said, repeating Christina's question.

Abegaile came back to life and turned to her.

"Well, I'm not *absolutely* sure, but while I was practicing, a string broke on my violin. Mr. Stittsdom had an absolute seizure while he fixed it, grumbling and carrying on, so I went to the windows and I saw an auto leaving."

"That's all?" Christina interrupted despite herself. No matter how hard she tried she always lost patience with Abegaile. Christina feared she was taking after her father.

"And whom did we see enter Mama's room as we came up the stairs?" Abegaile threw back.

"Mary Ann!" Katherine answered, beginning to understand.

"That's right," Abegaile continued, her tone buoyed with unaccustomed superiority.

Mary Ann would have no reason to speak to their mother unless the linen mistress were ill — or soon to be replaced.

The girls were silent for a moment.

"This is terrible," Katherine said, shaking her head as she thought of the situation.

Christina fought with her guilt and the rising fear that Stephen had been caught, too. It had seemed like such a wonderful joke. "We must ask Anna," she pronounced.

The twins nodded.

Anna was their chambermaid and had been forever. Katherine and Christina raced for the maid's pull.

Anna entered Katherine's room. She breasted her way in, a great white locomotive steaming into the forest of childishness.

"Mistress rang?" she asked, entirely superfluously.

It was always the same — she would be totally unapproachable unless one of the girls went to her.

"Anna! Anna!" Katherine exclaimed. "Whatever is happening here? What's happened to our linen mistress and the driver's son?" She thought that by not mentioning Stephen's name she could lessen his guilt.

Anna was a solid Irish woman who thought thoroughly before she spoke. She looked down at Katherine, surprised at the question, and then she smiled to herself as a piece to a different puzzle fell into place. *So that's how it was — the children involved. And Rudolph's son Scot-free once more!*

Christina watched the maid's distant eyes and knew Abegaile had been right — Rosey was gone.

"What of Stephen?" Christina asked quietly before Anna answered Katherine.

"Please do sit and tell us," Abegaile pleaded.

Anna reached behind her and closed the door. She smiled briefly then thought better of friendliness and became very stern, her brogue doing little to soften her tone.

"Lives have been torn up, young ladies. Claire did her job well — although I dare say she'll not be having a difficult time findin' another — but that's not be the point. If you girls were responsible," her eyes narrowed and settled on Christina as she continued, "then you should rightly be ashamed. There's nothing can be done now. 'Tis over. But if I was walkin' in your fancy shoes, I'd not sleep well."

Christina smiled to herself, careful to keep it hidden. *Who could sleep well in fancy shoes?* she thought, but then she remembered the boy and couldn't help asking again, "Stephen?"

"I suspected it might of been," Anna said. "It seems he was a bit more *careful* than Rosey." She thought briefly and then continued, "Are you saying he was similarly — ," she paused, "attired?"

Christina nodded without realizing it.

Anna couldn't help herself. She smiled broadly, fought it, and then chuckled through her set face.

"I've heard nothing, although I suspect he'll be creatin' his own problems soon enough. Even a clever fox is quickly caught if he visits the hen house often enough!"

"Anna!" Katherine teased. "Whatever do you mean? We don't have *hens*!"

"Well, you've a rooster, sure enough!"

Anna turned to the door and asked over her shoulder, "Will that be all?"

Christina answered, "Yes, Anna, thank you."

But before Anna left she added, "Aye, and young Rosey would of gotten into trouble sooner or later on her own, make no mistake; but it wasn't right — your helping her along. You're fine young ladies with the world spreadin' at your feet — be mindful of where you trod."

And she was gone.

After the midday meal Christina led the girls toward the walled garden. Abegaile trailed and glanced repeatedly back at the manor. "If Mama sees us we'll be in trouble," she warned.

No one but the gardener and the watchman was allowed to enter the hidden garden. Mrs. Van Luxall had somehow managed to turn it into a memorial for her lost baby.

"She *will* be angry, Chrissy," Katherine agreed. "Let's not make her angry while Papa is away."

The girls stuttered along cutting rose buds.

Christina couldn't stand it. It was as if the joy of life inexorably welled up inside her until she exploded. She threw down her snips and the basket she carried and looked at her sisters. "Can't catch — can't catch," she teased and ran off through a break in the bushes.

Both Katherine and Abegaile knew in a second where she would hide and neither was anxious to follow, but as usual, they found themselves incapable of restraint. They, too, dropped their snips and gave chase, pale dresses snagging from time to time on thorns as the twins wove after their older sister.

Christina circled far behind the hidden garden and entered by the gardener's door. Once inside she ran along the southern wall where she knew she couldn't be seen, even from her own perch on the keep tower. She passed beside the long reflecting pool and the rows of low flowers.

When she reached the stone benches of that morning she sank to her knees and searched under one. She probed the back corner with her fingers until she touched the paper she had hoped would be there. She pulled it out, brushed the dirt off of it, and sat on the bench. She then unfolded the paper quickly, picking out spare, crudely written words as she did.

Rosey — trick — trouble.

Then she settled into reading with care.

"You are a DEVIL," it said, "Rosey was caught. She knows it was your TRICK. YOU have a new ENEMY. Leave my CLOTHES here — I need them. I'm not rich, YOU KNOW!" It ended with the taunt, "I'LL GET YOU!"

Christina smiled and clutched the note to her. "'I'll get you,' indeed, Stephen Rheiner!" she whispered and laughed. Then she heard Abegaile stumbling along the outside wall. Christina jumped to the door to make her escape through the house tunnel, but the door was still locked. Just then Katherine and Abegaile ran into the garden from the far entrance. They went to opposite sides and raced toward Christina, who was now attempting to hide behind the fountain and its statues — a naked young woman with her arms outstretched stood above two frolicking and cherubic children.

Abegaile and Katherine reached Christina at the same time. They stood at her sides and asked simultaneously, "Well?"

Christina looked to each twin. "Well, what?"

"You know!" Katherine said, irritated to have to ask. "Did he leave a message?"

"A note — is there a note?" Abegaile begged as she tugged at Christina's arm.

The girl shook herself free and held out her hand with the folded paper.

"Read it! Read it!" Abegaile nearly screamed.

As Christina paused to be certain the twins were adequately attentive, she placed her free hand on the bronze woman's knee. Christina was the only one of the sisters who ever touched their father's precious statuary. She watched her sisters start when she did.

"Papa's lady!" Abegaile gasped.

Christina ignored her and read. After she finished she looked at her sisters and carefully refolded the note. Katherine was so delighted she raised to her toes. "You're in trouble, Chrissy! Rosey will try to get even!"

"Well, I'm certainly not frightened of a maid!"

"But Rosey's not like the rest of them;" Abegaile countered, "she's *crazy*!"

"*And* she's gone," Christina concluded as she ran her hand over the statue's leg. She did not feel the bravado she was masquerading. In fact, she was struggling with the guilt for Rosey's dismissal.

The girls looked at the standing woman. She was tall and thin with narrow shoulders and small breasts. She was life-size and with her pedestal she towered over them. Normally, water bubbled gently from her hands and fell onto the upturned and laughing faces of the cast children beneath her. But the water wasn't running now; Stephen had apparently forgotten after Christina's trick.

He was responsible for a myriad of odd jobs on the grounds and in the manor and one of them was to monitor the water valves for the garden. The sun was to rise on flowing fountains.

Christina felt the cool, smooth metal beneath her hand. "Some day someone will make a statue of me!"

The twins giggled as they pictured themselves naked and standing in a garden.

"Let's sneak down tonight and play statues!" Christina exclaimed and then challenged, "I dare you!"

"You're wicked!" Abegaile teased, blushing.

And then they noticed that the fountain was dry. Katherine stepped to its side and touched the empty pool. "Maybe Stephen was caught; he never forgets the fountains."

She had no sooner finished when a deluge of water burst from the woman's hands, cascading in all directions, quickly drenching the three girls.

The pressure abated. Water fell gently to the waiting cherubs.

Christina sputtered through soaking hair. Belatedly, Katherine jumped back, nearly tripping when she did. Abegaile stood in rigid disbelief. The yoke of her yellow sun dress was sagging wet in some places and clinging in others. Christina blew a strand of dripping hair away from her mouth and stamped her foot.

There was a laugh from the little building behind them. The door cracked open and three towels shot through the gap.

Christina turned and raced for the door. "STEPHEN!" she shouted. The door closed and the bolt scraped home just as she grabbed the handle. She pounded, her fists barely making a sound.

Katherine and Abegaile grabbed two of the towels and began to dry themselves. Christina continued pounding.

Until she heard the bolt dragged free.

She threw her weight against the big door. It creaked open and Christina raced in.

But there was nothing to discover in the slants of dusty light. The boy had fled and she was not about to pursue him through the tunnel.

She left the building, retrieved a towel and tortured her hair with it.

"Mama will be *so* angry!" Abegaile moaned. "Whatever will we tell her?"

Katherine looked at her twin and then down at herself. She started to laugh as Christina walked over to them, a big towel wrapped around her head.

Christina's towel shook free and she grabbed it and attacked her hair in renewed rage. "He knew we'd come for the note and he knew we'd go to the fountain! I hate him! I hate him! I hate him!"

The twins faked surprise at her outburst and then laughed in earnest.

Christina fumed. She threw down her towel and went back through Stephen's door. Katherine dropped her towel at the fountain and went to catch up with Christina. Abegaile stayed with her twin, folding her towel as she ran.

Christina led them through the tunnel. As they neared the middle, she slowed. She was listening. Abegaile and Katherine bumped up behind her. Christina stopped and raised a finger to her lips. She cocked one ear toward the far end of the tunnel.

"Don't you dare!" she hissed. "Don't you dare give it even one thought!"

She waited.

Abegaile held her breath.

Christina called, warning, "You'll get into trouble, Stephen! And then *you'll* be gone, too." She cringed at her words.

It was as if her last syllable had touched a switch. The lights went out. The bare bulbs gave a last pulsing glow and then died completely. Darkness raced through the tunnel.

Abegaile grabbed Christina's arm and squeaked. Katherine clutched the other arm. The cool void engulfed them. The girls stood rooted to the floor.

In addition to the cloying darkness, there were sounds. Frightening sounds. Water plinked.

Rodent-like rustlings traversed the stygian gutterways, echoing, seemingly surrounding them.

Stone rasped.

Katherine heard Abegaile swallow. Abegaile heard Katherine chirp when a stone skipped and rattled through the tunnel.

Christina turned to judge the distance back to the garden house, even though it was just as uninviting. At least Stephen wouldn't be there — but then they'd be back where they'd started and they couldn't just leave the garden from there and cross the grounds soaking wet.

She hesitated. The twins became more frightened. A faint sound came from the manor end of the tunnel. And then another accented the darkness. And another.

At first, Christina thought it would lessen her fear. It had to be Stephen. She told Abegaile and Katherine, "It's him. I know it is." But she didn't sound as reassuring as she had hoped she would. She didn't sound reassuring at all.

It's him! played in all of their fantasies.

It's him!

It's him!

Abegaile felt a scream building in her chest. She knew she shouldn't scream — it would mean disaster for all of them. They'd be in serious trouble and Stephen would be gone for certain. She swallowed the rising panic. Her fingernails dug into Katherine's arm.

"Rosey?" Katherine whispered to Christina just as the same thought teased her.

Now the thing coming toward them was dragging a foot.

It was absurd. Christina wished to feel relieved, for certainly Rosey wouldn't play *that* kind of game. But she didn't feel any better. She tried to control her imagination. *Maybe it isn't Stephen or Rosey. What if Stephen ran off and someone else — ? Who really knows what goes on in the cellar? Anyone could live there.*

Katherine's mind explored her own horrific scenarios. She remembered the men who delivered the mountains of coal. *What if one of them had stayed behind? And what of the stoker – he was an odd one.* "The coal men," she whispered.

An army of unfortunates brought coal, driving their sooty dump trucks and eyeing the manor all the while. "Ten tons of coal a day," the girls had been instructed by their father. "Ten tons of coal to heat fifty-eight rooms. Ten tons a day to warm five persons."

Two winters ago the watchman had found an old rag man hiding in the coal room. He was in the last throes of senility and pneumonia and looked more pathetic than frightening. Mr. Van Luxall had him dragged out and driven to the property limits.

The coal men — Christina and Katherine thought.

"The rag man's ghost," Abegaile whimpered so quietly no one heard her.

The shuffling stopped.

Christina could feel Abegaile now at her side, shaking and holding onto her arm. Katherine gave a brief sob.

"I'm sorry," Christina whispered down the tunnel. "I'm sorry — please don't frighten us any more." She surprised herself when she didn't use Stephen's name. She *wasn't* certain.

The thing in the tunnel groaned.

And laughed.

"Stephen!" Christina spat, and Katherine and Abegaile let out their breath in unison. Christina felt Abegaile's grip loosen on her arm. Katherine straightened.

Stephen called softly, "Walk to me; I won't do anything — I promise."

The girls started forward again. As they did, Christina and Katherine concentrated on the boy and how far in front of them he might be. Abegaile remembered the darkness behind and imagined things following. The cool air toyed with the back of her neck. Her wet dress chilled her.

"I'm here," the voice said and it was much closer than they had anticipated. "Reach out your hands."

Christina and Katherine extended their arms in front of them. Abegaile would have nothing to do with it.

At last, Christina and then Katherine brushed against his hand.

"Hello," Stephen said.

"Hello, Stephen," Katherine answered.

"Hello," Abegaile squeaked, relieved, but now anxious to get in front of the others. She went to crowd by and then realized that it was dark in front of them, too.

The boy laughed when he felt a wet dress brush against his arm. "Somebody's been in the rain!"

"You're not funny," Katherine accused.

Abegaile taunted, "You could get us all into trouble, Stephen. You probably ruined my new dress." Abegaile loved talking to Stephen. She was not as pretty as her sisters, and she was usually shy, but she couldn't help herself when he was near.

"Your new dress?" he chided. "I thought all your dresses were new. I bet you've never even touched old clothes, never mind mended ones. In fact, I bet I've seen more patches than you've seen stars!" he continued, exaggerating.

Stephen dressed well for his station but he played with the role of the downtrodden servant. "Christina, are you here?" he asked.

She hadn't spoken yet.

"You can't be angry with *me*, Christina, after what you did. Rosey and her mother are gone. That wasn't fair. You can't be angry." There was a touch of pleading in the way he spoke.

"Besides," he continued, "I know something you don't. In fact, I know two things you don't."

The three girls walked with the boy in silence for a few more paces. Each of them savored the thought of Stephen so near, in the dark. He wasn't particularly large — average height, actually — but he exuded strength even at seventeen. There was no room for danger when they concentrated on Stephen.

Finally, Christina couldn't avoid his bait.

"What are your *secrets*, Stephen?"

He didn't answer immediately. He cleared his throat noisily.

"Rosey and her mother were leaving anyway — they were hired off by Fairelawn."

Fairelawn was the home of Paxton Mansfield Wingate, industrialist. (People didn't hire servants; *manors* did. One worked for Fairelawn or Stan Hywet or The Chimneys.)

Christina felt as if a weight had just been lifted from her. And then she thought about Rosey and Fairelawn and the Wingate family. Nelson Andrew Wingate, several years older than she, was the only son of Paxton Wingate. And he was the boy Mrs. Van Luxall was always pushing on the girls.

It was not an unpleasant push; he was handsome, well mannered, and arrived driving the most interesting automobiles. But he was usually terribly boring and always very much in love with himself. And currently, Christina. Although he may already have switched to Katherine.

Never to Abegaile, to her distress.

And now Rosey's working for Fairelawn, Christina thought. *It shouldn't take long for her to discover Nelson — if she hasn't already. He'll notice her, that's for sure.*

They were walking carefully in the dark.

Christina pulled her thoughts back to Stephen.

Katherine and Abegaile continued thinking of Nelson Wingate.

"Well, I'm happy for her," Christina commented with no conviction. "What's the other secret?"

"A circus train is on the siding by Waltham's farm. They had the parade through town yesterday. I heard they set up two rings and have wild animals."

It was wonderful news and terrible at the same time. A traveling show had arrived — a circus — but the girls would never be permitted to go — not in a thousand years.

Unless.

"Papa is gone," Katherine said quietly, giving voice to the girls' hopes.

Stephen went as far as their elevator, the area again illuminated. He laughed at Christina's hair and at all of their dresses. He knew he hadn't ruined anything — it was just like Abegaile to think that water could ruin cloth.

"I'll leave you a note," was the last thing Stephen said as he closed them in and sent them aloft.

"Where?" Katherine asked of the paneled door.

"*I* know," Christina teased, and as the elevator rose she thought of Stephen.

The three girls descended the wide, curving stairs for dinner. They waited in the Grand Entry, Christina running her hand absently over one of the carved griffins at the base of the stairs. Abegaile fidgeted with her slip while Katherine tried to look like a serious woman in one of the ornate gilt mirrors. She frowned and knitted her eyebrows. She pursed her lips.

When they heard their mother approach all three girls stood straight and waited.

Mrs. Van Luxall passed around a far corner of the hall. She was at first preoccupied and then she noticed her daughters. She smiled at each girl, but still she remained distant, and they knew she was not feeling well.

"Good evening, Mama," Abegaile and then Katherine and finally Christina greeted.

Their mother looked each of them over from polished toe to shining hair. She stepped up to Abegaile and adjusted the shoulders of the girl's dress and then fussed with her hair. Abegaile smiled timidly.

"Hello, Mama," she whispered. "How do you feel today?"

It was entreating, and the older woman lost track of her hands as she looked into Abegaile's eyes. She smiled wearily and pulled her daughter to her.

"I'm not well, but it always makes me feel good to see you girls looking so fresh."

Katherine and Christina held their breath. Being hugged by their mother had the warmth of being drawn to a board.

Abegaile stood with her arms at her sides. Her mother sighed, released her, and looked at her two other children. "How could anyone be unhappy with daughters like you?"

It was meant as a kindness, but each of them felt it as a hot coal roiling in her stomach.

Daughters.

They were daughters.

And Papa so desperately wished for a son.

The four stood in the entry and embraced their failure.

Abruptly, Mrs. Van Luxall composed herself and led them to the children's dining room. She stood to the side as the girls entered. There were three servants at three chairs.

Once the girls were settled with napkins in place, their mother said, "Perhaps tomorrow we'll take a stroll in the Formal Garden."

"That would be nice, Mama," Abegaile answered absently, suddenly very sad with her life.

"Yes, Mama," Katherine added without enthusiasm.

Christina saw her mother's burden. She saw it and still she resented her for having three daughters — for having failed. If only she'd had a son — one who was healthy and lived more than a handful of hours — if only she'd done that, things would be different.

She realized her mother was watching her. Christina blushed. "Yes, Mama," she murmured and lowered her eyes.

The girls ate in silence in the children's dining room, their servants bustling about, a succession of platters of succulent meats and colorful, steaming vegetables appearing before them. After a dessert which seemed to swell in their throats, almost impossible to swallow, the girls rose and left the room.

They walked without speaking and at the foot of the huge stairway Christina turned and raced up their length. She wound to the second floor, and as she disappeared around the corner, still climbing, the twins saw that she was crying.

Evening absorbed the manor.

Katherine passed Christina's and Abegaile's rooms and roamed the vast halls. She walked beneath the masterpieces; mute Bruegels and Rembrandts and Turners and at last entered the first floor library where she absently traced her finger along its leather volumes like a child with a stick across a picket fence. At last she took down a collection of poems and settled into an antique chair in a nook by the leaded windows.

But it was not the book which held her attention. She was drawn instead to the sun's last warm shadows being cast across her body. Shades of crimson and apricot dappled the lap of her dress, and her chest was ablaze in jasmine, saffron and amber. She turned to the window. It was beautiful; hand made by Flemish craftsmen — a collection of hundreds of pieces of tinted glass — but its opacity was frustrating. It held her captive in her father's home. She couldn't see the last evening clouds, or the swooping birds, or the puzzled watchman who had found the scattered towels in the English Garden and now carried them lightly to the chambermaid he favored.

Katherine sat and lost herself, unfocusing, in the fiery colors.

Later, the sun set and quenched her window. The room dimmed, the upper shelves shedding definition until they were lost. Katherine heard her mother in the hall speaking to the housekeeper. She waited until they departed before she left the library, taking with her the slender volume of poems.

Abegaile spent the evening in her room, sitting on her bed, trying to read. At last she lost interest and dropped the book to the floor and stared at the canopy above her. When she was younger she had seen it as a cloud — a white, billowy cloud which would someday lift her into its midst. A cloud where her real family lived and nothing sad ever happened.

Abegaile knew she didn't belong at The Chimneys. Katherine wasn't her twin and Christina wasn't her sister.

They can't be, she always told herself. *I belong to a different family – a family that lives in a tiny house with a big fireplace and a father who comes home from work, dirty, and a mother who washes and cooks all day.*

That was her family, her true family. She couldn't be Katherine's twin; Katherine's twin was a boy. A handsome boy her father loved and was proud of. A boy who grew up to work in his father's business and carry on the family name. A boy to inherit their huge home and have his own children and teach *them* about the paintings and furniture and tapestries and all the other details.

A boy who would someday wrap his own daughters in The Chimneys and stand aloof while they smothered.

Abegaile stared at the canopy and thought of her other family.

Before she fell asleep — before she slipped away to awaken later in the darkness — she thought about death. Thought of it as a boy — as a brother — and when she did she couldn't stop herself from giving him Stephen's face.

Usually, Mrs. Van Luxall would bid each of her daughters goodnight, but she, too, was adrift, roaming different halls than Katherine; finally retreating to her bedroom where she sat by a window and stared across the vast lawn into the darkness.

After midnight, a moonlit owl landed on the peak of the Octagonal Tea House. She swivelled her head in the hovering silence and then glided noiselessly to a mouse crossing the open lawn by the Birch Allee.

Her prey hanging limp and long-legged beneath her, she pulsed her wings and slipped through the manor's glow and into the waiting forest.

CHRISTINA AND STEPHEN

Christina opened her eyes to the gloom. She lay across her bed, still clothed, and listened to the night noises of the house. Moonlight flowed through the windows, filling her room with its pale fog. She thought of her brother and of the hidden garden — the garden where years ago her mother had retreated to nurse her grief, ignorant of the children desperate to be consoled.

Christina pushed one shoe and then another from her feet.

She left her bed and unbuttoned her dress, letting it fall from her body as she walked. She continued until she stood naked, bathed in luminescence before her windows. Christina looked to the walls of the garden.

The garden of her brother.

The garden of the statue.

The halls were quiet as she passed along them and the stairs held her feet gently as she descended.

Christina walked in hushed defiance. She left the house and skirted the reflecting pool by the rear terrace. Stars shone in the black, still water. The grass was cool and wet. The night air embraced her body. She descended the gritty, hewn steps, hesitated and then passed into the garden, the flagstone path cold and smooth beneath her.

The walls echoed splashing water.

She went to her fountain.

Christina stared and then raised her foot to the pedestal surrounding the pool of the children. She climbed to it and stood effortlessly. Then, slowly, she raised her hands to the front, palms upward, mirroring her statue and spilling moonlight onto the children laughing silently below.

Her fingers nearly touched those of the other woman.

Stephen sat in the shadows on a stone bench, his knees encircled by his arms and drawn to his chest. He saw Christina enter the garden and he held his breath. He watched as she moved into the moonlight, her naked body distant, seeming to glide forward. She was ethereal, beyond life, present only as a dream, and Stephen sat and drank of her, aware with youth's rare intuition that the moment would never be surpassed. She was a goddess to him and he fell so deeply in love with her that the sun would not rise on a day that she didn't weave through his thoughts.

Nothing would replace the young girl at the fountain.

His heart pounded in his chest and he absorbed her presence.

Christina was lost within herself.

She didn't hear Stephen rise and walk to her, his hands clutching his wool cap. In fact, she didn't realize he was near until he stood beneath her. And then it was because she heard him dip his hat gently and raise it as he stepped onto the cast pedestal.

He lifted his cap, now bulging with the dripping water, and tipped it carefully into her outstretched hands. The water flooded her palms and passed between her fingers, escaping her futile grasp and falling through the air. The moonlight caught its twisting threads, sliding along them, charging them with its fluorescence, illuminating them as they splashed the shining faces of the infants below.

How long they stood, neither of them knew, but when Stephen removed his shirt and placed it over Christina's shoulders and finally took her hands as she stepped down, he felt that other than the lingering chill, they were dry. He put his arm around her as they walked to a stone bench. When he stopped he turned to her. She looked up at him, her face glowing, her features soft.

"You're so beautiful, Christina," he whispered, and as he spoke she knew his heart's secret.

He couldn't take his eyes from hers.

Christina rose and brushed her lips against his tentative kiss.

She shivered.

Stephen smiled, the corners of his eyes wrinkling, the happiness he felt spreading across his face.

She stared at him, trying to understand his feelings, who he was. "This isn't a game, Stephen," she gently chided him, her eyes betraying her fear.

He leaned back from her and looked down, ashamed.

"I know that, Christina," he mumbled, studying her bare feet so close to his rough shoes. "I'm sorry. It's not a game for me, either."

He looked into her eyes again.

"This isn't like anything I ever imagined," he began.

She shivered and then stepped from the flagstones onto the tops of his shoes.

"It's cold," she whispered.

Stephen barely registered what she had done although he wrapped his arms around her more tightly. It was torment for him to try to express himself. "I've watched you every day for as long as I can remember, Christina. You've been like a dream to me; a dream of being more than I am, more than my father is. I want to be good enough for you."

Christina watched his eyes as he spoke. She started to protest his last admission.

"No," he said before she could say anything. "I'm not stupid, Christina; I know what people think of me. I'm a fool to them; I'm the driver's son. But that's not all I am. Every day I wonder what I can do to raise myself. I mean, I look for ways to be somebody; to be someone you'd look at and think, 'He's really smart,' and 'He must really know a lot to have done that.'

"I want to be able to buy things — to have an auto."

At first he didn't know whether to continue. He feared if he looked deeply enough into her eyes he'd see that she was mocking him and so he looked away.

"Christina, every day I think about leaving here." He felt her pull slightly away from him.

She barely moved her lips as she spoke. "Why?"

"I have to go away. I dream about it at night. I think about it when I'm working. I leave and I get a good job and I get better and better. People start to respect me and I have a small factory or something and people work for me. I get lucky, maybe, but I work at it, too. I'm not afraid to work, Christina.

"I think about it. I see myself leaving and I imagine a thousand different ways I can make myself something more than 'the driver's son'."

He forced himself to look at her again. "I keep talking and telling you things and it's not what I really want to do now — I mean, it is, but — can I kiss you again, Christina?"

She moved her mouth to him and he felt her lips full and warm against his. He didn't kiss her back hard; he let her kiss him and it was like nothing he had ever experienced. He felt it through his whole body and then he began to tremble.

"Are you cold?" she whispered, her lips moving as they continued to lightly kiss his.

He couldn't stop shaking.

He turned his head to the side, embarrassed that his body wouldn't stop shivering against hers.

"Here," she whispered and grasped the sides of his shirt. She spread it and then pulled him to her. "I'll warm you," she teased, quietly.

Stephen felt the heat of her body and closed his eyes and sighed before he went on trying to explain. He was desperate for her to understand.

"I don't just think about going away, Christina. I think about coming back."

He had sworn to himself he would never tell her. Never.

"I come back for you — I always do."

He waited for her to laugh at him.

"I think about that the most. I come back to The Chimneys. I drive up in a fancy car — sometimes I have somebody drive me here — and your parents are glad to see me. I wait downstairs, and all the people who work for you pass me and they don't recognize me. Maybe somebody does and they can't believe it's me ...."

"Rosey?" Christina interrupted.

Stephen shook his head sadly. "You don't understand, Christina. I never see anybody but you. I see your face when I'm helping my Pop, I see you when I tinker with the fountains. I see you when I lie in bed, before I go to sleep. I don't think you're ever far from me.

"Christina, since the day my Pop and I came here I've sneaked around to see you every chance I get. I watch you and your sisters. I spy on you down the hall. I watch you play croquet. You couldn't guess how many times I've dreamed of you asking me to play, too."

Now Christina was embarrassed. For the first time she really understood the distance that Stephen must feel. She thought of herself playing croquet on the lawn and all she could see was Stephen far away, watching. She couldn't force his image into the game with her.

He saw her pull back from him.

"It looks like a stupid game, Christina," he added defensively.

She came back to him and smiled. She kissed him again. "It is a stupid game, Stephen." Christina lay her head against his chest. "You know something else?"

"I don't know," he answered.

When he did she felt his chest move as he spoke.

"Nobody has ever seen me — like this before. Ever."

"Oh, Christina," he said, shaking his head in frustration, "you're the most beautiful girl in the world. I've known that forever. And tonight — you're more beautiful than a statue, any statue. I wish this night was forever. I wish it would never end." He held her to him and they were silent. Stephen began to shake again. "Let's sit down," he said and then he began to take small steps backward, Christina's feet still on the tops of his shoes.

She laughed lightly, keeping her balance and feeling his rough clothing move against her body. He sat and she fell onto him and Stephen pulled her legs up so she was tucked under his shirt and on his lap.

"There," he said. "Are you warmer?"

"I wasn't shaking Stephen — you were. But yes, I'm warm."

He took a chance.

"Are you happy, Christina? Here, I mean. Now. With me?"

"Yes, Stephen, I'm happy." She hesitated. "I think about you, too, you know. At first it was a little girl crush. I knew that even then. I saw you with your father and around the manor and I used to watch you. You're handsome. You know that. I used to think a lot about kissing you. You're not going to believe this, but the other day, I almost did. I almost have a couple times."

"No," Stephen whispered, unbelieving, and also afraid if he said too much she would stop talking.

She kissed him quickly and continued. "This is a little confusing — I sometimes think of you as Papa's son, and you grow up and take over his businesses — and we get married."

Stephen laughed.

"Marry my sister?"

"It's just a daydream, Stephen."

"Marry my sister," he said quietly, his mind not on the fact that she would be his sister but that she actually thought of marrying him.

"You know what, Stephen?" She moved her hand to the back of his neck. "Dreams can come true. I know they can."

His shoulders sagged. "It's easier in your world than it is in mine."

"Then you don't believe in your dreams?" she asked with a hint of challenge.

Stephen stopped and thought before he answered. He started slowly, measuring each word. "I — know — they can, Christina. When I dream them — when I think them — I believe they can come true. They're not even dreams to me then — not really — they're what I'm going to do. They're dreams, later."

"Then you will come back for me?"

"Do you really want me to?"

She kissed his lips gently and then kissed his cheeks.

The moment passed and he couldn't let her answer, for his heart still refused to believe she could want him. And he couldn't bare to hear her say it. He tortured himself with doubt and then he changed the subject.

"What's it like to be rich — to have everything?"

Christina watched him warily. "It's not like anything."

Stephen laughed at her answer.

"But, how can you stand all that happiness every day?"

He felt her body tense. He looked at her. In the weak light he thought he saw that she was going to cry but she only blinked her eyes.

"I'm happy with Katie and Abbie — I think we're happy with each other — I love my sisters."

Her answer was icy and she didn't go on. Stephen was afraid he'd somehow insulted her or hurt her feelings.

"What did I say, Christina? I'm sorry."

She straightened, her body away from him. He looked down at her breasts, small and soft, her nipples at risk, their aureolas swollen with a young girl's early bloom. Stephen felt disappointment torment him. He wanted more from himself. He didn't want to be excited by her body. It was wrong; she was too good for him. And he wanted to protect her.

But he couldn't force himself to look away. She glowed in the moonlight, her smooth skin perfect, her innocence pulsing in the pale blue light.

She breathed slowly. Stephen watched her chest rise and fall. He was mesmerized by her breasts. And then she saw his fascination and moved his head to their softness. He listened to her heart, feeling its flutter — its plea for help — a call, faint and small. He heard her heart and felt the rising warmth of her breasts and wished she would hold him there all night. He realized he wasn't strong. He was helpless. He wished she would keep him against her chest and allow him to hide. And then he fought himself, knowing it wasn't right.

He should take care of her.

Perhaps it was the shadowed garden and the moonlight, for Stephen felt fear's nauseous grasp rising in him and he had a premonition that if he didn't guard her, if he didn't spend his life standing above her, something terrible would happen.

Christina lifted Stephen's face to hers and kissed him; gently at first, almost imperceptibly, on his cheeks and then the sides of his nose, and, finally, she touched his lips with hers, brushing them together, pulling away, feeling the heat of his breath and the humid warmth of his lips. She looked into his dark eyes and saw his honesty and his confusion. She kissed him harder then, opening her mouth to his, feeling his wetness, tasting him. She closed her eyes and knew only his mouth.

There was no garden and no night.

They kissed with silent desperation; her lips crushing his and Stephen holding her to him. They kissed, floating, weightless, oblivious to thought, conscious only of each other.

And as quickly Stephen was aroused and embarrassed as he felt himself pressing against her. His body awakened and he lost the night's purity, and with that loss he understood what it was he truly wanted.

He wanted her love.

And he remembered Rosey.

He fought it, but he couldn't keep her from coming into his thoughts.

Rosey wasn't like Christina. Rosey was sex. Rosey had taken him. Rosey had brought to him a romping, raucous sexuality; a reveling in waves of desire and fulfillment followed by a stark silence.

Christina wasn't offering sex. She offered herself. She was lost in his strength; the strength he didn't know he had, and in his gentleness and his friendship and in her dream.

Christina's kisses made Stephen ashamed that he had ever touched Rosey. Ashamed that Rosey had seen his nakedness and that she had teased him and handled him so boldly. Stephen hoped he would never see her again, that she would stay away from The Chimneys so he could forget her, pretend that they had never touched.

Christina kissed him and he held her, one hand resting on her shoulder, the other behind.

Christina pulled away to catch her breath and then she sought him once more. Her mouth moved over his face and to his ears, kissing them.

Stephen heard her breath and felt her lips. At first he couldn't help but tilt his head back, his lips parted, her mouth sending chills coursing through his body, until he thought he couldn't stand it and he moved his hand to the base of her neck and turned her head gently, bringing her lips back to his. He kissed their fullness. He tasted her freshness and couldn't remember Rosey's mouth.

He didn't wish to compare but he couldn't stop himself.

Rosey wasn't soft. She was all edges and urging.

Rosey didn't give herself. She took. She took him and she used him and she always left him spent. He was incidental. He was available. She was Rosey.

Christina sighed. She ran a finger along his face.

He moved his hand from the small of her back to her shoulder and as he did his shirt fell from her, sliding beneath his hand. He didn't arrest its fall. His hand left her shoulder and ran along her bare side, brushing the ridges of her ribs. And when he found that he was able, he paused and captured her breast; just the rise — just the side at first, and then all of it, caressing its smallness easily in his hand.

Christina drew her breath when she felt him touch her. No one had ever touched her body. No one had seen her. She arched into him and felt her tiny nipples harden. She whimpered softly and Stephen felt her tongue touch his teeth and then retreat. She felt his fingers move clumsily to her nipple. They passed it and then came back and touched, lightly and tentatively, and then more surely held it while he pressed his hand against her. Both of them breathed heavily, Christina's breast rising and falling against his hand, the boy's chest heaving as he tried to control himself.

By now he would have been in Rosey, moving heatedly with her, trying to hang on as she rode him past sex and into a graphic cartoon of love.

Christina arched her body still more and when she did he dropped his hand from her other shoulder. He traced along her body until he reached her waist and the rounding of her buttocks and then the side of her leg. He ran his palm along her leg and then brought it back to where she rested on him. He tucked his hand between them and felt her rise to let his hand slip under. He cupped her bottom and Christina couldn't remain still. She swayed on his lap, lowering and pressing hard onto him.

She whispered his name. And then she whispered it again. He was taking her from her smothering loneliness, breaking its web, pulling her free.

He kissed her and touched her downy wetness with his fingertips. Felt it, moved his fingers closer, and answered with her name.

He was dizzy. He wanted his pants off. He wanted her. He wanted to be in her. To take her. To take her on the cold stone of her father's garden, and as he thought those things he remembered the man — remembered him tall and overbearing — insulting — contemptuous.

And it was as if Christina heard him.

She struggled with herself at first, fighting the panic which engulfed her, fighting to come back to Stephen, to be alone with him, but she could not. Abruptly, she moved away, pushing as she did. Her father was there. He was in the garden. He was over them. He was ten times larger than the mansion and he blotted out the stars.

Stephen pulled his hand awkwardly from beneath Christina and slid his other hand from her breast to her back.

She was crying and the boy knew he had gone too far. He hated himself.

"I'm sorry," he whispered. "I'm sorry."

She didn't answer.

"I'm sorry," he repeated, his heart breaking as he spoke.

"It's not you," she said when she could, sniffling and then trying to wipe her eyes on her bare shoulder.

"It's not you at all, Stephen. I'm the one who's sorry. It's me."

She brought her hand up and rubbed her eyes, smearing the tears down her cheeks. She took a deep breath and then leaned forward and retrieved Stephen's shirt.

The mansion loomed unseeing in the fading night and the girl at the tower's crenelations disappeared before the first birds and the false dawn.

They walked in slow step through the tunnel and then to the little elevator where Christina, clothed once more in Stephen's shirt, brought his mouth to hers and kissed him one last time, cooly and with sadness.

STEPHEN AND CHRISTINA AND KATHERINE AND ABEGAILE

Katherine raced from her bedroom, through her twin's, and into Christina's. She flew through the door and leaped onto the bed.

"Wake up! Wake up!" she yelled as she pounded on her sister.

Christina rolled from her side and blinked at Katherine. "What time is it?"

Katherine ignored her question. "Get up and dress so we can have breakfast and then look for the note."

Christina sat up, looked around groggily, and then fell back to the bed. "Do we have lessons today?"

"No, silly; it's Saturday. We have all day, unless Mama has guests. Maybe she'll visit someone and we can sneak off with Stephen." Katherine grasped the hope even though it was very unlikely that their mother would leave the house.

"But she said we'd take a walk in the formal gardens," Christina moaned, reminding her.

"She'll forget. You know she will; she always does."

Christina sat up once more, rubbed her eyes, and swung her feet to the floor. "Is Abbie awake yet?"

Katherine shrugged her shoulders, said, "She wasn't moving," and then exclaimed, remembering her reason for awakening Christina, "Get dressed! Get dressed! I'll go get Abbie."

Katherine departed as quickly as she had arrived.

Christina walked across her room to the windows. She swung one open and leaned out. It was a pure, summer morning and Christina wanted a fresh start. She bathed quickly, vaguely unhappy with the unfairness of women having to take baths while men were allowed to shower. She washed and thought of Stephen and returned to their intimacy. Her eyes burned from lack of sleep, but it was the rebirth of her loneliness which bothered her. She had escaped it last night; had broken free and stood unfettered. But only briefly, for once more her father had brought his massive presence to bear on her life, and with his shadow had isolated her, had towered between her and Stephen.

Christina shook herself free of it all, put on the clothes that were set out for her, and went into the adjoining study. She was about to take the stairs to the fourth floor library when the twins burst into the room.

Katherine said in a rush, "We're late! You can't go up there now; Mama is waiting breakfast for us!"

Christina looked at her sisters, interested to see what they were wearing. Each of them wore the same white sailor dress as she. It was Saturday she remembered again. They dressed alike on the weekend.

When they entered the breakfast room — when they were led to the breakfast room, really, for their mother had sent a servant to escort them down, a sure sign that she was in a hurry — they found her seated, a cup of tea raised to her lips, and several triangles of toast on the plate in front of her, their corners nibbled away.

Mrs. Van Luxall sat with her back to six floor-to-ceiling leaded glass panels. They formed a bay beyond which was a fountain and a colorful flower garden. Opposite where the girls sat was a music stand with a poem printed in large letters. Mr. Van Luxall insisted the girls memorize what was before them at breakfast, and then recite it at dinner.

"Good morning Mama," the girls greeted.

"Christina, Katherine, Abegaile," she listed them, as always did, "good morning."

They started their meal in silence, the girls looking up from time to time to read the poem. It was not until Abegaile tipped a glass of orange juice, sending two servants into quiet apoplexy, that Mrs. Van Luxall spoke again. "I'll be visiting your aunt for the weekend, girls. I've gotten word she is too ill to travel and she doesn't have the accommodations for us all."

Christina's heart leaped. Katherine kicked Abegaile and then Christina under the table.

"Yes, Mama," Abegaile said. "Will she die?"

Katherine laughed and then caught herself.

Mrs. Van Luxall ignored Katherine's breach of etiquette. "No, she's not going to die, dear. But she's very ill."

"Mama..." Christina began.

Mrs. Van Luxall had her teacup raised once more. She hesitated.

"Could the twins and I take a long row on the lake and then have a picnic on the island?"

Her mother frowned.

"You promised we could walk in the gardens together. And now you're going away."

Before the end of breakfast, Christina had secured permission, placing the three of them beyond the eyes of The Chimneys for an extended period. They had the day to do what they wished.

"I'll have Alice make up a basket for you," Mrs. Van Luxall added before the girls left the room.

"Thank you, Mama," Abegaile said and kissed her mother's forehead.

"Thank you, Mama," the others parroted.

By eleven Mrs. Van Luxall departed and the girls quickly found Stephen's latest note. Abegaile and Katherine crowded Christina as she read it aloud, Katherine reading over her shoulder.

"Meet ME at The Hecksigone IF YOU DARE! I have a JOB at the boathouse. I'll see you."

Katherine laughed as she read.

"What's so funny?" Christina asked, piqued.

"Nothing — just the way he spells and capitalizes," Katherine replied.

"Well, he is just a worker, you know," Abegaile added, lamely defending Stephen.

"And what are we?" Christina demanded.

"Papa's daughters," Katherine answered.

Christina looked up from Stephen's writing. The girls were outside the doors by the East Terrace.

"Can't catch!" Christina taunted as she raced to the Hexagonal Teahouse.

Katherine and Abegaile flew behind, the tail to Christina's kite. They stopped halfway, all three too winded to continue running.

"We've got to exercise more," Katherine said, her breath coming in pants.

"We should all swim laps in Papa's pool!" Christina said, referring to the huge mosaic pool their father had constructed in the cellar of their home.

"I don't like it," Abegaile moaned. "It's so *hot* and so *damp*. I feel like a *mushroom* every time I go down there."

"Well, you *are* a mushroom, Abbie. A plain, grey mushroom," Katherine said and then added, "We all are — we're The Mushrooms."

And with that, they had a new nickname for themselves.

"I think I'm the toadstool," Abegaile muttered as they neared the teahouse.

Stephen had been puttering — starting projects and then interrupting them to go and see if the girls had arrived. Finally, he saw them just as they disappeared into The Hexagon.

He knew they'd go to the porch overlooking the water and so he circled below.

The lake stretched eight miles in front and five miles to each side, its perimeter a scalloping of coves and inlets. Fairelawn and three other manors bordered its shores. The remainder was either wooded or farmland fields. From where Christina and Katherine stood they could see the island and the distant grounds of Fairelawn, barely more than a light green scar in the woods.

In the winter when the ice was thick and the cold embraced the long nights, it was considered great fun to hitch a team of high steppers to a sleigh and tour the lake.

Abegaile sat on the porch and stuck her legs through the gaps between the stone banisters and swung her feet beneath her.

They were the feet which caught Stephen's attention when he crept below. He didn't know the owners, but he was aware of whose he hoped they were. He grabbed one dangling foot by the ankle, flipped its shoe free, and proceeded to mercilessly tickle the captured sole.

Abegaile was stunned and then electrified as she felt her foot trapped and tortured. She screamed. She fell backward. "Oh, stop! Stop! Stop!" she begged and laughed.

Stephen still didn't have a clue as to who it was he bedeviled. *They all sound the same,* he thought as he tugged downward, forcing Abegaile to slide toward the railing.

Abegaile feared she would wet herself if it didn't abate soon.

Katherine saw her twin being pulled toward the ledge. She took Abegaile under her arms and began to tug her back onto the porch.

Abegaile's screams shifted an octave higher, for her twin had inadvertently intensified her sensitivity.

Christina ran to Abegaile's side and leaned over the edge of the stone railing, her feet braced as she bent and peered under the porch.

"Stephen!" she reprimanded when she looked down at him. "Stop that this minute!"

The boy, recognizing Christina's voice, released Abegaile. He looked up at Christina and smiled, embarrassed. "Good morning," he said sheepishly.

Katherine, in the birth of a pull, fell backwards dragging her twin with her.

And Abegaile, her hopes that it was Stephen confirmed, continued laughing, though more softly.

The boy climbed one of the support posts and levered himself over the railing. In an instant he was seated, back to the lake, facing and talking to the girls. "Well, it took you long enough. Don't tell me you had a difficult time finding my note!"

Christina had wondered how she would respond when she saw him again. She had feared she would betray herself. Now, after the attention had centered on Abegaile, she was even less happy than if she had be caught, moonstruck. She was jealous.

Her tone was steeped with malice when she responded, "Believe me, Stephen, *you couldn't think of a place* for a note that I couldn't easily reach."

Stephen looked at her, mystified. "Oh, really? I couldn't?"

"Oh, really," Christina answered flatly.

Abegaile and Katherine sat up and watched the exchange, Abegaile more interested in Stephen than in actually listening. He had touched her. And he had teased her. She was reeling out of control with delight.

"Where are my shoes?" she interrupted.

Stephen tore himself from Christina's challenge. Abegaile's shoes were on the grass below.

He dropped ten feet to the ground, and then rolled and retrieved Abegaile's pumps. He dropped them into his shirt and climbed back up. Stephen pulled out the shoes with a gallant flourish, kneeled as a knight, and presented them to Abegaile.

Christina fumed and Katherine and Abegaile laughed lightly.

Stephen was aware of Christina's reaction; but her superior tone and its underlying meanness, rankled him.

Until he really looked at her again.

She was so fresh, so perfect, that he saw her as an ideal, not a person. He caught her eye and held her and for a moment they were back at the garden in the moonlight.

It was now Katherine and Abegaile's turn to observe.

Abegaile was hurt.

Katherine broke the spell. "Mama is gone for the day!" she pronounced.

"Then it's the circus!" Stephen proclaimed turning to her, once more full of youth and excitement.

"We have the whole day!" Abegaile added.

Christina couldn't allow herself to remain at the periphery. "Can we go, Stephen? Can we go?" she repeated.,

Stephen smiled broadly and then slapped his knee. "Can we go? Of course we can go! Give me half an hour and I'll meet you past the main gates."

"No!" Christina amended. "We've got to take the row boat. You meet us at the old landing; there's much less chance we'll be seen!"

"Yes, the landing!" Abegaile confirmed, and Christina and Katherine both looked at her. It was not like her to be so bold.

Abegaile flushed but wouldn't renege. "The landing!" she repeated defiantly.

"An hour," Christina said, being far more realistic than Stephen relative to the time the girls would need, although she knew an hour would be a rush, too.

Stephen sat and watched the three run down the alley to the Main House. As he did he allowed the danger associated with his bold offer to surface. It was one thing to talk with the girls in daylight, or to have a secret rendez-vous at night, but now he was going to *borrow* the gardener's vehicle, and take all three girls to the circus — in broad daylight! The old Model T probably wouldn't be missed, that wasn't the problem, but it was a variation on the theme of theft, and he was involving the Van Luxall girls. Plus, he knew they would be seen. He begged his God it would be by someone who didn't socialize with the older Van Luxalls — it was his only hope.

There wasn't a prayer for him if they were seen by someone who relayed the information to the girls' parents. He would be gone in an instant, and possibly his father with him.

He thought of meeting them at the landing and telling them that the old vehicle wouldn't start, or that the gardener was using it or fixing it or something, but the girls' disappointment — Christina's disappointment — was more immediate and real and so he went to get the car.

As the girls climbed the stairs, Abegaile prattled on in hushed tones about Stephen — how handsome he was, how funny he was — and it was all Christina could do to keep from throttling her.

Christina wanted to be angry with the boy, but she couldn't. Plus, Abegaile was as happy as she'd ever seen her, and so instead of irritation, Christina experienced guilt. She pulled that emotion down over her and wore it until at last she could see no reason for it.

He was Stephen. Stephen who had spoken to her of his life and who had shared his dreams. He wasn't just one of the help. He was a person and really quite bright and had ambition and didn't intend to spend his life doing for others. And she loved him.

His relationship with Rosey?

Well — Rosey was gone. Besides, Christina's attraction to the driver's son was one thing. Feeling threatened by a maid was quite another.

Katherine turned at her room and Abegaile felt strangely uncomfortable the few feet she had to walk with Christina. It wasn't that she felt they were in competition or anything as ridiculous as that, for Abegaile realized there was no contest. Not at any level. Christina was by far the most beautiful of the three, and certainly the wittiest and the most clever. She *knew* Stephen had chosen Christina.

But still, Stephen hadn't ignored her. And he wasn't put off when he discovered whose feet he'd captured. Abegaile smiled to herself. It had been such a lark. And he *had* gone to get her shoes. And he had been humorous even then.

She sat on the edge of her bed and listened to her sisters in their rooms and remembered the previous night. She, too, had awakened, and she had gone through Christina's bedroom, not the least surprised when she discovered that her sister wasn't there.

And she went the keep tower.

And stood in the moonlight watching.

Abegaile felt there was still, somehow, room for her. Room for her to be attracted to Stephen — she didn't dare think of his love; she wasn't worthy of it, she knew that — but she could dream of him. And if she were very lucky, she could laugh with him.

He was Christina's.

That was the way it should be. They would be happy. They would escape and start a life filled with themselves and their love. Her father couldn't hold them apart. He couldn't ruin everything — not forever. For the first time in Abegaile's life, she felt hope replacing the despair that had been her pillow, her blanket, and her bed.

And Katherine would have someone, too. Abegaile knew that. Maybe the Wingate boy.

Stephen was alarmed when the Model T wasn't at the potting shed. He ran to the side of the stables. It wasn't there. Near panic, he checked inside. It was in the shadows, the crank hanging loose below the radiator, the torn canvas top collapsed behind the back seat.

He checked the fuel and was surprised to learn the tank was almost full. But the water was low. He dumped a bucket over the radiator filler, spilling much more than he trapped. Finally, he took off his shirt and dusted the front and back seats.

The automobile was ready.

Anna appeared in Christina's room. "You'll find a basket with sandwiches and fruit and dessert downstairs in your dining room."

"Thank you, Anna," Christina answered absently, trying to find something to wear which would be even remotely appropriate for a circus. It would have helped had she been to one before.

Anna watched her.

Christina stopped and stomped her foot. She tore a dress from its hanger and threw it onto the floor.

Anna stepped forward, retrieved it, and ran her fingers over the rent.

"It doesn't matter, Anna. Throw it away."

Anna lay the dress gently over the back of a chair. "Hmmm," was the only sound she made.

"Well, it *doesn't*, Papa could buy hundreds more — *thousands* more, I'm sure."

Christina was neither bragging nor attempting to belittle Anna.

"Aye, I expect he could do that," Anna answered quietly.

"And you'd be lookin' for clothing to wear in a little rowboat?" she asked without expecting an answer.

Christina turned to her, realizing what she must know. They looked at each other.

"We're sneaking off to the circus, Anna. It shouldn't be a crime, but it is."

The big woman shook her head slowly. "No, it shouldn't be — but it is." Then she walked into the long closet and came out with a dress that was more earthy than anything Christina thought she owned — her father owned — and it was perfect.

"Yes, Anna! Yes!"

"I'll take a visit with your sisters and then I'll be back," she said. She found Abegaile and Katherine similarly stymied.

Christina was fastening the last button when Anna returned. She finished and went to Anna and embraced her. "Why does it have to be like this, Anna? Why can't we be normal?"

Anna wrapped her arms around the tall girl, stroked her hair and then released her.

"I know you'll not be going alone. You couldn't leave here without someone a'holdin' your hand. Be watchin' yourself is all I can say. You're quality, don't forget."

"We'll be careful," Christina answered, but she was thinking of what Anna had said — *You can't leave here without someone holding your hand* and she realized it was true.

Stephen put on a clean, collarless shirt, buttoning it to his neck, snapped his suspenders over his shoulders, and wet his dark hair and combed it. He took most of the money he'd saved and stuffed it into his front pocket. Finally he took his wool cap and pulled it down to one eyebrow. It was as jaunty and go-to-hell as he knew how to be.

He retarded the spark, checked the ignition, set the throttle, and gave the crank a whirl, careful to tuck his thumb out of the way should the engine backfire. He cranked the engine through a few times and then it sputtered to life, settling into a smooth idle before long.

Stephen cleared the low side door and landed seated behind the thick black steering wheel. He depressed the first gear pedal and banged and stuttered out of the stable.

So much for an unobserved exit.

He left the grounds by the utility road, making a wide arc until he intersected the dirt road to the old landing.

The girls weren't there, as he knew they wouldn't be and so he took the time to back the auto around and position it so he could easily depart once they arrived. He waited, sideways in the seat, his shoes propped on the opposite door. He surveyed the Model T, generally satisfied with its appearance, although he would have preferred it had both rear fenders. There was a hole in the floorboards at his feet, but he didn't mind that. In fact, he rather enjoyed watching the road pass beneath him. It added to the perception of speed, and in a Ford Model T, one had to embellish that perception in any way possible.

Stephen had seen a few of the old cars with their fenders stripped off and the body removed, leaving nothing but a steering wheel, the driver's seat, and a can of gas strapped behind it, and the overall impression had been of a racing car, but Stephen couldn't get the massive V-12's of Mr. Van Luxall's Lincoln out of his mind — *they* were speed and power! He was thinking of those engines with their even dozen little pistons when he heard splashing water and giggles.

The girls rammed the boat onto the beach and handed a basket out to Stephen. He helped them out, holding the hands of each of the girls as he steadied them. They went to the Model T.

Of course, Christina would sit in front. Knowing that, Abegaile climbed into the back to sit behind Christina so she could get a better view of Stephen as he drove.

Katherine sat in the back beside her twin.

Stephen helped Christina into the front and then raced around to give the little engine a crank. It started with a bang, causing Katherine to jump and Abegaile to shriek. Christina didn't seem to notice. She watched Stephen.

He drove them away from the fringes of their estate on a series of wildly bumpy dirt trails until he thought it was safe to take the main road. They rode for another hour, the girls mooing at cows and calling out to pigs and horses. At last they came to Waltham's farm. The girls cried out when they saw the top of a huge brown tent in a distant field. Near it was a crowd of cars, many of them already parked, others moving about like a swarm of scuttling dung beetles. A long curving line of cars inched across the field toward the writhing mass. Occasionally an impatient flivver would bound out of the line, creating its own short cut.

Stephen passed Waltham's farm, drove to the woods bordering the field and then turned into a gap in the trees. He and the girls bounced along a pair of parallel ruts separated by weeds and rocks.

"It's our secret entrance to the circus," Stephen boasted. "It's one less chance of being seen. And Old Man Waltham is sure to have his kids out collecting pennies to park in his field — I try to save my money when I can!"

The girls cringed. They had forgotten about money and now it was too late to do anything about it. Katherine looked at Abegaile. Christina turned back to them. They were all mortified. They were still just 'girls', relying on a male to get them through.

Stephen guided the bucking auto through the woods. Suddenly, he put on the brakes and groaned audibly.

The grove ahead was filled with automobiles.

He hadn't been so smart after all.

Circulating among the parked cars were various razorbacks — men who loaded and unloaded the circus train — and they were handing out fliers promoting the acts and sideshows.

"MIDWAY! MIDWAY" the nearest shouted, "SEE THE HUMAN ODDITIES AT THE MIDWAY!" He pronounced his words carefully, as if they were foreign. His clothing was particularly rough and his face was badly scarred. There was suppressed anger and challenge in his movement. He spotted the three girls with Stephen and started toward them.

"SEE THE BEARDED LADY! SEE THE STUPIFYING SNAKE WOMAN! WATCH HER SLITHER ON HER STOMACH LIKE A REPTILE. SEE HER FOOT- LONG TONGUE!"

The girls screwed up their faces.

The man stopped his spiel.

"Hey, Sonny!" he taunted Stephen. "Bring them Jills over here an' I'll give ya somethin'!"

Stephen went to pull the girls away but they had already started toward the razorback. He handed a flier to each of them. Stephen refused his. Then the circus man, bigger and twice as broad as the boy, took Christina's hand and placed something in it. "Here's a Annie Oakley for ya." He winked at her and then sneered with toothless defiance at Stephen.

Christina looked at the free ticket to the Big Top. One of her problems was solved.

"Thank you, sir!" she called after the hawker who had gone after another group of girls.

"Hey!" Stephen said irritably. "I thought you were with me!"

Christina showed the ticket to Abegaile and Katherine and then turned to Stephen. She smiled and took his hand.

"Of course, I'm with you!"

Abegaile added, "We're all with you, Stephen. Why is it called an Annie Oakley?"

Stephen really didn't want to discuss it, but he did. He pointed to the hole in Christina's ticket. "Annie Oakley's supposed to have shot it," he said and then shook his head in disgust. "I bet she's not even here!"

The sisters exchanged glances.

They walked out of the woods and across the field to the tents and the parked wagons. The smells of animals and candy and sawdust baked in the afternoon sun. There was noise and wild laughter everywhere, and the girls were lifted from their world of poise and hesitation.

Two dusty children ran by, bumping into Katherine as they did.

Stephen yelled at them and then turned back to the girls. "Let's go to the Midway S it's where the sideshows are."

Katherine hesitantly agreed but Abegaile and Christina balked.

"I don't want to see a *snake lady*," Abegaile protested.

"Let's go see the animals," Katherine offered. "Let's see the tigers!"

Christina supported her sister. "I don't want to see a bunch of freaks — let's see the animals."

Stephen would not be deterred. "We'll see 'em! Just hold on!

"Look," he added, pointing, "the Midway's right in front of us. We have to walk through it anyway."

Before Christina and Abegaile could think of a protest they were caught up in the crowd. Barkers on each side extolled the grotesques. Stephen ran off and came back with four tickets to see the Beguiling Human Mermaid.

Depicted on the side of the wagon they were to enter was a mermaid in a tropical setting. Painted palm trees leaned over a beach and white clouds were splotched across a blue sky. The mermaid was on the sand, smiling through chipped paint and coyly covering her chest with her hands.

Stephen led the girls up the steps and into the wagon. As their eyes adjusted to the diminished light they saw a mossy glass tank mounted in the wall. Something a foot and a half long swam at the rear. Stephen went up to it and tapped the glass. A fish with a tiny, fur covered, strangely human head swam awkwardly forward. It kept nosing to the bottom and then struggling upward.

Abegaile gasped and clutched Stephen's arm.

Christina turned away.

"It's a monkey's head," Katherine said solemnly and walked to the exit.

Out in the sunlight once more, Stephen dragged them ahead, oblivious to their reaction. Again, he went to a barker and came back with tickets. This time they were for Alonzo — The World's Largest Baby.

"This is the last one, Stephen," Christina protested.

The girls entered grudgingly, still unnerved by the mermaid. They were in a small tent with rows of wooden benches. Most were already occupied so Stephen and the girls sat near the rear. It smelled of hot canvas. There was straw on the floor. The crowd became rowdy, calling for the baby, until a man in a cheap, vested suit came out.

Christina stared at the floor.

"Alonzo — The World's Largest Baby," the man began, "weighs nearly four hundred pounds and is only ten months of age! Yes, ten months of age, ladies and gentlemen, boys and girls!" He looked the crowd over and continued, "His mother, a serf's wife in Tibet, died most painfully in childbirth. It was at great expense and unimaginable personal danger that Alonzo was brought to you." He paused and then proclaimed, "Ladies and gentlemen, Alonzo!"

A curtain was opened to the side of the man. He turned, extending his hand toward the thing that was now visible.

There, on a raised platform and leaning against a wooden wall, was an immense, pale and diapered human form of indeterminate age and sex. Its head was obviously shaven and the thing's features belied that it was severely retarded. Further, its skin indicated that it had seen little of the sun.

"Quiet, ladies and gentlemen!" the man said in a mock whisper, "We must be cautious to allow Alonzo his sleep!"

A few farm boys started calling out insults.

"WAKE UP, BLUBBER BRAIN!"

"I GOT A HOG BETTER LOOKIN' THAN THAT THING!"

The crowd laughed. Stephen elbowed Christina and smiled.

One eye and then another opened. The thing looked stupidly at the audience and then began a plaintive, screeching wail.

Christina was on her feet and halfway out the door, followed closely by Abegaile and Katherine, before Stephen knew they were leaving.

They didn't see who watched them depart.

The Midway was a disaster and Stephen was desperate to save their outing.

Abegaile was quietly crying. "It's so sad," she lamented. "That's a real person."

Stephen came up to her. "It's not a real baby, Abbie. It's a fat old moron or something."

Christina stared at him in disbelief. "It's a human being, Stephen. It's a person!"

He shook his head, still not getting the point. "I'm sorry; I thought it would be funny or interesting or something. Let's get out of here." He led them past the other wagons and barkers, past the Siamese Twins, and The Snake Lady, and The Albino Baby Elephant. The foursome was jostled several times as they encountered various crowds, but at last they were in the open between the Midway and the Big Top.

Abegaile dabbed at her eyes and looked at the ground. Christina was forlorn, too; only Katherine seemed to have weathered the assault. Stephen apologized again, wondering as he did what The Snake Woman looked like, but he was loathe to mention her.

"We'll go into The Big Top; it'll be fun there," he offered and dug into his pocket. His intention had been to pull out the dollars he had saved. It was far more than they could possibly need for the afternoon, but he wished to impress them somehow — show that even he could pay their way.

But panic painted his features as he dug deeper. He tried to appear nonchalant when he went to the other pocket. Color drained from Stephen's face as he remembered the various toughs who had brushed against him in the crowd. He had been so intent on keeping the girls together that he had not been careful.

They had passed a pickpocket.

Stephen was too deflated to be angry. He had ruined their day.

Christina watched him. She understood and offered her Annie Oakley.

He forced himself to look into her eyes. "That won't do any good, Christina. You go on in. We'll wait out here. There's plenty for us to see, honest."

Abegaile and Katherine nodded in agreement.

Christina held up the ticket and then tore it in half.

Stephen felt worse. "Do you want to walk around or something?" he asked.

"Let's go back," Katherine said and Abegaile agreed.

Christina thought for a moment. "Let's go back to the lake. We have the picnic basket. Let's —" She stopped and shared Stephen's depression with the mention of the basket. They had left it in the open car.

They skirted the sideshow as they went back toward the woods, passing a row of tents. Out of one of them a woman in a mended costume, her face heavily rouged and her mouth smeared with garish lipstick, led a string of elephants, trunk-to-tail.

Stephen and Christina and Abegaile and Katherine stood as the beasts swayed by. It helped to pick up their spirits. The last elephant emerged — a baby with a bright red cap and a gold tassel — and Stephen edged toward its path and then feigned pain as it passed. He hopped about on one foot, holding the other.

"My foot! My foot!" he complained. "I think it's crushed!"

A turbaned mahout watched Stephen's performance with dull fascination.

The girls laughed. Abegaile approached Stephen who now stood still but cradled his 'injured' extremity. She reached out with her shoe and stamped on the boy's earthbound foot.

Stephen howled and hopped again, alternately holding one foot and then the other. But he became overzealous in his performance and lost his balance and tumbled into a pool of mud by the pachyderms' wooden water trough.

Now, the girls laughed in earnest.

Stephen attempted to leap to his feet with face-saving poise, but he was so intent on appearances that he lost his balance and went down again.

Christina held her sides. Tears rolled off her cheeks as she fought to catch her breath. Abegaile felt sorry for Stephen, but the situation was too humorous to keep her from laughing. Katherine joined them.

When Stephen finally stepped from the mud, his hands were brown and his clothing a mess.

"You need a shower by the fountain," Abegaile teased, and Katherine laughed again.

Christina looked at Stephen.

Katherine and Abegaile watched them.

As they had feared, the basket was gone.

Stephen started the Model T and drove around the parked cars. Just as he was approaching the rutted path back to the main road, he spied the razorback from earlier in the afternoon. He was holding a thick sandwich in his broad mitt, leering at them and making a show of eating. He smiled at Stephen through a mouthful of food and winked at the girls.

Stephen tromped the pedals to the floor and aimed the car at him. The razorback read the boy's anger, dropped the sandwich and tried to dive out of the way, but was not quick enough. The girls screamed as the car's front fender brushed against him, pushing him to the ground. As he fell, they felt the rear tire run over his foot.

It was the man's turn to yell out. "I'LL KILL YOU ALL!" he shouted.

Katherine and Abegaile and Christina looked back and saw him rolling on the ground, gripping his foot in agony.

Stephen hooted the horn and then went to swing the car around to have another pass at him, but Christina grabbed the wheel and wouldn't let him. He fought her briefly until she caught his eye.

"Let's go home," she begged.

He nearly rammed a tree as he looked at Christina. But Abegaile screamed "We're crashing!" and Stephen looked up and instantly sawed the wheel to the side. He clipped the remaining rear fender and it ripped free and twirled on the ground.

"HA!" the razorback yelled after them, spewing half-chewed food as he did.

They laughed until they came to the road leading back to the manor.

Their spirits lifted, they drove in the late afternoon sun. Once more the girls yelled at barnyard animals and Stephen honked the horn and shouted with them. Finally, they turned into their woods and bumped along, laughing and screaming until they were back at the landing.

He helped them down out of the car, and as Katherine came close to him she turned her head and exclaimed, "You smell like the elephant tent, Stephen!"

The boy examined his clothes and then sniffed at his hands. He wrinkled his nose comically and started toward the water.

And he walked right in.

"Stephen!" Abegaile cried.

"You fool!" Christina chastised.

Katherine shook her head and laughed.

Stephen ducked and then sputtered back to the surface. He made a show of scrubbing his clothing with his hands. "First bath this year!" he proclaimed.

"Take us for a row!" Abegaile teased, but in a demanding tone.

Both Katherine and Christina were amused to see their sister so forward.

Stephen stepped bedraggled from the water and untied the boat. He lifted a soaking hand and helped the girls in, having them squeeze together in the rear seat, all three facing forward. He walked the boat through the shallows and then pulled himself into it, his clothing flooding the floorboards as he did.

Then he skillfully seated the oars and pivoted the boat, pulling on one oar and pushing on the other. He rowed slowly along the shore the remainder of the afternoon, telling the girls humorous stories and teasing them about ridiculous things.

Christina watched him as he talked, taking in his movements and his changing expression. His features never rested; they seemed to animate his tales. Abegaile, too, kept her eyes on the boy, thrilling when he laughed and enthralled with the things he knew. Katherine apprehensively observed the three of them, interested in what Stephen said, but anxious that there might yet be a problem between her sisters.

They continued into the summer evening, Stephen's clothing drying before the sun descended into the lower third of the sky and a coolness rolled across the lake. But more and more the boy's stomach began to dominate his thoughts and at last even the girls heard its growls.

"Perhaps we should start back," Katherine suggested, only to suffer killing stares from Abegaile and Christina, but Stephen agreed and then amended, "Let's meet tonight at The Hexagon."

"We'll bring food again and this time we'll keep it in sight," Abegaile said.

The allusion to the theft reminded Stephen of his lost money. He was saddened and then he recovered.

Of the girls, only Christina had truly understood the magnitude of his loss. She was determined to somehow make it up to him.

The girls would not allow him to take them back to the boathouse, fearing they would be seen by the staff, so Stephen rowed back to the landing and then drove alone to the stables. He pulled the old car through the open door and killed the ignition.

He sat, the quiet car now strange beneath him, and thought of the circus and of Christina. He wished he had been able to show her things she had never seen. He had pictured her in awe of the acts and laughing and having a gay time. He was afraid she now saw him for what he was — a dull boy who worked for her father.

A servant met the girls at the dock, secured the boat, and accompanied them back to the manor. He walked discreetly behind, curious that they did not have the basket they had taken earlier.

Before Christina changed her clothing she rang for their maid.

"Anna," she asked politely when she appeared, "could you see if we might have our dinner set out at the teahouse by the lake? And please leave instructions that we're ravenously hungry and will require much food—and tell them that after it's set, we wish to be left alone."

Anna, her hands clasped in front of her, stood immobile and expressionless.

Until Christina could remain aloof no longer. "Anna!" she exclaimed, "they stole our basket of food and the Midway was dreadful. It's full of unfortunate human beings. It's too disgusting to even think about. It was so horrible!"

Anna was always pleased when any of the girls demonstrated sensitivity, and as they matured she was rewarded more and more frequently. "It *is* sad; I'll be grantin' you that, young miss. Aye, how a man can be so pleased to see another's misfortune will remain a mystery long after these bones are gone."

"You're right, Anna!" Christina blurted, thinking of what her friend had said. "It's the *men*," she agreed. "They're the ones who seem to get so much joy from it. It's ghastly!"

"And remember that Miss Christina."

The girl stood and thought of Stephen — it had been his idea to look at the freaks and grotesques, and she was certain he would have stayed had it not been for her and her sisters.

Anna saw Christina lost in herself.

"Will that be all?"

"Yes, Anna, thank you," Christina answered, her thoughts still with Stephen.

Anna departed, closing the door quietly as she left.

The girls strolled through the dusk to the Hexagonal Teahouse. There was a cool breeze off the lake, filtering down the Allee.

Doves called back and forth and a dog barked by the stables.

The table was laid out, the light cloth rippling, and it was set for three; crystal and silver awaiting. There were mounds of food everywhere, some hidden beneath bright domes, some steaming in porcelain platters.

And as Christina had specified, once the girls arrived, the servants disappeared, unobtrusively descending the stairs to follow the tunnel back to the main kitchen. Christina looked from the table to the manor and then back again. An evil smile came to her face. With wicked indelicacy she ripped free a leg from a broiled chicken and went to the railing, eating as she walked.

Following her lead it became a game for Abegaile and Katherine to be as gauche as possible. Katherine dug her fingernails into slab of ham and pulled free a slathering of succulent meat. She stuffed it into her mouth and then blew on her fingers.

Abegaile took a handful of roast beef and another of steamed carrots.

Just then, Stephen came over the railing. He saw the girls attacking the food and shook his head in disbelief. But he remained at a distance even though he was starving.

His stomach punished him.

Christina was mystified until she understood his reticence and with embarrassment demanded, "Eat Stephen! It's for all of us!"

The boy would approach their beds with less trepidation than he now had as he faced their table. With stunned admiration he observed the girls' primitive attacks upon decorum. And then Christina's invitation finally registered and he joined them.

They ate for less than an hour, their savage abandon taking them quickly through the meal. Vegetables and meats suffered. Silver was flipped onto the flagstones and most of the glasses were tipped. The only one still standing floated an iceberg of mashed potatoes.

Stephen eyed the devastation and the remaining food. He had participated in the girls' game, but it had been with secret resentment. There were at least three meals left and he knew they would be discarded. It was such a waste.

They rinsed their hands in the water pitchers and then Stephen led Christina and Abegaile and Katherine down the stairs to the boathouse and out its long dock.

Evening took the lake. Swallows swooped overhead and terns whirled, their wing tips clipping the tops of the low waves. The sun settled behind the western woods, capping the trees with copper.

Stephen sat at the end of the dock, his back to the lake. His legs were crossed and he leaned forward onto his knees. The girls sat in a row, their legs hanging above the water. They wanted to range in a line across the dock, facing Stephen, but they couldn't bring themselves to be so obvious.

They talked quietly as the sun finally set.

Stephen told them of the death of his mother.

"For me, it's as if she never lived," he said evenly. "Pop says she was a great woman, and from the way he says it, I guess it must have been true, but still it's not easy to picture someone you never knew; no matter how well somebody else describes them."

"Stephen," Christina interrupted, "the way you talk about her — the way you tell what your father told you, I can see her and I thinks she's nice."

"I feel like I know her," Abegaile added softly.

"I do, too," Katherine concluded, and not one of them was exaggerating or attempting to cushion the boy's sadness.

"I wonder sometimes," Christina said delicately, turning the subject to the girls' family, "what our brother would have been like."

They were silent for a moment.

"I think he would have been like Stephen," Abegaile said and the girls nodded and the boy knew he had been given a heart-felt compliment.

The girls went on to speak of their brother, and from what they said Stephen learned how the girls viewed him.

"He would have been nice," Abegaile began, "and sensitive. I think he would have gone to college and been a writer or something like that."

"He wouldn't have been ignorant, that's for certain," Katherine interjected. "And most likely he would have gone into Papa's business." She thought about that for a moment and then concluded, "I'm not so sure they would have gotten along."

They were quiet.

Christina leaned back with her hands behind her on the dock.

"He would have been handsome — dark with strong features —"

"and sensitive hands," Abegaile continued.

"He would have laughed often. And he would have laughed at himself, too." Katherine smiled as she saw their brother teasing them. "It would have been so much fun. The house would have had so much more life — Mama and Papa so much easier to be with."

They paused after Katherine finished.

"Do you think —" Christina pronounced carefully at last, introducing doubt.

"Do you think — " she repeated, "he would have gotten all the attention? I mean, do you think Mama and Papa would have noticed us with a boy in the house?"

"Do you think Papa notices us now?" Katherine challenged.

"Your father? Not notice you?" Stephen demanded, incredulous. "Why, he's got to be proud of all three of you; you're all three as sharp as a set of whips and pretty, too."

Abegaile blushed and Katherine was stunned by his bald compliment, but Christina addressed his misconception. "He doesn't even see us, Stephen. We're not as important to him as the furniture he had sent from Europe."

Stephen shook his head, protesting, "I don't believe it!"

"It's true," Abegaile reinforced, sadly. "We're just girls to him."

"Just *girls*!" the boy laughed. "When I'm a man, I sure wish I'd be guaranteed some girls like you!"

He looked at each of them, genuinely the proud father.

Abegaile smiled and blushed after their eyes met.

Christina was looking out over the waves and missed him.

Katherine cleared her throat and studied the palms of her hands. "Is your father proud of you?" she asked.

Stephen calmed down. "Proud of me? Well, I never thought about it like that, but I can say we get along — he teaches me things and sometimes I teach him a thing or two." He laughed and the girls were envious of his easy relationship with his father.

"When I'm older I won't stand for my husband treating me the way Mama is treated," Katherine asserted.

Christina bristled. "Papa doesn't treat her any way, Katie; she's just another servant to him." And as she finished, she realized what she had said.

"What am I?" Stephen asked, his voice barely more than a whisper.

No one answered.

The boy allowed the pall to hang above them and then he dispersed it kindly.

"I can tell you this — I won't always be 'the help.' Someday I'll be important. I may not be as rich as your father, but I won't be as poor as mine."

He turned his gaze to the distant water.

"And when I have money I won't have people do the things I should rightly do for myself."

"Will you have a cook?" Christina challenged.

"No, I'll have a wife and she'll cook," he answered.

"I see," Christina acknowledged and then asked, "And who'll clean your home?"

Stephen was cornered.

Christina continued her challenge. "And who will mend your clothing?"

"And who will take care of your children?" Katherine added.

"You won't need servants, Stephen," Abegaile said, surprising herself that she was going to say what was on her mind. "You'll have a wife — *a girl.*"

They were silent again.

Stephen rose and stood over them, his hands in his pockets. "I never thought about it like that," he said lamely but with honesty.

"Who does?" Christina responded calmly.

Katherine concluded their discussion. "Just be glad you weren't born a girl, Stephen. It's not a lot of fun."

Fully fifteen minutes passed before anyone spoke again.

"I hid a note," Stephen said without spirit.

The girls were instantly piqued by his statement. They steamrollered ahead, anxious to break the spell of melancholy.

"Where?" Katherine demanded.

Stephen stepped up behind Christina. He lay his hand gently on the top of her head. "Well, Miss Smarty here says she can find one anywhere. I have a contest for her."

"I don't think you could really fool me," Christina said, enjoying his touch but bridling at his insinuation.

Stephen laughed. "It's in the mouth of the ugliest thing at this manor."

Abegaile opened her mouth and pretended to feel inside it.

"It's a contest;" he repeated, "you'll never find it."

The remainder of the evening they spoke of less weighty matters, Stephen content to hear Christina, and the girls warmed by his presence.

They had lapsed into silence when the door to the teahouse swung open a fraction and was then pulled closed.

"Pardon," a small voice said from inside.

It was enough to frighten them all. Under no circumstances would it be appropriate for the four of them to be conversing so intimately, particularly, at such a late hour. Reluctantly, the girls said goodnight and walked back the Allee together. They went to Christina's room and lounged in chairs and on her bed.

"He *is* a gentleman," Abegaile informed the others.

Katherine smiled and looked at her sister.

Christina tossed several of the pillows from her bed onto the floor. She propped those remaining, behind her. "I don't think he could ever be a gentleman, Abbie, and I don't mean to belittle him. It's almost as if he's too good for that."

Katherine used a maternal tone. "You two are so far in love with him I wouldn't ordinarily trust your judgements, but in this case I think you're both right."

"Aren't you attracted to him?" Abegaile asked.

Katherine smiled to herself. She raised an eyebrow as she thought of her twin's question. "In a funny way, he's too much like a brother for me," she said and then continued, "and in one fashion that's in his favor, and in another it's not. But if he were our brother I could love him dearly — as long as he didn't become like Papa."

She got up from her chair and walked over to one of Christina's Madam Alexander® dolls. She picked it up and toyed with its dress and then set it back on the stand. Abegaile and Christina could see that mentioning their father had set Katherine on edge.

"But I think I would hate him, too; Papa has spoiled a brother for us. For me at least."

"Do you think he's spoiled us for our own sons — if we have any?" Christina asked still on her bed, her arms at her sides, her legs splayed.

"I never imagine that I could have one," Katherine lamented. "I think it's beyond the women of this family."

Abegaile was sinking fast.

Christina saw it and tried to save her sister from one of her fits of deep depression. "Well, where *is* the ugliest mouth at our manor?"

Instantly, Abegaile was back. "Inside or outside, I wonder."

"Let's guess," Katherine said as she explored the possibilities. "The river mouth — is it ugly?" and she dismissed it as she said it.

"I don't know," Christina said absently as she mentally walked through the halls of their home and then went outside.

"Mouth — ugly mouth," Abegaile thought out loud.

"Oh no!" Katherine groaned.

"What? Where?" Abegaile begged. "Tell us!"

Katherine became irritated. "You can't do it, Christina — it's far too dangerous."

"Where is it!" she questioned angrily. "If he can put it there, I can get it."

"You'd better look before you answer so quickly, Christina."

Abegaile watched Katherine. It was unusual for her to use Christina's full name.

"Well?" Abegaile asked.

Without answering, Katherine walked to the hallway door. Her sisters followed. She marched them to the Grand Stairway and down its broad curves and then out the Main Entry and into the night.

Several chamber maids and the butler watched them pass but didn't comment.

Katherine walked her sisters along the front of the house until they reached the end of the West Wing. From there she took them to the terrace outside of the Music Room and finally halted.

Christina looked all around her.

Abegaile examined the statuary. A naked child caressed a bird's nest and stared fondly at the four baby birds' open mouths. Abegaile furrowed her brow absently.

Katherine waited until she had their attention.

She inclined her head and crawled visually past the first floor and then the second and finally to the peak of the third story. There, in the reflected light she locked her eyes.

Abegaile sat down without a word as soon as she realized what her sister was indicating.

Christina followed Katherine's gaze, and when she did she felt her knees weaken. "Oh!" was all she could say.

There, above them, poised at the pinnacle of the intersecting roof planes, was their father's gargoyle. Hideous, and imported for that reason, it protruded, its scaly wings bent, its taloned feet clutching the brick ledge, its leering mouth open as if to vomit forth a cry of subterranean horror.

"Oh, Chrissy, it's too much," Abegaile whispered.

"It is, Chrissy; you can't go up there," Katherine quickly and quietly agreed.

Christina locked her knees, regained her breath, and examined the beast.

There was neither a window nor a vent beneath it. He had to have reached it from above. From the roof.

Christina backed away from the terrace, visually following Stephen's probable path. He must have crawled or walked at least two hundred feet along the ridge of the house. "Of course," she murmured," he descended from the keep tower to the roof and went from there." She pivoted and strode off.

"No, Chrissy," Abegaile and Katherine insisted as they tailed her.

Christina stopped and faced her protesting sisters. Her breath was labored.

"Don't you see?" she demanded. "A boy can do it. A *boy* can put it out there. Well — a *girl* shall bring it down!" And she huffed off again.

No one uttered a syllable as they went back to Christina's room. There she took off her dress and threw it over one of her chairs. She pulled off her shoes and then her stockings.

She stood in the center of her room, clad in her bloomers and her overshirt, her hands on her hips.

Abegaile was afraid she was in the beginning of a nightmare.

Katherine feared she was about to lose a sister.

But neither said another word.

Silently, they followed her through the study and then up to the book-walled library and finally up and out onto the roof of the keep. The stars were brilliant, sparkling blue lights as hard and defiant as Christina.

She went to the front of the tower, leaned through a crenel and peered down to the roof below her.

It was at least a seven foot drop.

To the slick stone of their roof.

From there it was a sixty foot slide down the inclined slate and then another thirty foot fall to the night-shrouded ground below.

Christina imagined lowering herself from the keep and dropping the last few feet to the ridge and there losing her balance. She heard her echoing scream.

It was her phantom scream which made her do it. It was the fact that she would scream as a girl which propelled her over the edge of the tower, past the stone battlements, her sisters gasping when she did.

Abegaile failed to stifle the birth of a sob.

Christina hung, her hands grasping the lip of the crenel she had climbed through, her feet dangling far below, but not far enough.

Most important would be the second when she came in contact with the ridge. She had to break her fall. She had to keep her balance. And she had to immediately lower herself farther and keep from screaming.

It seemed their house stretched black beneath her forever.

Christina held her breath.

She released her hands.

Abegaile couldn't watch. She ran to the other side of the keep tower. She knew her sister would soon be dead.

Just as her brother was dead.

And their family was cursed.

Christina fell through the night until her bare feet slapped against the cold slate and she broke her fall and sank to the ridge. It had been little more than a shadow moments earlier. Now, she rode it.

She was astride, her legs to either side. She leaned forward and clutched the planes of the roof. It was as if she had mounted the huge black bull of their house. It was a medieval monster — a force of such magnitude that it did not even know she had straddled its back.

It was her father's monster.

No, it was hers.

And Abegaile's.

And Katherine's.

Christina found she was shaking badly. The cold from the slate crawled through her and for a moment she thought the house was beginning to undulate beneath.

She took several deep breaths and forced herself to look up at the night sky.

Katherine smiled down at her.

Christina smiled back.

Abegaile opened her eyes and crept over to Katherine. "Is she gone?" she whispered.

Katherine put her arm around her twin. "No, Abbie, she's still with us."

Abegaile gulped loudly and then tentatively leaned out to see her sister.

Christina smiled at her, too.

"How will you get back up?" Abegaile asked quietly.

Christina laughed.

"I'm not worried about getting *up*, Abbie. I'm worried about falling down!"

Christina breathed deeply a few more times and then tried to raise herself from the roof. She pushed her bottom into the air, her hands still clutching the v-shaped tiles of the ridge.

At first she couldn't force herself to release her hands and stand.

She attempted twice, but as she did she felt a tremendous lightness in her chest and air swirling madly about her ears. Each time she lowered her hands quickly to the roof. With the third attempt she regained her height. She slowly raised her arms so they extended out from her body.

Ever so tentatively she took a small step forward.

Her feet were on either side of the ridge and they matched the angles of the roof.

She took another step and then another, gradually lengthening them as she did. Her body swayed slightly.

Katherine and Abegaile forced themselves to look along the length Christina was to walk.

It disappeared into the darkness.

It was horrible.

"Oh, do come back, Chrissy," Abegaile called out to her. "Oh, do come back!"

Christina turned her head to Abegaile and that was a mistake. It so upset her equilibrium that she windmilled her arms. Her right foot slipped down several inches.

Abegaile blurted "Eeek!" and stuffed her fist into her mouth.

Katherine reached out as if to help her distant sister.

Christina lowered herself back to the roof and attempted to stop her heart from racing. "You have to leave me alone," she hissed back to them. "I can't look back. I just can't!"

"I'm sorry, Chrissy," Abegaile pleaded. "I was so frightened!"

Abegaile and Katherine heard their sister laugh.

"*You* were frightened!"

Christina got to her feet again and continued. Occasionally, the big house would appear to begin its own movements again, but each time Christina was able to control her fear and walk on, ignoring it.

As she got farther from her sisters she felt more and more alone. Even the house seemed to lose its overpowering strength, until at last she felt as if she were on a tightrope high in the air, above the world. She was performing.

The stars lowered and their brightness was frightening, white and fierce, and then they too changed and they were soft, calling to her, beckoning her to leave the house and go to them, and at those times Christina believed she could fly to them and they would welcome her into their midst. So consumed was Christina in what was above her that had she come to the end of the ridge she would have walked right out into the heavy night air.

She walked light footed and sure, and gradually she brought her arms down to her sides. She was above everything. She was not a part of her father's house. She was not a member of his family.

She was not his daughter.

It was as she thought of her separation that Christina did walk into the air.

She had been progressing at a sleepwalker's pace, oblivious to her feet, unaware of where she was, when suddenly she felt herself falling.

For a moment she mistook the motion for ascension, and then she knew it was not.

The ridge of the Tudor mansion was neither straight nor unbroken. Several times the roof line dropped three or four feet where it joined a lower section, and once it crooked to the left, above the conservatory.

Christina had reached a place where the roof line dropped several feet, and she had walked off of the main ridge.

She slammed to the roof below her, falling backwards as she did and striking her head against the brick of the higher end of the house. She didn't break her fall evenly; rather, she touched her left foot first and it collapsed under her. Then her right foot hit the slate and she was prepared and able to catch herself on that side. The overall effect was to send her tumbling to her left, over the front slant of the house roof.

She slid, losing all contact with the ridge.

Christina knew she was out of control, on her way for a very long slide and then the sure, fatal fall to the ground.

She crashed into something.

It was a chimney. Fortunately, she had fallen to the left, for there was no matching edifice on the right-hand slant of roof. Christina lay wedged against the brick and allowed her heart to stop fluttering. The chimney towered black above her, dividing into four, octagonal flues which seemed to scrape the stars.

Did I scream? she asked herself as she tore her attention away from the chimney.

If so, she knew she would hear her would-be rescuers soon.

But the night was still quiet.

She was able to prop her feet against the side of the chimney and stretch until she pushed herself back up to the lower ridge. She turned and grasped it with her fingertips and climbed back to the house's spine, there resting once more. From where she sat she could see the end of the lower roof ridge approximately sixty feet away.

Her fall should have frightened her into immobility but it did not. Christina, angry because she had been so careless, was once again able to convince herself that it was the same as walking on a wide slanting board on the ground.

Embracing that perception would have been more difficult had it been daylight.

But it was night.

The last distance was the easiest and Christina traversed it without incident. She sat astride the roof at its terminus and was delivered a double shock soon after.

The first came when she lay forward to view her gargoyle. As she did, the distance to the lighted terrace below became clear. It was a long, long drop.

Christina's stomach turned until she thought she would vomit. Then she lost her equilibrium and the house pitched smoothly under her.

Stop! Stop! Stop! she commanded, unsure if she were addressing her imagination or her father's house. She pressed her body once more onto the cold roof. The side of her face was flush with the slate and she trembled.

Slowly, she began to chant to herself, *I can do it. I can do it.*

The second frightful surprise came with the realization that her father's monster was perched far below the ridge of the roof. She had thought she would be able to reach down to its mouth.

That was folly.

The back of the gargoyle was fully four feet below her and its body extended the same distance outward.

It had appeared so easy from the ground.

How had Stephen managed? How had he gotten to that thing's hideous mouth?

Christina concentrated on the answers.

She knew what was necessary to reach the beast. She carefully raised herself to her hands and knees and turned so she faced the direction she had come, finally lowering her body until she lay on the roof once more. And then with heart-stopping caution she inched backward, her feet extending over the end of the house, brushing the dark night air.

Soon, her knees were free, above the gargoyle and the distant terrace.

She continued edging backward.

She was mid-thigh.

And Christina knew that in a moment her point of balance would shift as the majority of her weight was off the roof. She would begin to slide then and she knew there was nothing she could grasp to arrest her fall.

She would inexorably slip over the edge.

If the back of the gargoyle were farther below her than she had estimated — or if her feet skidded at the crucial moment when they touched — she knew there would be no chimney to save her.

They would find her on the terrace.

She pushed herself out farther and gravity began to pull her over.

Desperately, she tried to grip the smooth slates as they passed under her hands.

Her waist was in the air and she was falling.

She dragged her fingernails against the slate.

Her feet touched.

Christina gripped the monster's back with her flexed toes.

She stopped.

Her forearms were still stretched along the twin slopes of the roof. She hesitated and then allowed her legs to bend slightly at the knees to help with her balance. She still needed to turn so she faced away from the house.

She moved her feet, nibbling the stone with her toes, willing them to hold her steady. She twisted her torso until she was able to complete her turn, and then in one motion she lowered herself to the gargoyle's back.

His texture was rough, nearly that of poorly finished sandstone and Christina could feel the outline of each patterned scale on his back. She wedged her knees against the folds of the outstretched wings and clutched her arms around his neck.

She did not reach at first to retrieve the note, instead she lay against the thing jutting from the side of her father's house, preparing to fly off into the beckoning night.

What if it can't bear my weight? she thought. *What if it pulls loose from Papa's house and we both crash below?*

And then, strangely, Christina found herself in a floating calm, the stone warming beneath her, the air now hot and moist and soothing. She rested and then reached around to the thing's mouth, almost petting it as she did. She felt past the chiseled canine teeth and probed above its thick protruding tongue.

There was nothing.

There was no note.

At first she thought she had somehow missed it and then she began to anger and finally it was humorous and she laughed; lightly at first and then hysterically. It was all so funny. So ridiculously funny. She had risked her life for a bet. She had risked her life to prove that she was as good as a boy, and all along she had accepted his rules, his premise.

Christina laughed at herself and even continued chuckling when she rose and turned and hoisted herself back to the ridge.

She returned carefully, climbing the raised ridge by the chimney, and several times hesitating as she felt her control deserting her, but in the end she was below the keep tower, smiling up at her sisters who leaned out, holding onto the battlements. They looked down at her, their faces puffed and misshapen from crying.

Christina laughed again when she realized she stood beside a cast ladder extending upward, obscured from above by the projecting parapet.

That night all three girls stayed in Christina's room.

Abegaile and Katherine wished Christina to tell them more about her trip along the ridge of the house.

"I don't want to talk about it," Christina answered with conviction.

"Tell us!" Abegaile demanded.

Katherine gave Abegaile a long look. She had gotten so bold recently. Normally she sat back and listened and watched. Katherine had consistently taken her twin's reticence for granted but now she began to doubt it. Further, she saw that Abegaile was not the plain little girl she had once been. She was changing.

Abegaile realized Katherine was staring at her. "Make her tell us, Katie. Make Chrissy tell us what it was like!"

Katherine kept her eyes locked on Abegaile a moment longer and then turned to Christina. "Tell us, Chrissy," she said quietly, "or we'll go and find out for ourselves."

Christina looked to Abegaile to see if it was a bluff

Abegaile swallowed with effort and then said softly, "Actually, I think I can wait until Chrissy's ready to tell." With that she fell back to the bed and feigned sleep.

"Big help you are!" Katherine teased and punched Abegaile's side.

Then Katherine, too, fell to the bed and finally Christina came over and lay with her sisters.

Katherine fell asleep first, her breathing shallow and noisy while Abegaile and Christina tossed about, each aware that the other was awake.

Christina was thinking that the house was inordinately quiet for the middle of the night — until she realized the opposite was true — there were different sounds mixing with the normal overlay of creaks and groans.

Abegaile understood what was happening before Christina.

She sat up slowly, propping herself on an elbow.

Christina opened her eyes and saw Abegaile staring across the room to the study.

"It's the elevator," Abegaile whispered, her words barely carrying the short distance to Christina.

There was a distant whirring interrupted by muffled clanks and shuffles. And then there was silence.

Both girls heard the door quietly swing open.

"Papa?" Abegaile softly questioned her sister.

Christina was emotionally spent and in no mood to play guessing games. She didn't answer. But she listened carefully.

"Mama?" Abegaile whispered next. She didn't hesitate with the hushed remainder of her list: "Anna? Stephen?" and finally, "*Rosey?*"

Christina was now sitting, also.

"Sssssst!" carried into the girls' room. And then "Sssssst!" came again.

It had to be the boy and both girls knew it.

They pulled the covers to their necks.

A black form appeared in the doorway.

"What are you doing in here!" Abegaile demanded, still cautious to keep her voice very low.

Stephen didn't think it sounded like Christina.

"Who's that?" he whispered back and as he did he became frightened that Christina had a visitor. He prepared to leap back through the study and into the elevator.

This time there was no mistaking Abegaile. "Who do you *think* it is, you fool!" The tone was more aggressive than normal, but the voice was definitely hers.

"Abegaile! What are you doing here?" be asked incredulously.

"What am *I* doing here!" she responded, incensed, her voice rising.

Under any other circumstances she would have been awash in embarrassment, so obviously was she interfering with the boy's plans, but she had gone through much in the time she waited for her Christina's return — in the time she awaited her scream and fall — and somehow, Stephen-the-boy was now more a bother than an amorous adventurer.

Stephen realized there were two shapes sitting at the head of the bed.

"Are you frightened?" he asked. "What I mean is, has something happened? Is something the matter?" He couldn't figure why they were in bed together.

"Don't be silly," Abegaile answered shortly.

At last Christina spoke. "Fixing the elevator, Stephen?"

"Christina!" he responded.

Katherine stirred and asked from the borders of sleep, "Is this a party?"

Stephen began to question whether it was worth the risk to talk to all three of them. "I was just wandering around ...."

It sounded stupid when he said it.

"Papa would be impressed," Christina taunted.

The boy was very uncomfortable with her tone. "Say, you didn't find the note, I'll bet."

Christina waited.

"Did you even look yet?" he asked.

Abegaile fumed in the darkness.

"It doesn't matter, Stephen," Christina answered calmly. "It really doesn't matter."

The boy was truly baffled.

Abegaile couldn't remain silent. "You could have killed her, Stephen. Is that the kind of person you are? Is that your idea of a joke?"

"Killed her?" he questioned. "What are you talking about? Who's going to get killed reaching into a statue's mouth? Tell me that." He took a step forward as he spoke and then he stopped. He was, after all, in a bedroom with three girls.

Abegaile continued berating him. "She could have fallen — don't pretend to be so high and innocent!"

Stephen stepped closer.

"How can you fall reaching into that stupid thing's mouth?" he argued quietly. "You might trip on the step, but I think Christina can manage a step or two."

"What are you talking about?" Abegaile demanded.

Katherine lay with her eyes open, amused with the heated exchange that was taking place between once-quiet Abegaile and Stephen, *in Christina's bedroom, in the middle of the night!*

"What are you talking about? I put the note in the mouth of those ugly things by the entrance to the Birch Allee."

"Papa's Foo Dogs!" Katherine exclaimed and broke into hysterics.

Stephen waited until Katherine calmed down, and then he asked Christina, "What's going on?"

"I really don't want to discuss it, Stephen," Christina answered.

Abegaile jumped in. "We thought it was on the roof, Stephen. We thought it was in Papa's gargoyle and so Christina climbed up and walked along the whole *roof* and it wasn't even *there*! She could have fallen! She could have died!" Abegaile finished with, "You are so *stupid*!"

As she spoke, Stephen backed to the wall and then slid down it. By the time she finished he was seated on the floor, his mouth hanging. He couldn't speak once Abegaile finished.

All four of them were silent, the house shifting as a freak night wind rubbed along its length.

At last he struggled back to his feet. "I'm sorry, Christina. Oh, my God, I really am sorry."

He edged out of the room. "I could have killed you," he whispered.

The thought of Christina on the ridge of the mansion churned his stomach.

I'm not good for her, he berated himself. *I've got to leave all of them alone.*

He pictured the girl falling through the air and then he saw her broken, on the ground, and he was sickened. He didn't for a second see any of what had happened as a joke.

The image of Christina's fall haunted him as he entered the elevator and closed the door. It was the most horrible thing he had ever imagined and it didn't matter that Christina was still safe — that she hadn't fallen.

He went to his bed, physically sick.

STEPHEN AND ABEGAILE

Early the next day Mrs. Van Luxall was back from her visit. She had learned her husband had abridged his meetings and would be coming back earlier than expected, that evening in fact, and so she added that knowledge to her current burden.

And took a nap.

The girls saw nothing of Stephen and they were uncertain if he were avoiding them. Christina realized it was probably a combination of factors which kept them apart — their mother's return, the preparations for their father's arrival, and the fact that none of the girls made any attempts to make themselves available to be 'found'.

Not one of them sought his note, even though each thought of it.

Christina attributed her aversion to disdain for the childishness of it, while Abegaile was restrained by residual anger. Further, she knew it wasn't intended for her, and Katherine had no desire to further involve herself in the confusing three-some.

Stephen kept himself as busy and as distant from the girls as possible. He spent his day in trivial maintenance at some of the more isolated buildings on the estate.

He decided he loved Christina too much for her good.

He was an interloper in her life. He didn't belong there yet, even at its fringes.

And as he thought these things, Stephen toyed with the idea of leaving. He was sick of skulking about her father's estate, sneaking through the grounds and corridors like a thief, hoping to get a glimpse of Christina. He would leave and do things to make her proud of him. When he faced her father again he would be a man with a future and with power.

As the end of the day approached, Stephen returned to the carriage house. He was surprised when he saw Mr. Van Luxall's long touring car motoring in from the gatehouse. He took a fresh interest in the man and watched intently as the vehicle approached. Soon it would veer toward the Main House.

It did not. It stopped.

Mr. Van Luxall strode from the back of the vehicle. Stephen sensed what had happened and so knowing, drew himself up and waited.

He started to greet the girls' father, but was cut short.

"Here's your pay." The elder Van Luxall spat the words. "Remove yourself from my property before sunset; if you return I'll have you arrested and thrown into this state's darkest jail. If you attempt to communicate with my daughters — " he hesitated as he weighed the wisdom of unveiling a homicidal threat. Instead of finishing verbally, he concluded with his most hateful, loathsome glare.

Stephen's father was at the side of the idling car, his cap in his hands, his head lowered.

The sight of his father so defeated humbled Stephen more than any of Van Luxall's scathing words. As the boy looked from his father to the man who was looming over him, a thick hand thrust forward with a thin white envelope.

Stephen looked directly at his former employer and wished for all of the world there was something he could say, but there was not. He turned his head toward the Main House and when he did — when he averted his attention from Mr. Van Luxall and so obviously sought his daughters — the big man took it as the final insult.

Stephen's father watched his employer crumble the envelope in his fist, draw back and slam the boy across the drive.

Stephen was knocked cleanly off his feet. His head hit the gravel and a black curtain fluttered down. But it lifted as quickly and Stephen shouted to his father who was now advancing behind Van Luxall.

"Stop! He's right! I had it coming. Go back to the car. It was my fault." He shook his head to clear it and massaged his jaw.

Mr. Van Luxall feared no attack from behind and so he made no effort to see if his driver were near. Instead, he remained above the downed boy, staring at him, until at last be dropped the envelope and walked to the Main House, nearly stepping on the Stephen as he passed.

The girls learned from Anna.

While it was customary for them to dine formerly with their father when he returned, that evening they did not. They were at the children's table — Katherine moving smalls bits of food about with her fork; Abegaile forlornly and quietly crying, her tears falling freely onto her napkin, while Christina sat rigid, her eyes blank and unfocusing. They had been thus for half an hour when their father entered the room, left three small packages on the seat of a chair by the door and departed without speaking.

Abegaile renewed her sobbing and Katherine rose and left the room.

The following day they endured their tutorials and then spent the afternoon in their rooms. The next day was the same, and the next.

The weather changed and a summer storm banked in from the west, dumping rain on the mansion and grounds for three days. The downspouts rushed water, storm drains clogged, and the Grand Lawn was flooded.

The sky cleared late the third night and in the morning the last moisture dripped from the open mouth of Mr. Van Luxall's gargoyle.

With the morning and the new sun, the little Oriental grounds man flip-flopped to the Walled Garden. He carried several plantings from the greenhouse and hummed softly to himself as he proceeded, cautiously remaining on the flagstone paths. Once inside the garden he passed the reflecting pool and the still fountain. He put the pots down on one of the stone benches at the serving shed and swung the big door open.

He was the first to see Abegaile, her body cold and naked, a note crumbled on the floor beneath her slowly turning feet.

THE FIRE

The summer passed.

Katherine and Christina rarely spoke.

Christina went to the family mausoleum every morning and sat sobbing on its steps. And in the evening Katherine walked to the marble building, bringing with her a handful of flowers which she left in an increasing pile against the bronze doors.

Mrs. Van Luxall had her sleeping quarters moved to the back of the house, and there she remained, in her bed, staring through the windows to the Walled Garden. She took her meals in her room, and other than those who attended her, she would see no one.

Mr. Van Luxall did not appear to notice.

The fall came wet and cold, the leaves turning and tumbling to the ground soon after. The gloom and depression was so pervasive that it insinuated itself into the servants and soon their despondency permeated the manor no less thoroughly than the family's. A lucky few sought employment elsewhere.

Christina and Katherine mumbled through their studies while their mother withered in her room, unavailable.

Mr. Van Luxall's trips became more frequent and of longer duration. There were rumors that his businesses were failing, but no one knew for certain. Then one early winter morning word riffled through the manor that he was taking Mrs. Van Luxall with him on an extended cruise aboard the liner, Ile de France. They would depart after he returned from a short business trip.

Mrs. Van Luxall seemed not to understand, or if she did, to care.

Her husband left on a Tuesday. There was a light snow the following day and it brought with it a winter chill. At noon Mrs. Van Luxall surprised the butler by calling him to her room. She didn't turn from the window as she spoke.

"Coal is too expensive. We'll heat the manor by fireplace only."

It was a ridiculous notion and the butler feared she had finally slipped from everyone's reach. Fortunately, Mr. Van Luxall was due to return soon.

That night, stacked logs burned brightly in all of the fireplaces.

After midnight the wind picked up, rattling some of the windows, and just after two in the morning Mrs. Van Luxall rose.

She started at the conservatory in the West Wing, first swinging open the vast double doors and then walking directly to the fireplace. She levered several burning logs across the hearth and onto the Persian rug Mr. Van Luxall had commissioned for the room. The wind wove past her, immediately suckling new flames from the scattered, glowing coals.

She left the conservatory and loosed the fire in each of the rooms she entered. By the fifth room the flames were raging in pursuit down the wide hall. She proceeded into the dining room, there opening the tall leaded windows with their colored medallions. Looking outside, she saw the fire's glow reflecting from the turned faces of the terrace statuary.

The manor was afire and it was awake. Above the crackling roar servants and maids screamed and called to one another. A thick fog of searing smoke poured through the downstairs hall, forcing those who were able to escape to cover their faces.

The flames raced along the oiled wooden floors, fingering upward as they did, consuming artwork and antiques. Ancient Chinese vases toppled from crumbling stands. Flemish tapestries gave birth to curtains of fire. Furnishings that had survived hundreds, even thousands of years erupted in volcanic fury.

The flames sought the second and then the third floor of the manor.

Anna burst into Christina's room.

"GET OUT, CHILD! GET OUT! THE HOUSE IS BURNING!"

Anna had come in through the study but when she went to propel Christina out the closer hall door she opened it to thick smoke. Anna banged the door shut and grabbed the girl and pushed her toward the study. Smoke was beginning to fill that room, too.

On the other side of the study was another bathroom and beyond it the stairway.

"GO THROUGH TO THE STAIRS!" Anna shouted. "I'll GET KATHERINE!"

Christina stood dumb for a moment and then turned to run with Anna through Abegaile's room to Katherine's. Anna stopped and grabbed the girl and violently shook her. "THERE'S NO TIME — NOW GO!" she screamed. She spun Christina about and pushed her out of the room.

Anna then flung open Abegaile's door and disappeared into the smoke. Christina turned and watched her open Katherine's door to flames.

Anna charged through them.

Christina found her voice. "ANNA! KATIE!" she screamed. She screamed again.

The flames spread in waves into Abegaile's room. Her bed exploded with fire. Burning curtains fell to the floor and windows popped and burst outward with the escaping winds.

The incredible heat slammed into Christina. She covered her face and backed away. Every time she tried to rush forward she ended up losing ground. Flames spread through her bedroom.

She backed out. The floor was hot beneath her.

Christina turned and ran through to the stairway. Smoke billowed upward. The steps smoldered. Wallpaper curled and paint dripped from the paintings lining the walls.

Christina went down and down and down through the smoke, her lungs aching, the roar of the fire and the screams and shouts of others accompanying her. She broke from the back door and fled across the terrace. The heat from the fire followed her, only lessening when she reached the Formal Gardens.

Christina turned.

There was fire everywhere.

The house seemed larger, the flames extending its height another fifty feet. Fire roared from the windows; amber rivers climbed the walls and licked through holes in the roof. Smoke blotted the heavens. Windows shattered and breaking glass impossibly punctuated the night. The roof above the West Wing collapsed and a mad whirlwind of sparks mushroomed from it.

Christina could not leave the walled garden. She curled in refuge against the stone shed of her sister.

CHRISTINA

Mr. Van Luxall sent Christina to boarding school.

ROSEY

From a chambermaid's perspective, Fairelawn was not much different from The Chimneys.

Fairelawn was Provincial in design and had a few more rooms. The Chimneys was Tudor Revival and had elevators. At The Chimneys, Rosey had worn a black uniform with a white apron until after dinner when she changed to burgundy with white trim. Fairelawn required pale blue in the morning and a white in the evening. Her aprons were white. Mrs. Van Luxall had her linens folded; Mrs. Wingate insisted everything be rolled. There was not a crease to be seen at Fairelawn.

But another difference was soon discovered.

Rosey met with several of the other maids, and took an immediate liking to a petite, mousey-haired girl named Doris. As luck would have it, they were to share a small dormer room in the service wing of the mansion.

Doris took her new friend up to their room. Rosey entered the room in a rush and dumped her cardboard suitcase onto the bed.

"Well, tell me!" she insisted, referring to the question she had just asked Doris. She was wasting no time before she got the most vital information about Fairelawn.

Doris leaned against a wall and looked out the window. At first she made no attempt to answer. Finally, she turned to Rosey, who now stood with her hands on her hips.

"The boys are pretty plain, really. Peter is about the best of the lot, but he's odd. Doesn't seem to notice the girls."

Doris smoothed the front of her apron. "What were they like at The Chimneys?"

Rosey laughed. She had opened her suitcase and was transferring its contents to a small dresser. She thought of Stephen.

"There was one boy —" She stopped mid-sentence and sat on the corner of her bed. She rested a dress in her lap and ran her fingers idly over its material. Until that moment she had taken Stephen for granted.

He was fun. They had played together often and be was handsome. These things Rosey had known, but now she thought of him at a different manor. She realized she would miss him.

"Of course, there *is* Nelson," Doris said, tired of waiting for Rosey to finish her sentence, and taking the opportunity to tempt her.

"He's a real Valentino; laughs a lot, and has the girls fighting to be near him."

"Nelson?" Rosey asked.

Doris laughed. "He'd be perfect for you, Rosey. Absolutely perfect — except —"

Rosey was back on her feet. She discarded Stephen's memory, tossed the folded dress aside and ran to Doris, pretending to throttle the girl.

"Tell me! *Except what?* Is he married?"

Doris laughed. "No — he's not married."

"Then, what?"

Doris grinned impishly. "He's the master's son—his father is *Andrew Paxton Wingate. The Third.*"

Rosey released her hands from her new friend's throat and went back to the suitcase.

"How handsome *is* he?"

Instead of answering, Doris fell onto the bed, pretending to faint.

"That *handsome*?" Rosey teased.

Doris opened one eye. Then she rolled over, spreading her arms.

Rosey laughed as she watched.

"That handsome!" Doris exclaimed and got back to her feet.

As she did, the door opened and the housekeeper stepped into the little room.

Rosey was about to learn the biggest difference between Fairelawn and The Chimneys.

Eleanora, the housekeeper at Fairelawn — the woman who was in charge of all of the female domestics in the manor — would brook no nonsense.

She was a tyrant.

She looked at the new wrinkles in Doris's apron and uniform and her eyes narrowed.

"Press it again, missy," was all she said, but Doris immediately disappeared out the door.

"*Rosey*, is it?" Eleanora asked slowly as she and the girl stood in opposition.

Rosey raised herself to full height.

"Yes, mam." She didn't like the housekeeper already.

Eleanora stared at her for a minute. Then she pivoted and left the room without another word.

The next day Rosey saw Nelson, confirmed Doris's appraisal of his attractiveness, and realized who he was.

"I know him," she whispered to Doris, walking beside her with her own stack of rolled, fresh linens. Nelson had just crossed the hall before them.

"Oh really!" Doris answered in mock surprise.

"He goes to The Chimneys all the time," Rosey whispered, "to see Christina Van Luxall — the oldest daughter," and as she spoke and remembered the girl, she angered.

Doris saw the change in her friend. Rosey's eyes were pinched and her jaw was set.

She was about to comment when Eleanora hove into sight at the end of the corridor. Doris turned smartly into the next bedroom. Rosey continued toward the housekeeper.

Just as Eleanora and Rosey were less than twenty feet apart, Nelson reappeared in the hall. He saw the housekeeper and nodded and then noticed Rosey.

He stopped.

"Good morning!" he intoned, cheerfully.

"Morning, sir," Rosey answered without inflection.

Nelson looked Rosey over from head to foot. Satisfied, he turned back to Eleanora.

"Please bring some fruit to my room," be said, and from his bearing the housekeeper knew he intended for her to do it personally.

It was demeaning and it set Eleanora on edge. Her skin prickled. She opened her mouth and then shut it. She was less than five feet from a house telephone she could have used to call the kitchen and have the fruit sent up.

Nelson smiled at the housekeeper. "Thank you, Eleanora."

The big woman turned to the stairway. She couldn't help looking over her shoulder as she descended.

Eleanora ceased to exist for Nelson. He studied Rosey. "Miss — ?" he asked.

"Rosey, sir," she answered and looked down as she did. It was a movement which usually pleased the men.

Nelson was pleased.

"You're new with Fairelawn?"

She kept her head low and slowly drew in her breath to expand her chest.

"Yes, sir."

The boy continued to judge her. She was young and pretty and her red hair tempted him immediately. He wondered.

"Welcome to our home, Rosey," he said after she again raised her head.

He met her eyes and held them.

"Welcome," he repeated.

"Yes, sir," she answered, "Thank you, sir."

"And you're in room. . . ?"

The maids' rooms were numbered.

Rosey knew, but pretended to have forgotten. She wished to remain in his presence a while longer.

"Twenty-seven," she said at last.

"Twenty-seven," he repeated, evenly. "Well, well — I used to hide there as a child. It's a small room as I recall. We rarely assign it. Only two beds."

Nelson Paxton Wingate, at eighteen, exuded the assurance and grating superiority of a man three times his age. When he spoke to Rosey it was as if he were granting her an audience — which in many ways he was.

Rosey watched and determined it was not quite time to abandon her role as the fawning, subservient girl.

Soon enough, Master Wingate, she thought. *Soon enough, you'll be looking up to me,* she whispered silently and then dared to glance at him again.

A new challenge, he teased himself and then amended, *A new diversion; the help is never a challenge.*

"I shall look forward to seeing more of you, Miss Rosey."

He smiled as he backed away and returned to his room.

Rosey stood by his closed door and then heard Eleanora puffing up the stairs. She went quickly back to where she had seen Doris disappear earlier. Rosey was through the door and had it closed before the housekeeper reached the hallway.

Doris was bent over a bed, stretching a sheet. She saw Rosey and was about to speak when Rosey raised a finger to her lips. Doris stopped fussing with the bed and waited. Both girls heard Eleanora knock at Nelson's door. She knocked again.

An assured voice called through the closed door, "Thank you, Eleanora, but I've changed my mind; you may return the fruit to the kitchen."

Eleanora came close to dashing the fruit onto the floor but restrained herself.

That boy has the same damning attitude as his father, she thought and then moved back down the hall, all the while muttering, "That new girl's in his room — I'd bet the Christmas ham!"

Fortunately, Rosey realized what the housekeeper would think. In a flash she threw open Doris's door and dashed out into the hall, nearly running into Eleanora.

The housekeeper stood and sputtered. She looked down the hall to Nelson's room and then back at the girl and realized she had been wrong. It did nothing to assuage her anger.

Unfortunately, Rosey couldn't help but smile.

With that, the housekeeper thrust the bowl of fruit to her, stacking it on Rosey's linen.

"Take this to the dumbwaiter — send it down — it's at the end of the corridor," she said, pointing.

When she placed the bowl on Rosey's linen, she was not content with that alone. She depressed it there, nearly succeeding in pushing the entire bundle, fruit and all, from the girl's hands.

Rosey sank with the pressure, tightened her grip, and recovered sufficiently to act as if she were curtseying.

"Yes, mam," she answered and left before Eleanora could do anything more.

"That one's trouble," the housekeeper said to herself, attempting to mollify the embarrassment of her earlier error. She continued her cruise through the upper corridors, thinking as she did of the complications associated with the new girl:

First, Rosey's mother was top-drawer. It was obvious already that she was quick and would soon be ingratiating herself with the Wingates. Further, Rosey had already gained favor with Nelson, the family's overindulged son. And worst of all, Mr. and Mrs. Wingate frequently traveled, leaving the older boy as the titular and sometimes actual head of the manor while they were away. It would be too easy for the elder Wingates to return from a voyage and find a new housekeeper in charge.

Far too easy.

But that was not enough to keep Eleanora from attempting to wend her way around the various traps and cause trouble for the girl.

She checked the linens and the bathrooms, and grudgingly satisfied, returned to the first floor.

It was a week before Rosey had anything more than a fleeting glance of Nelson. She and Doris were in their room, preparing to dress for bed, when the service light over Rosey's bureau was illuminated. Rosey turned and lifted the maids' phone.

But Elisabeth, the house operator, was not on the line.

"I'm sorry — ?" Rosey said, unsure of what she had just heard.

The male voice repeated, "I need fresh towels, immediately."

And then, "This is Nelson Wingate — please remember I'm not used to being kept waiting."

Rosey glanced over to Doris and smiled with tempered evil.

"Yes, sir, *immediately*," she said and stepped away from the mouthpiece.

"Nelson," was all Rosey said to her roommate as she dressed and then departed.

"Nelson, indeed," Doris whispered with delight after her friend was gone.

Rosey was surprised to see that Eleanora's door was not open. Normally, the housekeeper peered out from her bed at anyone who passed to enter the Main House. She slept on her back with her face toward the open door a pale, twisted, leviathan hovering near the maids' escape. And with any sound, regardless of how soft, she always opened at least one eye to investigate. Doris told Rosey that Eleanora never really awakened, that her eye opening was a nervous twitch.

Both girls laughed and neither believed it.

Rosey went to the vast linen room, took three thick, rolled towels from a stack, and proceeded to Nelson's quarters.

The house was quiet as she passed through it, her footfalls muffled on various rugs. The majority of the hall lights were extinguished and a breeze gently coursed through the louvered doors separating the various rooms from the hallway. 'Bombay doors' Doris called them. Each was constructed so the louvered outer door and the regular door built flush with it could be closed as a unit or separately. With the louvered door closed and its mate open, air could circulate through the rooms and into the hallway, thus cooling the entire house while allowing privacy.

When Rosey approached Nelson's door she saw it was ajar.

She smiled to herself as she tapped lightly on the door and then pushed it inward. It was time to discard her 'awestruck servant' demeanor.

She had been thinking of what to expect and her suspicions were confirmed.

He was not in the huge bedroom.

Rosey smiled again when she heard the shower running. She stood in his bedroom and waited.

Eventually, the water was turned off. Nelson was humming.

He padded into his bedroom, making no attempt to cover himself as he dripped across the room to Rosey.

"Ah, yes, thank you," he said and took the top towel.

She stared at his eyes, defying his nudity.

Nelson made a show of drying his hair. Twice, he abruptly stopped and checked the direction of the maid's glance. Twice, Rosey met him with a vengeance, her eyes never wavering from his face.

Finally, she passed him and went into his bathroom. She lay the remaining linens on the shelves and saw at her feet a row of sodden towels. Still rolled. She retrieved them and carried the dripping cloth logs into the bedroom.

Nelson stood facing her, the towel now draped across his shoulders and behind his neck.

Rosey couldn't resist. She could play his game.

She slowly walked her eyes down his body, admiring his chest and arms and flat stomach. She paused and then looked at his manhood.

She hesitated.

"Will that be *all*, sir," she asked, her eyes still lowered.

Nelson was quiet for a moment and then he chuckled softly.

Rosey raised her eyes to meet his.

She smiled.

He pulled the towel from his shoulders and wrapped it around his waist. He did so unconsciously, not realizing what he had done until after the fact.

This time his laughter was genuine.

"Well, well," he said and continued laughing.

The dripping water from the towels was beginning to pool at Rosey's feet. Additionally, much of it had run onto the front of her uniform and by the time Rosey noticed it, it had soaked through to her undergarments.

Nelson stepped to her and took the wet towels. He pitched them gracefully across the room and into the bathroom.

"They'll get them in the morning," he said.

His use of 'they' irritated Rosey.

"Yes," she answered, "we will, sir."

The bib of Rosey's apron was not sufficiently wide to cover her chest. Her white uniform, now thoroughly wet, clung to her.

Nelson made no attempt to hide his interest. He examined her breasts.

Rosey steeled herself for his comment. She was about to be stung by her own bee and she knew it.

Nelson had "Will *that* be all," halfway to his lips when he hesitated.

He looked at her face. She was beautiful, really, in a common, coquettish way. And he was certain that when he used her, she would be using him right back.

Rosey waited for his words until she realized he had stopped himself.

She smiled at him with renewed respect.

He took a heavy robe from the chair at the foot of his bed and put it on, loosening the towel from his waist as he did and allowing it to fall to the floor after he tied his robe closed.

"Rosey, Rosey," he repeated to himself and turned full to her. "We shall have fun Rosey, if you wish."

He allowed her a moment before he asked, "Do you think that possible?"

He was asking and the girl was flattered. He had stopped at the best time and regained control of their meeting. Rosey was mildly startled when she understood what had happened; it had been accomplished deftly and with consideration.

She felt her chest chill from the wet uniform.

Nelson saw and smiled.

"We must be careful, Rosey; Eleanora would love to send you packing. She doesn't like you, you know."

At the mention of the housekeeper, Rosey became tart.

"I think she frightens you more than she does me."

"Oh, you do, do you?" Nelson teased. He combed his fingers through his hair and Rosey was taken with the gesture.

He was a very attractive man in a feminine way.

"A comb would do a better job, sir," she said lightly.

"Would you mind terribly?" he answered.

It was not what she had meant, but Rosey went to the bathroom and came back with a tortoise-shell comb, set in a tooled silver handle.

Nelson seated himself on the edge of his bed and Rosey walked up to him and began to gently comb his wet hair.

Her proximity, along with the translucence of her uniform and the attention she was yielding to him, was intoxicating. She toyed with his hair, first arranging it one way and then another, and all the while he sat and watched her move before him. He had intended to take her to bed, but the more time he spent near her, the more determined he became to defer that pleasure.

Finally, Rosey stepped back.

"Finished?" he asked.

She grinned.

Nelson rose and went to a wall minor.

"Very handsome, indeed," he said. "Exactly correct for sleeping." He brought his hands up and pretended to examine the details of her work. "I'm afraid I'll never be able to achieve this on my own. Would you mind terribly if I asked again for the favor?"

Rosey was about to answer when he continued, "It won't do, though — your sneaking down this way. Eleanora isn't the easiest woman to —" he seemed to struggle for the correct word. " — divert," at last pleased him. He raised a pensive finger to the side of his face. "Let me think of a plan to facilitate your egress from the grasp of our omnipresent and odious housekeeper."

It was plain to Rosey that he didn't expect a response. He was having too much fun listening to himself.

"If my plan is of sufficient merit, will you agree, Rosey?"

"*If* it is of sufficient merit," she responded, teasingly articulating each word.

He looked at a clock on his desk.

"You'd better get back. 'Our friend' is due to return to her room, soon."

Nelson accompanied the girl to his door. Before she left he lifted her chin and pressed his lips to her forehead.

"I believe I underestimated you," he said.

She was about to leave when he stopped her.

"And Rosey — go directly to the third floor before you cross to your room. Our housekeeper is prowling the North Wing."

He closed the door quietly as Rosey turned and stepped softly toward the stairs.

Rosey was certain she had encountered a formidable opponent; Nelson had lost control only briefly. She was also certain her stay at Fairelawn would be interesting.

When Eleanora returned to her room she was fuming; she had been manipulated, she was sure. She glared at the doors of the maids' quarters, running through their numbers until she came to the end room, the room whose door faced her.

Twenty-seven.

The housekeeper imagined its two occupants mocking her.

Rosey bit onto her wrist to keep from laughing. Doris stuffed the corner of a pillow into her mouth.

Moments earlier they had alternated time in front of the keyhole. Doris was watching from her knees when the big housekeeper drifted into the hall like a silent dirigible. The girl moved to the side to allow Rosey the spectacle.

Eleanora's hair exploded in all directions from her head. Her ample robe was wrapped around her body, and the oversized, soft-soled slippers she wore flopped wildly until she stopped, her arms crossed over her chest and her eyes riveted to the girls' door.

At first Rosey feared the housekeeper could somehow see her eye at the keyhole. She was about to back away when Eleanora turned and clopped off to her own room.

"She doesn't question for a minute who's to blame, does she?" Doris whispered.

"Why should she?" Rosey answered. "We took each other's measure the first day."

Later, in the darkness, Doris asked, "Do you think you'll be staying?"

Rosey thought and then answered, "My mother's happy. I know she wants to stay."

She had seen very little of her mother since they had arrived at Fairelawn. Rosey knew it was partly because of the tremendous responsibilities her mother had assumed in her new post at the Wingate's manor, and partly because she was still angry with her daughter. The fact that she had insisted on Rosey staying in a different room indicated that she was distancing herself from the girl. Rosey was hurt, but she also understood — their departure from The Chimney had been timely. And Rosey knew she was no longer a child. From now on she would have to stand or fall on her own.

The next time Nelson called Rosey, he'd had a direct connection spliced between the two rooms.

"Miss Rosey?" he asked, hoping he had not reached Doris.

"Yes, sir," she answered, rubbing her eyes.

"Rosey, listen," he whispered. "Go to the dumbwaiter outside of your room. Wait a minute and then get into it. Close the door and I'll lower you." He waited for his message to register fully with her. "Now remember to be quiet. And be careful."

The girl didn't bother to put on her uniform.

She whispered to Doris, "I'll be back," and then slipped into the hall.

Doris peeked through the crack at the door as Rosey went to the dumbwaiter — the one they used to haul the big baskets of linens to the various floors. Doris was confused and then aghast as she saw her friend crawl into it and pull the door closed behind her.

At first, Rosey feared Nelson would not be ready. There was a lock which immobilized the apparatus, but it had to be set and then released from outside and since she could not release it, she dared not set it. Consequently, if he were not ready, there would be no one to hold the pulleys and arrest her descent. She would plunge to the cellar.

It would not be an enjoyable experience.

But she felt the large wooden box dip as she crawled into it and then rise as the slack was met and checked. She sat with her knees drawn to her chest and descended slowly through the walls of the manor. It was black and the only sound was of the ropes as they rolled over the pulleys. The tiny elevator slowed and then stopped. The lock was set. The door opened and Nelson reached in to help her unfold and depart from her prison.

"Well, well," he whispered.

He grabbed her hand and they ran lightly down the hall to his room.

Their meeting was nothing like the first. From the beginning he was offhand and teasing. Once more, Rosey was set back as she attempted to adjust to his tone. She had expected more jousting.

He took her in his arms as soon as they were in his room.

"Rosey! Rosey!" he teased. "*We are* naughty children!" He released her and went to his bed. He was wearing a satin robe, its material swirled with black and shades of burgundy.

She had been expecting him to kiss her and was disappointed when he didn't.

Beside him on his bed was the comb.

"You promised," he said, indicating.

She saw that his hair was wet and disheveled and she was surprised that she had not noticed it earlier, in the hall. Rosey felt ridiculous in her night gown. It was plain and threadbare — she could not remember what possessed her to risk the halls in that attire.

Yet, Nelson looked at her with approval.

"You are really quite alluring," he said, and she knew he was not teasing.

She went to him and took the proffered comb. He slumped his shoulders and leaned forward, resting his forearms on his knees.

"Do be gentle," he softly implored.

And so Rosey once more combed his hair. She did so slowly and carefully and she felt herself being drawn to him more and more.

It would have been so easy had he taken her the first night.

She would have allowed him.

It was what she wished for.

Now she began to wonder if he would do so the second night.

He didn't.

After she combed his hair in silence for what seemed to be half of the night, he suddenly lay back on the bed and raised his hands and locked his fingers behind his head. He didn't act as if he expected her to lie with him.

"What do you think about at night?" he asked, his manner quiet and trusting.

Rosey was at a loss.

"I don't know," she answered weakly.

"*You don't know!*" he teased, whispering, "*You don't know what you think of before you fall asleep?*"

Rosey turned to him. *Surely, he doesn't want to talk about what I think!*

She tried to see if he were making fun of her. He didn't appear to be.

"I'm serious," he said and repeated his question.

Rosey answered haltingly at first, cautious of the strange ground she was on.

"I think about what I've done, of course," she began and gradually allowed him access to those things which mattered to her.

"Sometimes I imagine myself really living in a grand house — owning it, you know — and arranging the furniture for myself and actually sitting in it." She laughed quietly at how she must sound to him but then she continued, allowing him a glimpse of the skirts of her dreams. At last, he interrupted her. "It's late, Rosey. We'll talk about it again tomorrow night." And they did.

For two weeks he called her in the middle of the night, and each time she stuffed herself into the little service elevator and emerged in a different world.

From the beginning she went easily to his bed and sat opposite him as she combed his hair, and by the end of the second week, they talked reclining — Rosey with her head upon his naked chest and one hand on his shoulder.

At first she suspected he didn't have any sexual interest in her, but that concern was addressed when she lay her leg across his middle.

He was interested.

During the day Rosey wondered as she cleaned, curious as to what exactly was happening. She had been prepared to battle him, to make him suffer a bit, but she found that he presented nothing to strike against. From the moment she emerged from the elevator until she once more closed the little door behind her, he behaved civilly and as a friend, even.

A close friend.

Eleanora was beside herself. The new girl was efficient, though slow — preoccupied, most likely — and she appeared to be keeping away from the Wingate boy. *The Wingate boy.* Each time Eleanora thought of Nelson Wingate as a boy she was repulsed. *Ought to be earning his keep, that one!* she repeated to herself in her nastiest tone.

Several times the housekeeper remained awake most of the night, but no one passed her room to access the door and the rest of the house beyond. Two nights she rose and locked the door to the stairs and the hallway.

Those had been her worst nights for she knew locking that door was strictly forbidden by Mrs. Wingate. After the Triangle Shirt fire, such things weren't done.

She watched the girl at her job and tried to relax. Perhaps she had judged her prematurely. But every time she decided that was the case, years of experience leaped before her, declaring, "You're wrong! You're wrong!"

Lack of sound sleep was beginning to exhaust her.

Nelson was enjoying himself.

Rosey was fortunate to have gotten Doris as a roommate; she wouldn't have dreamed of speaking to anyone about her friend's visits, and so the two girls remained fast friends, delighting in their secret. Rosey began to think of Doris as a sister.

Doris had viewed Rosey as hers from the beginning.

And neither of them could figure out what Nelson was up to.

No matter how relaxed Rosey was in his company; regardless of how much they talked through the night and how often she combed his wet hair, she still felt deep within her the fear that something was happening beyond her control.

By the third week they spent the last half of each night lying on his bed, their clothing on several chairs.

But still they only talked.

The fourth week, halfway through its length, he was telling her a story, when he gently worked her one leg completely over him. He continued talking in the darkness, but by the end of that evening they had made love.

Rosey went back to her bed very much alone that night. She had never experienced anything like what he had done with her. It had been so gently and so tenderly accomplished she feared she had dreamed it all.

The next night it was the same.

Rosey could not have been more ensnared had a net fallen over her. The greatest subtlety she had experienced previous to Nelson was when Stephen-of-The Chimneys hesitated before he made love to her. Before that night she had viewed sex as an attack on her body — an enjoyable attack, to be sure, and one which invariably guaranteed her attention and kind words, but still, it was always an attack. After Stephen she realized the attack was sometimes briefly delayed.

Nothing had prepared her for Nelson.

What she didn't understand was that he enjoyed her. He quietly reveled in her presence and her femininity. He drank her in, savoring her body as he had learned to do with an exceptional meal or a fine wine.

But he did not love her — that was as foreign to him as his sensitivity was to her.

Rosey spent her days dreaming of her nights.

Nelson spent his days visiting other girls. Wealthy girls — girls of his station — and they generally bored him half to death.

He had been briefly saddened when he learned of the fire at The Chimneys, and Abegaile's and Katherine's deaths, and he had been inconvenienced when Christina was sent off to finishing school, but he survived it, shifting his attentions to girls from other proper families.

Rosey was aware that he spent most of his days away from Fairelawn and she suspected it was in pursuit of amorous adventures elsewhere, but she knew Nelson would find no match for their nights. She was unshaken in her conviction that what they had was different.

It amazed her that as time passed they didn't run out of things to talk about — things to quietly discuss as they lay in one another's arms. And their passion remained slow and tender and nearly matter-of fact.

At their periphery, Eleanora finally worried herself to illness. The third month after Rosey's arrival, the housekeeper took sick. The doctor feared it might be influenza, and the mention of the word brought back images of The Great War and the influenza epidemic. If she did not recover soon, she would be moved to the Pest House, and there she would suffer with the others who were thought to have any contagious disease. Less than half of those who entered a Pest House left it upright and breathing.

Eleanora remained bedridden and worried about Nelson and Rosey, troubling herself constantly with the overpowering belief that something was going on behind her back — under her nose — at her very feet.

Those were her concerns when she awakened one night. She remained in bed as long as she could, alternately staring into the corridor or listening attentively, when at last she decided to attempt to walk to the hall.

She rose quietly, leaning first on her bed and then shifting her bulk to her dresser and finally the side of her opened door. She thought she heard something. She took a moment to catch her breath and then poked her head slowly out from her room. Her eyes widened. Her fleshy, pallid hand went to her mouth.

There at the end of the hall, disappearing into the dumb waiter, was a bare foot.

Eleanora experienced a strange feeling that the service elevator had just eaten someone.

The little door closed and the housekeeper momentarily doubted what she had seen. She looked back at her bed expecting to see herself there, asleep.

Probably, because she was so run down, and possibly, because she did not wish to admit her own stupidity, it took her an unusually long time to understand what was happening. She stared at the closed door of the dumbwaiter and listened to the ropes and pulleys whirl.

When at last she understood, Eleanora had the presence of mind to see that it would not be as easily addressed as it could have been had she discovered it months before, for in the interim, Rosey's mother had steadily risen in the domestic hierarchy. In fact, Eleanora's illness had left a vacancy which the woman quickly filled. Worse, the Wingate elders were on another of their trips abroad.

It would require much thought and careful planning if she were to salvage the honor of the manor while retaining her position — regaining her position. The days passed as she plotted and listened and planned, and her strength returned. Eleanora was nearly well when a plan of brilliant simplicity presented itself.

She had learned to her horror that Rosey's escapades were nightly and so she didn't have to wait long to initiate her scheme.

The ex-housekeeper had conceived her solution in the morning and that afternoon she lumbered to the kitchen and retrieved a large knife. In the evening, after the house had quieted and all were to have been in bed, she crept to the service elevator, lowered it until its ropes were exposed, and then sliced two-thirds of the way through each of them. She reset the little box, closed the door, and returned to her bed.

The magnitude of Eleanora's humiliation insulated her from even a shred of doubt or concern. She knew the girl would be badly hurt; *If the little hussy wishes to play in the dumbwaiter, let her.* It didn't cross her mind that the accident could be fatal, but if it had, she wouldn't have cared.

Rosey no longer waited to be called to Nelson's room, for they had set a time. With his parents gone there were no parties and there was no entertaining. The entire manor settled into a predictable pattern of quiet evenings and early retirement.

She put her hand on Doris's shoulder and gently squeezed. The girl moaned and rolled to the side.

Rosey whispered, "I'll be back," and Doris made a little sound.

Rosey cracked her door slowly and then tiptoed into the hall, there turning and pulling the door until it faintly latched behind her.

She crossed to the dumbwaiter and swung its small door open and depressed the platform of the elevator. It dipped and then rose as Nelson pulled it back to its stop. He awaited her. Rosey crawled part way into the suspended box. She took the book of verses Nelson had given her and set it beside her. Then she worked herself around so she could pull the door closed.

The elevator took her weight and one by one the strands of rope parted and untwisted. As less of the rope was left to bear her, the disintegration accelerated.

Nelson began to lower Rosey.

She approached the second floor stop where Nelson would arrest her descent, set the lock, and help her out.

Nelson had the door open. He moved one hand to the lock. The bottom of the wooden box appeared and then strangely, the girl flew by, her mouth agape, her eyes startled.

Rosey was silent as she passed the first floor, her stomach in her throat. A fraction of second before she slammed onto the cellar stone she began her scream. There was a clatter and her sounds abruptly shifted to a wailing moan.

Rosey was driven, screaming, to the hospital where a doctor worked on her for the remainder of the night. She had broken both of her arms, injured her back, and badly damaged her left knee.

Nelson sent Eleanora packing before the sun set on another day.

Rosey's mother and Doris visited her the evening after the accident, and later, Nelson appeared. Before he went to her room he was waylaid by the doctor and informed, as her employer, that the baby was still apparently healthy. She had not lost it.

"That girl's carrying a fighter," the doctor told him. "One hell of a fighter."

Nelson left the hospital without entering her room. The following day he went to her mother, Fairelawn's most recent housekeeper.

"Does she have a boyfriend at the house?" Nelson asked without prelude.

Rosey's mother hesitated and then shook her head. She was competent, but she didn't have her daughter's fire; Nelson Paxton Wingate frightened her.

"Did she have a boyfriend at The Chimneys?" he pressed, adding, "I must know."

"Stephen," she said timidly. "Mr. Van Luxall's driver's son."

She tried to raise her eyes to Nelson's but found she could not. "I heard he left shortly after we did," she mumbled hastily.

Nelson forced her to meet his gaze. When she finally did, he pierced her with his hatred.

"If you wish to remain, find out where he is," he spat before he turned and walked away.

STEPHEN

The day Stephen was fired he walked out the driveway from The Chimneys at twilight, carrying a small rucksack with his belongings. He approached the gatehouse.

An old man called from his window, "Hey! Where are you off to, boy? It's too late for a walk!" When he saw that Stephen was carrying a bundle he quickly withdrew his head and reappeared at the door.

Stephen forced himself to smile; Clarence was like a lost grandfather. His hair was white, his face was deeply lined and he was so thin he appeared ill, but actually he was hale, despite his crippled walk. He had teased the boy since Stephen had come to the manor on his father's shoulders. But Stephen was in no mood for anyone.

"Mighty large dinner you packed there, laddy!"

Stephen turned from the road and walked over to his friend.

"I thought I'd be gone without having to say goodbye," he answered forlornly.

"So it's goodbye," Clarence said and shook his head sadly. He thought a moment, shook his head again and then looked across the wide lawn to the manor house. "I figured you'd go one of these days."

"You did?"

A look of secret wisdom crossed the old man's wrinkled face. Even in the diminished light Stephen could see the freckles and liver spots shifting.

"Stephen, my boy, that musty old place is both too damn big and too blessed small for you. Too big to let you feel any bigger than a little can of beans and too small to give you any room to grow. You needed to get away."

For the first time since his confrontation with Mr. Van Luxall, the boy began to rebuild his self esteem.

"But I'm leaving because I've been sent off," he protested. "I took the girls to the circus. We must of been seen."

Clarence laughed out loud, then mellowed into a quiet chuckle and finally wiped his eyes and cleared his throat a few times.

"Caught, were ya? Well, what you did wasn't wrong; somebody ought to show those girls a good time or two. Believe it or not, I've always felt sorry for 'em." He continued, "Everything always proper. Everybody always linin' up to do what they say."

"They're real nice girls," Stephen interrupted, thinking of Abegaile and Katherine. He moved his thoughts to Christina and he was once more deeply saddened.

The old man watched the boy and saw the clouds.

"Got a place in that fresh heart for one of 'em, do you? And now you feel whipped."

Stephen shrugged his shoulders.

The old man dug into the pockets of his baggy pants. He rooted past various useless articles — a broken pen knife, a pencil stub, a chipped marble — until at last he found what he was seeking.

Stephen thought he was searching for a cloth to blow his nose on.

"Here it is," Clarence said and pulled out what looked like a black knot roughly half the size of his finger.

"See that?" he asked as he handed it to the boy.

It was the shape of a clinker, but heavier.

"That's a Gatling gun bullet, boy. They thought it would have me down for life. Never walk again."

Clarence and Stephen stared at it.

"Well, it was too small to do that to me, lad. I got well on my own — learned to walk again — and I'll keep walkin' 'til the day they put me under."

Stephen went to hand the bullet back but he was waved off

"Let me tell you," the gatekeeper continued, "when things got bad I always took that old hunk of metal out and held it. Now I want you should take it. I don't need it no more — nobody shoots at me these days and the family's all gone. Both boys died, one way or another, and so'd my wife. Epidemic got her. Couldn't hold out. Besides, I musta used up all my luck by now — bad and good. You take it."

He pushed Stephen's hand away.

"Now keep it, laddy. And when you hold it, you just think of me — and think of them tellin' me I'd never walk again."

He put his boney hand on Stephen's shoulder.

"You're young. Go take the world if you want. Go on now, git."

Clarence turned away from the boy and shuffled back to the gatehouse door. He paused and lifted his foot to the step and then shifted his weight forward and rose and went into the darkness.

The boy spent his first night in a barn halfway between The Chimneys and the trolley. He awoke before dawn, the roosters clamoring. Goats and sheep added their voices to the morning mayhem.

Stephen rose and brushed the straw from his pants.

The road to the trolley stop tunneled through a full, green canopy. A few squirrels were about, leaping overhead, and birds chattered at his passage. He reached the tracks before the trolley arrived from town. There was a wooden shelter, roofed in slate and tucked up to the tracks, and Stephen paced around it, attempting to decide where he would go.

The trolley jogged into view, silent at first, casting miniature lightning as it approached. It grew larger. By the time it sparked to a stop, he had made his decision.

"End of the line!" the conductor called.

Passengers climbed down — to the number they were employees of one manor or another. Several recognized him and nodded. Soon various manor jitneys would drive out to pick up the workers who now kicked about the dust and waited.

Although the trolley was always punctual, the buses from the manors were always late — one more way to let the workers know they were at the disposal of others.

Stephen's irritation grew.

"All on!" the conductor shouted to the boy. The driver threw a few switches, adjusted a lever, and proceeded to the opposite end of the trolley to power it back to the city. Stephen climbed aboard and gave the conductor a token.

It's time to leave, he thought. He'd made up his mind to take the trolley to the other side of town and walk to the freight yards. He'd ride the rods. It didn't matter where. He just needed to be somewhere else.

He hadn't hopped a train before, but he'd heard it wasn't difficult as long as you were careful.

"First thing to know," a well-traveled gardener told him, "is that they're always goin' faster than they look — 'cause they're so big and all. Hop a slow one — one so slow you think she's barely movin'. And boy, *never* hop the door. She'll sure as hell look temptin' — don't get me wrong — but that's the best way there is to lose your pins."

Stephen remembered flinching when the gardener told him that.

"You fall, you're gonna tumble your legs across them tracks and before you got any kinda chance to move, WHACK! WHACK! — WHACK! WHACK! you got two sets a trucks runnin' over you. Knowed two brothers. Hopped an eastbound. Younger brother goes for the door, loses his grip and the older brother watches as the rest of the train passes over the boy's legs. Cut 'em off! Tried to carry his brother on his back from there, but said he kept feelin' them empty pants-legs afloppin' against the back of his and down he'd go. Passed out cold. Younger brother kept havin' to bring him around. Older brother'd pick him up and walk a few steps and then pass out again. Just kept happenin'.

"You grab the ladder on the front side of the car — not the one at the end, neither. That way, you fall, you got time to roll under the train and wait for it to pass, or if you can, you can roll out to the side before them back trucks hits ya. I prefer stayin' put in the middle, personally."

The idea became less appealing.

The trolley stuttered through the city and then glided toward the opposite terminus.

Passengers boarded and departed while Stephen sat and the conductor eyed him.

"Last stop! End of the line!" the conductor announced to Stephen. He leaned toward him. "You are gettin' off here, aren't you, son? You don't look like a 'rider' to me."

Stephen ignored him and rose from the wicker bench.

The two ends of the trolley line were quite different. He now looked across open fields. The freight yards were about three-quarter of a mile from where he stood. Had he been blindfolded he could have followed the steam whistles now hooting distant instructions to the yard men. All he needed was to cut across a ragged corn field and he would be among the shunting engines. He could have let his nose direct him; the tempting, sweet smell of burning coal reached out from the fireboxes and settled over the countryside, its fine, black grit dusting the rows of broken stalks and covering the stoney ground between.

Stephen was hungry. His stomach cramped and rumbled as he shaded his eyes from the sun.

The rail yard was mayhem compared to where he'd spent his life. There were stacks of orange rails and small fortresses of black railroad ties. Three engines rusted near one end of the yard, and a tiny caboose — a 'bobber', its sides now a parallelogram — lay tipped into a shallow gully, broken cattails a testament to its recent fall.

And everywhere there was junk. Scrap iron. Trash. Engine parts. Up-ended wheels and broken couplers. He spotted two burned box cars on one siding and a grey work train smudged between two strings of freight.

Blackened men moved about slowly, waving flagged arms. Grey-capped engineers jutted from narrow windows. Locomotives crawled. The only thing which appeared clean was the steam shooting in white bursts from around the wheels and shrieking from the whistles.

It looked hot to Stephen. Hot and dirty.

He dropped his rucksack to the ground and reviewed his decision. It didn't look like much of a life if the switching yard were any indication.

A stubby engine backed to a spot in front of a tall, leaking, wooden water tower. An urchin in bib overalls scrambled up to the side of the tower and pulled a rope connected to a huge spigot rising from the tower's side. Another boy clambered onto the locomotive and opened a port on top of the boiler. A torrent of water rushed forth, most of it swooshing down the engine's black sides.

The boys shouted soundlessly to each other.

Time passed.

The engineer hooted the whistle and the spigot was raised.

The boys were filthy.

Depression clung to Stephen.

He was unaware of how long he stood motionless. A crow cawed and a hot summer breeze brought more sounds from the rail yard. A string of flat cars rolled into a line of mixed freight and seconds later a deep, repetitious whumping reached the boy.

And then a fresh wind brought a different sound. It came from behind and above, and it waxed and waned but gradually built in volume, its insistent drone thinner than the noises of the trains.

Stephen turned at the hips and looked up.

A tan biplane with long, narrow wings fought toward him, jogging with different currents of air, bucking its way through them. It passed high over the boy and Stephen waved and imagined a peculiar bob of the wings to be the pilot responding.

His heart pounded in his chest.

Then one wing dipped and remained low and the craft slowed and then walked through the air on an inclined curve, the tops of the upper wing and the horizontal tail surface clearly visible, the little engine popping and backfiring as it idly kept the aeroplane aloft. At last it straightened and the motor picked up and then slackened again. Stephen watched it gently settle as it approached a distant field.

The boy looked a last time at the mottled freight yard and smiled.

His wasn't going to attempt to ride one of those filthy, leg-devouring monsters.

He was going to fly!

He snagged his rucksack and ran back across the field. He crossed it and the road he had arrived on earlier and continued through a different, fresher field. The farther he got from the yards, the cleaner the grasses became until he could smell the country smells once more. He crossed field after field — it seemed he would never reach his destination.

Not that it mattered to Stephen. Every foot he raised and each little stream he leaped did nothing more than confirm his decision. The aeroplane had passed over all of it so quickly!

You can bet that pilot isn't winded. Or dirty, either.

Stephen raced on.

To an unjaded eye, the primitive airfield was neither particularly clean nor tidy.

Two rows of squat buildings with low, rounded roofs faced one another. Half had wide doors rolled shut while the others had open fronts with no doors. Dust swirled around the bare soil before the hangars and there was, of all things, an automobile junk yard not far from the grassy field used for take-offs and landings.

A corrugated roof corner on one of the buildings flapped with every breeze.

Stephen saw the airplanes.

No two looked alike.

He was in awe.

In the shadows inside the open hangars he could make out diagonal propellers and horizontal wings. There were planes of every shape; a Curtis JN4 biplane, a Jenny, he later learned, was parked beside one of the hangars. A Nieuport-Delange 29 and a Verville-Packard R-I were side by side next a makeshift hangar, the R-1's single outboard wing strut looking peculiar to the boy. There were at least fifteen more craft parked in long lines beyond the hangars.

Stephen was surprised to see the aeroplanes were held down by ropes dropping from their wing tips to tie-off points on the ground. It was as if someone feared the aeroplanes might take it into their minds to fly off on their own.

Stephen smiled to himself.

"YOU, BOY!"

Stephen saw a man standing beside an aeroplane, motioning to him.

"YOU, BOY, COME OVER HERE!" he repeated, insistent and controlled.

Stephen dropped his rucksack and ran over to the man.

"Yes sir?" he answered, but the man now had his head stuck inside an open panel on the side of the aircraft. The boy feared he wasn't needed after all.

"Yes, sir?" he said again adopting the man's earlier tone.

The man grunted a few times and then pulled his head out. He had the friendliest face Stephen had ever seen. Wide streaks of grease painted his cheeks and patches of oil sprinkled his forehead.

The boy grinned widely and so did the man.

"What's so funny, boy?" the man asked. They both were smiling at some unknown joke between them. The man then took a rag from his back pocket and wiped his hands.

Stephen watched him as if he were learning a new skill.

"You got time to help me here, boy?"

"*Stephen,*" he informed the man, "My name's Stephen," and then answered, "I've got more time than I know what to do with."

"You a runaway?" the man asked, tilting his head as he did. Stephen would learn that anytime Mr. Boisvert angled his head to the side, he was serious.

"No sir," Stephen answered carefully. "I just left my job at The Chimneys; I'm lookin' for work."

The man stuffed the rag back into his pocket and thrust out his hand. "Jacob. Jacob Boisvert. A job just found you, boy. Step over here and help it along."

He didn't wait for Stephen to acknowledge. Instead, he instructed, "Hold this fuel line. When I tell you to, blow on the end. We got to clear it out. Some kind of obstruction in it." He indicated a narrow tube to the boy.

Stephen grasped it.

"Now, boy, now."

He put his mouth on the end but before he could take a breath and blow, his mouth filled with fuel. He tried to expel it, but it was so aromatic he choked.

Stephen coughed and gagged.

Jacob laughed.

"First taste of aviation fuel, boy? She's not so bad, but I don't want you to drink a lot of her. No more than you have to. I won't charge you for the first swallow. And by the way — any fillings in your teeth? Be careful — one spark and you'll explode." He chuckled at his joke.

Stephen spit ineffectually and then wiped his tongue off on his shirt sleeve. Instead of acknowledging his new employer's remarks, he went back to the tube and blew heartily.

"Good. Good. Now hand me that spanner down by your foot."

They continued, Stephen doing as he was told — handing tools, holding various items, and running around the aeroplane to satisfy Jacob.

"Well, boy," Jacob said as the sun headed for the horizon. "From the looks of you I'd bet you don't know where your next meal's comin' from; although I expect you've had enough high octane for one night. And I'll bet you don't have a bed."

Stephen was too embarrassed to answer. He had been preparing to ask the man if he could spend the night in one of the hangars or under the wing of an aeroplane.

"Listen, now," Jacob Boisvert continued, "come out to the house with me. You can have a square meal and then I'll drop you back out here. There's a cot down by my office. Not fancy, you understand — but it's clean and I don't believe anyone will bother you." He scratched his head and then caught Stephen's eye. "That suit you? You can be my night watchman. You don't take to the city at night do you? Not a wild one?"

"Yes sir," he answered and then seeing his employer's reaction, corrected, "I mean, No, sir — no, sir, I don't take to the city and yes, sir, sleeping here suits me." He looked around at the aeroplanes. "It suits me fine, sir."

Jacob then said several things to Stephen, but the boy wasn't listening; he was attempting to hide his disappointment that they hadn't at least started an engine.

He looked forlornly at the big propellor.

Jacob saw him.

"Oh, I see. You were thinkin' that I'd go up today, and maybe you'd hook a ride or somethin'."

Stephen had not dared to hope for such a thing. Not yet.

"No, sir. I mean, that would of been wonderful, really. I was just thinkin' I'd like to hear this engine just once. She looks like a beauty to me, sir."

Jacob laughed.

"Well, she is a beauty. She's a dependable old workhorse, that's for certain. When she swings that big piece of lumber around you can be darn sure she'll keep turnin', too. And son, when you're in the air, the most comforting sound you'll ever hear is a solid engine. She misses once and you're heart'll stop with her."

He ran his hand over one of the wings as he walked along it. Stephen came behind and Jacob added, "But this aeroplane — she'll glide for miles. Cut your power, and if you have even a little altitude, she'll give you plenty of time to find a pasture. She's one forgiving aeroplane."

The boy was impressed with the respect and affection he heard in the man's voice.

They passed the wing tip and Jacob stopped.

"Let me tell you one more thing on your first day — Stephen? — is that what you said your name was?"

The boy nodded.

Jacob returned to the craft and placed both hands on the wing. "Now this may sound strange to you, but understand it's comin' from a man who's spent as much time in the air as just about any pilot still alive today.

"You treat an aeroplane right, Stephen — you love her — and some day when she's giving you all she's got — when she's doin' everything she was designed to do — you ask her, and she'll give you more.

"Don't laugh, son," he said, even though that was the farthest thing from the boy's mind.

"I was carrying the mail one night and I was forced down in the dark in a field half the size of your girlfriend's bed. I spent the night thawing a frozen carburetor and that morning I looked and saw there was no way I could fly out.

"There was a blizzard comin' in, and I knew that if I didn't *fly* out it'd be the rest of the winter before I *thawed* out.

"Well, I got her goin' again and we taxied down to the end — swung her around — the wind in my nose — and I stared down the length of that field.

"It wasn't long enough, not nearly.

"But I had a choice: Either I tried her or I shut her off right there and prepared to become a snow man."

Jacob paused and Stephen could see he was back at the field.

"I remember I wiped off my goggles and put them back on my leather helmet. Had my sheepswool collar up, scarf wrapped around it. The engine was ticking over nice, its heat warming me some. Snow started to fall. The size of acorns.

"For the longest time I just sat and stared, until something told me we could do it.

"I started to run that old engine up and this voice says, 'You two can do it, Jacob.' So I did, and we began our roll, the storm coming dead at us, the sky gettin' dark as thunder. We bounced across the frozen ground, but the farther we went and the more speed we picked up, the more certain I was that we were gonna run outta room.

"There was a row of trees just staring me in the face, son, getting bigger every second."

He was silent.

Stephen was bouncing down the cold field with him, a row of trees looming ever closer.

"I had my gloves on, of course. Big sheepskins, and I slipped one off; I don't know why; I just did. And I patted the side of that aeroplane and whispered, 'Come on sweetheart, you and me, we can do it.'"

He looked at the boy.

"Son, after you've flown awhile you'll know what I'm talkin' about. You'll learn to judge when your ground speed is fast enough to let your wings do their work. Well, we weren't going fast enough. Not nearly. I could tell. But the trees were almost over us; we were that close — and I gave her another pat and pulled back on the stick.

"I had no right to do that; I knew she couldn't fly — we just didn't have the speed.

"Well, Stephen, I'd always been good to that machine, and you know what? She grabbed the air and jammed it under her wings. The tail was raised and we raced along and then she just went 'whoosh' and we were off the ground.

"We cleared those trees — well, we almost did — I snapped a few branches with the landing gear, but basically, we made it. Beat the storm to Richmond.

"I found a hangar for her that night. Tucked her in, and you know what? I turned down a bed so I could sleep out with her. Turned down a warm bed and slept rolled in a blanket under her wing.

"Can you beat that?"

Stephen looked at the aeroplane in front of him as if it were the one of Jacob's story.

"No sir, I can't," he answered softly. "I'll remember that, sir; truly I will."

The Boisverts lived close to the airfield, their house much larger than Stephen had imagined. It was not The Chimneys or Fairelawn, but it was certainly bigger than a workman's home. The furnishings were obviously expensive, and on the way in the boy saw a Cadillac touring car in one of the stalls of the stable.

Mrs. Boisvert was as friendly as her husband, showing no surprise when Stephen walked through her kitchen door with Jacob. "Hello, young man," she said as a greeting. "Excuse me," she added and turned back to discuss dinner with the woman who was obviously the cook. As if remembering something she turned back to her husband with frown and wagged her finger as she accused, "There's no reason to bring folks in through the kitchen, Father."

Her husband stopped her before she could finish.

"He's helping me, Esther, and I don't think you're going to impress him with your fancy parlor — he just left The Chimneys."

She raised an eyebrow and straightened the front of her dress.

Stephen ate well, but was disappointed when Mrs. Boisvert made no effort to stop her husband from driving him back to the airfield for the night. She did offer that there was an extra blanket in the room behind the storeroom.

"Hope you rise early; I'll likely beat the sun."

"Yes, sir," Stephen answered.

But he didn't sleep well; in fact, he slept very little. At first he lay on the small bed, his hands behind his head and thought of Christina. He remembered their night at the fountain and then he pictured her walking the ridge of the mansion and he was miserable. He missed her already, even though when he was at The Chimneys he sometimes went a week without seeing her. Not often. But sometimes.

In the middle of the night he felt he had to get outside, so he swung his feet around, pulled his shoes back on and left the building. It was quiet, with only the crickets and an occasional, far away dog interrupting the silence. Half of the sky was clear, the stars bright, but across the remainder heavy clouds were advancing.

Stephen thought of the storm of his new employer's story, and he was heartened to take his mind away from Christina and concentrate instead on the fact that he was actually at an airfield, surrounded by aeroplanes. He looked about him and saw their dark forms here and there, some near the hangars, others parked apart.

He walked to one of them, a small biplane with bigger tires than Stephen expected. He touched the wing, surprised at the feel of the stretched and painted fabric. *It's so thin!* he thought. He went to the end of the lower wing and placed his hand through a hole at the tip, obviously intended to be used as a grip. Stephen found that the wing rose easily when he put his weight under it and lifted. *There's not much to 'em.*

The smell of the engine drew him to the front of the aeroplane. While he had overestimated the thickness of the wings' coverings, he found himself in awe of this plane's huge wooden propellor. He ran his hand over its lower section, exploring the nicks and chips knocked from its leading edge. He had expected it to be smooth, but it was not.

Luck was with him that night, for when he pulled himself up so that he could look into the cockpit, he stepped on the small section of the wing which was designed to sustain weight. Had he ventured out farther or attempted the opposite wing, he would surely have felt his foot pass through the tearing fabric.

Stephen leaned in and explored the gauges. They would have made no sense to him in daylight, and at night they were little more than shiny discs. He saw a leather helmet over the control stick in front of the seat.

Stephen was not aware that there were steps built into the side of the craft and so he awkwardly hefted himself up and finally into the cockpit. And he was in heaven, although he sat much lower than he thought he would, the padded rim touching his shoulders, the distant windscreen very high.

There was not a chance in the world he would be able to resist donning the leather flying helmet. He put it on, several times tangling the goggles with the tightening straps before he had everything straightened properly. He lowered the goggles. There were two lenses for each eye — the main section which he peered through when he looked ahead, and a smaller side lens for peripheral vision.

He felt the toggles and switches at the side of the cockpit, running his fingertips blindly over them, then he lost interest in their mysteries and gripped the control stick. Stephen found himself imagining flying high in the air, flying perfectly, bursting through clouds and diving and swooping over fields.

His fantasies were strictly aeronautical until he remembered Christina.

It was a glorious summer afternoon and Stephen flew high above the countryside. He looked below him and saw the lake and circled it, finally locating The Chimneys. It was small from his height, and the boy enjoyed its diminished size. He was appreciating the view, thinking of Christina and wondering where she was, when he noticed a gathering of tiny people out on the Grand Lawn.

They were having a picnic.

He put his plane into a gentle, spiraling dive, the people growing as he lost altitude. Soon Stephen could see that the entire family was there in their white wicker chairs, the girls in flowing white dresses. And they were waving to him.

He accomplished a wide turn so he could straighten out far from them and then fly back low across the Grand Lawn. He passed over them once, wagging his wings gallantly as he did, and he saw that even Mr. Van Luxall was waving.

On the next pass he lowered the aeroplane so it barely skimmed above the grass and then he shut off the engine and glided the last few feet to the ground. His aeroplane came to rest and as he climbed out of the cockpit, he saw Christina running across the lawn to him. The twins and their parents still waved slowly, obviously pleased and perhaps even excited that he had come.

Christina ran to him and Stephen saw himself in polished brown riding boots and tan jodhpurs. He wore an expensive white shirt and he had on a pair of fine leather gloves.

She was in his arms and they both laughed and he twirled her around.

But then —

They heard another aeroplane overhead. It was insultingly loud and everyone recognized it immediately as a Hun. A Hun with machine guns blazing, ripping a twin row of death across the Grand Lawn.

Mr. Van Luxall dove to the ground and cowered beneath a chair.

Stephen kissed Christina once more and then turned and ran to his aeroplane. It was still running. Two brutish machine guns were now on the cowl in front of the cockpit.

A dog barked nearby and the boy jumped.

He was embarrassed as he took off the helmet and goggles. He climbed out of the cockpit, stepping carefully down the wing, and then jumped to the ground and walked away.

Germans diving across the lawn at The Chimneys!

He tortured himself further.

Good thing those machine guns appeared. I could have rammed him, though — crashed my plane right into him — right over the heads of the Van Luxalls — Christina would have raised her hand to her forehead and then fainted as my burning plane plunged to earth.

Stephen was now doubly embarrassed. He found that he was actually visualizing the newest ridiculous scene.

He went back to his bed and spent the remainder of the night fighting a series of air battles and enjoying a spate of reunions with Christina. He always ended them abruptly, pushing them out of his mind, and no sooner did he do that, when he flew back into view, his aeroplane increasingly powerful, his flying skills improving with his much needed practice.

By dawn he had made several loop the loops over the manor, once actually flying through the wide opening in the Octagonal Tea House. Many particularly onerous Germans perished, and unfortunately, the boy died a time or two himself.

The sun had not risen when Mr. Boisvert honked the horn on his automobile — the beloved and battered 1913 Abbott-Detroit Battleship Roadster.

"Stephen!" he yelled as he stepped down from the car, patting the steering wheel before he released it completely. "You awake yet, son?"

"I'm over here," the boy answered from behind a huge two winged aeroplane beside one of the hangars.

"We've got work to do, follow me," Jacob called and went into his office.

When Stephen entered, blinking against the bright lights, he was handed a broom. He could barely contain his reaction. He stood dumbly for a moment.

Mr. Boisvert laughed and took the broom back. "We use it like this," he said and began sweeping the floor. "It's not as difficult as flying — I think you'll get the hang of it."

Stephen was startled. With the mention of flying he realized he had half convinced himself that he had learned that night.

He began sweeping the floor. "Is it hard to learn?" he asked.

Jacob understood his question.

"For some. Others seem to pick it up pretty easy." He watched the boy attack the floor. "I'll make you a promise, son; you work hard here — don't complain or try to find ways to dodge your work — you do that, and I'll teach you."

Momentarily, he regretted his promise, for Stephen was suddenly creating a whirlwind of dust swirling from the floor.

"Careful, there, son. If you're going to be an aviator, you've got to learn that you do things carefully — with precision."

The two words, 'aviator' and 'precision' would eventually rival Christina for dominance of the boy's thoughts.

Stephen cleaned the office, ran a few errands, and accomplished nothing even vaguely associated with flying. In fact, there was no other activity at the field. Each time a man would approach one of the parked aeroplanes, the boy held his breath. And each time he was disappointed.

On one of his forays in Mr. Boisvert's automobile, Stephen purchased bread and a few slices of meat. At noon he was sitting on a box in front of his employer's office when Jacob appeared from behind one of the larger hangars.

He cupped his hands and called, "Son! Come here!"

The boy rose and looked at his half finished sandwich. *Leave it or carry it?* Stephen was anxious to foster the image of a mature, responsible person. He didn't believe walking with two slices of bread and a slab of meat contributed positively. He jammed the remainder into his mouth and chewed and walked, his cheeks chipmunked.

He wiped his mouth with the back of his hand before he reached the little man.

"Just got a call this morning — the engines should be shipped in the next few days — new Wright Whirlwinds. We'll be able to begin work again, finish these models, and test 'em." Jacob unlocked a side door and walked into the hangar.

Stephen followed and as his eyes adjusted, he counted four, then five of the sleekest aeroplanes he had ever imagined.

"Aren't they beauties?" Jacob asked, now standing with his back against one of the wings.

Stephen couldn't believe his eyes. In fact, all of his senses were overwhelmed, for the air was close with the smells of thinner and paint and varnish, and when he placed his hand on the nearest craft, it was as if he were touching one of Christina's fine dresses.

The thought of Christina in a similarly colored dress nosed into his mind, but it was gone in a flash as he ran his fingers over the wing. Even in the hangar the aeroplanes looked as if they were streaking through the air though still and earthbound.

"There's only a lower wing!" he proclaimed when he realized what had been bothering him.

Jacob smiled. "Well, that's true enough, sonny. But it's no new idea. It's just part of a big argument. Most think two wings are the safest, most reliable way to fly."

Now Mr. Boisvert looked at his aeroplanes with appreciation. "They may be right — about safety and reliability — but I think they're way off the mark when it comes to speed."

Stephen turned away from the closest aeroplane. It sounded so foreign to hear Mr. Boisvert speak of speed. He couldn't imagine the little man going fast. Some pilots did, of course; the young daredevils and barnstormers, and the army pursuit pilots, but the man before him, all smiles and baggy pants was the last person he imagined racing through the air. Stephen knew Jacob was a pilot, but he had imagined him to be one who plodded through the air. And then a horrible thought cruised through his mind: *How do I know Mr. Boisvert can really fly an aeroplane?*

He said he could.

And he's always around the aeroplanes.

Stephen knew Jacob owned the airfield — but he hadn't seen him fly.

The boy's stomach sagged. He had been so excited. He'd allowed his boss to rise as some sort of hero to him. And now — he didn't know if the little man's feet had ever been off the ground. Stephen was all too familiar with the tales men told.

Jacob saw the boy's consternation. "You feeling alright?"

Stephen tried to smile. He was facing disaster.

"Mr. Boisvert —" he began, finally. He didn't know how to phrase his question without either appearing stupid or insulting. He plunged ahead. "Can you really fly an aeroplane?" he blurted.

Stephen had never seen anyone laugh so hard.

The boy laughed a little, himself.

Jacob eventually stopped, and then he tugged at his right ear. He motioned with his head for Stephen to follow, and they walked out and headed for the well-worn Jenny beside the hangar. It was ungainly compared to the planes Stephen had just seen, but he was excited; he knew he was going to witness a takeoff and landing.

Jacob climbed onto the wing with surprising grace. He got into the rear cockpit and did something the boy couldn't see. He then climbed out and down and went around the wing to the engine.

Stephen was mildly confused. He had thought the front cockpit was the important one; that's where the pilot sat.

"Give me a hand here." Jacob had his hands on the blade of the propellor. "You do it like this," he said, indicating how he placed himself, all the while adjusting his hands until he was satisfied with his grip. He raised his leg. "Then you swing it around, balancing on one foot and using the foot you have in the air to help you put more weight behind your pull. You got that?"

Stephen stepped up beside him and grabbed the wooden propellor.

"Now swing it through."

He was awkward. The propellor barely moved and so he tried again. And again. Gradually, he got the knack of it.

Stephen smiled.

"That's good, son. We're pullin' oil into the cylinders now and we're getting some fuel into 'em, too," Mr. Boisvert said and put his hand on the boy's shoulder.

He became very serious. "Listen to me, Stephen. Listen carefully.

"The machine you see in front of you knows a thousand ways to kill a man. It's a machine you have to be careful with every second you're around it. Some people think these things fly themselves — well they don't. They're powerful and they're dangerous. On the ground and in the air. That piece of lumber you're holding could chop you into a thousand pieces before you could blink an eye, son. And once you're in the air, you'll find that an aeroplane always wants to get back to the ground, and it's not particular how it gets there.

"It's like an aeroplane is a tired horse that's ready to go back to the stable. You have to make it stay out. You have to work with it."

Mr. Boisvert took a step away from Stephen.

"You swing it through, son, and you get out of the way. Always. She may catch — she may not. If she doesn't, you step back to her and try again. But always assume she'll start."

Stephen nodded and then Mr. Boisvert explained the rote he was soon to employ.

Jacob went around and climbed into the rear cockpit.

Stephen was confused again but he placed his hands on the huge propellor.

"CLEAR IN THE FRONT?" Jacob shouted.

Stephen looked around. "CLEAR!" he answered. He was embarrassed that he was shouting but he was excited when he thought of the aeroplane engine starting and whirling the propellor in front of him. He wasn't afraid.

"SWITCHES ON!"

"SWITCHES ON!" he shouted back and tensed in preparation for throwing his weight behind the wooden propellor.

"CONTACT!"

Stephen pulled the prop through a portion of an arc as he yelled, "CONTACT!"

He jumped back.

Nothing happened.

He stepped up to his job and tried again.

On the fourth pull, there was a popping sound and the propellor jerked through a complete circle.

A cloud of smoke belched out one of the exhaust pipes which traveled from the engine compartment, over the front of the craft and then turned at a right angle to end above the top of the upper wing. A cloud then flew from the other exhaust.

Stephen backed way from the aeroplane. The engine was running and he was so excited he thought he would be unable to contain himself. He ran to the side and saw Jacob. He had his leather helmet on and his goggles lowered. Stephen could see the propellor's wind blowing over him. He raised his thumb to the boy.

The noise was louder than he expected, and he immediately smelled the tartness of the aircraft's exhaust.

Jacob leaned out one side of the cockpit and then the other. He repeated the movement several times and then the engine revved and the wind from it increased. The airplane bumped forward.

Jacob pointed to the right wing and Stephen ran to it. He grabbed its tip and raced forward with it, forcing the aeroplane to pivot between the hangars, finally pointing toward the field beyond.

Stephen watched the control surfaces on the aeroplane raise and lower as Jacob tested them. The engine slowed to an idle once more, the big propellor loping around, barely visible.

Stephen smiled at Jacob who was now holding up something.

It was another leather helmet.

He pointed to Stephen and then to the front cockpit.

Sex with Rosey couldn't compare with what he felt.

He was proud. He was thrilled. He wished he could leap around in a few circles.

He controlled himself.

Stephen climbed over the wing and into the delicious, oily wind as he took the leather helmet and goggles, a smile illuminating his face. He settled into the front cockpit, surprised that there was a complete set of controls there, too. He placed his feet carefully away from the rudder bar on the floor.

Some day —

He craned around and gave Mr. Boisvert a smile.

The little man was deadly serious, but he managed to nod.

The wind and noise suddenly peaked and they began to roll. Dust and debris was blown into Stephen's face, the tiny wind screen doing little to protect him. They rolled by the hangars and then onto the grass, bumping ahead.

Stephen was perplexed as to why Mr. Boisvert kept steering from side to side, traveling a snake's trail as they taxied into the field, but when he looked back once more he realized that Jacob could not see directly ahead because of the angle of the aeroplane, its nose elevated in front of the man.

They slowed to a stop and then idled for what seemed to be an hour until the boy began to suspect something was wrong with the engine. Just as he turned to see what was the matter he felt Jacob advance the throttle. Again, they bounced across the grass, this time accelerating as they did, faster and faster. Stephen felt the tail of the aeroplane lift. The bounces became longer and less pronounced. He thought he was in a racing car, the ground whizzing past, the propellor wash impossibly increasing.

And then with a swoop they were in the air.

Stephen drank in the experience. It was indescribable. He could compare it with nothing he had ever done before.

They climbed farther.

He looked over the side and ahead and was surprised to see the trees so small. The aeroplane was climbing much faster than he thought possible.

They flew for almost an hour, the last half of which Mr. Boisvert erased entirely the boy's earlier opinion of his boss. They dove at cows, sending them running in all directions; they plunged into sweeping passes over the airfield, and they made steep turns in the air.

Stephen shouted and whooped, unable to manage his excitement. Even after they landed and jolted back to the hangar, the boy's heart raced. It was much, much, more than be dreamed it would be. From that afternoon on, he would never view Mr. Boisvert as anything less than a god.

It was the first of many surprises.

The engines arrived and he helped install them on the noses of the sleek aeroplanes. Stephen shadowed his employer every work day, and neither was disappointed in their partnership.

Summer passed and Stephen often flew with Mr. Boisvert. Eventually, the little man allowed the boy to take control of the aeroplane, and with time, he helped the boy through increasingly difficult maneuvers. Stephen devoted the days to doing whatever Mr. Boisvert bid and the evenings he spent either reading the aviation books he had borrowed or daydreaming about his reunion with Christina.

Stephen learned of the fire at The Chimneys before he heard of Abegaile's death. In a stroke, Christina's sisters were gone. Stephen's father had driven to the airfield to tell him. He and his son had communicated a few times since the boy's departure, but a wall of mutual uneasiness had made the visits uncomfortable for each of them.

When he told Stephen of the fire, he gave him only the barest details and then left, saying he had much to do.

Stephen grieved for several days and then borrowed Mr. Boisvert's Battleship Roadster and drove out to the gatehouse at the manor, hoping to learn from the gatekeeper where Christina had gone.

Clarence hobbled out, obviously pleased to see the boy.

"Welcome back, Stephen!" he said, thrusting his hand to him. "This your automobile?"

Stephen shook his head. He didn't answer, for he had just caught a glimpse of The Chimneys.

What was left.

It was horrible; brick walls stood roofless and empty windows gaped charred and stark. The trees surrounding the manor had died in an arc of death.

Stephen's reaction was entirely visceral. Never, in Jacob's wildest aerial maneuvers, had the boy known his stomach to be so upset. He had heard that Christina had survived, but as he viewed the burned-out shell, he feared it could not be possible. He turned back to Clarence. "Christina?" he asked softly.

The old man turned away from Stephen, leading the boy to believe he had heard incorrectly. But then he realized the devastation and the deaths of so many would have been a tremendous burden for the old man.

Stephen was embarrassed he had been so insensitive. "I'm sorry," he said, "It must have been horrible."

When Clarence once more faced the boy, he looked at him with rheumy, distant, eyes. "It was," he replied quietly.

Stephen repeated his earlier question. "Christina — did she survive? Is she alright? I heard she didn't —" and then he stopped.

"*He* sent her away from here," Clarence answered, and when he did he indicated the Gate Lodge behind him. It was much larger than one would expect a servant to be allotted. In fact, Clarence stayed in a small cottage behind it.

"Is that where he lives?" Stephen asked.

Clarence nodded. "When he's here."

The old man didn't know to what school Christina had been sent, and when Stephen forgot the situation and asked if Anna would know, he realized his error. He didn't wait for Clarence to speak.

"I'm sorry," Stephen said once more. He pictured big Anna smiling and hovering in the vicinity of the three girls. He looked back at the manor. The gatekeeper had turned away once more.

"I've got to get back, Clarence," the boy said and started Jacob's automobile. "I'm sorry."

He left, trying to push The Chimneys from his mind. He had forgotten to mention the keepsake Clarence had given him.

Flying required heavier and heavier clothing but Stephen didn't mind. He saw the changing countryside from the air, and he flew saddened that he had been unable to locate Christina.

One afternoon he was helping replace a cracked propellor when a cobalt-blue touring car pulled up in front of Mr. Boisvert's office. The driver got out and opened the door for a well dressed young man who carried himself aggressively into the building. He reappeared shortly and looked around until he spotted Jacob and Stephen, and then strode over to them.

Mr. Boisvert made a point of ignoring the visitor.

Even when he cleared his throat.

Stephen turned and Nelson raised an eyebrow.

"I am looking for one, Stephen Rheiner." He seemed to find mentioning the name a distasteful experience.

Stephen narrowed his eyes and looked the stranger over. "That's me," he answered at last.

Nelson's derisive look required he be silent briefly. He spoke through its remnants. "Really?" It was his turn to run his eyes over Stephen.

Jacob watched the two, angering as he did. "This man's working. If you've come to tell him something, spit it out. Some of us *earn* our money."

Nelson turned haughtily to Mr. Boisvert.

"Well said, sir; I shall therefore minimize the interruption." He stared at the old man's greasy clothing. "Your need to earn your money appears to be significant."

He turned his attention back to Stephen.

"*Stephen,* indeed," he said and then continued in mock seriousness and haste; "Congratulations are in order — consider yourself informed that Rosalind Baker is carrying your child. You will find her at the City Hospital."

Stephen stood, dumbfounded.

"You do remember, *Rosey,* don't you?" Nelson asked, enjoying himself.

Stephen didn't realize it, but he nodded in shock.

"Well then, back to work, gentlemen," Nelson said and returned to his automobile.

STEPHEN AND ROSEY

Rosey surveyed the other patients in the ward with her. The majority were asleep and so it was unusually quiet; the random moaning and futile complaining temporarily abated. Even the nurses had padded off, adding to the unexpected hiatus. The cloying aseptic oppression of the institution wreathed the patients as completely as their silence.

Claire Baker and Doris made the trip to the hospital every few days. Rosey knew Nelson had come that first night, but he had not returned. Each day confirmed the cast of his intentions.

She lay on worn sheets, one hand on her stomach, her red hair splayed on the striped ticking of the bare pillow. Rosey tried to adjust her arms and thought of her baby and their future; she harbored no delusions regarding the child's father. They had been discarded.

She was on her own.

She bitterly thought of supporting herself and the child. Currently, her mother was paying her bills, but that couldn't go on. It wasn't fair.

And she hated herself for her feelings for Nelson; they confirmed her foolishness. He had ensnared her while she lay with her eyes open. She had gone to him time after time and she had dropped every defense she had so carefully constructed through the years. When she thought of the nights they spent together she despised him and at the same time she missed him so desperately she loathed herself as well.

At first she determined to seek revenge against Nelson, but as she stoked her anger it grew until its intensity included all men: She disliked the doctor who roughly attended her healing body and she found herself irritated when the colored man passed through, mopping the floor, always so damned cheerful. She hated any man who came into the ward.

And then one day Stephen walked down the narrow corridor between the beds.

The windows were closed and the shades pulled. As Stephen passed through the close air of disinfectant and misfortune he felt himself smothering. The walls were brown and the beds were bulky and depressing. Women, sweaty with fever, their hair oily and matted, tossed about and called to him, mistaking him for a doctor.

Stephen wished he were in the air, high above the suffering. The deeper he walked into the room the more sickened he became.

But he had conceived a child.

And he was to be a father.

After Nelson Wingate came to the airfield Stephen spent the night cursing himself for his stupidity. Every dream of Christina was gone and his chances to make something of himself destroyed. *Rosey* had ripped his future from him. She had taken him and thrust him back into a life of subservience with no escape. She had dragged him back. She had tricked him. She had used him.

He remembered he once liked her and now he wished she were dead; she had no right to do this to him; she was from his past — from his childhood — how could she crawl back into his life and demand so much? When he thought of her daring sexuality he was repulsed. It had all been so cheap.

He saw her pale and defeated on her bed, her belligerence tempered by fatigue.

Rosey watched him approach and sensed his anger.

He was still handsome, although he had lost his boyish charm. In the moments before he reached her bedside she compared his crude and cheap clothing to Nelson's. Her stomach constricted; she would be a pauper.

Our child will be raised in poverty.

As she thought 'our', Rosey felt her own meanness rage through her veins. It was her child. Her child!

When her mother had told her that Nelson was searching for Stephen, she had known why.

And she would not deny it.

They looked blankly at each other, their mutual resentment a thick wall. Stephen swallowed visibly and then looked to a moaning girl two beds down. An ancient, withered woman in the bed next to Rosey's gasped something through cracked lips. The blue-gray skin of her bare shoulder draped loosely over the sharp bone. The flattened husk of her breast lay exposed. Stephen looked away.

He let out a long breath and moved to Rosey's side.

He was confused by the extent of her injuries.

"When can you leave?" be asked dully and then added, "What happened?"

Rosey hated his ignorance. She glared at him before she answered.

But when her eyes met his, Stephen saw the old Rosey in spite of her attitude. He saw her young and well and he remembered their fun. He didn't see Rosey's anger and he wouldn't think of Christina or of his future.

Rosey had been his friend.

He smiled at her and forgot where they were.

She watched him smile and she, too, momentarily forgot.

He cautiously touched a cast.

"How exactly do you *have* a baby?" he asked. "You don't jump off a building or anything, do you?"

Rosey smiled back at him. She couldn't help herself.

She had allowed Nelson to sweep her away — to tenderly take her — but he had never made her laugh as Stephen could, and she had been too enraptured to miss it. It hurt her side when she laughed now, and Stephen saw that she was in pain. He sat beside her and took her hand in his. He held it loosely, afraid he might hurt her further.

His hands were rough and calloused.

She would never have noticed had she not spent time with Nelson.

Rosey lay and wished to quench the hatred she had allowed to poison her. She closed her eyes, but she clenched her teeth when she did. The thought of grease and blisters and roughness set her on edge.

Those hands would never touch her.

Fall embraced the farm and woodland. At Fairelawn, Nelson was left in charge as his parents went on yet another holiday.

Christina bridled with her school's attempts to prepare her to be an interesting wife.

Rosey left the hospital and she and Stephen were married in the cheerless formality of documents and mumbled promises. They moved into a small cabin on the edge of the Boisverts' property. Rosey was to work in the Boisvert home while Stephen went to the airfield.

Humor died. They nurtured their resentment until its cancer spread unaided, wrapping itself around their dreams. The baby grew inside of Rosey and drained from her the sensuality which nature loans briefly to poor girls. That allure was replaced by an anger both angular and bitter.

Stephen still thought of Christina, but she was no longer a goal. He saw no way to rise above his domestic morass, realizing it would be worse once the baby was born. He became moody and Jacob Boisvert found his helper settling into preoccupied sluggishness.

One morning after Stephen crossed the hard ground to one of the hangars he found Mr. Boisvert standing in the shadows watching him.

"Son, come here," he said, and Stephen put a crate of pistons on a bench and walked over.

"Yes sir?"

Jacob didn't respond right away.

Stephen shifted his weight from one foot to the other. He was chilled and he wished to drive the cold from his body. When he looked up it was with sullen eyes.

The older man shook his head slowly.

"Stephen," he began at last, "I want to tell you something and I'm not sure how to do it; so I'm going to tell you two different stories and hope you'll listen."

Stephen almost rolled his eyes, but fortunately he didn't.

Mr. Boisvert began.

"Now, an engine is a mechanical thing; a marriage of machined parts. They're oiled and bolted into place and everything is measured and designed so it'll run just so. And that's what usually happens — it runs — for years most times, and it does what it's designed to do and everything's fine.

"Well, that can't last forever, of course, and eventually, something wears a little too thin and things get out of balance, and where once there was an almost liquid power, a vibration starts and it grows into a thumping until a part which used to revolve smoothly, doesn't anymore — it tries to tear itself away from the rest of the machine and it gets so bad that you can actually hear it — you can hear that machine thumping and ripping itself apart."

Jacob stopped. He waited a moment and then concluded, "That's one story."

He walked over to an aeroplane in the hangar and placed his hand on the fabric of a wing. "You've flown enough to understand something about aeroplanes, son. In fact, I had an idea you'd be going up alone soon."

Stephen didn't like the sound of 'had'. Mr. Boisvert owed it to him; it was his right.

He listened more carefully to the second story. .

"Remember when you first took the controls?" He waited for the boy to nod.

"It was different for you then than now, because you fought them. You weren't certain and so you tried to force the aeroplane to do what you wanted.

"It doesn't work that way — it never does.

"You learned — I've watched you do it — to work with an aeroplane. You've learned to work within its limits and you've learned to coax it gently, carefully.

"And each aeroplane's different. What works well in a Jenny is just another fight in an Overland. So you learn to approach each aeroplane fresh — you listen to it — you feel it — you let it *tell* you how it wants to be handled. You've got to do that if you're going anywhere with it."

Stephen had also put his hand on the skin of the airplane and both he and Jacob were unconsciously running their fingers over the fabric.

Jacob saw what they were doing and smiled.

"Son, you're like an old machine — you're tearing yourself apart — and there's no reason for it. You're too young to be thumping like you do. When you came here you had one life and one view of how it was going to be, and you were determined to work with it. I admired that in you, Stephen — I admired it from the first time I talked to you.

"But things are different now. Rosey's here and soon she's going to have a child. And all I see you doing is trying to force the controls. You keep acting like you're in the same aeroplane you started with and you aren't, son. You're in a different one now. Wake up. Quit trying to fly it into the ground. Because that's what you're going to do. Life is too valuable to waste, son. And it's gone before you know it."

Before Mr. Boisvert left he added, "It's not my business — I know that, Stephen. You're a man now; you've got to take responsibility for what you do. I'm just disappointed to see what you're doing to yourself."

He turned and left.

Stephen watched him walk away. He had listened, particularly toward the end, but it would have been lost on him if Mr. Boisvert hadn't added the last sentence — *what you're doing to yourself.*

It hit him.

I'm doing it to myself.

I'm making Rosey suffer because of something I've done, and am not man enough to own up to it and make the best of our lives. I'm going to be a father. I have a family. And that's crushed me? Mr. Van Luxall had three children and look at what he's done.

Then he remembered Christina. For the first time, Stephen didn't hide in her. He forced her from his mind.

I've married Rosey, he thought. *I'm not a boy running errands or playing pranks to get a girl's attention. I have a man's job and I'll do something with it.*

That night he walked to their home. He looked it over as he approached — *old paint — low roof — crumbling chimney —field stone foundation. Home.*

When Stephen entered, Rosey was seated on a wooden chair, her arms on the table and her head on her arms. Her back ached, her stomach was upset, and she was depressed by everything. She heard Stephen but didn't look up.

He knew that soon she'd be crying, if she weren't already. It was the same every night — Rosey would cry until she fell asleep and then later, with the darkness, she would get up and grudgingly put something together for them to eat.

Stephen usually went directly to their bed and reclined, fully clothed. There he waited with his hands behind his head and anticipated every move and complaint of Rosey's. *Her back hurts. Her stomach's upset. Mrs. Boisvert made her work too hard. There's not enough money. They would be poor forever*

Occasionally, because it moved Stephen to the lip of violence, she would blame Christina for their failed lives.

"A filthy joke to her — I lose my job and it's nothing but a laugh. She's never worked a day in her life but she had the time to get me fired."

And on and on.

Stephen would do everything to avoid being pulled in by her. But she continued until he couldn't remain silent.

"YOU WERE LEAVING ANYWAY!" he would shout. "YOU AND YOUR MOTHER WERE GOING TO FAIRELAWN — YOU BRAGGED ABOUT IT! WE'RE THE FAILURES, ROSEY, YOU AND ME, NOT CHRISTINA!"

Then Rosey would go crazy, also shouting, "YOU STILL LOVE THAT PRECIOUS BITCH — THAT'S YOUR PROBLEM!"

And after, Rosey would turn to Stephen, stare at his face for a moment and then laugh. "A rich girl! A little rich girl! You couldn't pay to shine her shoes and she still has you following her memory like a puppy! Do you think she remembers you?"

Then she would invariably remind him of their current failure.

"Look where we live, Stephen — look at this place. We're like slaves — and you were going to impress *Christina? With what?*"

It was always said with piercing vehemence; for as Rosey spoke she always thought of Nelson and the resulting tone was predestined to hit the mark with Stephen. On those nights they would shout until they had said everything several times and then they would go to their bed, Rosey crying and Stephen sunk into mute hopelessness. Neither would sleep.

Only once had Stephen attempted to bring Rosey's injuries into their arguments. It had never been clearly explained to him what she had been doing and he had hurled that topic at her at the wrong moment.

"ME, ME, ME!" he had shouted. "YOU ALWAYS TALK ABOUT *MY* FAULTS! *MY* FAILURES! LET'S TALK ABOUT YOU — YOU'VE NEVER TOLD ME HOW YOU ENDED UP THE HOSPITAL WITH OUR BABY! WHAT HAPPENED?"

"I FELL, STEPHEN; NOT THAT IT'S ANY OF YOUR BUSINESS! I FELL DOWN THE STAIRS — DOES THAT SATISFY YOU? DOES THAT MAKE YOU HAPPY?" And then Rosey attacked him with anything she could reach. Chairs flew, dishes were smashed, and even a window pane suffered. Stephen retreated to the bedroom and closed himself in as Rosey's anger consumed everything fragile they owned.

"YOU DON'T CARE! YOU DON'T CARE! YOU DON'T CARE!" was the chant she adopted and used to buttress her wall of guilt. He had come too close to the source of her bitterness.

And she would make him suffer for it forever.

When he came into their home that night, he came quietly. He pulled the other chair to Rosey's side and he sat with her. At first he did nothing, but gradually he allowed himself to see her as she had been; to see the old Rosey, full of life, teasing and tempting with her flaming hair.

He placed his hand softly on her shoulder and he began to move it carefully, gradually bringing to her his acceptance of their life. He smoothed her dress and then he rose and stood behind her and massaged her back with both of his hands.

Rosey didn't move.

He rubbed her gently and took the pain from her and soon he began to speak.

"I'm sorry, Rosey. I'm sorry. I don't mean to get you mad at me. I don't mean to hurt you. I guess I just don't think much anymore. I guess I am a failure.

"I just had all these dreams — dreams of being somebody, of working for myself and earning a good living. I don't want to scrabble for a quarter every day, Rosey. I don't want us to live here forever. I don't want you to scrub floors and clean other people's houses. The Boisverts are nice and everything; I know that, but I — I didn't used to see me being a mechanic forever."

It was after he began to run his fingers through her hair that she responded. He was combing softly with his fingertips and Rosey didn't feel Stephen's hand — it was Nelson's. She was with Nelson and he was speaking in the manner which Stephen had adopted. He was caressing her and they were together again.

Stephen felt her relax beneath him. He combed her hair and he ran the flat of his hand along her body as he told her of the future they would have. He shared with her the dreams he had permitted to die and he swore to her they would realize them together.

The sun set and they remained in the front room, Stephen moving his hands over Rosey, and she feeling Nelson and listening to him.

Perhaps it was the strength of her subterfuge which guided the boy into his own, for as the room darkened and he could no longer see the red of Rosey's hair, it was Christina beneath his hands. She was with him and she loved him so much that she would stay with him while he bettered himself. She would remain at his side and in that way he could prove to her both the power of his love and his ability to make a better life.

It was a bargain Rosey and Stephen struck; a better lie they would use to survive.

CHRISTINA AND NELSON

Every day Christina thought of her sisters.
Every night she remembered Stephen.

The school where her father sent her specialized in preparing young women for their role as an appendage to a successful man, and Christina bristled with the first word of her first professor.

"*Ladies,*" he had pronounced and it was with similar unctuous condescension that he continued his introduction. And his attitude was mirrored in every class.

She learned to hate etiquette, despise fashion, abominate subservience and absolutely become violent when she was instructed to take a place in society which enhanced the achievements of her husband.

She wrote to her father demanding she be transferred to an institution which allowed her to study what she wished.

Mr. Van Luxall's secretary passed on the request.

She was soon enrolled in a nearby state university. There, Christina lost herself in business, engineering and science.

And she excelled.

A year passed.

She also succeeded in making it difficult for Nelson Wingate to track her down, although that hadn't been her intention. When he finally did he motored to her campus to see her. They went out together, Christina aloof but surprisingly relieved to be with someone who was from the past. She had made no friends, content instead to spend her time studying.

In fact, Christina had lost more than her family at The Chimneys. She had lost her compassion, her sport, her humor, and her desire to be with anyone. For most purposes, she too had lost her life.

It was early fall when Nelson first visited her. The leaves had turned and most of the other girls in Christina's dormitory were at a football game. Nelson arrived wearing coffee trousers and a rich brown sweater under a tweed jacket, all of which was smothered in a cumbersome raccoon coat. Christina watched his roadster pull up and she was vaguely sorry that there were not others around to see him. She had the reputation as something of an odd bird and only her beauty saved her from becoming an object of active derision. Nelson in full regalia would certainly have given them something to consider.

He examined himself unnecessarily before he switched off the vehicle.

Christina pulled away from her second floor window and waited.

She was buzzed from downstairs but she ignored it.

Finally, one of the house girls climbed the steps to her room and knocked on the door. "Visitor, Miss Van Luxall, — male."

Christina opened her door and affected her most bored countenance.

The girl couldn't resist adding, "*Very* handsome, too. And a *beautiful* convertible."

Christina looked at the girl as if she had just said, "And he has two arms and two legs."

"Nelson Wingate?"

The girl nodded.

"Thank you."

Christina was aware that the other girls of her floor would be apprised of her visitor when they returned. Fully apprised.

Days earlier Nelson had been reviewing his lady friends when he remembered he had lost track of Christina. When he decided to reintroduce her to his admiring stable he wasn't prepared for the girl who came out to meet him.

Previously, Christina had been polite and attractive. She fit in well with the others he visited. And her sisters were fun.

The girl descending the stairs was striking; nearly breathtakingly beautiful. She took in Nelson in a glance and appeared neither impressed nor anxious to spend much time with him.

"Christina?" he asked cautiously, unable to believe she was the Van Luxall girl.

She looked at him as she would a new servant. Gradually she allowed herself to show signs of recognition. "Nelson?" she answered, but without the obvious pleasure he had shown.

He looked at her hopefully.

"You've changed, Nelson," she added and gave no indication if the changes were for the better.

He thrust his hands into his pockets and attempted to strike a jaunty pose. He did, after all, arrive in a new Stutz roadster. He was, after all, Nelson Paxton Wingate.

And he wasn't used to being dealt with in such an off hand manner.

"Christina," he offered, "you look stunning."

Which was accurate.

She wore a mid-calf heather wool skirt and a buff colored sweater under a cashmere coat. She was no longer a little girl.

Nelson beheld a young woman of consummate composure — the essence of the women he saw himself impressing.

She didn't appear to notice.

Finally, he blurted, to his absolute chagrin, "Would you take a spin with me. Around campus. In my auto. A new Stutz —" And with each word and every stammering ejaculation he found himself cursing his lack of poise and control. He was crestfallen when he heard himself mutter, "It's a Bearcat."

What's the matter with me? he asked himself. It is only Christina Van Luxall, after all. Her family is in total shambles. Who knows what's really left of their fortune — of her father's businesses? No one seems to have a finger on him. Plus, he's an awfully queer one these days.

Nelson stared at Christina. Was she beyond the edge, too? Was that what had him so unnerved? He couldn't find an answer but her effect on him was unrelenting. He was waist deep in a flood tide. He absolutely couldn't get his balance.

He walked her to his vehicle, opening the door so she could seat herself on the soft leather. And then he swung it closed, satisfied when the latch caught and the solid metal on metal contact let itself be heard. It was a magnificent machine and it was expensive and quick and unattainable to nearly everyone who watched it gleam by.

As he matured Nelson found himself infatuated with quality automobiles and speed. There were moments when they, as twins, approached his fascination with his own reflection. Only recently, following his father's acquisition of a tire factory and its aviation division, had the boy turned to the skies. He had earlier viewed flight as a proletariat interest, but things were changing.

Nelson and Christina motored out of the campus and into the countryside. She answered all of his questions politely and inquired as to the health of his parents.

"Fine, all fine," Nelson replied, and as he did a squirrel bounded across the dirt road in front of them. Nelson skillfully turned the large steering wheel first one way and then another, barely missing the animal.

"Is it difficult?" Christina asked, at last showing animation.

"*Is what difficult?*"

"Driving, I mean," she answered, and with her answer Nelson found a way to move in the direction he required.

"You've never tried it?" he asked in jubilant discovery.

Christina had never thought of it before. She was driven everywhere too distant to walk. And that realization made learning to drive immediately necessary.

"Do stop!" she exclaimed. "Show me!"

Nelson could hardly believe the change in her attitude.

Even Christina was surprised.

He swung the Stutz to the side of the road, disengaged the gears and hauled back on the parking brake. A cloud of following dust passed and Nelson raced around the vehicle to open Christina's door. She was out before he got there.

He taught her what he could; usually keeping his own hand on the wheel as he directed the coordination between her hands and feet. And they laughed more and more frequently as Christina lost herself in the task.

"I can't believe we have drivers, Nel!" she exclaimed. "This is fun. I'm going to learn so I'll never have to be driven again!"

Her comments returned her to an old conversation with Stephen.

Nelson saw her slipping from him. A turn was approaching. A sharp turn.

Christina was wallowing in reverie when she felt one front wheel and then another leave the road.

A covey of partridge flew from the field she subsequently invaded, and as the roadster bounced forward through them, Nelson released the steering wheel, anxious to allow Christina full responsibility for their foray through the countryside.

Christina pulled her foot from the gas pedal and braked with all of her might.

The Stutz halted. They were in a clover and bramble field. Christina turned to Nelson, who now affected total surprise.

"It appears we've lost our way," he said.

"Your motor car — have I hurt it?" Christina asked, embarrassed.

Nelson reached to the ignition switch and killed the engine. He pulled off his driving gloves and leaned against his door, watching to see what Christina would do next.

"Are we stuck?" she asked. "I mean, can we drive out?"

Nelson stretched over the door and looked to the ground.

"Can *we* drive out, Miss Van Luxall?" he queried.

Christina answered his challenge. "*I'll* drive us out! But first let's walk; motoring is exhausting."

She was out and over to Nelson's door before he could respond. She opened it.

They walked together to a rise and sat beneath a spreading tree. The sky and trees were too clear, the clouds too white and the scene too perfect. Christina didn't wish to be so content.

"I have a bottle of very decent wine," Nelson offered and rose to retrieve it.

She watched him walk back to his Stutz, stopping occasionally to free himself from a briar. She drew her knees up and rested her elbows on them. *What do I want?* she asked.

When he returned, he brought not only the wine but a small wicker basket from whose depths he produced a wedge of cheese and a stack of wafers wrapped in linen. He also unwrapped two crystal goblets, setting them on the small table top he created by closing the basket lid.

Nelson held the wine bottle for Christina's approval and was surprised when she took it from him. A corkscrew appeared in her hand and she deftly inserted it and removed the cork.

"A lady is always prepared," she informed him. "Which means a lady travels nowhere without the proper means of extracting a cork!" She laughed then; the second time she'd released herself in many months.

Nelson smiled and proffered his wine glass.

"But can the lady pour?" he teased.

"Poorly," she said, being careful to spill some of the liquid onto Nelson's hand.

They laughed together and their afternoon progressed. Occasionally, Christina would fight the loss of her unhappiness and distance, but she'd been cold for so long it seemed to fall away on its own.

Nelson allowed Christina to drive them back to her dormitory and there he asked if he might visit her again.

"I am awfully busy, Nelson," she protested, but it was weakly done and Nelson brushed it aside.

"I'll call soon," he assured her and returned to his Stutz.

Nelson drove to the campus three weeks later and then three weeks after that. It became a ritual.

She was invited to spend the second weekend in November at Fairelawn. The invitation was carefully worded, and written in the hand of Nelson's mother, but Christina knew it was Nelson requesting her presence.

Christina had driven The Chimneys from her mind just as she had displaced her father and had attempted to do the same with her thoughts of Stephen. But recently they had returned in a flood.

"Thank you, Nelson," she said over the telephone, "I'd love to go, but I have a million things to do. Please tell your mother that I'm disappointed...."

Nelson didn't let her finish.

"I'll not do any such thing. To a manor born, my dear —" he teased, "and all that guff. But you must be missing the seclusion *and* the attention. Fairelawn is quite nice this time of year, you know. You can study if you must. We'll leave you alone. And if you fancy, perhaps we could go riding."

Christina hadn't permitted herself to admit how much she missed the opulent life she'd become accustomed to at The Chimneys. She knew it would be much the same at Fairelawn.

Her final protest was therefore more feeble. "I really haven't the time to pack on such short notice, Nelson," she said, but they both knew it was a formality.

"Friday afternoon, then. What time?" he asked.

"Six," she said with absolutely no resignation.

"It shall be!" he said and she could tell he was smiling. "And you'll drive us!"

There was an early snow the evening they arrived at Fairelawn. The fires were blazing in the fireplaces and at first Christina wished she hadn't come. But the manor was sufficiently different from The Chimneys to allow her a respite.

Mr. Wingate fancied everything French and old. The house was precious and feminine, unlike The Chimneys' Tudor bulk.

Christina and Nelson were seated near the Music Room fireplace. He watched her as she stared into the flames, her fingers nervously touching the sleeves of her dress. He guessed by the sadness of her eyes that she was thinking of The Chimneys.

"Have you been back?" he asked at last.

"I haven't," she answered curtly, once more aloof.

"Will your father rebuild?" he persisted.

She turned to face Nelson. "I hope not. I hated that house. I hated everything about it!"

Nelson was oblivious to her outburst. "It's a pity, really; it was a magnificent home. Tudor revival. Splendid. Plenty of weight to it. A man's home."

Nelson was speaking honestly, for he had always enjoyed the manor. He'd spent many afternoons at the Van Luxalls' playing billiards, and Nelson consistently found the dark paneled room with its cumulus cigar smoke the proper antithesis for the gilding and the delicate legs of the furnishings at Fairelawn.

Christina realized Nelson was back at The Chimneys.

She had lost him to her father's house and she resented it.

"I may rebuild it one day," she said with quiet defiance.

Nelson turned and eyed her warily.

"I beg your pardon, Christina?"

"I said, 'I may rebuild it one day.' It only requires money."

"And money is available?" Nelson asked. He, too, had heard the rumors regarding the precariousness of the Van Luxall fortune. And he was curious enough to let manners suffer and ask.

"I wasn't speaking of Papa's money," she answered with dark eyes, daring him to dispute her.

Nelson listened as the subsequent silence emphasized Christina's words.

She willed her body to hide her discomfort. She watched Nelson, her face devoid of emotion while inside she felt herself adrift.

Oddly, it was neither the talk of money nor of The Chimneys which had discommoded Christina. It was how she had referred to her father; she had not thought of him as her 'Papa', much less called him that, since the fire.

"You do hate him, don't you, Christina?" Nelson asked, once more prescient.

She ignored him.

The fire crackled and she heard the roar of the flames which had kept her from Katherine's room.

She came back to Nelson's comment and was determined to respond honestly. Or at least to try. She thought it through and then answered, "I don't hate him, Nelson. We never hated him. But I *am* angry that he made us hate ourselves — hate ourselves for being unable to please him. He taught us that we weren't enough — that we couldn't measure up, and for that reason we were failures.

"And Mama didn't do any better. In fact, I think she was the one who ultimately convinced us he was correct.

"I think *she* hated him, though, toward the end. We girls didn't."

Nelson listened, his hands folded together on his lap, his feet stretched in front of him. He added nothing to what Christina said and he didn't question her further. He hated *his* father, and his mother had absolutely nothing to do with it.

They sat in silence.

Christina leaned back and rested her head so she looked at the ceiling. A maid bustled quietly down the hall and after a few minutes, returned. Later, the butler stepped to their door, noted the waning fire and sent a man in with additional logs. Nelson waved him away and the fire guttered until there were only coals casting muted light.

Before they ended their evening together Nelson took Christina's hand in his own. She turned sleepily toward him but didn't speak.

"If you're serious, Christina," he said at last, " — if you truly intend to rebuild The Chimneys —" he paused again and then finished, "I could help you."

She looked back at Nelson and attempted to judge him.

She rose and departed the room.

Christina and Nelson met through the early winter, but it didn't interfere with the girl's rape of knowledge. She devoured every practical science, painfully intent, frequently the only female in her class; alone in a sea of boys and unforgiving of any who attempted to defer to her.

Had she not been so beautiful, the nicknames she attracted would have been more cruel.

Some of the girls in her dormitory continued to attempt to befriend Christina but she remained aloof, impenetrable, buoyed only by her relationship with Nelson.

Rumors spread: They were secretly married — Christina had a child which she left in Nelson's care — or, they were actually brother and sister, involved in an incestuous tryst.

The possibility of their being related by birth was not difficult to believe, for Nelson was feminine and his features were similar to Christina's.

One rumor mired in a base of facts held that Christina's parents were insane; her mother having perished in the fire she had set to kill them all. Further, it was whispered that Christina was in a school so far below her station because she was hiding from her father, a madman who had detectives searching for his surviving daughter. It was conjectured he didn't intend a cheerful reunion.

Nelson's appearances in the shiny Stutz always generated new variations of the established stories.

Christina was oblivious to the whispering which trailed her, but she still fought to insulate herself from the past. It was only when she awoke in the dark that she could not control her memories. Alone, in her room, she always went back to Stephen.

Even though he had left her — that was painful enough — and had never attempted to contact her again, Christina forgave him. But when she learned from Nelson that he'd married Rosey and that they had a child and were living in a shack somewhere, Christina felt betrayed.

Sometimes, Christina felt herself to have been a young fool. Yet, in spite of those feelings, she missed him and couldn't completely abandon their dreams. Their night at the fountain was still with her, and she held it as a moment of perfection, a moment when the evil of the world had fallen away and left them together. She could still feel the water he had poured into her hands and she believed he had offered her his love and his soul.

On those nights Christina rose and dressed and wandered through the campus stillness, giving rise to a different set of rumors. She always ended up at the fountain at the intersection of six campus ways and waited for Stephen to come to her. One winter evening, light snow tumbling quietly around her, Christina closed her eyes and stood in the silence, her face raised to the darkness and the snow, and prayed that the strength of her will would bring him back to step once more from the shadows.

Christina didn't wish to spend the Christmas holidays with the Wingates, but the campus closed and everyone was required to leave and she refused to return to The Chimneys. It was snowing when Nelson arrived in his maroon Stutz, the parking area beside the dormitory choked with snow-capped cars, a snowball fight progressing near the Hall entrance.

Nelson wore his raccoon coat. He pulled off his driving gloves a finger at a time and walked to the door of the residence hall stepping around patches of snow as he did.

"Christina!" he raised his hand and called when he saw her exiting a different end of the building.

Those who weren't already watching turned.

"Christina!" he repeated, anxious for everyone to see him.

She stopped and tried to locate Nelson and just as she did a snowball slammed into the back of his head. Its trajectory had been flat and hot; there was no chance it had been an accident.

Everyone stood and waited. Nelson turned slowly after he was hit and faced a short, broad, student standing twenty feet away with his hands on his hips in a carefully positioned attitude of challenge. He sneered at Nelson, his look brimming with contempt born of the middle class.

"Hey, sorry chump," he called out, with no hint of apology in his voice. "I thought you were some kind of wild bear in that coat." Like Nelson, he reveled in the attention of others.

Those persons who stood in the middle distance between Nelson and his antagonist moved away.

Christina was interested. She wished to see how Nelson would react.

He didn't.

He brushed the snow off the back of his head, most of it falling inside the upturned collar of his coat, and then he cut across to Christina.

He didn't mention the incident and he wouldn't look again at his tormentor.

He's a coward, she thought. *He's weak.*

With that realization Christina was at first maddened. And then she wasn't, for she realized there could be no fights with Nelson. And no commands from him. And no shadow to stand in.

Christina drove.

She'd adopted his style of driving and was no longer cautious; now putting the big Stutz through its paces, sliding through corners and ravaging the straight-aways, leaving a swirling cloud of snow to settle behind them.

As they raced away from the campus, Nelson reached behind the seat and produced an insulated jug of hot chocolate. He carefully poured some of the steaming liquid into a mug and held it for Christina to take.

She looked at it and smiled, but they were approaching a turn and she was attempting to massage the Stutz into a lower gear with one hand while she gripped the thick steering wheel with the other. She'd been thinking of Nelson's weakness and comparing him with her father.

Once through the turn she looked briefly at Nelson and the cup.

"Feed me," she said, simply.

Nelson looked at her.

She didn't pay any attention to him.

He uncomfortably accepted it as a joke and raised the cup to her lips. She drank and then nodded and he lowered it.

She neither thanked him nor acknowledged it had been done in jest.

Nelson drank slowly from his own mug and thought things over. It was his first hint that their relationship had changed.

Christina found it satisfying. She drove and thought of how things could be.

They motored for some time, the road now clear and straight. Nelson had been silent until he asked, "Would you care for more chocolate?"

Christina had her right hand resting on her leg.

"Yes," she said but made no attempt to reach for the cup after Nelson poured the steaming liquid into it. She turned her head slightly toward him and parted her lips as if she expected the chocolate to be appearing there soon.

Nelson hesitated and then held the cup to them.

She drank.

"I am to feed you now?" he laughed.

She thought a moment, her eyes scanning the gauges.

"When we're alone," she answered without humor.

He looked at her and she ignored him, intent on the road, instead.

"Oh my, oh my," Nelson said quietly and then spent the remainder of their journey attempting to evaluate their situation.

It wasn't devoid of appeal to him but its subtleties were unfathomable. The best he could do was allow himself to view it as their game.

Christina drove between the stone towers topped with snow-covered, rearing lions and down the entry boulevard to Fairelawn. She stopped the Stutz in front of the manor and two doormen descended the stairs and made for the automobile.

"Take my luggage to my room, Nelson," Christina said, still not deigning to look at him when she spoke.

Nelson laughed uncomfortably. "I'll have that done for you, of course, Christina."

She turned to him.

"Nelson —"

He had an uncomfortable feeling he knew what she was about to say.

"I want *you* to carry it, Nelson."

"Aren't we taking this game a bit far?" he asked, allowing a wisp of frustration to surface.

Christina bore her eyes through Nelson's pitiful resolve.

"Take me back to school."

"You can't be serious!"

They were silent.

He smirked at her.

That was a mistake.

Christina switched the ignition to on and engaged the starter.

"You *are* serious! What if I don't always wish to play *this game*, Christina?" Nelson whined weakly.

The Stutz engine rumbled back to life. The doormen hesitated and then retreated to a respectable distance. It was obvious there was a confrontation occurring in the automobile.

"Well, it's not a game to me, Nelson," Christina answered evenly, each word laden with resolve. "If you want to be with me, you'll do as I say. You can consider it a game if it makes it easier."

Nelson's mouth dropped open. He wished to speak, to protest, but he couldn't think of anything to say. The situation had become so ludicrous.

Christina engaged first gear.

"Alright! I'll take care of your luggage, Christina," Nelson said, his voice feminine with defeat.

She switched off the automobile and shoved her door open before a doorman could help. "Good," she replied over her shoulder and walked ahead of Nelson into his home.

He tottered in behind her, glaring at a footman who rushed to help with Christina's suitcases. The servant halted in deference to the scathing silent warning he received from Nelson.

That evening Christina sent down her apologies to Nelson's parents. She wasn't feeling well enough to join them at dinner.

Nelson spent the evening struggling with how he would handle things. Not once did he more than fleetingly consider confronting Christina. He knew she'd ask to be driven back to school — closed for the holidays or not.

He reviewed their time together since he'd arrived at the school and attempted to determine if he had somehow offended her. Nothing made sense. One minute she was one of his interests, the next she had him on beck and call.

Nelson did know Christina well enough to be certain she wasn't doing it to humiliate him. Still, he couldn't make any sense of it. Perhaps it was some recently manifested familial aberration. It *was* a queer family. Her father *did* now live alone in the gate house, and the manor was *still* a burned-out hulk, untouched since the fire; and the rumors *were* that Mrs. Van Luxall had started the conflagration. But Christina — there had never been a hint that *she* had problems, too.

Twice, he nearly went to her room but decided it would be a mistake. Instead, he decided to wait and see what the morning brought.

The new day came and the sun shot white rays across the thick, smooth ice of the lake. The snow had blown away — white armies whipping madly in panicked retreat — and the ice reflected grey, rutilated with a fine webbing of silver. Along the lake's border, trees cast skeletal shadows and three distant deer stepped from the edge of the woods and stood, poised and alert.

It was a perfect morning.

A fire was set in Christina's fireplace. Frost edged the windows. She bathed and dressed slowly for the day.

Nelson came to her in the second floor library where she sat reading. He was apprehensive and seated himself on a small and uncomfortable chair near her feet.

He waited.

Christina read quietly, turning pages in silence.

Nelson knew he should be angered by such treatment but he was beginning to find it oddly satisfying.

He continued to wait.

At last, Christina instructed, without actually looking up from her book and in a quiet but authoritative voice, "It's a beautiful day. Let's take a sleigh around the lake, Nelson. Bring along a basket of warm breakfast rolls — cinnamon and maple — and a huge tumbler of fresh milk and a jug of scalding tea."

She turned to Nelson.

"I expect you to prepare it."

Instead of bridling, he felt happy inside. It was as if a wish — a monumental and secret wish — one he had never even been aware of — had just been granted.

Things were strange, indeed.

And then Nelson went beyond Christina.

He lowered his head as he left the room.

He didn't tell her how soon these things would be ready for her, and he didn't ask her when she wished to have the sleigh brought to the house; he would do it and he would wait.

Of course, Nelson neither baked the rolls nor hitched the massive horses to the sleigh. But he hovered over the cook as she prepared the breakfast, and later he slipped into the stable and followed the groom as he led a team of brown Belgians through the Carriage House and harnessed them to the sleigh by the large double doors.

It was not unusual for Nelson to drive the sleigh; he was an accomplished horseman and at Fairelawn the men of the house often took the reins, but it did seem odd to the help that he sat for such a long time waiting for Christina to appear.

The Belgians steamed and threw their heads about occasionally, sometimes dragging a front hoof through the snow, or whinnying impatiently, but Nelson remained unperturbed.

When Christina exited the front doors, she kept her hands in her muff and her head tucked down to her wrapped scarf.

Nelson could see nothing of her facial expression.

She climbed onto the sleigh and sat behind him, pulling the covers over her lap and positioning her feet over the flat heated stones.

As soon as he knew she was settled, Nelson drove the sleigh away from the front entrance of Fairelawn and took them to the road which led to the lake. The big animals were delighted to be on the move. Jangling bells on their collars and reins kept cadence.

Nelson slowed the team as they approached the lake. He was about to ask Christina where she wished to go when he felt her leaning near his shoulder.

"Take me to The Chimneys," she whispered and then placed her warm mouth on his neck. She didn't kiss him quickly and pull away; she kept her lips on him until he felt chills radiating outward from where she touched.

Finally, she raised her mouth and, still whispering, said, "Thank you, Nelson, drive on," and returned to the covers and her seat.

They flew across the ice then, the Belgians' shoes spiked for its slippery surface and tossing storms of chipped ice as they ran. The sleigh's runners hissed and bit through the cold and Christina felt she was weightless, flying across the sharp blue sky.

Nelson kept the horses edging the limits of safety and as he followed them through a shallow turn he felt the sleigh's runners sliding sideways beneath them. It was unlike him do anything so incautious with a sleigh, but he attributed it to the strange and exhilarating effect of the new Christina.

He hadn't expected her kiss.

Had she not kissed him, he might have been able to continue pretending it was a game. But he was hers now and he suspected her new unpredictability would temper his infidelities.

The Belgians devoured the lake that morning, thumping across the thick ice until they were below the dark scar of The Chimneys.

The site was imposing; the scorched orange brick and the tipped black timbers outlined against the snow and sky. Only a portion of the roof on the Main House and the East Wing remained, the rest tumbled inward, an undulated sweep of broken slate.

The front wall of the West Wing was also collapsed, as was the back wall opposite the Grand Terrace and the Reflecting Pool.

Christina stepped down from the sleigh.

Nelson was about to join her when she turned and said, "Not yet, Nelson," and walked up the bank past the Hexagonal Tea House and the ice-locked docks.

Christina had not returned to The Chimneys since the fire and now she thought that with the snow and the morning quiet, it was like an ancient dream; this shell before her its frozen leavings.

She walked down the Maple Allee and as she approached the house the trees showed wider scars until their trunks were almost entirely charred on the fire-side, checked black by the heat.

Christina left the Allee and skirted the Breakfast Room, its windows gone. She walked along the front of the manor and at the Grand Entrance she looked up to her keep tower, still standing at the back of the house.

She followed what remained of the manor's ridge and remembered her father's gargoyle.

Has it fallen?

She ran lightly through the snow to the West Wing, its interior now an exposed jumble of snow and rafters. She walked over the rubble of the fallen wall, careful to pick her way through the loose bricks and the cross-hatching of burned beams.

Finally, Christina reached the end of the wing. She violated the clean snow of the music room terrace and from its expanse stood and tipped her head. Above her, defiantly perched, its wings half folded, its hideous mouth open and screaming, the stone carving remained.

Papa's monster, she thought, *it's still there.*

Christina wondered if her recent resolve to rebuild The Chimneys would have survived had it fallen.

It mocked her.

Christina remained a moment more and then continued, passing to the back of the manor. She walked to the outside of the Reflecting Pool, the snow falling dry from her boots, a freak wind from the lake scudding along the surface of the pool, eddying the snow in its trail.

Unconsciously, she raised her collar and stopped at the base of the keep tower.

The doors she had escaped through were propped against the brick wall, their insides charred. Now, so near the path of her flight, Christina could smell the memory of the fire, its acrid and oppressive fingers finding her heart once more.

She entered the manor and stood at the foot of the stairs. The spine of the spiral was burned away, leaving treads stuck into the surrounding walls. Those which remained appeared firmly imbedded.

Christina stepped haltingly onto one and then another, and although they gave a little with her weight, she was able to climb to the second floor and then halfway to the third.

Were one of her successive perches to fail, Christina knew it would be a barely interrupted fall to the first floor. She held her breath and looked up. The walls moved.

The remaining steps were more precarious than those she had already used in her ascension.

In fact, the next step broke free as she bent and tested it with her hand. It clattered briefly as it hit the stairs below her and then found the open air of the stairway center where it tumbled as it fell.

Christina stood frozen, but she was not afraid.

She was five feet beneath the third floor doorway and at least twenty-five feet above the entrance. She stood, both feet and all of her weight on the one good step, and again tested those which remained.

Christina tore loose two steps and found the third to be relatively solid. She raised her skirt and coat over her knee and stretched until she had her foot on the third step. She pulled herself onto it, grasping two others as she did.

One she was holding broke free just as she advanced her center of balance to the third step.

Christina wavered and then caught herself.

Unwilling to listen to its fall, she did not discard the loose tread. Instead, she placed it carefully on another. She needed to take only one more step upward and she could get her hands to the exposed brick of the door jamb. She reached to check the steps she would use. The first snapped off brittle, as did the next. Her fingers were smudged with the char.

The third moved tentatively when she tested it. The one above it was better. The others seemed secure. Christina balanced and slowly took off her coat and dropped it to the steps below.

She took a deep breath, hesitated, and then flung herself upward, grabbing what she could to steady her advance. She quickly mounted the steps, hastily attacking those above as she leaped upward.

Two gave as she left them.

Had she hesitated she would have fallen.

She lunged through the doorway, the floor secure, her heart pounding.

She rested against a wall and listened as the two freed steps tumbled and banged downward, one sailing into the second level hall, the other reaching the entrance far below with a distant and hollow echo.

There was no roof above her. The sky was winter blue hung with white clouds. Christina felt the house sway. She closed her eyes. It was like her night on the roof.

Christina walked through the bathroom and into the study she had fled more than a year earlier. Beyond it was her bedroom and then Abegaile's and finally, Katherine's.

Abbie's and Katie's.

Abbie and Katie.

She had not allowed herself to use those names since the fire. And no one had called her Chrissy. Especially not Nelson.

She walked through her bedroom, entranced, unconscious of her surroundings until she entered Abegaile's room. Half of it was gone — burned, the roof fallen and propped against the outside wall. Beyond, most of Katherine's was smothered in timbers and debris.

Christina stood in what was left of Abegaile's bedroom and looked to the back wall. There were two windows with panes shattered or missing; those remaining were soot-blackened.

Set in one of the windows, a colored medallion caught what it could of the sunlight.

Christina went to it and grasping her cuff, wiped the glass. It was lavender. She bent to a piece of brick and used it to break the surrounding pieces. She then twisted the tinted section free of the lead channels still holding it.

Christina slowly massaged the glass between her finger and thumb and thought of her sister, Abegaile.

Gone.

She went to Katherine's door. There was just enough floor left to allow her to get through to the window.

The roof angled over her and Christina had to stoop to get past.

She reached Katherine's window, most of it blown out by the intensity of the fire and now covered by the fresh snow far below. She stared at the blackened sill and moved closer. As she did she felt glass underfoot.

Christina bent then and brushed through the accumulated rubble — through the bits of plaster and splinters of wood, past half of a brick and the many ill-shaped marbles of grout. She had nearly forsaken hope when she found several long shards of glass and then two medallions, one falling apart in her hand when she lifted it, the other remaining whole and sound. She held the oval lightly in her hand.

Katherine's cleaned to pale blue.

She held her prizes and knelt in the corner of Katherine's room. The absence of her sisters flowed through her arm and into her chest and Christina felt her heart expand painfully. And then she couldn't stand it any more. There was, at last, no place for her to hide.

Christina crouched in the ruins of her father's home and wept.

She left her sister's room, passed once more through Abegaile's and then her own and wondered how she was going to get back to the ground level. She went to the hallway, the one which had been choked with smoke when Anna had turned her toward the study.

Christina had forgotten Anna.

There would be no glass medallions for her; no elegant bedroom in ruins.

Anna had nothing and had given everything. She had given everything and still she'd failed.

Christina could not weep for Anna.

And she didn't know why.

She went to the hall and found the east end intact, though darkened; she walked through it to a different stairway.

The flames had been arrested at last before they reached the East Wing. Christina did not remember any fire apparatus arriving, nor had she seen anyone employing the equipment her father had stored in the Carriage House.

All she remembered was her flight to the walled garden.

At first, Christina thought the walled garden looked much the same as it always had in winter. The pool in its center was empty but for the snow, and the vines along the stone walls wore white sheathes over their twisting length.

She stood and gazed down the garden's length, slowly coming to the realization that something was wrong — something was missing — and then she saw that it was the statue — it was gone.

Her first thought was that Stephen had come for it and had somehow managed to remove it from the garden. He had come and stolen it because it was all that was left of their dream. In his own way, he had returned.

But as she went to its pedestal she saw it, tipped to the side, now outlined beneath a blanket of snow.

Christina tried to move the statue but only succeeded in rocking it to the side, the snow falling away leaving the cold green metal exposed. She attempted twice and then ran from the garden to the foot of the Maple Allee and shouted to Nelson.

"COME QUICKLY! NELSON, COME HERE!"

Her voice carried clearly across the snow and soon she heard the horses and then saw the sleigh as Nelson paralleled the Allee.

"COME TO THE WALLED GARDEN," she called and then went back before he had stopped the sleigh. Nelson tied off the horses and strode through her trail in the snow. Once back in the confines of the garden Christina raced to her statue. She heard Nelson behind her. "Help me lift it; it must be standing! It must stand!" She was nearly maniacal in her insistence. He went to the statue and grasped it by the neck and head, and with Christina struggling at the girl's chest, they raised it to a standing position. Christina backed away immediately. Nelson rocked the statue until he was satisfied with its stability.

Despite its fall, it was intact. Nelson returned to the pedestal. He thought he had kicked a rock but saw instead an infant's carved head looking up at him from the snow. It was unnerving. He stared at it quizzically and then whispered, "Someone has smashed one of the little statues, Christina." He dragged the toe of his boot through the snow around the head, uncovering a shattered torso and then another head and finally a collection of arms and legs and feet. "Who would do that?" he asked of no one. "And leave her unharmed?" Christina retrieved her coat. They returned to the sleigh and Nelson kept the horses to a trot as they continued around the lake.

That afternoon Christina dined alone in her room and later she deferred from joining the Wingates for the evening meal. Nelson's parents — his mother particularly — expressed concern as their dinner progressed. "Is she all right, Nelson?" Mrs. Wingate asked and he could hear in her voice the edge of the rumors concerning the Van Luxalls. "*Quite*, mother," he answered, his voice chilled to hoarfrost. Paxton Wingate harumphed and supported his wife. "Haven't seen her since she arrived. A bit odd, wouldn't you say?"

Nelson turned on his father. "Were you expecting a performance? She does have studies and examinations, you know." He regretted his words as he spoke them. Nelson knew he had just given his father two avenues for attack.

He used them both.

"Yes, well, I can't imagine things are too challenging at a state school."

Nelson was prepared.

"Perhaps they've raised their standards since you attended, Father."

Paxton Wingate touted himself as a self-made and self-educated man when in fact he had attended two different state universities and found himself unable to keep up in either.

Mr. Wingate reddened and tried again.

"And you, Nelson? Are you going to spend *your* life thinking about going to college?"

"Well, Father," Nelson answered without pause, "You've accomplished a fair amount without an education; I should be able to do at least as well."

Paxton Wingate hated his son. He wished desperately to see Nelson mature and fail. Very soon he would be able to demand the boy either choose a college or a career and stop dancing at his mother's skirts.

"Now, Father," Mrs. Wingate intervened, "calm yourself. It's Christmas and we have a guest."

"Do we?" the older man demanded before he pushed his chair back, drew himself up and left the room.

A collection of stone-faced servants enjoyed the exchange.

It snowed again that evening and fires blazed in Fairelawn's fireplaces.

Nelson went to Christina's door and knocked lightly. He wore a forest green smoking jacket and black velvet trousers. His feet were tucked into the black slippers his father detested.

He knocked again.

Christina knew it was Nelson, but she was in her bed and did not intend to answer.

"Christina!" he whispered through the door.

She sat in silence.

He whispered her name again, his voice ridiculously hoarse, "Christina!"

She smiled malevolently and reneged.

"Yes, Nelson, come in!" she almost shouted.

He opened the door slightly and slipped through, mortified.

"Christina! My parents!" he said to her, his voice barely louder than before but carrying the fear that he would be discovered in her room.

He attempted to understand why Christina was affecting him so strongly. Perhaps it was the game she had begun to play — no one had dared to trifle with him before — but he had deluded himself with the conviction that he would put an end to their charade once he tired of it.

Christina rested against the pillows on her bed and watched Nelson. She had a sheet pulled just above her breasts, and while her absolute lack of vulnerability unhinged Nelson, her eyes, her unrelenting stare, actually frightened him.

STEPHEN AND ROSEY

Rosey rested with her hands on the crown of her belly. Beneath them she felt the movements of the child Nelson had given her — left her with, actually — before he had pushed her out the back door.

She hated him and she loved him and she also harbored the belief that eventually he would come back to her. He would ride up in whatever expensive automobile he owned at the moment, and he would beg her to divorce Stephen and return with him to Fairelawn.

She embellished the reunion in a thousand ways — Nelson contrite — Nelson depressed — Nelson ripping in and taking her away forcefully.

"*I couldn't live without you, Rosey. Our nights together. Our love. The things we said to each other. My God, it's been torture; terrible torture for me.*"

"*Oh, come back, Rosey. I desperately need you with me.*"

"*We can live together at Fairelawn. No — I'll build a manor for you! Yes, yes, dearest Rosey! Our own manor!*"

Rosey usually had two problems at that point:

First, how would she react? The variations included making him absolutely grovel, followed by a gradual reduction of her resolve to punish him further, or running to him at once, and even Rosey laughed at the thought of her ungainly shape involved in the act of running to anyone, throwing her arms out and attempting to get close enough to instantly forgive him.

Scenes involving retribution dominated, four to one.

The second dilemma concerned the name of their new manor.

Grand Place? Grand Home? Large Manor? Breezy Manor? Faire Home?
Each sounded sophisticated and entirely appropriate.

"Thank you again, Rosey, dear," Mrs. Boisvert said, interrupting the girl's reverie as she always did. "How is the little one?"

Rosey bristled. Mrs. Boisvert consistently expected her to perform every menial, disgusting task with a smile and a quick movement and then to be anxious to discuss her personal life as if they were old friends.

If I hear one more time how that old sow's mother worked right up to the day before she delivered her child, she thought, *I'll kill her with my own hands. Baby or not.*

"Rosey," Mrs. Boisvert continued, "you're doing so well. I remember my mother, bless her departed soul, told me...."

Rosey shot her the most evil look and her employer visibly cringed. She could barely tolerate Mrs. Boisvert. It was as if the child growing in Rosey put her above all but the very wealthy.

Mrs. Boisvert tried to be kind and to draw Rosey into conversation, but the girl shunned her.

Stephen and Mr. Boisvert became closer each day. They enjoyed working together and their respect for one another grew.

That evening, winter brushed against the walls of their home while Rosey fueled the fire in the coal stove and grudgingly began to prepare dinner. Stephen stepped through the door as she banged through their meager collection of pots and pans. He shut the frigid night wind behind him and went to her, enclosing her in his arms.

"It's us against the cold."

Neither addressed the other by name and each thought it went unnoticed, and so Stephen was not speaking to Rosey anymore than she was hearing him.

"Our baby won't be still. I don't think he'll wait until spring," she said in response. Talking to Nelson about their child always pulled her away from her crushing reality and telling Stephen the baby was their's was her newest joke.

When at last they lay in bed, Rosey on her back, Stephen facing her, his eyes closed, his mind back at The Chimneys, Rosey spoke. "It's got to be our only child; I don't want another." Her voice was leaden with finality.

Stephen thought about what she had said. In most ways it suited him perfectly, for he didn't wish to be welded to her any more securely than he already was.

When he didn't protest, Rosey sank into her own analysis.

Maybe he knows, she thought. *But why did he have gone along with it? Why did he marry me at all?*

As she lay in the dark and thought these things Stephen began to question her motives.

Why does she want just one baby?

But the answer was immediately clear to him — Rosey was far too selfish to wish to be burdened with any children. The first was an accident. She would not want a second.

Stephen had flown alone and even the rigors of winter flight could not deter him from getting aloft as often as possible, and in this he was encouraged by Jacob Boisvert.

"Fly when you can, son; life's short," he'd say. "There's nothing finer on this earth!"

He always chuckled with the irony of the remark.

And so Stephen flew.

He still was the one who did the distasteful work around the airfield, but he was also becoming increasingly involved in aeroplane construction. He learned to stretch fabric over the wooden spars, and to apply the fresh varnish which made it indistinguishable from sheet metal. He learned to work with engines and that was the easiest because they were almost the same as automotive power plants; essentially more simple without the cumbersome transmission attached, and in the case of air cooled engines, they were simpler still, stripped of the water pump and radiator and hoses.

Jacob Boisvert took the opportunity to explain the design theory associated with every piece the boy touched.

"Time for the Jacob Boisvert College of the Air!" his employer would joke before he began a lecture.

Winter progressed.

Rosey found it more and more difficult to clean the Boisvert home. She waddled from room to room, half heartedly dusting where she cared to reach, but spending most of her time resting in one chair or another.

"Tired child?" Mrs. Boisvert would inquire when she came upon the girl avoiding her work.

Rosey would usually answer as if holding the woman responsible, "Yes, and I've been sick every morning for three months."

Rosey and Mrs. Boisvert became increasingly uncomfortable in the other's company. Rosey moped around the Boisvert home irritated with all they owned. It was no manor but it was large and had a grace the girl recognized and hated. At first she attempted to belittle it.

Ain't no Fairelawn, she would sneer, or *You could put the whole thing in the Music Room at the old Chimneys,* but her taunts were hollow. It was so much more than she and Stephen had and so she tried to find other ways to mock the Boisverts.

She found her mark late one afternoon.

Rosey was in the kitchen passing the time with the Boisverts' cook, when Mrs. Boisvert returned unexpectedly from town.

"Rosey, dear," she began, "would you clean up the parlor once more — we're having guests later."

Rosey didn't move at first. She glared at Mrs. Boisvert's back. Then the older woman turned to her.

"Tired child?" she asked.

Rosey exploded.

"You can't know how horrible it is carrying this *thing* around all the time. You're always sick. You never feel good. Nothing fits. It's terrible. Terrible!" And with her eyes fixed on Mrs. Boisvert, who had turned to face her she repeated, "You can't even guess how horrible it is!"

The cook, Emma, a young woman from France, quietly drew in her breath.

Mrs. Boisvert reacted to Rosey's challenge as if she'd been hit. She recovered and attempted to accommodate the virulence of the attack.

The girl realized she had finally found what she had been searching for. She watched the woman struggle with her failure.

"Oh, Mrs. Boisvert," she said at last, her voice now contrite and fawning, "I'm *so* sorry; I didn't know it was like *that!* I just thought you and Mr. Boisvert didn't *want* children."

Rosey smiled weakly at her employer. "I'm so sorry," she repeated. "It must be *terrible* for you!" She made a show of struggling to her feet and then went off to the parlor, a sluggish, oversized but smug beetle.

Rosey dusted a few things and then settled into a chair and dreamed of the home she would one day own.

Stephen turned some of his dreams toward owning an aeroplane.

"What does a surplus Jenny cost?" he asked Jacob as they warmed their hands near the stove in the corner of a hangar.

Mr. Boisvert laughed.

"I was wondering when you'd ask that, Stephen. Took you a little longer than I thought it would."

"Well, we don't have much money," the boy answered, apologetic.

" No, no, son, I know that. What I mean is, it doesn't cost a cent to wish for something. Of course you don't have a lot of money yet. But you're young. And from what I've seen you're gonna do real well for yourself, son. You're going to make Rosey proud of you, too, I'm sure of it." He put his hand on Stephen's shoulder as he finished.

"Cost?" he answered, finally. "Well, just after the war they were cheap enough, that's for certain — and they're still not so bad today. I've seen 'em go for as little as fifty dollars."

Stephen was pulling his greasy gloves over his hands in preparation to return to the engine they were overhauling. He handled the bulky items while Mr. Boisvert, bare handed, attended to attaching those smaller.

Jacob looked at the boy for a long moment.

"Follow me, son," he said at last and led Stephen from the hangar. "You know what I'd do if I was you?" he asked as they walked.

"No, sir, I don't."

They walked by the hangars and toward the auto junk yard in new silence.

When at last they were near the snow covered wrecks, Jacob pointed to an aeroplane fuselage, its tail and rudder surfaces intact and the tips of various wings protruding from an adjacent snowbank.

"If I was you, Stephen, I'd take this tired old soul and I'd mate her with that engine we have in the back of hangar two."

The boy attempted to understand what Mr. Boisvert was suggesting.

"How much would this cost?" he asked cautiously. "This and the engine, I mean."

As usual, Jacob smiled.

"Son, two things break my heart every time: The first is an aeroplane that can't fly anymore. The second is a man who doesn't own one."

He extended his right hand to Stephen and said quietly, "You get old Number Eleven back in the air and we'll call it even."

Stephen didn't see rotting fabric and tangled wire and broken spars; he saw Number Eleven glistening in the morning sun on a summer day. He smelled her engine and he felt her sweep him upward, away from the earth, above the homes and trees and little people bumping from place to place.

He was so moved by what Jacob had just done he didn't think for a second of shaking the man's hand.

He hugged him.

The baby was born in early spring and Number Eleven took off soon after.

Stephen loved the baby — loved holding him and loved his very existence, and couldn't wait until the child was old enough so Rosey would allow him his first ride in Number Eleven.

Rosey held Nelson's child to her breast. *He's as beautiful as his father,* she thought, and when he moved his clasped hands against her skin she remembered the nights at Fairelawn and wished she were there.

"Nelson," she said quietly. "Take me away from here." Rosey touched her child's head lightly with her fingertips and added, "Take us, Nelson — I have our son."

She stared at the suckling child and lost herself in his mouth and in his weight cradled in her arm. When she finished touching his hair she lightly stroked his cheek and the baby turned to her finger, a bubble of her milk at his lips.

"He'll take us," she assured the baby. "He'll come for us once he hears about you."

But as Rosey thought of Nelson and her last statement she knew he would not come to them and so she amended, "Then we'll go to him. I'll go first and then I'll take you to him. He can't resist us both."

The baby had turned back to her breast and Rosey allowed herself to drift. She awoke to the sound of Stephen coming through the front door.

He carried himself differently now that he had an aeroplane and a son. He was more assured and he was older and Rosey saw the change. She watched him and asked herself, *Why don't I love him? Why can't I be content with the lie?*

She no longer questioned their poverty, for on one hand she had lived her life in it, and on the other she was beginning to realize that Stephen would rise above it. She could see Mr. Boisvert favored him and that Stephen was learning something new every day. He had taken to reading in the evening and he often showed her sketches and rudimentary technical drawings he had made of aeroplanes and the improvements he wished Mr. Boisvert to try in one of his aircraft.

They were meaningless to her, but Stephen's excitement and the fact that he brought them back later with corrections and new ideas suggested by Stephen's employer indicated that they were not without merit.

His latest excitement and interest centered around a mechanism to raise an aeroplane's wheels into the body of the plane once it was in the air.

It had elicited one of her few comments.

"Why bother?"

"The aeroplane can go faster, don't you see?" was his reply, but Rosey persisted.

"Why do they need to go faster? I think they're fast enough already. And what if they don't come back down when you want to land? What then?"

Stephen stared at his drawing.

"But they'll come down! They have to!" he added, joking.

"You hope so," was Rosey's final word.

She was sitting with the child in a stuffed chair the Boisverts had given them. More accurately, it was a chair Mrs. Boisvert had told Jacob to have Stephen pick up. Rosey and Mrs. Boisvert rarely spoke.

Rosey had not worked for the month since the baby was born, and the first day the woman had visited and asked to hold the child, Rosey had refused.

"I really shouldn't," she said, gloating over Mrs. Boisvert's disappointment. The woman never returned to the little house

"Stephen," she addressed him as he took off his heavy, greased shirt and hung it by the door, "I'm not going back to the Boisverts."

It was a pronouncement.

They had discussed it before and Stephen now bridled with its re-introduction.

He didn't respond.

He walked across the front room and into the bedroom. He clumped around as he attempted to keep his anger under control. When he returned to the room, Rosey had her eyes closed. The baby was asleep.

"I've been thinking —" Rosey said and waited for Stephen to ask her to finish, and when he didn't she went on, her eyes still closed, "since we're so hard up for money — you haven't gotten us out of this shack yet — and the new girl working for Mrs. Boisvert has her mother take care of *her* child; I was thinking I might leave the baby with her mother, too, and go back to Fairelawn."

Stephen stopped; he couldn't understand what she was suggesting.

Once he did, he protested, "The trolley fare will eat up most of what you earn and Elly's mother won't take the baby for free — what would be the advantage? I don't understand why you can't work for the Boisverts."

"You don't have to understand;" she answered hotly; "*I'm* the one who makes that decision. You don't *own* me — you never have and you never will."

She glared and Stephen could not for the life of him figure why she was so bitter.

"But you said you hated Fairelawn — you said you'd never go back!"

She was prepared.

"I have *friends* there, Stephen, and my *mother* is there. Why is it so wrong to want to have people I can talk to. You're always either working, or reading, or playing with your aeroplane. Do you know how *boring* it is living here?"

Somehow, the baby managed to sleep through her tirade.

Stephen held his tongue even though he was very upset. He turned and went back out the front door leaving Rosey and the baby alone.

He strode toward the hangars, attempting to decide whether he would finish the carburetor work on Mr. Boisvert's aeroplane as he had promised and as he had intended to do later that evening, or if he would take up Number Eleven.

His compromise was fatal.

He rushed through the last stages of his work on Mr. Boisvert's aeroplane, attacking the job, thinking not of what he was doing, but of Rosey and the hell she had been putting him through since the birth of the baby.

Once he was finished he didn't check his work. Instead, he went to Number Eleven, pulled the big propeller through a few times, switched on the ignition, and went back to the front of the aeroplane.

"Clear!" be called to no one and threw his weight behind the upper propeller blade. After the third pull there was a cough and then an internal rumble and the engine came to life, idling, the propeller spinning around slowly, its circuit interrupted by ragged coughs.

He and his boss had done so much flying since the departure of winter that they had taken to leaving their aeroplanes parked downwind — the prerogative of the owner of the field — ready to take-off. Occasionally, the wind shifted and they would require the assistance of someone walking with the wing to turn the aeroplane windward, but usually it was possible for either of them to go to his plane alone, start it, and take-off.

Stephen ran around the right wings of the aeroplane and climbed into the cockpit. He accelerated the engine as he pulled on his leather flight helmet and adjusted the goggles. It was all second nature to him now, nothing like the first night when he had clambered over the side and sat staring dumbly at the darkened instruments.

He sat for awhile, allowing the engine time to warm up, then leaned out the side of the aeroplane to be certain it was still clear in front of him.

He was in the air quickly, and immediately worked the aeroplane high over the blooming countryside. There was still plenty of light and so the boy felt no hurry.

He performed a variety of aerobatics, testing himself as he did, requiring precision and smoothness for each maneuver. It was as he was flying inverted, a lake far below him, that he realized he was somewhere near The Chimneys. He rolled slowly to level flight, investigating the landscape as he did.

He located the manor easily, the jagged outline of its walls and the blackened heart of the large building as clear an indicator as he could have required.

And then, as he had the night he lay awake and thought of flying over Christina and her family, he dove toward the Grand Lawn. He skimmed over the grass, lower than he had in his fantasy and as he did, his imagination took over and the girls' mother and Christina and Katherine and Abegaile waved to him. Mr. Van Luxall was not present.

Stephen couldn't resist. He made a circuit, shed his altitude and landed.

He came in hot through a cross wind and while he still had enough speed to maneuver with his rudder he spun the plane around on the broad lawn, finally parking in position for take off.

No one ran to him as he climbed down from the cockpit and there was no picnic — no table and no line of attentive servants. There was only the charred hulk of The Chimneys.

Stephen walked Christina's winter path around the mansion. He did not venture into the rubble strewn interior, instead he descended to the English Garden and sat and remembered the night she had stood on the lip of the fountain. He drew his knees to his chest and leaned against the wall, the ghost of the girl he loved hovering before him.

The plantings were lost in the weeds and the water in the long reflecting pool was full of floating sticks and flecks of green. But the statue still stood. It was no longer on the pedestal above where the children had been, but it was upright, the woman entranced, her palms upward as if to catch the very air around her.

Stephen rose slowly and walked to her, and as he did he felt the loneliness and the disappointment of his life flow through him.

I've been wrong, he thought as he approached the statue. *I've done nothing right, Christina, and I miss you so much.*

He realized in the end that he was addressing the statue.

He stood opposite.

"Christina," he said and touched her fingertips. "My God, I've missed you. What happened to our dream?"

Stephen held her cool hands. He looked at her and then clenched his lower lip between his teeth to fight the tears. The love from his youth overwhelmed him.

The spring sun touched the horizon as Stephen started Number Eleven and swept across the lawn once more. In the last seconds before he was airborne he caught a glimpse of Clarence at the gate house and he waved and shouted to him.

The old man slowly raised his arm and Stephen and his aeroplane were gone.

The boy returned to his home.

Rosey stood over the table pressing her nicest dress. She had bathed and Stephen could tell she had put something in with the water, for the little house smelled as sweet as she. To the left of the table and beneath a chair her shoes were tucked side by side, cleaned and waiting for morning.

He looked at her warily.

She ignored him.

"You're going to more trouble for Fairelawn than you've done for me since we got married," he complained, his heart still aching from The Chimneys.

Rosey placed the flat-iron back on the stove and turned to him.

She's alive again! Stephen thought, startled to see the Rosey of their youth, and he began to wonder if her return to Fairelawn weren't a much better idea than he had originally thought.

Her eyes changed to haughtiness and Stephen felt their challenge.

"I'm going to bed," he said and went into the other room.

That night they lay together and Stephen was back at The Chimneys remembering Christina and their love and the dreams he had nearly forgotten, while Rosey's apprehension for the coming day crawled through her, tearing her apart.

What if he doesn't want me — she questioned — *what will I do?*

She felt Stephen's heat and knew who would be punished, and instead of that thought tempering her hatred for him, they served as a prelude to the act itself. *You'll pay — like never before!*

Rosey fed the baby in the night and rose and fed him again before she dressed to leave.

Stephen dreamed deeply and didn't hear Rosey until she was dressed and preparing the baby to be taken to the new housekeeper's mother. In a motion he was out of the bed — he had intended to rise early and check the work he had done on Mr. Boisvert's aeroplane. He knew the little man was leaving early and an uneasy feeling regarding his repair work haunted Stephen.

"What time is it?" he called out to Rosey.

Rosey looked toward the bedroom but didn't answer.

"Rosey!" he shouted, more angry with himself than her.

She snatched the bundle and the child and was out the door before Stephen could ask again.

Mr. Boisvert was surprised to see that Stephen had not come out to help him. He walked sluggishly around his aeroplane, idly looking it over, finally stopping by one of the panels below the engine. He opened it and could see that the boy had done what he had been asked.

The sun sliced between the horizon and a low layer of grey clouds as Mr. Boisvert reached into the cockpit to begin the start-up procedure. He climbed down and went to the front of the aeroplane. He pulled the propellor through several times to lubricate and prime the engine and then he caught his breath and rested against the leading edge of the wing.

"Boy," he muttered, "where are you when I need you? I'm too old for this."

It was not really a complaint. He had started many engines on his own — it required more work, but it was not as difficult as he made it sound.

He went back to the cockpit, reached in, called, "Switches on," and then hurried around once more to the propellor. He grabbed the upper blade firmly and prepared to heave it around.

The sun passed into the bank of clouds.

"Clear!" he called and pulled.

The engine did not catch and so he stepped to it again. What he did not see and could not know was that while the carburetor choke was closed, the throttle valve was stuck wide open — the worst possible combination under the circumstances.

He grasped the wooden propellor blade.

The great engine caught this time, sputtering and coughing as Mr. Boisvert stepped back, and then as if clearing its throat, it built to a roar. The old man's eyes widened and his stomach jolted as he stole a glance to see if the wheels were chocked — had they been, the aeroplane probably could not have rolled forward, and even if it had enough power to jump the chocks, Mr. Boisvert would have used the time to get out of the way of the propellor — the big piece of lumber.

But there were no chocks and the aeroplane began to move. Instinctively, the little man held his hands out as if to stop it, and before another second passed they flew from his body. In a flurry of gore he was reduced to a sluice of pieces.

The aeroplane rolled straight until one wheel struck a leg and veered to the right as it bumped over the appendage. The craft taxied perpendicular to the field, at last striking a tree on the other side. One blade of the propellor hit the trunk and broke off short and then the other shattered. Without the counter-balancing resistance of the propellor, the engine howled.

From where Mr. Boisvert's violated body lay it sounded like a death wail.

Stephen ran by the hangars, hoping he would see the two aeroplanes at the end of the field. But when he saw Mr. Boisvert's auto he knew he had missed him.

The boy stopped and looked around.

He saw the aeroplane abutting the trees.

Oh god! he moaned.

He saw the shapes in the grass where Mr. Boisvert's aeroplane had been, and Stephen walked slowly forward, hesitating with each step until he could not proceed.

He became sick and retched where he stood.

Rosey took the trolley through town and waited at the last stop for the omnibus from Fairelawn. She sat with the others while birds rushed from bush to bush. The sky was overcast but it was a warm spring morning.

At last the vehicle drew up to the trolley stop. Someone inside was waving madly. Doris had ridden out to meet her.

"Rosey!" she shouted and jumped from the bus. She ran to Rosey, embraced her and then withdrew, holding her friend at arm's length while she examined her.

"You look so good!" Doris continued. "How's the baby? I want to see him again, soon! Bring him next time; I have someone who'll watch him!"

Doris put her arm around Rosey's waist and walked with her to the omnibus.

After they were seated away from the others Doris leaned close to Rosey and whispered, "Does he know? Does *Master Wingate* know you're returning?"

Rosey didn't answer at first. The bus had started with a jolt and she waited until it had shifted through its whining gears before she responded. She turned full to Doris and startled her with the bitterness painting her face with strident lines.

Rosey answered simply, "No."

"I didn't think so," Doris murmured but then became more animated when she added, "Did you hear that Nelson's father died?"

And the rest of the way they discussed the circumstances of his death and the changes that had already occurred with Nelson at the helm of his father's businesses and the manor.

"He's not as pleasant," Doris complained. "It's like he thinks he can impress the Van Luxall girl that way — but *she* runs *him*, make no mistake of that!"

"*Van Luxall?*" Rosey asked.

Doris frowned at her ignorance.

"Christina Van Luxall — the sister who lived through the fire. Cold and far off, that one! But she gives Nelson his due!" and as she finished, Doris feared she had said too much.

But Rosey only smiled.

"Does she really," she answered with no hint of a question in her voice.

At the manor, Rosey went to her mother, something she would have had to have done under any circumstance, for the woman was the head of the domestic staff. They met in her mother's quarters — a surprisingly large accommodation — much nicer than Eleanora's had been.

Mrs. Baker reviewed for Rosey the changes that had taken place since her daughter had left and when she was finished she warned, "There can be *no* nonsense, Rosalind. I won't have you ruin what I've worked my life for — and I warn you, if there's even a hint of trouble, I'll have you out of here in a minute!"

Rosey stared at her mother's moving mouth, and when it stopped she said flatly, "Thank you for asking — the baby is fine."

Mrs. Baker softened momentarily and then drew herself up again.

"Rosey, you don't know how hard it was for me to convince Nelson Wingate to let you come back."

"No mother, I don't know how hard it was — and I don't care, either. I've no plans to come near the master of this house. I'm here to work and get away from the Boisverts — they're the ugliest, meanest family I know." Rosey paused. "You may not remember, mother, but I have a baby and a husband — I'm not a little girl anymore."

Unconvinced, her mother stood with her hands at her sides and shook her head slowly.

"I hope you remember those things, Rosey. I really hope you do."

Rosey didn't answer but there was something about her mother which didn't sit well with her — something had changed and she couldn't decide what it was.

The funeral for Mr. Boisvert was attended by an astounding number of persons. Then, a week after her husband's death, Mrs. Boisvert summoned Stephen to her home. In the interim, he had been going through the motions of finishing one of the projects he and Mr. Boisvert had begun.

Stephen walked to her house, forcing himself forward with each step.

I'll tell her, he thought. *It isn't fair that she don't know.*

He was met at the door by Mrs. Boisvert. She shook his hand formally and then put her arms around him.

"I'm sorry, Mrs. Boisvert," he said and waited for her to release him. She did, finally, and he could see she was having difficulty controlling her emotions. She didn't lead him to the parlor, as he had expected, but to Mr. Boisvert's office, instead.

Stephen knew why she had called him — she was going to sell the airfield and Mr. Boisvert's business. An unrealistic hope was that the buyers would allow him to continue working, but he knew that once Mrs. Boisvert learned what he had done — that he had killed her husband — she would send his family packing.

Mrs. Boisvert dabbed at her eyes with a small handkerchief before she spoke.

"Jacob loved you, Stephen; he thought of you as a part of our family. He always talked about you." A new tear moved slowly down her check. She hesitated, regained control and continued, "Every night at dinner he talked about how much you had learned and about your ideas for his aeroplanes. He said you were the smartest young man he knew, Stephen, and he was proud to have you working for him."

Stephen looked at his shoes. The more time that passed before he explained to her — confessed to her — the more difficult it became. He thought of himself as neither bright nor creative; he thought of himself as a selfish monster — a murderer who had negligently put his own needs before the safety of the one man who trusted him.

I should have checked it. I should never have worked on it in the first place, he taunted himself. *He told me never to touch an aeroplane if your mind's somewhere else.*

He had known what had happened before he retrieved the aeroplane and took the carburetor apart. What he had done was stupid and unforgivable.

"It's what he wanted, Stephen. Will you do it?"

Her use of his name brought him back. She looked at him kindly and Stephen bridled with his guilt.

"I'm sorry, Mrs. Boisvert," he answered honestly. "I didn't hear what you said."

Once more he hung his head, but this time he forced himself to listen to her words.

"He told me many times, Stephen, that if anything happened to him you were to take over the company — I was to make you full partner. He wasn't well, you know...."

"I didn't...." he tried to interject.

"No, you wouldn't;" she continued, "he didn't want anyone to know. He was so determined to teach you everything before he died. It was his purpose. It's what made him go to work every day. He needed you, Stephen. And he needs you even more now."

He looked up at Mrs. Boisvert.

"I need you, Stephen; I don't wish to sell the airfield and I am going to keep the business going — to see it grow. It's all we have left of him."

She was silent then as she waited for his answer.

Stephen sat for a long while before he forced himself to begin.

"Mrs. Boisvert — you don't understand — he trusted me too much...."

"No, son," she interrupted, not allowing him to finish. "No, he recognized you for what you are, Stephen. Please say you'll help him now. He saw the man in you and he respected it, Stephen, just as he loved the boy."

Stephen took a deep breath and held it while he tried to think of a way to explain to her, to remove himself from the unbearable situation which had embraced him.

And then he thought of the little man, always smiling, always forgiving and laughing, and a sob choked Stephen as he sat.

"I will," he whispered at last. "I mean, I'll try, Mrs. Boisvert."

For two days Rosey did not encounter Nelson. Once she saw his back as he departed in his auto, and once she heard him calling across the lawn to the grounds keeper, but it was not until the third day that they stood face to face once more.

Rosey was carrying a basket of fresh flowers to be placed in a guest suite when Nelson left the room she was about to enter.

"Good morning, sir," she said with mock servility, careful to temper her words with a touch of levity.

Nelson smiled thinly.

"Rosey," he said.

Every day she had been careful to appear neat — certain her hair was as she wished it and her uniform clean and pressed. She had once been more beautiful and she knew it; now she worked to recapture what she had taken for granted before.

His eyes covered her, finally settling on her hair. It curled loosely and he wished to touch it. He didn't bother to look to see if they were observed as he raised his fingertips and lightly traced a curl.

"Your hair is what I remembered most," he said quietly.

She looked at him and could not speak.

Then he broke the spell and asked, "You're well?"

She didn't answer but Nelson continued as if she had.

"And the baby? Your baby is well?"

Then he added clumsily, "A boy — I had heard you had a little boy."

Rosey could not be angry in his presence. She smiled at him and answered, "Yes, Nelson, we —" and then she didn't finish. She lowered her eyes and clasped the flowers in front of her.

"Could we talk, one day?" she asked. "Alone, I mean — and quietly? I miss it, Nelson. I miss it more than anything else."

She was so comely and she spoke with none of the anger he had expected. Nelson thought of their situation and then answered, "I think we may, sometime, Rosey. Allow things to settle here for a bit and then I'll make arrangements. You've only just come haven't you?" He asked the latter as an afterthought.

She was close enough that he could smell her freshness and he didn't need an answer. He held her with his eyes a moment more and then he turned and passed down the long, wide hall.

CHRISTINA, NELSON, AND ROSEY

Christina and Nelson saw one another through winter and spring. Christina was not at first aware that Rosey had returned to Fairelawn, and Nelson, knowing nothing of their past, did not anticipate trouble.

He attempted to see Christina every weekend, but as he buried himself in his father's businesses, finding time for her became more and more difficult. At first he ceased seeing his other friends in an effort to maintain his relationship with Christina, but it was not enough and he began to miss an occasional weekend and then several in a row.

It did not immediately create a problem; Christina had a full week of business and science classes and her course work kept her busy. When she wasn't studying she attended evening and weekend lectures. Her second year at school passed quickly and rather than return to The Chimneys and her father at the gatekeeper's lodge, she enrolled in a full schedule of summer classes.

When it was necessary, she communicated with her father through his attorney, William Paget, the semi-retired senior partner of Paget, Plumb, and McDonald, a dusty firm serving the catatonic widows of the captains of industry. Mr. Van Luxall had enlisted them years earlier when a minor heart problem gave birth to fears that he would predecease his wife.

After the fire he turned Mr. Paget's focus to the financial needs of Christina.

She saw little of Nelson that summer. It wasn't until the following spring that any sort of regularity regarding their visits was resumed.

Christina gave no thought to seeing anyone else. In fact, she never really considered herself to be seeing Nelson. He was a convenient and known quantity. She was using him and she would continue to do so when she could.

Nelson was determined to prove his father wrong. Consequently, he allowed the responsibilities of business to overwhelm his life. He was driven to improve the family's financial base.

Once Nelson came to understand the complexities and inter-relationships of their various companies, he began to divest the family holdings. First the peripheral and later some of their primary sources of income and power were sold. Most of the funds were plowed back into expanding the family's new base industry: rubber tires and aviation.

Some of his choices were brilliantly propitious. Others were not.

He sold their steam-automobile factory and the last of their canal stock. He liquidated the coal gasification plant and the incandescent light factory. He then sold the railroad short-lines, along with the controlling interest in a steel plant in the southern part of the state.

Nelson could barely believe his father had involved the family in the production of books for children to color. He sold the publishing house. Additionally, he removed virtually all of the family funds from the stock and bond markets, preferring to keep the funds in short-term government obligations.

After two years of selling, investing, and accumulating capital, Wingate Tire and Aviation was the only jewel that had not been pried loose from the family crown.

At first Nelson thought he could steward his involvement in aviation from behind a desk, but the industry technology was changing quickly. Before long he knew he was too far removed to keep up.

So he learned to fly.

Nelson did not fly well; he was not a natural student. He didn't experience any thrills or succumb to any joy. Flying was a process. A process to allow him the insight necessary to more easily understand his engineers.

He had embraced aviation not out of love, but from a stroke of cold vision. And he would expand beyond manufacturing tires, and build aeroplanes because that's where he knew the future lay and for no other reason. He hired the best and paid them well and listened to what they advised. He ignored their faraway looks and their excitement.

His luck held.

And so at a time when Christina was obsessed with her education, Nelson was up to his elbows in business, his silk shirt sleeves folded neatly back, his hands insulated.

Nelson breathed business, but balance sheets couldn't sublimate his sexual desires.

Had she the inclination, Christina would still have been physically unable to slake his lust, but she was at school and those few times when they were together, she kept him at bay with variations of her theme of mastery. They no longer pretended it was a game, and still he did what she wished. She hadn't taken dominance beyond its brutish genesis of service and denial, but Nelson learned to serve with more facility than he had taken to flying; perhaps because perfect flight required grace and feeling, and subjugation did not.

Christina was perfectly aware that he would eventually turn to others for sex, and in that she had no interest; Nelson was free to do what he wished with anyone else.

At first he resisted returning to Rosey, but she was available and he knew from experience that she was capable of discretion under the most taxing circumstances.

He rekindled their relationship gently.

One late summer afternoon an electrical storm raged over the city, casting lightning randomly about. Before it passed, poles were struck and limbs crashed across transmission wires, and in a colossal flurry of sparks and surges, the electric generating plant in town ceased producing power. Trolley service was discontinued for three days.

Rosey would not leave Fairelawn. She believed the baby to be safe and so she allowed herself the glorious respite of two childless nights.

Stephen would have driven out to pick her up had he known, but he was out of town expanding the Boisvert interests.

Doris had moved to a larger room, and now Rosey had twenty-seven to herself. She felt young once more and blissfully unencumbered as she undressed for the night. Nelson had driven off that morning and Rosey believed he hadn't returned.

In fact, Nelson had driven back to Fairelawn well in advance of the storm. He had sequestered himself in his office — his father's old office — and he was alone; his mother was off on a Mediterranean cruise and so Nelson was enjoying a spate of undisturbed work.

He enjoyed the storm, feeling its violence, while he wrestled with a shortage at one of his production facilities. Fairelawn supplied its own power and so Nelson was unaware of any problem until he spied the omnibus returning through the rain with its earlier compliment of passengers. It splashed through the deep puddles and pulled beyond his office windows, headed toward the servants' entrance.

Nelson stood at his desk and watched the bus pass. He grabbed a telephone from the cradle — one of the direct outside lines which did not pass through the manor's switchboard — and found the line silent. Next he rang the manor.

"Lines dead?" he asked.

"Yes, Mr. Wingate," the operator answered.

He lowered the receiver.

He went back to his work then but his mind didn't remain on the availability of lamp black for coloring tire rubber and neither did it explore the storm.

That evening he waited in his bedroom. His premonition was that Rosey had remained at the manor and would later come to him.

He was only correct by a half; she did not come to him.

He quietly trod the manor's halls after the others were in their beds and his patience was exhausted. The staff had created a brief commotion when they'd arrived, but soon they took to the extra rooms. The event itself — a circumstance mandating that those who lived away from the manor must spend the night — was not that unusual. It occurred at least ten times every winter.

By the time Nelson walked the corridors, everyone was asleep or at least in bed. He went to Rosey's room unerringly and gently turned the knob to allow himself entry. The small room smelled of her and he closed the door behind him and adjusted to the darkness.

Rosey sighed quietly.

Nelson started. He composed himself and walked across the room to her bed.

She was covered but still he ran his hand lightly over her back and shoulders. Rosey moaned softly but did not awaken. He touched her hair next, feeling its light curls against his fingers and then he combed through the curls, keeping his fingertips gently touching her head.

"Rosey," he whispered.

Still, she didn't stir.

He said her name again and as he did he placed both of his hands on her back and massaged her.

Rosey was used to Stephen coming to their bedroom late and she had also grown accustomed to sleeping with a wiggling, kicking baby. Nelson's attentions went unnoticed.

He rose from her bedside and stood above her.

Nelson went to the other bed. Had he been in his own room he would have dropped his clothing to the floor. Instead, he neatly laid out his shirt and then his pants. It was the way he believed Christina would have wished him — *required him* — to act.

Undressed, he walked across the wooden floor to Rosey's bed. He carefully pulled her covers aside and crawled into bed behind her, embracing her as he did. At first he lay quietly, but her warmth aroused him and he began to move gently against her. He spoke, rekindling old conversations, regaining immediately his lost familiarity.

At first, Rosey moved away from him, but he followed and his voice seemed to penetrate her sleep at last. She did not turn to him as he had thought she would, instead she reached up to his arm, ran her fingers along it, and then carefully held his hand.

"Good evening, Rosey," he whispered.

She responded by moving her body closely into the contours of his.

He kissed the back of her neck.

"Nelson...." she murmured from the edges of sleep.

He hugged her in response.

"We have a child, Nelson," she finished and drifted away again, only to awaken later when Nelson became bold with his wandering hands.

He held her the rest of the night, rising before dawn and returning silently to his room.

The next day he drove to Wingate Tire and Aviation to assess the damage, and saw that only one plane which had not been properly secured had flipped over. The damage was not nearly as bad as it could have been.

But for the watchmen, the factory was deserted.

Nelson drove back to Fairelawn after briefly prowling the dark halls of the office building.

That night he wondered if Rosey would come to him. He didn't remain alone for long, for he had no sooner posed the question when his door opened without the prelude of a knock.

"Nelson," she called softly.

After the storm Nelson and Rosey met during the day.

Rosey sometimes questioned what she was doing. She had not mentioned their child after the first night and neither did she speak to Nelson of their future. As if by magic they picked up where they had left off years before and Rosey was afraid to alter any of it.

It was so comfortable.

CHRISTINA

In November Christina was summoned to the offices of Paget, Plumb, and MacDonald. That in itself was unusual for it was Mr. Paget's practice to require nothing of Christina other than her signature, and he had never asked her to leave school during the term. He always visited her at school.

But this time he sent a car and as she waited for its arrival she wondered if perhaps her father had died.

The long, black vehicle took her to the city and there, in a dark paneled office set with leather winged chairs, musty oriental rugs and boring nautical paintings, she learned that her father was quite healthy, actually — at least physically.

"We are apprehensive, Miss Van Luxall," Glenn Paget began, "and we thought it wise to apprize you of the situation, given our legal and fiduciary responsibilities." His face was pinched as he spoke, giving the old man the concerned countenance he had achieved by practice and from repeated visits to his proctologist.

He continued, hedging constantly with "We *believe*," and We *conjecture*," and "We *fear*."

He was correct in his use of 'we' for he had fortified his office with a collection of somber partners. Christina thought at first that their presence was warranted merely by the size of her father's fortune, but as Paget droned on it became clear that they had been called forth because of the precariousness of her father's mental state and the enormity of her solicitor's request.

"We think it most wise that we work with him in his lucid moments...."

Christina frowned at the sound of 'moments'.

" — to turn control of his enterprises over to our firm. We shall require your signature, of course."

Paget nodded to one of the younger men along the wall. As the junior partner bought forward a sheath of documents, Paget seemed for the first time to notice Christina's rising anger. He amended hastily, waving off the boy, "Were you older, and, well, (he attempted to laugh off the impossibility of his suggestion) if you weren't a *Miss* Van Luxall, Miss Van Luxall, we would have recommended grooming you to work in your father's stead, but as you know, that is not the case."

He saw her distress was still increasing.

"Are there questions? Something you wish to discuss?" He began to punctuate his last statement with an embarrassed laugh but apparently decided it was inappropriate and switched to a quick cough.

"Is my father at The Chimneys?" Christina asked, cutting off the old man in the middle of an extended series of harrumphs and throat clearings.

Mr. Paget raised his bushy eyebrows. It was pathetic and amusing to hear her speak of a pile of charred rubble as "The Chimneys."

"Well, yes, he keeps his residence there. . ." he paused for effect, "in the *gate house,* if I'm not mistaken."

A partner of sufficient stature to be permitted a chair at the august gathering nodded to Paget. "Indeed, he is there," he confirmed and settled back into legal silence.

"Then I'll speak with him," Christina said, glaring from man to man, trying to let them all know she had little use for them.

She stood and faced Mr. Paget. It was too much — another man was attempting to push her around, to force her to do what he determined was necessary.

"*We* shall," she began, stammering as she attempted to control her fury and search for correct words, "*We Van Luxalls,* " she said at last, "shall require no *more* from your house than we have in the past, *Mr. Paget.*"

"*In fact,*" she threatened, "I suspect we may be requiring *less.*"

She was out of the room before old man Paget had time to assess the damage.

It had been paramount to secure the permission of the sole heir before he could declare Van Luxall incompetent and tuck the Van Luxall fortune under the protective wing of P. P. and M. And now that Paget had apparently failed, there was not an individual in the room who dared to look at him.

The partners, junior and senior, filed out of his office, their eyes unfocussing, their steps light with deference, a somber wave of grey and blue wool.

Paget had intended the meeting to be his farewell performance. He tapped his fingers on a stack of papers and stared at Christina's empty chair. It was the same color as the spots on the backs of his hands.

Christina stepped to the curb and hailed a taxi.

"Smithson Automobile," she announced, glaring at the driver.

He shrugged.

Christina picked the vehicle which suited her, and drove off, leaving a stunned salesman staring at her check.

From there she returned to school, packed her clothing and was gone in less than an hour. It was dark when she arrived at The Chimneys. She went to the gatekeeper's lodge, sensing the burned-out manor across the Grand Lawn, and moving ahead of the sorrow which pursued her anger.

Mr. Van Luxall was seated near a window facing the manor. He did not look up at first and Christina passed by him, exploring the cottage. Locating a small, empty bedroom she left her luggage on the bed and returned to her father.

He turned slowly to her, laying a moist unlighted cigar on the arm of the chair as he did. The room was poorly lighted and that could have been why he did not acknowledge his daughter.

They stared at one another until the old man spoke.

"Yes?" he asked as if the young woman had come to request something of him.

Christina did not answer, rather she looked around the room for lamps to light. She saw several and lighted them all, brightening the room measurably and causing her father to shield his eyes momentarily with his hand.

He was not the strong, overbearing man she remembered; not the male force which towered above her through her childhood, never mildly interested in what she said or did. She had steeled herself for the moment of their encounter and Christina now realized she had waited too long. There was nothing left to confront. She wondered if he could possibly have amassed the fortune his solicitors had suggested. The fortune they now feared he would squander without their help.

"It's Christina," she said finally.

She dragged a straight-back chair from a corner and positioned it in front of the man, for standing above him gave her an advantage which seemed unfair.

Christina sat and waited for his reaction.

There was none.

"I want to talk to you about business. I need to know what's happened — what's happening to our holdings and to you." She spoke forcefully, giving him no quarter.

Mr. Van Luxall squinted at her.

"Christina?"

He was like a man awakening in a dark, strange room.

Unconsciously she softened her tone. "Yes, Papa."

"*Why aren't you in school?*"

She was about to respond when he continued.

"And Abegaile and Katherine — where are they? Are they here with you? They should be at their lessons."

Christina didn't answer. She sat and watched. At first his eyes moved nervously everywhere but toward her. She waited. When finally he looked, first at the clothing she wore and then at her face, she saw that he did recognize her and then the more he investigated her features, the haze seemed to lift from behind his eyes.

When he spoke again, irritation had crept into his voice.

"Why aren't you at school?"

Where the same question asked earlier had carried with it the almost gentle questioning of a parent to a young child, its repetition was of someone reprimanding an inferior.

Her father was back.

Christina was heartened to return to her pent-up rage.

"I am home to learn *our* business," she almost shouted. "You need me now and I've returned for you to teach me what you know."

He looked at her — she was beyond belief — then he laughed through his nose, his derision precluding a verbal response. He glared. He grew before her and his eyes narrowed and Christina became more erect in her chair while her father relaxed with unthreatened insolence.

The silence filled the massive void between them and though they were barely a yard apart Christina felt as of she were looking down a long, long hall to her tormentor.

And then she saw he was fading again and Christina flashed at the thought of his retreating from their confrontation.

"DAMN YOU!" she intoned and he returned with a shake of his head. It was as if she had slapped him.

"I'M NOT YOUR SON — YOU HAVE NO SONS! I'M YOUR DAUGHTER AND I'M ALL THAT YOU HAVE LEFT!" She had risen from her seat, and now, above him, she shouted, "YOU'RE LOSING YOUR MIND — IF YOU HAVEN'T NOTICED —"

She laughed out loud as she said the latter and Christina feared that she, too, was being tipped over the edge. When she continued she did not speak loudly but her words had the same force, and they rolled from her, uninterrupted.

"You're going to teach me what you know. I'm going to be with you every waking hour and you're going to help me learn our business, and every minute you're not mentally sound I'll make the decisions. Hide now, if you wish, and I'll take over immediately. I'm all you have, Papa; you'd better make the best of it."

He didn't answer at first but Christina knew he understood it all. She saw embarrassed anger sweep through him, carried along by his own knowledge that he was losing control, that he was old, and that he was mortal. He blinked his eyes repeatedly and shifted them from side to side.

She waited a moment longer and when he still had not spoken she added, "I talked to Mr. Paget today; his firm wishes to take control of our businesses. They told me you're no longer competent — know that, father, for you have no friends."

She could see that he was still with her. He watched her speak, his eyes now sharp and penetrating. They softened briefly and Christina saw what she had believed him incapable of — his eyes moistened and she could see him fight emotion she had thought he lacked. He stood from the chair and looked up to her.

My god, he's smaller than I am! she marveled. Then somehow, he became larger than she.

Arrogance briefly puffed his body. "I leave at five-thirty in the morning — be ready," he said curtly and then collapsed back onto his chair, dismissing her with a wave of his cigar.

In the weeks that followed Christina watched him struggle with his ability to remain cogent. He fought and usually he won, but sometimes he lapsed into lethargy, immobilized in his downtown office, staring out his window, always looking off at some unseen vision. At those times Christina took over.

During the first incident, Mr. Van Luxall's secretary, Thomas Woolsley, didn't do as he was bid by Christina and she brought to him a storm as bad as any he had ever weathered with her father.

"If you wish to remain in our employ you'll change your attitude immediately, Mr. Woolsley — or when my father returns (she spoke of her father as if he were not present, although, in fact, he was in his chair a few feet away) he will find that you have left our employ." She cut him with her eyes and finished, "You can't be so stupid that you fail to see what's happening.

"The choice is yours, Mr. Woolsley — understand that I'm tolerating you because I believe you can help us — now make up your mind to do as I say, or pack your desk."

Over the years the thin little man had wrapped himself in the tail of her father's mantle and she had just jerked it from his narrow shoulders.

Christina pursued him.

"Well?" she demanded.

He cleared his throat nervously. "My apologies, Miss Van Luxall. You are, of course, right.

"We've been at a loss here for awhile," he added, glancing nervously to Mr. Van Luxall. "I guess I haven't helped by pretending everything is all right, but really there's been nothing I could do."

After his defeat he went on to remind her of several obligations scheduled for the afternoon.

"If you wish, I can call and tell them you'll be conducting the meeting in your father's — Mr. Van Luxall's — place."

Christina smiled to herself; but she wasn't gloating, just pleased that he was staying. Woolsley was educated and competent and he could provide continuity during the transition.

Sometimes when her father would 'leave her', she got the impression that he hovered at the edge momentarily; listening, observing, testing, even. And then, once satisfied, he would slide silently into the distance. And when he did, it was as if she could actually see him leave the room.

The Van Luxall empire was spread as wide as the Wingate's had been before Nelson began paring it away. But Christina loved the diversity. The farm implement business fascinated her, the Ever-round Tire factory, its penetrating smell and suffocating heat an elixir to the young woman used to perfumes and scented rooms. She visited the fledgling paperboard box plant and the brick monster of a steel mill and they too drew her in.

It was business and it was a man's world and Christina couldn't get enough of it.

And then, strangely, as she immersed herself, her father began to improve — slowly at first, and then with increasing rapidity — and Christina found herself concerned that fully recovered, he might throw her out.

She sought ways to ensure her future but found none.

It was not as if he had openly begun to push her away and it was not that she detected any fresh hostility in his manner — it was just a feeling, an unsubstantiated fear.

Their working relationship remained distant and demanding; her father dumping mountains of statistics and evaluations and projections on her and Christina consistently wading through them and reporting her recommendations.

He took them, and when he did what she had suggested Christina never knew if it were because of the weight of her arguments or because it was what he had intended to do in the first place. If his refusal to follow her advice led to a reversal in their fortunes, he would then adopt her recommendations tardily, never mentioning that he had.

When they were both wrong he bulled ahead in silence.

They remained at the gate house cottage and there they didn't speak at all. Mr. Van Luxall took his meals in town and Christina cooked for herself.

Christina's concern for her future festered through winter and spring, and then finally, in early summer he called her from her office. He glowered across his desk at her before he spoke and she knew what he was about to say.

"I'm well now and your education is finished. I don't have the time to tutor you any more."

He slid an envelope across the desk to her.

Christina reeled. She had at least expected a long lecture; an extended belittling. She could not take her eyes from the envelope and she couldn't make her hand reach for it.

"Now take it and get out," he commanded.

For all of the control she had wielded, for the many times she had steered their ship through shoal waters, in the end she felt she had been betrayed. The ancient hatred welled up inside her until she pushed her chair back so violently that it slammed onto its back on the floor.

She measured the man, her eyes narrowed, her fists tight. Her chest heaved with anger. She couldn't attack his decision, but she could attack him.

"I haven't always hated you," she began evenly, leaning slightly forward as she talked. "It wasn't until I grew up and learned what a small, evil man you are that I've learned to do that. I was afraid of you when I was a little girl — I was afraid of you and still I wished so hard to please you — to be a boy. To be your precious little boy!"

Christina tried to control herself but couldn't.

"We all wanted to please you — we all tried so hard —" and she began to cry as she named her sisters, "Katie and Abbie — they loved you so much and they needed your approval so desperately — and Mama — you killed her, too — you drove her crazy the same as you did the rest of us."

Christina smeared the tears away with the back of her fist. And then, she couldn't speak. She looked over his office as if saying goodbye, snatched the envelope from his desk and walked out of his business and his life.

She returned to the gate house cottage and packed in the same flurry she had when she left her school.

She threw her luggage into the back of her auto and tore out past the main gates. Unconsciously, she raised her hand as she always did to the gatekeeper, forgetting he had died a year ago.

Christina drove to the intersection where the old dirt road from the landing joined the one she was on. Her big car slid to a stop and she jammed it into reverse, tires spinning on the lose gravel, and then she turned and bumped down the road, finally stopping at the shore where she and her sisters had met Stephen before their doomed circus trip.

It was there that Christina remembered the envelope her father had given her — the last pay she was damn well certain she deserved — and it was there that she took out the hand written check and gasped.

Six million dollars.

Christina dropped the check and frantically went back to the envelope. There was nothing else. Not a note or a letter or even a simple good-bye.

She clutched the top of the steering wheel and rested her forehead against it and cried — for her mother and her sisters — and for her father.

CHRISTINA AND NELSON

Of course, everyone in the business community had talked about the Van Luxall girl's apparent apprenticeship to her father; it was perceived as a bit of a joke by all who had not encountered her, and then when she was no longer at her father's side, the stories shifted to address the change.

Christina felt as if she were watched everywhere she went, and it was as bad as when she had been at school. At first she was tempted to take her father's check and leave the city so she could truly start fresh, but she only entertained that idea briefly, for it sounded too much like running away.

Finally, she ensconced herself in a hotel room downtown and stared at the check for hours. At the back of her mind was the nagging doubt as to its actual value. The next morning she walked to her father's bank. Once seated in the president's office she slid the check across to him.

"I'll be demanding funds against this soon. Will it create a problem?"

He glanced quickly at the amount and appeared quite nonchalant.

Briefly.

He then cautiously pulled the check toward him and lifted it from his desk. He looked at the writing and then at Christina and then back at the writing.

"Your birthday?" he asked with strained humor.

When she didn't respond to his wit even though he was only off by less than a week, he looked at the check a final time and said, this time steeping his voice in banking wisdom and hiding his fears, "Miss Van Luxall, while it is an extraordinary face amount for one check, I believe there will be no problem if you will give us adequate time to prepare for the withdrawal. There are stocks to be liquidated and we will consult with Mr. Van Luxall."

Christina felt her whole body react. Until his last words she had insulated herself from the magnitude of her father's gesture. She rose slowly from her seat, reached across and shook the man's hand and then paused in the doorway of his office.

"Please deposit it in my account and prepare the funds to be transferred as soon as possible. I am staying at the Carlton Arms, suite twenty-three ten."

From the bank she went to the three largest investment houses in the city and spoke to the manager of each. Fortunes were expanding hourly in the van of the stock market's incredible protracted advance and it was only by putting the accent on her last name that Christina was able to be worked into their schedules.

She came away from her meetings with the uneasy feeling that each of the men with whom she had spoken was on some sort of wild, gambling holiday, anxious to draw in new money. Additionally, she knew that any money she put into the stock market would invariably end up underwriting the empire of men, and that had limited appeal.

And so she was determined to do what had tempted her from the first. She would either buy an established company or start a business which she would manage. The difficulty was deciding which industry and which company to select, for in the sustained euphoria of the current business climate, every company seemed a money maker and all of them had their stock prices run out of sight.

Had she not spent the time with her father, Christina's choice would have been easier, for before her apprenticeship she had not understood fully how he had managed to amass his power and wealth. Now she knew that it had been done through a combination of opportunity, attention to detail, and absolute belief in himself. Along with a healthy dose of ruthlessness.

There appeared to be opportunities everywhere, and that frightened Christina. It seemed too good to be true, since at the rate the nation's industrial base was expanding, the country would soon be blanketed with factories from coast to coast. It couldn't be possible. She remembered the concern of one of her economics professors — one of her *unpopular* economics professors.

In terms of understanding the details associated with manufacturing firms, that was much easier if one were watching a few companies, but Christina stood with virtually all of them to choose from. The problem would be narrowing the field. She was tempted to mirror her father's investments, as she was most familiar with them.

Regarding her belief in herself, Christina would not allow a doubt to surface. She could succeed because she had to succeed. All she needed was to decide a direction to take.

Three days passed and Christina was no closer to making a decision. Instead, she was crippled with the crushing number of choices.

On the morning of the fourth day she rose early, dressed, and retrieved her vehicle. She drove out of the city proper and toured the sprawling complex of factories reaching out into the surrounding countryside.

Black smoke poured from hundreds of tapering brick chimneys and endless clouds of workers choked the sidewalks around the factories. Field upon field had been converted into parking lots and everywhere she looked railroad spurs crossed the intersecting roads. Trains of hopper cars mounded with coal were an integral part of the landscape, some backing into sidings, others static in long parallel lines in switching yards, still others crawling in bunches of a hundred or more, snaking along, sometimes stretching out of sight.

Christina was in love with it all. The filth, the coal dust, the crowds — they represented success and power. They were the might and the backbone of the country and she was poised to become a part of it.

She drove on, and the smells were as integral a part of the complex as the factories themselves. There was no fresh air, only thick sulfur fumes from the coal, and clouds of choking chemicals from nearly every plant. The air was blurred yellow or orange, or grey, or shades of each, and in some places it was actually black. In addition to the omnipresent coal dust, a fine liquid mist covered her windshield as she drove past more than a few factories.

It was an elixir to Christina, for she knew that once past the amorphous, moving, smudges of workers; once inside the buildings and into its offices, the smells would fade until they were unnoticed, and all that would remain was the feeling of raw, heady power which fueled manufacturing.

She drove the entire day, hoping that eventually something would reach out and help direct her.

Nothing did.

And so, late in the afternoon, she drove beyond the factories and into the country.

Earlier, Christina had driven down the street beside where Nelson sat in his office and listened to his three chief engineers argue. Two were adamant that the firm should involve itself in the air racing circuit. It was the best way, they said, to put pressure on the entire engineering and production team and to quickly test and evaluate their latest innovations. Further, it would give the firm the recognition it sought as a force to be reckoned with in the aviation business.

Nelson was unconvinced.

The dissenting engineer, a big German, argued, "You want to speed up development — start a war. You want people to know the name of your company? Build the biggest, the best, and the most handsome aeroplane. Otherwise, don't play around. We design aeroplanes. We build aeroplanes. We don't have to fly them in dizzy circles or race from city to city. Racing is a waste of time."

Nelson listened quietly, his fingers touching as if in loose prayer. Eventually, he dismissed the men and sat alone in his office. He would make a decision by morning.

Christina drove back to her hotel room with a new stack of papers. Tomorrow she would absolutely make her decision. And the same day, the eighth day of October, she would celebrate her birthday.

She did reach a decision with the morning, but it was not what she expected. She had slept little, but had come to realize that she was being far too precipitous. The magnitude of her future course warranted more than a few hours or days of deliberation. She decided she would dedicate adequate time — a month or more if necessary — to think through what would surely be the most important decision of her life.

She didn't realize she had just made it.

ROSEY AND STEPHEN

Stephen had what he wanted. The government, after months of impossibly complex negotiations, had agreed to purchase ten of the Boisvert P-22 Pursuit aeroplanes, with a potential back-up order of fifty more, the first purchase hinging on the speed and performance trials to be run in early November before the Army Air Corps and the back-up order relying on dumb-luck, favorable winds, and possibly a senator or two.

Stephen was confident the P-22 could deliver everything he had promised, and more. It was a powerful scrapper and capable of every dream Mr. Boisvert had shared with him. It was fast, reliable, and built to take punishment, and it was beautiful like a frightening animal, fully a third of its stocky length dedicated to engine cowling; its wings thick and blunt.

The only embarrassment he had encountered so far was the sidelong glance he received when he admitted he did not intend to enter the machine in the 1930 National Air Races at Cleveland. With his manufacturing facilities less than a hundred miles away from the pylons, it did seem odd, indeed.

Stephen stood in the hangar with the prototype and her four sister ships. Painted jet-black with brown wheel pants and pin-striping, the aeroplane did look ferociously canine.

"You *are* a bulldog," Stephen accused, tenderly, and he had no sooner said it when the realization of what he had said hit him.

"The Boisvert Bulldog! By god, that's what you are!" and he immediately began to mentally design the script logo. The name did something else, too. The Boisvert P-22 Pursuit aeroplane did not beg to race. It was a concept realized in wood and metal, the answer to the Army Air Corps' demanding specifications; but the Boisvert Bulldog — the Boisvert Bulldog was already looking for a fight — it *had* to race.

Stephen and Rosey moved into a small home closer to the airfield. Mrs. Boisvert had given it to the couple as a thank-you gesture for Stephen's staying on and agreeing to step into Mr. Boisvert's shoes. It was nice enough that it took a week for Rosey to find something wrong with it.

"It's too far from the trolley stop, Stephen. I need to learn to drive and I need a car."

Stephen was thunderstruck. They had just begun to save money in earnest and already Rosey had a use for it.

"What do you need to drive for?" he asked. "You don't work anymore, so you don't have to spend every minute at Fairelawn. Stay home with our baby for a change."

Stephen knew the tact Rosey would take and so he tried to head her off.

"Have your friends come out here."

He no sooner said it when he realized the error in his logic.

Rosey paused to see if he could understand the ridiculousness of his suggestion before she blasted him in anger.

Stephen forged ahead. "I know, I know;" he amended, "they have to work. And you have to have friends. But why can't you spend more time with Billy?"

Rosey had held her temper as long as she could.

"I have a life too, Stephen. And I don't want to spend all of it in this dumpy little house."

And they went on from there, Rosey demeaning Mrs. Boisvert's gift and Stephen allowing his recent resentment of Rosey to surface in the guise of their argument.

He should have questioned who would have the time to spend with her when she was at Fairelawn, but he didn't. He had learned with difficulty that the less he questioned her the more peaceful their home was, and so he tended to let things ride. In fact, he had begun to ignore Rosey when he could. When he came home late in the evening, it was his son he visited. And his son that he brought little presents, including the miniature Boisvert Bulldog he'd modeled just large enough for the child to sit in.

Rosey became more and more distant and Stephen refused to notice.

In truth, Rosey didn't spend much time with anyone at Fairelawn; she was still distant from her mother, Doris was working, and Nelson was usually in the city. But when Nelson did return early, he was always pleased to find Rosey awaiting him. And she didn't wait in room twenty-seven anymore, either; as long as Nelson's mother wasn't around, (since her husband's death she spent most of her time in Europe and so she wasn't around often) Rosey gave herself the run of the manor. Nelson was aware of it and he didn't object. Actually, he found it amusing,

With business consuming so much of his time, the convenience of having Rosey available was undeniable. She was his release and to a limited degree, his confidant, although he suspected she didn't understand most of the things he told her about his business dealings.

Fortunately, in the months since the beginning of Rosey's newest arrangement, Nelson had not seen Christina, and so there was not yet a problem regarding the two women.

So Rosey spent her days wandering about Fairelawn as if she owned it, walking through rooms with an eye toward rearranging them, and baiting her mother mercilessly. "Hello, mother," she would call after her any time Mrs. Baker happened to pass a room where Rosey was lounging.

The housekeeper had confronted her daughter once, but the tables were so effectively turned that the older woman knew immediately where the new power resided. Rosey's latest comments to her mother ran along the lines of, "Do a good job; I don't want you *jeopardizing* Nelson's and my *relationship*."

As much as anything else, the woman resented her daughters toying with Nelson Wingate's words.

It wasn't long before she was muttering to herself the same as Eleanora had.

"'Jeopardize a relationship', my foot! Grown too good for her own mother, that's what's happened!" And she determined that if the opportunity arose to slam her daughter down from her lofty heights she wouldn't hesitate to use it.

Most ignominious was the fact that Nelson had begun to leave his daily instructions regarding the running of the manor for Rosey to review and then deliver. Nelson recognized that the girl was surprisingly imaginative and efficient — she would have made an excellent housekeeper.

Rosey found herself remaining later and later at Fairelawn. She was desperate to be there when Nelson came home, and when he finally did, she was loathe to leave at all. Several times she had actually remained through the night, and while Stephen was beside himself, it was more because of the baby than his actually missing his wife.

He suspected that she virtually lived at Fairelawn when he was out of town on business, and he was right. His phone calls to check up on her resulted in such horrible arguments when he came home that he resisted them. It took only one call to Fairelawn to finally cure him of the habit. He had called Rosey's mother and had her get her daughter to the phone.

"AND WHERE ARE *YOU?*" Rosey shouted back, entertaining the staff at Fairelawn with her attitude. "WHAT DO YOU CARE ABOUT ME? AS MUCH

AS YOU'RE GONE YOU'RE NOT A FATHER OR A HUSBAND! ALL YOU CARE ABOUT IS YOUR AEROPLANES."

While Stephen shuddered silently through her hysterics, it was the moment when she finally exhausted herself and lowered her voice that he most dreaded. He had confided to only one person his responsibility for the death of the man he loved, and it had been a poor choice.

"I know why you're doing this, Stephen," she hissed. "I know why you're trying so hard to make that woman richer than she already is — and it won't bring him back, Stephen — and it won't make you any less of a killer.

"Stay away, Stephen. Stay away forever, for all I care, but don't you dare try to tell me what I should do while you're gone."

More than a few times he thought of divorcing her, but he knew she would take his child, and he feared she would also tell the world what he had done.

NELSON AND STEPHEN

Business was flourishing and Nelson should have been happy, but he wasn't. His firm was producing a handy little sports aircraft which was selling well to the young men of the wealthy set, currently enamored of Lindbergh's fame, but he wanted to break into production for the government. He wanted a contract — any contract so that he could get his foot in the door. Nelson recognized that military aviation had the potential to be a particularly lucrative business. It was still in a relative slump after the debacle with General Billy Mitchell, but it couldn't last. For all but the most ignorant, the handwriting was on the wall.

Additionally, he was toying with the idea of founding an airline, but unfortunately, hauling the mails had absolutely no appeal to him — it was somehow beneath him — and since virtually all of the existing companies in the transport business carried both passengers *and* cargo as a consequence of the demands of efficiency, Nelson moved ahead with hesitation.

And so when he learned that tiny Boisvert Aviation had just received a government contract to purchase ten of its aeroplanes, he was beside himself. He raved through his offices and then called his senior people in for a meeting.

Nelson remembered Jacob Boisvert from his trip to inform Rosey's old boyfriend of her pregnancy, and what he remembered about the little man made him angrier still, and although he was not ordinarily a desk pounder, Nelson thumped his desk more than once as he attacked his staff

"HOW CAN ONE MAN — ONE OLD MAN AND A HANDFUL OF EMPLOYEES — GET THE JUMP ON THIS FIRM? WE ARE WINGATE TIRE AND AVIATION, GENTLEMEN; NOT A SLAM-UP OUTFIT IN THE BACK OF A TIN HANGAR!"

One of Nelson's vice-presidents corrected him.

"There's really more than a 'handful' of folks working out at Boisvert's these days, Nelson. They have quite a tidy operation."

"And it isn't run by Old Man Boisvert, either; he died a while ago," another interrupted. "It's headed up by some fella he hired as a kid, years back — and he's taken the old man's ideas and from what I hear, he's doing a damned good job of producing a quality aeroplane."

Nelson boiled over when he realized he knew the person his employee was referring to.

"ARE YOU TELLING ME, THAT WITH THE SALARIES I PAY, A KID AND AN OLD MAN CAN PUT TOGETHER AN AEROPLANE THAT OUTPERFORMS OURS?" He was absolutely beside himself, ignoring the details of what he had been told, reacting instead to the tone of the message.

The fellow who had given Nelson the bad news about Stephen's involvement, a manager of production named, Jim Schmidt, sealed his own fate for early retirement when he sanguinely tried to assuage his employer's anger.

"Aviation's still a new thing, Mr. Wingate. An old man — a kid — it's still possible for someone like that to come up with some fine innovations at a backwater airfield. It happens all the time. But, we'll get them in the long run; we have the muscle, and the depth, and the resources. Sure, he can build a few planes that are fast as hell, but can he set up a real production line to build ten, fifty, even a hundred of them? I don't think so."

Nelson had widened his hatred to include the man who was speaking.

"Well, in that case you may be just what he needs. Get out — you're through." He glared at the others around the polished table "This meeting is over."

There was no doubt about what Nelson had meant. Schmidt was gone.

Stephen was back at the airfield filling out what seemed to be his thousandth form for the United States government and the Army Air Corps. He didn't look up when a well dressed man came into his office and stood over his desk. Salesmen were always stopping by.

Stephen swore and threw down his pencil.

"Damn! They're going to kill me with paperwork. I just want to build aeroplanes, not start a library."

He surveyed his visitor. The man was older, wore a dark grey three piece suit, and carried his hat in his hand. Stephen realized he was too well dressed to be a hawker.

The man spoke, "Don't tell me you do that all yourself?"

He wasn't entirely correct in his observation, since Stephen had hired two secretaries to work with him, but they were currently at lunch.

Stephen laughed. He liked this man already.

"Are you going to fill 'em out for me?" Stephen asked, curious as to the man's answer.

Schmidt stepped closer to Stephen and offered his hand as he looked at the forms Stephen was working on.

"You'd better do those in triplicate and make copies of each — they always lose the first two sets."

Stephen laughed. "This *is* the third set. They don't have any record of the first two."

"Then you're done," the man laughed. "They're just particular about throwing out the first two. James Schmidt. Jim. I'm here to see if an overworked man like you — you are Stephen Rheiner, aren't you —"

Stephen nodded and Jim Schmidt continued, "I'm here to see if you're deep enough in shit to realize you need help with your production facilities."

"Did God send you, or did the competition?" Stephen asked.

"I'm afraid you're not going to like my answer," Schmidt warned. "The first thing I did this morning was stick up for you at Wingate Aviation. The second thing I did was pack my desk. You know the third."

Stephen was having a hard time believing the fellow before him. It was just too good to be true.

"Now, wait a minute," Stephen cautioned. "Nelson Wingate pays the best salaries in the business. I can't come near what you made with him. And how do I know he didn't just get rid of you for building airplanes sideways?"

Schmidt laughed.

"Well, I've built a few *backwards* in my day."

Stephen looked him over and was surprised he wasn't intimidated by a man twice his age dressed in a better suit than he could afford. "You fly? You don't look like a pilot."

"I flew with Eddie in '17, if that counts, and I still do a little when I have the time."

Eddie Rickenbacher. Who didn't know him! Stephen was impressed.

"I guess you flew with the best," he said, lamely.

Schmidt still smiled. "So'd your old boss. I ran into Jake a time or two over there."

"No," Stephen protested.

"He wouldn't have told you, even if you'd asked — that's the way he was."

Stephen shook his head. "I'll be …."

Then he became more suspect. "If you were such good friends, why haven't I seen you out here, and why were you working for the competition?"

Schmidt saddened visibly. "You really want to know?" He didn't wait for Stephen to answer. "He was a better pilot, I can tell you that." And then he was very serious, humbled even, when he continued, "And at least one person thought he was a better man —"

Stephen didn't get it.

Schmidt saw and added, quietly, "You ask Mrs. Boisvert. She wasn't a Boisvert then. Mayer — she was Esther Mayer — prettiest girl in town."

Stephen and Jim Schmidt walked through the various hangars now used for production facilities and then both of them went up in Number Eleven. Stephen would never get rid of Number Eleven and he now used her as a gauge of people. If she let them handle her, they were okay by Stephen.

Jim Schmidt did everything with the old aeroplane except walk out on the wings. He was the smoothest, most assured pilot Stephen had ever known, let alone flown with. When they were back on the ground Stephen asked, "And you say Jacob Boisvert was a better pilot?"

"Fighting pilot. He was better in a dog fight. His reflexes were like lightning; he could sense the enemy's next move before be even thought of it, and he was fearless to the point of recklessness. We never expected him to finish the war."

"But he did," Stephen said, proudly.

"Yeh, the louse got influenza and was sent home a year early; I heard he never really recovered — weakened his heart or something."

And with Schmidt's remark, Stephen quickly changed the subject.

They worked out a salary and Jim Schmidt was hired. Stephen recognized his good fortune immediately.

CHRISTINA

Christina took her personal sabbatical seriously. She loaded up her automobile with financial reports, newspapers, a score of notebooks, and copies of the balance sheets of each of her father's businesses. She was determined to drive to the middle of nowhere, check into a roadside cabin, and not make any further contact with civilization until she had reached her decision. If it took a month or more, that was fine with her.

She drove west until she could turn north and head into Michigan. Late in the day she was in the lakes region and was able to find a little cabin on a lake advertised at a service station where she stopped to get fuel and stretch her legs. The man who pumped the gas owned the cabin and was more than pleased to rent it to Christina with an open departure date.

He was a ragged fellow, tall to the point of implicit awkwardness, missing a few teeth and sporting a half grown beard.

"She ain't fancy," he warned Christina. "Water runs from the pump outside and the john's out back. Got a wood stove and a fireplace and plenty of wood; gets cold at night — you'll be all right."

He looked Christina over. "Just thought I'd warn ya," he concluded.

"Sounds fine," Christina assured him, and that was exactly how she felt. She suspected that in spite of the owner's rather rugged approach to cleanliness the cabin would be spare but clean.

And she was right.

She had bumped several miles down a dirt road when she crested a hill and saw the lake spread beneath her. It was a small lake and it appeared there was only the one cabin, and that suited her, also.

She parked in the shadow of a tall pine and sortied back and forth into the cabin with her hastily packed luggage and the arm loads of food she had picked up at the general store beside the garage. The fellow who owned the cabin and the gas station owned the store, too.

He had introduced Christina to his wife; a dumpy woman with a handsome beard of her own who kept eyeing Christina warily as if the young woman might be up to something with her husband. She looked from Christina to her sheepish husband and back to Christina again, certain she would catch them exchanging secret looks.

Christina stared back at her blankly, attempting to assure the lady that bedding disgusting men was the last thing on her mind.

There were oil lamps which Christina fiddled with until she finally figured one out, and there was kindling and a small stack of logs beside the fireplace and the wood stove. The floor was bare and clean and the bedroom, an area segregated from the rest of the cabin by a five-foot surrounding knotty pine wall, had a bed smothered with quilts, and a series of nails pounded into the wall to take the place of a chest of drawers and a closet.

Again, it couldn't have suited Christina better.

It was nearly dark by the time she was finally settled in so she took a quick walk down to the lake, saw a small wooden boat up-ended against a tree not far from the water, a shaky, narrow dock, and a raccoon trundling from the rocky shore back to the safety of the trees.

She decided to launch the boat in the morning, and to dedicate the dock as her place to watch the sun set. She wished the raccoon Godspeed and prayed he wouldn't encounter Nelson's furrier.

She hung her clothing on the bedroom nails, wrapped herself naked in a quilt, hopped into bed, and bulked the rest of the quilts on top of her. She would claim for years it was the first of a series of blissful nights which would remain unsurpassed.

Christina slept late the first day, rising barely before noon. She fixed herself eggs and bacon and a pot of coffee, using a blackened iron skillet that weighed a half a ton, and a dented coffee pot that looked to be about as old as Christina. It didn't take her long to realize that the battered cookware enhanced the flavor of everything it touched.

Although superlatives kept coming into Christina's mind, it wasn't as if the beginning of her stay was without incident. She had filled the stove with kindling and several larger sticks of wood and located the big stick matches. In no time at all the fire was roaring. She did not, however, know to open the flue. "What's wrong?" she choked as the cabin filled with smoke.

She figured out the problem, aired the cabin, and proceeded to crack a half a dozen eggs into the hissing skillet. It wasn't that she actually wanted to eat that many eggs, but the process was so cathartic she couldn't stop herself.

And then as the eggs and the strips of bacon sputtered and cooked, the coffee started to heat up, and the cabin was filled with the smells of her country breakfast.

There were chipped, black porcelain and tin plates and a similar cup which she carried to the dock, the eggs and bacon shifting as she walked, and the coffee spilling rich and black in little surges at her feet. She walked out and sat cross legged on the dock, the lapping water and the wind in the trees the only noises other than her fork scraping against her plate as one, and then two, three, four, and finally five eggs disappeared before Christina saw how many she had eaten.

She laughed to herself, ate the crisp bacon strips, and then finished off the last egg.

The metal cup was still hot and the coffee scalding, but she stared across the lake and sipped her coffee without noticing. Christina marveled at the wisdom of her decision to leave the city.

The Chimneys had been in a rural setting, but it was also its own contained metropolis. And her hotel room certainly had provided solitude, as had the Gate Cottage for much of the time, but there was no comparison with the sublime freedom she experienced at the cabin. She was determined to see if she could buy it before she returned to the city.

Christina studied, as she had promised herself, and she spent most of her time deep in the analysis of various businesses, But she also took early morning rows in the small wooden boat, and walked the trails and sat on the porch and watched the sun rise and set.

A week passed and she had to return to the store to buy more provisions, again suffering the jealous scrutiny of the owner's wife. She spent another week unwinding and reviewing her options, and then another.

Her only complaint — absolutely the only thing which bothered her — was the army of spiders in the outhouse.

There were that many.

She attacked them with a broom, poked at them with sticks, and had a series of heart attacks when they lowered themselves in front of her at inopportune moments.

Christina had narrowed her career field to three choices, certain that she would reach a decision in the next several days. That was fine until she discovered she was once more out of food. She bounced back out to the highway and then drove to her general store.

The owner's wife was now brazen in her distrust. And she had what she considered to be a secret.

"By that fancy car I'd guess you must come from money," she began.

Christina continued walking down the narrow aisles, picking up cans and blowing the dust off of them before she dropped them into the reed basket she carried. She chose to pretend she hadn't heard the woman.

"You read the newspaper?" the woman persisted.

Christina answered, irritated, "Of course I do. Not recently, though. Why? Amelia cross the Pacific this time?"

"Bet she wishes she had," her tormentor answered, cryptically.

The woman had a newspaper spread on the counter in front of her. Christina walked over, and even upside down, the news reached out and grabbed her by the throat.

MORE BANKS CLOSE. STOCK MARKET CONTINUES CRASH.

Christina ripped the paper away, devoured the headlines, and then skimmed the articles. With every word the news worsened.

NELSON AND ROSEY

"It can't be," she gasped and the owner's wife added, "Why's that? Anything can be. Even a fool knows that."

Christina went back to the front page and slowly read it through in its entirety. She tuned out the owner's wife and went through page after page. When she finally put the paper back down she felt as if she had aged ten years.

She then looked at her basket of food and went to return the items to the shelves.

"I must get back...." she said as she put the food back randomly.

"Think they need you, do you?" the woman asked, and with her comment Christina stopped, a can halfway to a middle shelf. She dropped her arm to her side and the can hit the floor. She blinked away the tears for a moment, inflated her chest, and then let her breath out slowly.

"How much is that cabin a week?" she asked and then calculated what she had spent so far.

"I think I can afford another," she sighed and then went around and once more picked out her supplies.

She paid, acutely aware of the cost of each item, and left knowing she had a different set of decisions to make.

Nelson lay with Rosey and tried to remember the last time he had seen Christina. He had called her school and learned she was gone, and, later, he had heard that she was working with her father.

"Talk to me," Rosey said, interrupting his thoughts.

Nelson turned onto his side and looked at her. She had never quite regained the daring, almost boyish sexuality she'd had when she was younger, but she was still a temptress. She wore her hair shorter now, and was looking presentable enough for Nelson to consider being seen with her.

"I must buy you some clothes, one day," Nelson idly teased, and Rosey was on him in a minute.

"Really, Nelson? Will you?" She pressed her breasts onto him. "You'll buy me clothes?"

Nelson laughed. "I thought perhaps we might go to the theater and dinner one evening. Can you get away?"

Rosey couldn't contain her excitement. She suspected it was the prelude to a proposal for marriage, but it wasn't. Rosey had known in her heart that sooner or later Nelson would want her, truly want her for what she was, and she believed it had finally happened.

She was correct, but not entirely; Nelson wanted to show her off, but it was because of who she was — Stephen Rheiner's wife.

He had learned of Jim Schmidt's defection and he was livid. He'd expected Schmidt to slink away, his tail between his legs, and disappear, but he hadn't. No, he was still out there, trying to make a fool of Nelson Wingate. It was one more humiliation and one more reason to get even with Boisvert Aviation.

Nelson came back and heard Rosey.

"When, Nelson, when?" she begged playfully as she unbuttoned his shirt and ran her hand over the flat of his chest.

Nelson took her then, tearing off her clothes and bringing to her his hatred of her husband. He took her violently, and without prelude, and it was the first time Rosey had known him to be rough. Afterward, she lay spent on the bed, her body a rag. Nelson rose immediately and left the room for a shower.

Rosey felt as if she were his wife, and she liked the feeling. She would sacrifice the tenderness and the words if a manor and unlimited wealth were offered in replacement. She lay and thought of the clothing she would buy and the places they would travel.

Nelson stood beneath the steaming shower and thought of Rosey and her husband and his damnable Boisvert Bulldog. He had learned that the boy was flying it at the '30 National Air Races, less than eight months away. Wingate had announced its intentions shortly after, but Nelson wasn't entirely sure they'd have a plane that could beat the Boisvert. He needed to know more about the Bulldog. He needed the plans.

Rosey watched him walk from the shower and remembered the first time she had seen him. She rolled to her side and knew Nelson was watching her breasts move as she did. He smiled at her but he seemed angry.

"Will that be all?" she teased.

Nelson made the connection immediately.

"I don't think so, Rosey, my dear. I don't think so. What exactly is it that you'd like?"

CHRISTINA AND STEPHEN

Christina had tried several times to call her bank, but there was no answer, and with each new newspaper she picked up at the store, her depression deepened. Hourly she fought the urge to race back to the city and attempt to get her money by force, but each time her reasonable nature won out.

She recognized that her own situation was as bleak as the nation's. She couldn't return to school; she had lost her appetite for academia and she didn't have the funds for it anyway. She had effectively cut herself off for Paget, et al, so there was no money to be had from that quarter, and she absolutely could not go back to her father, either for money or to offer to help him, since it was likely that he was at least nose-deep in the current financial morass.

There was nowhere to turn.

The photographs of the lengthening unemployment lines assured her that finding any job would be a challenge. And it wasn't just the job situation which distressed her. Soon, she would be out of money and she wouldn't have a place to live. She wasn't even entirely sure she had enough money to address her current hotel bill. Unfortunately, she had not checked out when she had left for the country — it hadn't occurred to her that paying for an unused room for a month was less than thrifty. Her only hope was that she could negotiate a reasonable settlement with the hotel manager.

She laughed bitterly when she thought of her plan to buy the little cabin she was staying in. She *knew* she couldn't afford it, now. Suddenly, that insulting woman and her run-down husband were wealthier than she. *Wealthier.* She laughed at the word. She didn't have wealth — very soon she wouldn't even have trolley fare, never mind being wealthy!

Stephen noticed the change in Rosey immediately. At first he thought it was a passing good mood, but when it persisted he was suspicious and then grateful.

And then one evening, for the first time for as long as he could remember, he came home to a warm meal. Rosey had changed Billy and put him to bed and the table was set for dinner for two. Stephen looked at the table and the rest of the kitchen, which was actually tidy. He was still in awe when Rosey wrapped her arms around his waist and kissed him full on the mouth.

"I missed you today," she cooed demurely and then kissed him again.

Stephen pushed her away and eyed her warily.

"I've flown near thunderstorms more predictable than you, Rosalind Rheiner. What are you up to?"

"Stephen Alan!" she answered and kissed him again, quickly this time. And then she became serious.

"I was just thinking about the old days, today, and I miss them. I miss the fun we used to have — you used to be so funny, and I miss going to bed with you," she giggled with an effort Stephen didn't register. "I miss going to bed with you and making wild love. Do you remember all the places we used to do it?"

Stephen was pulled in.

He listed, "The Octagon, the basement, the elevator, your room, the greenhouse — " He slowed a little, but not much. "The boathouse."

"The rowboat!" Rosey interjected, laughing.

Neither would mention the hidden garden.

Stephen pulled Rosey back to him. He grabbed the back of her head and tilted it roughly. He kissed her hard, his breathing loud and gusty through his nose.

Rosey was repulsed but stayed with him, managing to kiss him, too. She struggled free at last.

"Dinner first! I went to a lot of trouble for you!"

He eyed the table as Rosey went to the oven and removed a pot roast.

"My God, that smells great, Rosey!" He retrieved a sheaf of rolled technical drawings which had fallen to the floor earlier.

Rosey watched him, suddenly interested.

"What are those?" she asked as casually as she could manage.

"Nothing — the usual," he answered without thought. "Some things I'm working on."

Rosey brought over the steaming roast and frowned petulantly. "You used to tell me about what you did — you used to be excited and want to show me your drawings and talk about them."

Something was wrong and Stephen couldn't figure out what it was. Rosey saw the confusion on his face and set the platter down and went to him. He was now seated, so she bent over him, pressing her breasts onto his shoulders. She moved slowly from side to side and then moved to his right and teased the side of his face.

"How hungry are you?" she asked, careful to keep a breast lightly moving against his cheek.

Stephen turned and kissed the cloth of her dress and then nuzzled the outline of her nipple with his nose. He felt it harden. He glanced at the roast and then returned all of his attention to Rosey. She was now standing so that he couldn't resist reaching for her bottom.

She bent at the waist, moving away from his hand as it came for her. Stephen leaned in pursuit, tipping his chair to the side as he did, until he was balancing on the two chair legs closest to her. Rosey stopped and took his hair and smothered him against her chest. Stephen kept tipping until he had gone too far. As he fell, he pulled her down with him.

"Stop it!" she protested. "After the meal I made you, all you can think of is sex!"

He was on her, running his hands over her body, pulling her clothing loose as he did. He lifted her dress with his knee and held his knee against her. Rosey felt the pressure and rode him, rocking as she did. She had her mouth open, cupping Stephen's ear.

She tried to pretend he was Nelson, but it wasn't working. There was no gentleness, only the rough and tumble groping she had tolerated when they were younger. Rosey laughed to herself. She had taught the boy everything he knew.

Rosey felt her panties being dragged down her legs and then off of one and at the same time Stephen had raised himself and was sliding his own trousers down, too. He was in her then, quickly, finally settling into a semblance of rhythm.

Stephen came with a shudder soon after, and Rosey held him to her. She was lost as he did, wandering the deserted rooms of Fairelawn. As suddenly as it had started Stephen was up and off of her, still breathing heavily and helping her get to her feet.

They ate later than Rosey had expected, but Stephen didn't seem to notice or care that the roast had cooled considerably. He teased her all through the meal and Rosey found that to be the most tolerable part of the subterfuge she was forcing herself to play.

"Should we have saved the best part for desert?" he asked.

Rosey was certain there wasn't a 'best part' but answered, "Maybe you can have 'seconds' later if you want."

Stephen couldn't believe his good fortune.

"You didn't go to Fairelawn today did you?"

Rosey shook her head. "I stayed home, cleaned the house, took care of the baby, and got dinner for you."

"But you were there yesterday?"

Rosey tried not to return the suspicion she felt in his words.

"Yesterday?" she stalled. "That was Wednesday — I spent the day talking to my mother. She's having back problems and staff problems and every other kind of problem, I think."

She hoped she had assuaged Stephen's unexplained discomfort.

Stephen decided to think it through, later. Something was wrong. Something was going on, and he couldn't figure what Rosey was after.

Then he knew and he couldn't believe how blind he'd been.

His first impulse was to confront her and get it over with, but the more he thought of it the better he figured it would be if he gave her time. Plus, the dinner was good and the romp on the floor was absolutely unheard of; if he waited, perhaps there could be more. As he thought of it he became increasingly determined to use Rosey's tricks to his own advantage. He knew he should have been angry with her for using him, but the more he thought of it the more humorous it became.

My God, Stephen thought, *do all women think men are stupid?*

"What are you smiling about?" Rosey asked as she cleared the table.

Stephen allowed himself a little chuckle.

"Nothing really," he answered.

He realized Rosey was truly wasting her time; he had already decided to buy them a car. He would still use the Battleship Roadster during the day, but it was a little beat-up for family use. He laughed again to himself. *All this and she was going to get a car anyway!*

That evening he humored her as they looked at the plans he'd brought home to work on.

And they made love again that night.

NELSON AND CHRISTINA

Nelson could barely believe what was happening in the city around him. It looked more like the pictures he'd seen of the Russian revolution than anything else. Everyone was in a panic, and it hadn't settled down appreciably since the banks closed more than a week earlier.

It had helped that his family, for all purposes, controlled a bank. Better still was the fact that he had miraculously little of his personal and corporate funds in stocks or cash. T-bills, T-bills, T-bills. His father had been correct when he had taught Nelson to use only government obligations when it came to salting away money.

"I don't give a good goddamn if we do own the bank; I want Uncle Sam behind every nickel I have to keep in his currency. If I can't keep it working in a company, I don't want it lying around as paper. Loan it to Uncle Sam not some weak kneed banker — that son-of a-bitch will pay it back or else!"

Nelson had suffered through that lecture at breakfast and dinner for as long as he could remember.

"Sure, we own the bank," his father would embellish. "And I own a Colt revolver too, but I wouldn't put it in my mouth and trust that it isn't loaded, even if I just got done emptying it myself. Trust the government or buy cattle — that's your only hope. At least the shit you get from the government you can spend!"

So Nelson had done it and now he could reap the reward.

Prices for everything were tumbling. But then again, so were orders. A day didn't go by that another sports aeroplane contract wasn't cancelled. Even the folks that Nelson knew would weather the storm were backing out.

They'd call and ask to speak to Nelson. "We're gonna wait and see, Nelson; can't be sure what'll happen next. Wait and see."

If Nelson heard it one more time he would throw the telephone out the window. The tire company's orders shrank daily also, but that side of the business didn't interest him — it was the aviation division which was exciting.

At the end of the second week he let half of his employees go, trimming his management staff even more ruthlessly. He had just fired another round of workers when Christina walked into his outer office and asked to see him. He was surprised when he caught a glimpse of her through his nearly closed door. It had been ages!

"In a moment," he told his secretary and then leaned back in his chair and thought of the Van Luxalls. He'd forgotten all about the old man. He reviewed the Van Luxall businesses and attempted to evaluate their chances for survival. Dismal, moderate, hopeless, moderate. It all depended on the cash they could lay their hands on. Then he thought about Christina. He hadn't seen her for as long as he could remember — somehow they'd just drifted apart. Ever since his father's death he'd been sucked up by the family businesses. The last time he managed to break loose to call on Christina, he learned she'd left school. The rest was basically rumor; her *job* as her father's assistant and then her disappearance from the face of the earth.

And after the crash he hadn't thought of anyone but himself.

Nelson realized that wasn't entirely true. He was having a good time with Rosey. He wondered then if his infatuation with Christina and her silly games would have survived during a time when he was having wonderful sex with Rosey. He had seen that Rosey's adulation not only bolstered his already soaring ego, but actually made him embarrassed when he thought of the subtle degradations Christina had subjected him to. He looked up toward his outer office and wondered if it weren't perhaps pay back time.

He'd know soon enough.

He rose then and walked to the door.

"Christina! Darling!" he called to her.

As usual, he found her beauty incredibly discommoding, but he forced himself to rise above it.

Christina had been pacing his office, straightening magazine piles, drumming her long fingernails on a window sill, and generally driving Nelson's secretary crazy. When he appeared, finally, Christina was close to leaving. She wasn't looking forward to what she wished to ask him.

"Come in, come in!" he said as he ushered her into his office, pushing her gently ahead of him with his hand in the small of her back. "Christina, heavens, it's been absolutely forever since I've seen you. How are things? How have you been? What are you doing in these absolutely maddening times?"

He could hardly wait for her answers.

Nelson sat behind the expanse of his desk and leaned back in his chair. He had not yet offered her a seat and she was now standing uncomfortably at the head of his desk. She was still stunning. Nelson watched her chest rise and fall beneath her silk blouse and wondered how he had ever managed to spend so much time with a woman he'd never touched. Never been *allowed* to touch.

Nelson remembered and hoped the news of her life was devastating. The thought of toying with the future of the Van Luxall girl was suddenly very appealing.

"May I?" Christina asked indicating one of the wing back chairs behind her.

"Christina! Of course! Silly of me. I never dreamed you'd feel you had to ask! Sit, do sit."

He was firmly in control of their meeting. Christina knew it and also knew there was absolutely nothing she could do save walking out. She was close to the same level of frustration and humiliation Nelson had felt when she had demanded he carry her luggage into his parents' home.

She sat on the edge of the chair and crossed her leg at the knee. Nelson watched her with undisguised interest.

"Beautiful legs, Christina; I always thought they were absolutely beautiful. How tall are you, anyway?"

She nearly answered him.

He was already making it much more difficult than she had feared.

"How have you been, Nelson?" she asked instead, attempting to gain some time.

"Well, Christina; I've been well." He stared at her in silence for a moment. "But never mind me; I'm not the enigma. What of you? Last I heard you were with your father, and then you disappeared."

Christina forged ahead.

"Nelson, I really don't have time for small talk, I'm sorry." She laughed to herself as she said it; she had all the time in the world for small talk — as long as she didn't get hungry or tired.

"Nelson, you know what's going on in town — who's hiring? What's available at the management level?"

Christina bridled at Nelson's laughter.

"Oh, Christina," he said between guffaws, "I was afraid that's why you were here. I suspect you just passed two of my officers on your way in. I had to let them go."

Christina shot to her feet. She couldn't get out of his office fast enough. It wasn't as bad as it would have been had she gone groveling to her father or his law firm, but it was bad enough.

Nelson rose slowly. He extended his arm toward her and made a sweeping gesture dismissing her intended departure. "Sit girl, sit! It's bad, but not that bad. We'll survive it here; we've the resources and I do see an occasional glimmer of light now and then."

He then adopted a more professional tone and continued.

"We lost a third of our aeroplane orders before the end of the first week. In fact, we lost another third this week, but strangely, already some of our earlier cancellations are calling back to re-establish confirmed delivery dates.

"We're in for a horrible time, Christina, I don't want to delude you, but Wingate Tire and Aviation will survive it, I'm certain."

Nelson grimaced. "Although, I'd give my right arm for an army contract, right about now. Damn, what I wouldn't do to line up with the United States Army Air Corps!"

Christina's mind was reeling as she tried to remember everything she knew about government contracts and procurement. It was frightfully little.

While she thought, Nelson watched her with increasing interest. She was such a beautiful woman. He determined he would not allow her to leave his office until he had somehow gained some degree of lasting control over her. It became his game, his quest.

"These are difficult times, indeed, Christina, and I'm sorry for the discomfort you must be feeling right now. I'd guess you've been tossed out on your ear by your father; you don't wish to go back to school, and you'll be damned if you'll go back to the old man with your tail between your legs. Is that a pretty good summary?"

Christina didn't answer at first and Nelson saw that he had hit the nail on the head all three times. He didn't wait for her to speak. He tried once more to prod her.

"Every good company needs good help, Christina; I'm sure you learned that in school and saw it when you worked with your father. Even now — perhaps especially now — quality management, resourcefulness; all of those things are more necessary now than ever before. And I believe in you. I always have, you know that, surely."

Christina smiled thinly but she had the feeling she was being walked into a trap.

"We've had a lot of fun." Nelson paused as if he were reviewing all the things they had done together. He laughed through his nose and then shook his head slowly as if he were dismissing the childishness of it all. *"Anyway,"* he continued, stressing the word, "we're talking business now. We can talk about fun after we're finished."

Christina felt two giant unseen steel jaws being pried apart.

"I suspect you came here with some sort of proposal, Christina; a proposal that would demonstrate to me that with your unique capabilities, your drive, and your determination, Wingate Tire and Aviation could not possibly survive unless it adds you to its dwindling list of remaining employees." He looked up at her. "Am I correct so far?" It was a rhetorical question, for he waved off her silence as if it had been filled with an embarrassing barrage of begging and pleading. "I don't need to hear it, Christina. You've convinced me already."

The forged metal jaws of the trap were set. Christina swore she could hear a dull clack as the tripping mechanism snapped into place. *Just step forward, my dear, onto this raised metal platform; you'll be so glad you did!*

"Alright, Christina, you've convinced me, and I'll take a chance."

She could not bring herself to feel relief, particularly since he hadn't finished with his own proposal.

"A while ago I fired my production control manager. I wish I hadn't, but I did. My proposal is that you work the production line — yes, actually work it — help build aeroplanes — for a few months and then if we both agree you can handle it, step into the management position. Fair?"

It was more than fair, but Christina sensed there was still more.

A malevolent smile formed on Nelson's face like a pale mushroom in a dark cave. His thoughts were miles away, but Christina knew he was thinking of her. He laughed out loud. "Christina, I've never admitted this to anyone — but I am a wicked man!

"Allow me to escort you to dinner this evening and we'll formalize our agreement with a toast and your acceptance of my only stipulation." He saw her narrow her eyes. Nelson laughed again. "Christina, Christina! It won't be as bad as all that — we'll make it fun — great fun! Remember the fun we used to have? Where are you staying? I'll pick you up at eight."

Christina forced herself into the spirit of his banter. She was, after all, off the hook. As she left his office she said over her shoulder, "Don't be late, Nelson."

Nelson chewed on the corner of his lip. *Late*, was the last thing he would be.

Rosey would probably be upset, but she'd live through it.

STEPHEN AND BILLY AND ROSEY

Stephen couldn't get enough time with Billy. It was the only real regret he had after he took Mr. Boisvert's place at the head of Boisvert Aviation, for he found he had less and less time to spend with his son. And so he made time for the boy. Stephen got up earlier and went to bed later than he was used to. Additionally, he stole home at lunch when he could so he could play with his son. Occasionally, Rosey would take the child with her, but usually she left him with the woman next door, and those times Stephen could play with the boy uninterrupted.

Not that Rosey's interruptions were as bad as they used to be. Actually, they weren't bad at all. Rosey, the wild and raucous girl of The Chimneys who had changed into Rosey, the sullen mother and angry wife, had changed once more. It was as if she had suddenly matured.

True, he had bought her the car she had asked for, but he was surprised by her reaction when he drove it home.

He'd called her first, and feigning anger, had said, "I know what you've been up to, Rosey; I'm coming home!" There had been an uncomfortable silence after his accusation. And then when he pulled into their driveway, he thought he saw relief and not excitement steal across her face.

And then the market collapsed and Stephen thanked the gods he'd bought a used car.

It took a barrage of letters and inquiries before he was assured that the Army Air Corps intended to go through with its original order and further, that they were still interested in the back-up order of fifty aeroplanes, provided this and that and the other thing happened.

Rosey was close to indifferent about their car. It was a 1925 Buick, in perfect shape and particularly forgiving of Rosey's halting attempts to master it. Stephen didn't have the time to instruct her, but a retired man, a neighbor and the father of one of Stephen's employees, was more than willing to spend time with Rosey.

He was a big man, and heavy, with a happy face, a bowler and a black suitcoat he wore every time he took Rosey driving. When she ground a gear or stalled the vehicle he would cajole her, "If all it took was beauty to drive a car, you'd'a been born in the driver's seat, sweetheart. Now let's try that again." He was perfect for the job; oblivious to her disdain of him, patient as a pastor in a one cow town, and happy to be seen with a pretty lady.

"Gears are worn a little smoother, and the brakes are probably burned out, but I think you've got'er," he informed her one day. Rosey passed her test, got her license, and never spoke to the man again. She wouldn't even wave when she passed him as he walked to town.

With her vehicle, Rosey savored her new independence. She was always popping up at the airfield, following Stephen around and asking about the various things he was doing, and then she'd roar off again.

Stephen's biggest disappointment was that no matter how hard he tried to convince her, Rosey refused to go for a ride in Number Eleven. She used the line she'd heard from her erstwhile driving instructor. "I'll fly any time you want — as long as I can keep one foot on the ground."

Stephen had heard that old saw so many times he couldn't believe Rosey quoted it so freely.

He had to admit, though, that his marriage and life were about as satisfactory as they had ever been, and the change he'd witnessed in Rosey was just short of unbelievable. True, she still spent most of her time ignoring the baby, but her mood was good, she didn't complain nearly as much as she used to, and she was showing a genuine interest in Stephen's work. She was still driving out to Fairelawn all of the time, and she did stay over with her mother or Doris frequently, but Stephen had finally shrugged it off as 'playing-pretend'. His theory was that Rosey went to Fairelawn and pretended she was the mistress of the manor. Ever since he'd known her she had dreamed of living in one and he figured it was her fantasy world.

Stephen understood that, because he spent so much of his own time daydreaming of Christina. His love for her, if anything, had grown since he had begun to experience the responsibilities of business and the pleasures of his success. He was on the right track, he was sure of it. Granted, he had a wife and a child, and he'd probably spend his life with Rosey, but the fact that he was succeeding fueled Stephen's dreams. He had determined to make something of himself to show Christina that he was more than just 'the help', and that's exactly what he was doing.

He wondered, sometimes, if he would ever see Christina again. He hadn't heard a word about her for years and he began to question if she had perhaps married and moved far away. He pictured her in a manor with an unbelievably handsome husband and a house full of children. He tried very hard to, but he couldn't imagine her remembering him.

CHRISTINA AND NELSON

Christina sat across the table from Nelson. She was in a very uncomfortable position. After a fair amount of bargaining, she had convinced the hotel manager to accept a reduced settlement for her bill, assuming that she moved out at the end of the next week; but as good as her compromise was, it wasn't *that* good, for it left her with no funds and the prospect of either begging her father for money, going to his solicitors and begging *them*, or asking Nelson for an advance on her salary.

She would have been more comfortable if she'd had enough cash to pay for their dinner, but that was out of her range, particularly when she thought of the restaurant Nelson had chosen.

Worst of all was the knowledge that no matter what little game Nelson cooked up for the final stipulation for his hiring her, she had already decided to agree to it. She believed, to her mortification, that Nelson was going to give her a sexual assignment, the likes of which she could guess, and the thought of going to bed with him for a job was lower than she ever imagined sinking.

She was beginning to doubt whether she would agree to it after all, when he broke through her reverie.

"It appears we're one of the few couples in town still able to afford this place, Christina. The least you could do is pretend you're enjoying it!"

She caught the last of what he said and started, embarrassed.

"I'm sorry, Nelson," she apologized honestly, "everything is upside down these days."

"So you went to the country after your father precipitously let you go, did you?"

Nelson was not aware of the final check from her father.

Christina had been toying with her meal. She put her fork down and took a long swallow of wine. She looked into her glass as she spoke.

"Okay, Nelson, you can quit playing with me now. We can talk small talk all night if you want, but you know what we're both waiting for."

"Oh, yes!" he marveled as if it had completely slipped his mind. "Indeed! We haven't actually reached an agreement yet, have we, Christina, my dear?"

Christina was repulsed by his superiority. She changed her mind. She'd sell apples and live in her car rather than sleep with him.

"Well, I suppose you are correct, Christina; we should be getting our tedious business negotiations out of the way so we may enjoy the remainder of our meal." He pulled a gold and faience fountain pen from inside of his vest pocket and then took a white linen napkin from a nearby table. He wrote a figure on it, folded the writing to the inside of the napkin and then passed it across to Christina, his distaste for discussing money apparent.

Christina was tempted to accept without looking at the figure. Since it really didn't matter as long as it was adequate to address her primary needs. But then she realized it would be playing to Nelson, showing her willingness to take the job at any price. She unfolded the napkin as matter-of-factly as he had folded it. She was surprised to see the figure was neither insulting nor a gift. It was fair.

"Thank you, Nelson, it's an attractive offer."

Nelson smiled.

Christina put the napkin to the side. "What else?" she asked, simply.

"Well, Christina," Nelson began, "that's an excellent question — 'What else?'" He continued tapping his pen on the table. "We go back a very long way, you and I, Christina. We played together as children — we've grown up together, really. And the games we've played ...." he paused as if remembering them all. He closed his eyes and spoke softly. "Oh, the games we've played Christina — the fun we've had. But we are adults now, aren't we, and the time for games has passed."

He opened his eyes and leaned forward, resting his forearms on the edge of the table. "Let's play one more game, Christina. Just one more game. It would be great fun. A game similar to one we've played before, but let's be fair. You are still a fair person, aren't you Christina? You always were." He acted as if he were waiting for her to answer, although he knew she would not. "Well, I remember you as quite fair. At any rate, the world is falling apart, businesses are failing daily; who knows about tomorrow. I think we must take the time to play one more game for old time's sake."

Christina sat expressionless. Nelson didn't need to remind her of her current situation; she hadn't forgotten it — especially since the dinner had not been paid for. He was playing with her, and Christina didn't like it, but she felt he had that right. She had toyed with him.

"For our game, Christina, let's pretend." He smiled when he continued, "For one week, let's pretend we've never met. Let's pretend we've never met and you are working for me."

He looked into her eyes. "Fair so far?" This time he refused to continue until she answered. At last, Christina nodded almost imperceptively and repeated quietly, "We don't know each other."

"Now, the last part may be a bit of a shock, but before you answer, I want you to think of all the games we used to play, Christina. All of them. I want you to remember them and then ask yourself if it isn't fair if we were to play one of them again. Except this time — this time, Christina — it's only fair if we exchange roles. I mean, how fair is it if you always get the good parts?"

Christina knew where he was going — at least she knew the direction if not the destination.

"Let's play Lord of the Manor, once more — I know we never named it that, but it could have been the name of our game. Had we been younger I'll wager we would have named it that. Or, *Lady* of the Manor, perhaps.

"The rules are as simple as ever, Christina. For one week we do not know one another, and for one week — the week before you begin employment at Wingate Tire and Aviation at a fair wage in a reasonable position — for that week before you join the firm, you come to Fairelawn — as a chamber maid!"

Nelson sat back as the last words left his lips. He sat back and watched every muscle in Christina's face. He watched every movement, every shift of her eyes, and even the slightest parting of her lips.

Christina could have stood and left without a word. She could even have laughed in his face and told him there was no job she needed that badly. She could have done any of those things, as each was passing through her mind, had Nelson lacked the sensitivity to say one more thing.

"I understand, Christina," he began, quietly, "that I'm asking you to ignore all those things your father taught you or gave you. I'm asking you to discard all the advantages he made possible; I'm asking you, Christina, to start on your own. To stand on your own, however briefly."

Nelson waited, and when he saw no reaction from Christina, he added, "No meal is complete without dessert, Christina. I didn't bring you to dinner to cut it short."

Nelson raised his glass to her. The candlelight reflected in the glass and danced along its crystal lip. "Shall we raise a toast to our agreement and then order dessert, my dear?"

"A toast, " Christina said quietly as she brought her glass to his. Nelson smiled.

ROSEY AND CHRISTINA

Rosey's mother had never seen her employer in such a good mood. Mr. Wingate was simply beside himself.

"We have a new girl coming in today — very bright, anxious to work."

Mrs. Baker couldn't figure out why he had hired another maid; the staff at Fairelawn was more than adequate, and all of the girls were anxious to please with jobs so scarce. Rumors passed through the manor daily regarding expected firings, although none had yet occurred. Hiring an additional maid was daft.

"Remember — no favoritism — put her right to work. And I expect to be informed if she isn't pulling her share of the load. Understood, Mrs. Baker?"

"Yes, Mr. Wingate." *Inform him of a problem with a domestic?* It just didn't make sense.

Yet.

Nelson hated to do it, but he had to leave for the office. He was determined to return earlier than usual.

Mrs. Baker saw the Cadillac sedan pull past the front entrance and park at the rear of the manor, near the delivery door. She wasn't expecting anyone other than the new girl, and the car that had just arrived was far too fine to be bringing a chamber maid. No doubt, *she'd* arrive in the manor jitney.

The housekeeper tried to place the woman's face as she strode from her car. She was striking; tall and quite elegant, although her dress was surprisingly simple. It was Christina's hat which kept Mrs. Baker from recognizing her until she was at the servants' entrance.

"Miss Van Luxall," she pronounced carefully, unable to keep some of the surprise out of her tone. The girl had certainly grown into a beautiful woman. Her thoughts raced through the possibilities. If she had come to see Nelson, it was quite odd for her to use the back entrance — plus, it had been so long since she'd been visiting, surely she'd come later in the day. Then she wondered if perhaps Christina had come to attempt to hire her back to The Chimneys — but it was still rubble from what she'd heard. Things just weren't making sense.

Christina extended her hand. "Good morning," she said, surprising the woman.

"Morning, mam," Claire Baker answered while she wondered why the Van Luxall girl had taken her hand.

"Where can I change?" Christina asked, and Mrs. Baker was triply confused.

"Change, Miss Van Luxall? I don't understand."

Christina let her breath out slowly. She hadn't expected to have to explain.

"Nelson — Mr. Wingate — hired me. I'm to start as a chambermaid." She rushed ahead. "Where will I find a uniform and what do you wish me to do?"

Mrs. Baker rocked back on her heels as if she'd been struck. She examined the young woman's features to see if it were some kind of joke. "Well, yes, I mean, they're down the hall, yes, um, follow me," she sputtered. Times were bad; horrible, really, but she hadn't heard of *this* sort of thing before.

Her uniform was starchy and uncomfortable and her shoes looked absurd.

"I suppose you can start by gathering the dirty laundry from upstairs. You'll find Marilee up there now, in the East Wing. It's up these stairs and to your left." She pointed as she spoke.

It was absolutely unbelievable, and Mrs. Baker still had trouble pounding its reality into her mind. It was so *devilishly* unbelievable that its sweetness took some time to edge its way into her. Not that Christina had ever treated her badly; she was always pretty much aloof — apart from and *above* the staff. *Better* than everyone else.

And then a story Rosey had told her wormed forward. Christina hiding Rosey's clothes the day they prematurely departed The Chimneys. Christina tormenting Rosey.

Mrs. Baker smiled to herself and wondered if Rosey would be stopping by later.

"Somebody's a simp! A complete simp!" Marilee teased over the laundry she had bunched to her chest. "Why, you're rich — you can't do this!" She thought about what she had said and then hastily asked, "You *are* still rich, aren't you? I mean you must have had *so* much money! You couldn't lose it *all*."

Christina grimaced and then smiled. "I'm not rich, anymore, but I do want to eat, and so here I am. Now tell me what to do before we both get into trouble."

Marilee looked over her shoulder. "Well, alright then," she said and passed the load of towels and sheets to Christina. "Take these. And I can call you Christina?"

Christina was embarrassed. "Yes, Marilee, you can call me Christina." She followed her into the hall and down to the dumbwaiter.

"Stuff them in here," the girl said after she opened the little door. "Careful," she teased and then added mysteriously, "This is the one that ate Rosey." Marilee leaned to Christina. "Do you want to hear a story?" She looked around then as if she were about to disclose a great secret. "You won't believe it, but it's true! I swear it is!"

Christina was interested. It had to be her Rosey — *Stephen's* Rosey.

Marilee grabbed Christina's arm and squeezed it confidentially. "Well, you have to promise you won't tell a soul! Her mother's still the housekeeper — and it's about Mr. Wingate, too — it's such a whopping good story!"

And she started to whisper its beginning to Christina as she worked the dumbwaiter's pulleys

"Rosey used to stay with Doris — you'll meet her soon enough — sweetest girl — I love her. And *Rosey* used to sneak down to Mr. Wingate's room — before he was master — this was before his father died ...."

Just then Mrs. Baker came around the corner from the stairs.

"Miss —" The housekeeper stopped herself. "Christina, come here, dear, I've some work for you in the kitchen."

And that's where Christina worked through the remainder of the day. As little thought as she had given to silver before, she came to see it in a new light. By noon her fingers were smudged and by mid-afternoon her hands were blackened to the wrists. Christina would no sooner finish polishing one cupboard full of tureens and salvers, when the housekeeper would appear, incredibly reject the luster on at least one object, and then go to a different cupboard for another army of pieces. The wide kitchen work table was stacked with teapots, pitchers, plates, serving platters, creamers, serving implements and silverware of varying sizes, each one ornate, rippled with roses and vines and scrolling.

It was nearing three in the afternoon when Christina, her arms aching, her fingertips raw and burning, heard hysterical laughter coming from the hallway beyond the kitchen. The laughter approached and faded and Christina could tell that whoever was having such a jolly time had stopped at the other side of the kitchen door.

Rosey composed herself; it was too wonderful to fully comprehend.

STEPHEN

He loved Number Eleven; loved her clacking, noisy engine, and the fabric and wood of her awkward body. And he loved the gentleness she brought to flying; her turns as docile and smooth as her wings were long and narrow. She was Stephen's first aeroplane, and so she would always be his favorite, but there was no denying the thrill he felt every time he thought of flying the Bulldog.

The Bulldog always seemed to be on her haunches when she was earthbound, poised and ready to leap forward, her muscles bunched and taut, forever spoiling for a fight. She was a reliable craft as far as engines and structure went, but she was a demon mistress; unforgiving of mistakes, and ragingly aggressive with anyone didn't know what they were doing.

"She's a suicidal bitch when you let her take the lead," Stephen said to Jim Schmidt, who immediately agreed.

"She's that, Mr. Rheiner — that and more. But she's tight as hell and she'll take the fight to anyone stupid enough to try to share the sky with her."

They stood beside her, their prototype, and the only Bulldog Mr. Boisvert had lived long enough to fly. Stephen remembered the day he had waited on the ground as his old boss took her aloft for the first time.

There had been no aerobatics that day, no steep turns or diving passes at the field. He had merely gotten her aloft, tried level flight for a short distance, banked through a few shallow turns and then brought her back to the ground.

Mr. Boisvert climbed down from the stubby aeroplane, visibly shaken. There was still fear in his eyes when he gave Stephen his first impression of the flight.

"Jesus and Mary, son — we've created a monster," he said, and his grin was respectful and diluted with trepidation. "She can be tamed, I'm sure of that, but the man who flies her during the day will have angry dreams of her at night!"

He hadn't let Stephen take her up that day, instead he had required Stephen to fly with him in Number Eleven, the old man in the front cockpit and Stephen in the back. Before they took off Mr. Boisvert had instructed Stephen, "I'll use the controls too, son, and I'll try to give you a feel for how the P-22 reacts."

It had been a wild ride.

All Stephen had to do was begin a maneuver and Jacob Boisvert would immediately magnify any movements of the stick or rudder bar that the boy initiated. They were all over the sky, Stephen desperate to learn to minimize every motion he made.

And the landing had been worst of all. He'd had to fly by the field several times before he was able to coax his old friend, Number Eleven, to line up and settle into a non-lethal rate of descent.

"Are you kidding me?" Stephen demanded after Number Eleven's propellor windmilled to a stop and Mr. Boisvert had climbed down from his cockpit.

"Stephen," he'd said, "I'm sorry son, but that's just a fraction of what you can expect."

Stephen did take up the Bulldog the following day, and his maiden flight had been significantly longer than Mr. Boisvert's, but it was because the boy was afraid to try anything other than level flight.

"If I thought I'd had enough fuel to just fly around the world in a straight line and landed back here later, I'd have done it," Stephen confessed. "That aeroplane's mad as hell about something." It had reminded him of the first time he'd ever ridden a horse. The animal had sensed the boy's weakness and shot like a bolt over fields and then into the woods, trying with every step to either shake the boy free or brush him off with a low branch.

But Stephen had persisted with the Bulldog, especially after Mr. Boisvert's death, and with time he'd learned to master the machine. He was good with it now, but he still tempered every maneuver with respect and wariness. Although it didn't look like that to others.

He sat in the rumbling cockpit, the magnificent metal propellor a glittering arc in front of him, the noise from the engine pounding into his sternum while the powerplant was still at idle. He was strapped in, and had already closed the access panel in the streamlined windshield he'd used to lower himself in through. Little needles jerked in the gauges and the control stick shook with the aeroplane's vibrations.

Stephen checked the field in front of him a final time, gave the thumbs-up signal, and waited while his ground crew pulled the wheel chocks free. Stephen nodded and bumped the throttle forward a fraction. The aeroplane was rolling forward in an instant and Stephen took a deep breath and advanced the throttle farther for take-off power.

It was still a thrill — a frightening, gut wrenching thrill when the engine exploded with power, at last free to whirl the massive propellor in cyclonic fury. They jarred down the runway, Stephen concentrating and the Bulldog roaring, until he massaged the stick carefully into his lap and they were airborne.

His crew stood far behind him, their hands on their hips or shading their eyes as they watched and waited. Their boss never disappointed them.

With a howl the Bulldog pivoted onto her tail and clawed her way perpendicular, rocketing into the low clouds above. She disappeared in the billowy mist, and it seemed to absorb much of her sound too.

And then the crew turned as one, for they knew what would happen next. They listened intently, hearing the engine fade and then begin to increase in volume until it was screaming, still out of sight, and apparently diving toward the earth.

Stephen and the Bulldog exploded through the cloud cover, the engine now thundering, and then pulled out just above the grassy field. They streaked by, the Bulldog's wheels barely skimming the grass. Then the plane jerked up twenty feet and spun onto its back, its flight path a step higher but still level across the field. Stephen flew upside down for several hundred yards and then jerked upward, climbing back through the clouds.

The men on the grass shook their heads and walked toward the hangar.

"Best damned pilot I've ever seen," one of them said, and the best dressed of the three smiled and added, "He's a natural, boys; I wished we'd had him back in '17."

The others turned to Jim Schmidt and smiled.

His exit performance over, Stephen sought a comfortable altitude, relaxed the throttle some, and scanned the gauges in front of him and the sky outside the little glass canopy. He never stopped moving his head around as he flew, constantly searching for the unexpected.

He was loaded with fuel, and the engine was running well; Stephen has intent on spending the best part of the morning checking out the performance of the craft now that he'd finished a new series of modifications. He thought about them as he flew, and laughed to himself when he remembered Rosey's consternation as he'd tried to explain them to her. She was an eager student even if she wasn't particularly quick at grasping concepts. And it sure beat the hell out of her constant complaining.

By mid-morning the clouds had begun to break up and Stephen put the Bulldog through its paces, smashing entry into the diminishing clouds and checking flight performance at different power settings. He had just blasted through a formation at three-quarters throttle when he saw the lake below him. He banked the plane around, trying to locate The Chimney. Instead, he saw that he was almost over the distinctive crescent-shaped lawn of Fairelawn.

Fairelawn — normally he avoided it.

Stephen wondered if Rosey were there. He tried to see if he could pick their blue Buick out from the other automobiles clustered in the back parking lot, but he wasn't certain.

Fairelawn.

Wingate Tire and Aviation. He'd heard the rumors that they were trying to make a pursuit craft, too. Trying to nose into military aviation when they already had a good business with their sports planes. They were also sounding out the possibility of starting an airline — nothing was truly secret in the city — or in the flying business, for that matter. More than a few large Douglas aeroplanes had come and gone from the Wingate hangars at the airfield, and the word was that Nelson Wingate was trying to decide which to purchase.

Stephen knew that while Wingate Aviation might start with another firm's aeroplanes, soon enough they'd design and build their own entry for the transport business.

Stephen had been doing a lazy, throttled-back circle high above the Wingate estate when he finally recognized Rosey's car — their car.

"What the hell," he muttered to himself. "If Rosey can visit, then so can I."

He goosed the Bulldog's loafing cylinders and dove on the manor, the exhaust screaming by the time he pulled out above the tree tops.

A horse-drawn mower bolted out of control near the Wingate's boathouse. Stephen turned to look at the manor as the fellow trying to calm the horses risked freeing one hand from the reins to shake his fist at Stephen.

The last mile or so of the wide boulevard leading to Fairelawn's front entry was arrow straight, and Stephen couldn't resist. He advanced the Bulldog's throttle another notch and quickly grabbed several thousand feet of altitude. Then he nudged the nose down and dove on the far end of the entry boulevard, the Bulldog's engine now howling like a stricken Valkyrie. He leveled out barely fifty feet above the drive, inverted his aircraft at over a hundred and seventy five miles an hour, and then settled another twenty feet toward the roadway.

Stephen roared over a roadster he hadn't noticed earlier and then pulled up in time to clear the roof of the manor. It seemed that most of Fairelawn's occupants had spilled outside from his earlier pass and now surrounded the manor, craning their necks to catch a glimpse of their tormentor.

Stephen decided his life as a madman with a pilot's license would be extended if he resisted the urge to dive on the manor one more time. Instead, he streaked out over the lake, skimming the wave tops and blowing up a line of short waterspouts with his prop-wash.

He had scared the driver of the roadster half to death. Nelson had been deep in thought when the Bulldog had ripped overhead, nearly deafening him and startling him into momentarily veering toward the edge of the driveway. He skidded the Stutz to a stop and looked up through his windshield. The black and brown blur had just popped up in time to clear Fairelawn and then had settled out of sight once it passed over it.

Nelson's ears were still ringing when he realized the aeroplane had been inverted, the pilot's head less than twenty feet over him when he had passed.

"A goddamned Bulldog!" he cursed, for he recognized the radial engine's throaty roar, the craft's stubby profile, and the performance characteristics of the fine aeroplane.

Everyone had taken to calling it the Bulldog, these days.

And then as he seethed, Nelson's temperature soared higher when he understood who would be brash enough to make low altitude passes over Fairelawn.

"Goddamn that cheeky little bastard!" Nelson cursed and pounded on his steering wheel.

CHRISTINA, ROSEY, AND NELSON, AND STEPHEN AND THE BULLDOG

Christina, a silver rose vase in one hand, the polishing cloth in the other, watched the door as it swung open. The bib of her apron was blackened from the polish and her hair hung in loose strands over the left side of her face. She was hot, she was tired of work, and she was in no mood for the woman who now stood opposite.

Rosey began laughing once more.

"Welcome to Fairelawn," she said through her hilarity, "It's not often a *Van Luxall* gets to see the kitchen. And in *uniform*, too, I see!"

Christina slammed the vase onto the table behind her. "Well, Rosey," she answered levelly. "Why don't *you* put *yours* on and join me; there's plenty more silver here."

Rosey stopped her. "You don't seem to understand; *I'm* not the *help* here, you are! I come to Fairelawn to visit; *I* have friends here and *I* don't have to work anymore."

She looked Christina over, absolutely loving her dirty, ill-fitting uniform. "If you haven't heard, Miss Van Luxall, I don't work any more. I have a child and a husband. *Stephen*, remember him? He supports me." She set her jaw and then went on, "But I'd bet you don't remember Stephen, do you, Miss Van Luxall; he was one of *the help* at The Chimneys, too. You got him fired, too, didn't you? That's about all you did — the poor little rich girl, getting everyone into trouble."

Rosey saw the change in Christina's attitude at the mention of Stephen and she couldn't believe it — the Van Luxall bitch was interested — she *cared*.

"Oh you *do* remember Stephen? How sweet. He remembers you, Miss Van Luxall, oh, he remembers you!" She looked Christina over from her shoes to her disheveled hair. "And he still *hates* you, if you're wondering."

She saw Christina flinch and knew she had opened a wound. "Why does he *hate* you so much?" she persisted, "Why does he say the things he does about you? What *else* did you do to him, Miss Van Luxall? What did you do to make him call you the names he does?" She paused to give Christina time to absorb what she was saying. She was now open-mouthed, gripping the edge of the table behind her.

"'The rich bitch,' he calls you. 'The rich little Van Luxall *bitch!*'"

Rosey adopted an embarrassed attitude. "Oh, excuse me, Miss Van Luxall, why, I didn't mean to swear in front of you. And I didn't even remember to mumble or lower my eyes. *Oh please don't fire me, Miss Van Luxall. Oh, please, don't fire me, again! Whatever would I do?*" She paused and then continued, now acting as if she had just realized something. "But — look!" She held her clean hands up. "I'm not working here, *you* are!"

Christina released the table behind her. Unconsciously she balled her hands into fists.

But, something was wrong — something she didn't understand — not Rosey's tirade, for Christina knew she deserved it — but something deeper was happening and she couldn't put her finger on what it was. She opened her mouth to speak, but at the same instant the kitchen and the manor around it shook. The windows rattled as a tremendous roaring filled the room and the chests of the two women moved too.

The aeroplane was far from the house before Rosey realized what it was. Her first thought was that someone had crashed nearby and then she heard the aeroplane's roar receding.

"*It's Nelson!*" she exclaimed and bolted past Christina and out of the manor.

It's Nelson! Christina repeated in her mind, mimicking Rosey's obvious delight. *Nelson? She called him, Nelson! Who the hell is she to call him Nelson!* And then she, too, went out the kitchen door to see if he would pass again.

They stood apart but both of them searched the skies; Christina with barely more than idle curiosity and interest in the aeroplane itself, and Rosey, obviously enthralled with the possibility of catching a glimpse of her romping knight.

They heard the aeroplane approaching again, apparently from the front of the manor, and the two listened as its engine's howl increased in volume. Christina looked from the sky over the manor to Rosey and then back again. There was a rapt smile on Rosey's face, an almost visible longing apparent in the way she leaned toward the sound.

The black and brown Bulldog passed ripping overhead, too fast for them to see more than the fact that the craft was flying upside down. The girls turned with it and watched as it rolled to heads-up flight and then diminished as Stephen roared across the lake. Almost at the other side, they saw him swoop into the clouds, little more than a dot.

Christina smelled the exhaust fumes settle over her.

"The Bulldog," Rosey spat, disappointed and then angry. "What the hell is he trying to prove?" She glared in the direction of the departed aeroplane. "Stephen, you son of a bitch, stay out of my life."

Christina turned and stared at Rosey. She couldn't believe the virulence in her tone. *She hates him*, Christina realized, and when she did she studied further the abrasive features of Rosey's face.

Rosey felt Christina's eyes on her. She turned and glared back, understanding that she had let her guard down to the wrong person at the wrong time.

"Don't you have work to do?" Rosey nearly screamed even though her voice did not raise above a hiss. "Don't you have *silver* to polish, Miss Van Luxall?" She did not expect an answer. Rosey spun around and strode back into the house, slamming the door, oblivious to Christina not three feet behind.

Once in the kitchen, Christina heard Nelson rage into the manor also. "THAT CHEEKY BASTARD!" he shouted and then barked orders to several servants.

"Out of my way!"

"Have someone fuel my automobile!"

"I'm taking dinner in my room tonight and I'll fire the first person who comes near me!"

Then Christina heard him lower his voice and speak to someone else. There were too many closed doors for her to tell who it was, or to catch what was said. But soon a door slammed and then another. Shortly after, Christina caught a glimpse of an automobile pulling away from the back of the manor, Rosey's fiery hair clearly visible inside.

Nelson didn't come around to harass Christina that first day as she had been certain he would.

"Not too bad," the housekeeper said as she inspected the silver.

Christina wasn't listening and couldn't have cared less what Claire Baker thought. She leaned over the sink trying to clean her hands, but the black, the worst of it under her chipped fingernails, wouldn't come off.

She shook her hands and then wiped them on the skirt of her dress.

"We'll have none of that!" the housekeeper admonished tartly, and after she did, Christina glared at her from heights the woman hadn't known existed.

Christina walked up the stairs to her room, determined to spend some time later with her new friend, Marilee.

CHRISTINA AND MARILEE

Christina changed into her evening uniform. She had bathed even though Marilee told her she would get into trouble if she took the time to do it before they were done for the night.

"You mustn't need a job as bad as you say," Marilee said cautiously. The new girl was a mystery to her.

"What do you mean?"

Christina liked Marilee. She was unassuming and totally honest from what she could tell of her so far. She reminded Christina of Abegaile, perhaps because Abegaile had been timid, too.

Marilee sounded worried. "You could get in trouble, that's why, and you don't act like you care. Everybody I know does the best they can, at least for the first week or so. And I don't think you're going to get along with the housekeeper at the rate you're going."

"I know her; she's not so bad."

Marilee was not impressed. "I know her, too, and even though she's not Eleanora, the mean cow we had before her, she's not a lot of fun. It's like she's waiting for all of us to try to be as wild as her daughter was."

"Rosey?" Christina asked, knowing full well who Marilee was referring to. "How wild was she? You started to tell me earlier."

Christina had just finished putting on her evening uniform and adjusting her apron.

"She used to room with Doris in twenty-seven," Marilee said, indicating with a movement of her head the room at the end. "It's almost right above where we were this morning."

"By the dumbwaiter, you mean," Christina said, helping her along. "You were going to tell me about Rosey and something about the dumbwaiter."

And Marilee did. When she had finished; embellishing the story here and there, and leaving out details no one but Rosey and Nelson knew, the puzzle Christina had mentally begun to piece together was well along toward being finished.

"Let's get downstairs, now, before we *both* get into trouble," Marilee warned, and Christina absently agreed.

"Alright, let's," she said, but her look was far away and her heart had returned for the first time since Rosey's tirade about Stephen hating her and calling her the 'rich bitch'.

They worked together, cleaning their assigned rooms, and then went to the laundry room to help until they were dismissed at nine. As it turned out, Christina and Marilee were alone once more.

Marilee held a towel away from her body and looked at Christina who was struggling with a sheet. "I still don't understand why you're working here, Christina. I mean, lots of people lost money and everything, but I don't hear about them becoming maids." She thought about her own statement for a moment, rolling a towel as she did.

"*Rolled* linens?" Christina asked, attempting to divert Marilee. "I've never heard of such a thing." She almost went off on a tangent about how things had been done at The Chimneys, but stopped herself.

"It's so they don't have any fold marks," Marilee explained and then plowed ahead. "Don't you have any family — rich relatives or something — who can take care of you until this is over — until everybody gets work again?"

Christina bridled. "I'm a grown woman, Marilee. How could I go to a relative to support me?"

"Well, what did you do before you became poor?" Marilee asked, still confused, but anxious to understand the situation and then help her new friend.

"I went to school — college — for three years."

"Well, did you work or anything before that?" Marilee persisted and when Christina didn't answer right away, she knew she was only embarrassing her.

Christina *was* embarrassed, and with her discomfort she remembered Stephen and their conversations.

"I just want to get married," Marilee said, her voice full of hope. "A husband — that's the answer to my dreams. Why haven't you gotten married, yet,

Christina? You're beautiful — I'll bet lots of rich fellas have asked you." She looked Christina over. "*Begged* you, I'll bet." Then she made a joke. "Before you had black hands and all, I mean!"

Christina raised her hands in front of the two of them. She shook her hair away from her eyes and laughed. "Can't we wear gloves or something? This is absolutely the most disgusting thing to do to yourself!"

Marilee examined her own hands. While Christina's were black, for sure, they were also delicate, with long fingers and splendid nails — a bit chipped today, but Marilee could see how they had been — her own fingers were gross and blocky. "Never mind your gorgeous looks — that beautiful hair, your pretty eyes, your smile and your white teeth — I'd just be happy to have your hands, Christina. Is there anything about you that isn't pretty?" she asked with honesty and innocence.

Christina appraised her friend. She was full of life, and she didn't appear to have suffered any grave misfortunes. And she was young. And very poor — a chamber maid in someone else's manor.

Christina relaxed and spoke the words which had meant so much to her years before. "What are your dreams? What's the most wonderful thing in the whole world that could happen to you?"

Marilee didn't hesitate. "I already told you; I want a husband. Handsome would be nice, but I'd settle for good-looking." She laughed at herself. "I'd settle for *alive* and under a hundred. I'm tired of being alone, Christina. Aren't you?"

They were now both rolling towels as they spoke.

"Yes, I'm tired of being alone, but it's because I don't feel like I'm alone with me — I feel like I'm with a stranger. Do you know what I mean?"

Marilee was lost. "No," she answered, honestly, "but I can pretend I do if it makes you happy."

Christina smiled and didn't say anything more for awhile. Then she began again as they were straightening up the laundry room for the night. "Sure, I'd like to have a husband, Marilee. And I'm tired of being alone, too."

Christina was glad she had decided to live at the manor the week she worked there. The thought of driving all the way back to her hotel room exhausted her, never mind the prospect of paying for the gas and the nightmare of facing the manager again. She hadn't walked away from their negotiations feeling particularly successful.

That night as she lay in bed, she was sorry she had not told Marilee that she was only going to be there for a week — it was like a subterfuge and she was afraid Marilee would ultimately see it as a betrayal and a further belittling of her own work. Then she remembered Rosey and her mother and decided it was just possible she wouldn't make it through the week anyway.

The next morning Christina's right hand was so cramped she felt it could neither open nor close if her life depended on it. She sat on the edge of her bed and massaged her hands and became aware of the pain in her lower back and in her shoulders.

"I'd kill for a long, soaking bath and a massage," she said as she unrolled her uniform for the day. She was momentarily confused when she saw that the circle of cloth which would have covered her chest had been cut away. And then she understood and threw the dress down and went for the door, cursing with each step. "That red-haired tramp will pay for this!"

But she was smart enough to stop before she opened the door. *Oh really?* she asked herself. *And how will you make her pay? Run to her mother? I don't think so. Have her fired?*

Christina went back to the dress on the floor and retrieved it. She examined the size of the hole and then unrolled her bib apron. If she were careful, she could keep herself covered with it and then steal downstairs the first chance she got and get another uniform dress.

She put on the uniform, feeling totally ridiculous as she adjusted the top of her apron to cover her slip and brassiere.

"This is going to be a long week," she muttered to herself as she joined Marilee in the hall. "How do I look?" she asked the girl. "Truthfully," she added as she took a breath and expanded her chest, calling Marilee's attention to it.

Marilee blushed. "I told you, Christina, you're beautiful — all of you." She stared a while longer and said, "If I had *those* I think I'd already be married."

Christina felt better for several reasons. She laughed and good naturedly poked at her friend. "Can you keep a secret, stupid?" she joked.

Marilee was hurt by the nickname but happy to be teased by Christina. "Of course I can, as long as you don't make fun of me."

They continued walking down the hall and as they did Christina circled Marilee's waist with her arm. "I like you, Marilee, I really do. Now look at me and don't laugh out loud."

Christina stopped, moved Marilee around so they faced one another, and then slid the bib of her apron aside. Marilee's eyes doubled in size.

"Christina! Why did you do that!"

"I didn't, you …." She stopped herself. "Rosey must have. Now don't tell anybody; I've got to get a new uniform before long. The first time I have to bend over there's going to be hell to pay."

Marilee imagined the scene. "You'd better hope it's in front of Master Wingate — Nelson — I don't think *he'd* mind."

"No, probably not," Christina laughed.

It was midmorning when Marilee stole into the room Christina was cleaning. She tossed a new uniform dress onto the bed she was straightening.

"You're a sweetheart," Christina said as she hastily peeled off her apron and the dress beneath.

"The door to the uniform closet was locked — I had to use a special favor to get that one! Boy, somebody's really trying to get to you!"

"Well, with your help maybe I can survive!"

Marilee smiled. It was great to be needed by someone like Christina.

Once dressed, Christina was finally able to settle into her morning routine and allow herself some time to daydream. She had meant to try to work out the situation with Nelson and Rosey and Stephen the night before, but she had hit her pillow and fallen asleep in one motion.

She went back to when she had first heard of Stephen's wedding and wondered. From what Marilee had told her, Rosey had been entertaining Nelson nearly every night for quite awhile. Christina wished she had exact dates; they would help to figure things out. But then again, if their little games had begun soon after Rosey started at Fairelawn, Christina knew there would really only be one person — if that many — who could positively point to the father of Rosey's child.

Christina wondered how much Stephen knew.

And she wondered if any of it altered what she thought of him. The more she learned, the less accurate the picture became that she had drawn of Stephen's life after he had left The Chimneys.

When she thought of his stunt flying over Fairelawn she laughed to herself. He had himself a marvelous — if somewhat noisy — aeroplane. And he did know how to fly, that was for certain.

Christina remembered Stephen ripping off the rear fender of the gardener's car the day of their circus trip and she laughed again.

And that started a new mystery. The shock of Stephen's being sent away, followed by the tragedy of Abbie's death, and then the fire and Katie's and Anna's deaths, had kept her from ever really questioning how her father had learned of their trip.

Rosey? she asked herself. *But how could she have found Papa to tell him? That question eliminated her involvement.*

And then Christina remembered her father and her thoughts veered in a different direction.

ROSEY AND STEPHEN

Rosey went directly from the maid's lockers at Fairelawn to the field at Boisvert Aviation. She pulled up in a cloud of dust and was into Stephen's office before it settled. She brushed by his secretaries without a word and they were grateful, for they had no inclination to involve themselves with Mrs. Rheiner if they could avoid it.

"WHERE IS HE?" she raged when she came back out of his empty office. "IS HE BACK YET? IS HE BACK WITH THAT GODDAMNED AEROPLANE?" she screamed.

The two seated women rolled their chairs away from Rosey as she continued.

"Is he back? Is he here? Or did he go to old lady Boisvert's!" she said, absolutely shocking the women.

Rosey laughed madly, "*She's* the Bulldog! She's the one who looks more like a bulldog than any damned aeroplane!"

With a whoosh she was out the front door again, already certain the secretaries would offer no useful information. "STEPHEN!" she screamed at the top of her lungs.

He appeared from a door in a distant hangar and came running. His first thought was that Billy had been hurt.

"I'M HERE, ROSEY, I'M HERE!" he yelled as he crossed to her. "What's wrong? Tell me what happened!"

When he was within reach she slapped him hard across the face.

Stephen rocked, stunned.

"Leave me alone, you bastard," she seethed. "What the hell do you mean coming out to Fairelawn. You made me look like a goddamned idiot. Can't you grow up? Can't you just be content to build your goddamned aeroplanes and make your goddamned money?"

She caught her breath and forged ahead.

Stephen was still too abashed to speak. He knew he'd been wrong buzzing the manor. He'd been showing off and he regretted it before he landed. It was no way for a man — a responsible man — to act.

"Showing off!" she continued as if reading his thoughts. "What kind of man are you?"

And then it was as if Rosey understood what she had missed before.

"It was for her! You knew she was there and you just had to do it for her and make me look like a fool!"

They remained in the middle-ground between the hangars and the office, Rosey waving her arms wildly, the secretaries peeking through the front window of the office, and a gaggle of Stephen's employees watching the exchange from the shadows inside the hangars.

He struggled to figure out who Rosey's 'her' was.

Rosey saw his look of consternation and jammed it down his throat.

"Don't tell me you didn't know — don't lie to me, Stephen — CHRISTINA! — your precious Christina Van Luxall — Van WHORESALL was at Fairelawn! And don't ask me what she was doing!" she spat. "It was too wonderful for words!"

Stephen was reeling now. *Christina? She was there?* he asked, oblivious to everything else Rosey had said, forgetting her tone, even forgetting her accusations. His life centered on the fact that he had been close to Christina.

"What was she doing there?" he asked, his attitude now a combination of desperation and daze. *Christina's back. She's returned!* Then he remembered Rosey had struck him — his wife had hit him, and Stephen began to feel anger building in him, too.

Stephen went back to Christina and reviewed his flight and inanely wondered if she had been impressed. He wished he could ask Rosey, but she had turned on her heel and stomped off. Her shrieking had changed to uncontrollable grumbling punctuated with "You bastard, you bastard!"

Rosey backed away from Stephen's office, nearly ramming into a parked car, spinning the Buick's tires as she did. Gravel rattled against the other car after she jammed the Buick into forward and sped away.

Stephen walked slowly back to the hangar, said a few things to Jim Schmidt who was looking as hangdog and sheepish as Stephen, and then went to the Battleship Roadster and looked at the damage.

He had never seen Rosey so angry. She had been insane — And the whole horrible scene was flooded with his knowledge that Christina was back. It was a slap worse than Rosey's, especially when he questioned whether Christina was with Nelson Wingate — engaged or married to him.

Then he remembered Rosey's challenge, "Don't ask what she was doing!" and he was absolutely tormented. He didn't wish to return to Rosey, but she was the only one who knew about Christina. He certainly couldn't go out to Fairelawn. He started to drive away from his office, then changed his mind. It was way too soon for Rosey to calm down — if she were going to — and he was not anxious to walk into another hail storm.

And so, he went directly from his car to Number Eleven. He was almost to her when he saw that the propellor was already spinning and heard the engine popping and snapping. There in front of her, leaning against a wing, the ropes to the wheel chocks in his hand, was Jim Schmidt — 'Smitty' he had come to call him.

Stephen veered toward him, feeling he should thank him or something, but Schmidt waved him away, pointing to Stephen and then to Number Eleven and then to the sky, finally poking the corners of his own mouth into a comic smile.

Stephen nodded forlornly and then couldn't help smiling back. It was great to have a friend. He wished Smitty knew Christina, and he was sorry they both knew Rosey. Things had been going so well, though, and that fact confused him. And then he remembered Billy and knew that if it weren't for Rosey he wouldn't have a son, and with that thought everything was worse again.

He climbed into the cockpit and checked everything. He pulled on his leather flight cap and goggles and then gave Schmidt the thumbs up. He bounced Number Eleven by him, losing him briefly in a cloud of dust and blowing debris, and then saw him again, this time pointing to his own head, reminding Stephen of the cardinal rule of the air — always keep your mind on your flying.

Stephen and Number Eleven flew slowly and well.

It was dark when he drove up in front of their house. The lights were out, and Stephen suspected Billy was at the neighbors for the night. He entered his home tentatively, closing the door behind him and resisting turning on any lights as he advanced through the hall into the dining room. In the kitchen he filled a glass with water and walked with it to the stairs leading to the bedrooms. He heard Rosey sniffle upstairs.

He had thought it all through.

"Rosey?" he said softly. "Rosey, I'm sorry," he called ahead as he took the stairs two at a time. "I was wrong, Rosey, and I *was* showing off."

He went to their bedroom and feared he would find the door locked, but when he twisted the handle he found that it wasn't. He repeated his apology as he went into the darkened room. Still, Rosey didn't answer and an inexplicable fear settled into Stephen's stomach. He stopped and listened. He could hear her breathing evenly. He walked to their bed and sat on the edge when he reached it. He had expected Rosey to shift away from him, but she didn't.

"Rosey?" he said again, and this time she answered him. He jumped when her voice came from the corner by the window. She was on the floor, sitting with her back to the junction of the two walls.

Her voice was whining and defeated. "You go and ruin everything, Stephen — you can't keep ruining things."

She gave voice to the same thoughts he'd had earlier in Number Eleven.

"I know I do; I'm sorry, Rosey. Do you want me to leave?"

She didn't answer. She came near flashing into destructive anger when she thought of him wanting to leave her so he could go to Christina, but she controlled herself.

It had been turned it into a nightmare at Fairelawn. First Stephen's flight and then Nelson's reaction. Nelson had been demonic in his fury over Stephen's stunts with the Bulldog and he was beside himself when he deduced that Rosey had been taunting Christina.

Little rich girl, Christina. Everyone's concerned about poor, helpless, Christina!

But then, back at her house — on the way to it, really — Rosey had finally come to see that if she weren't very, very careful, she could truly lose Nelson — he wouldn't tolerate any more nonsense from her after the scene at Fairelawn, and now, with Christina back in the picture, it was just possible that she could lose Stephen, too.

Rosey had never understood how Eleanora could cut the rope cables that night at Fairelawn and risked another person's life just to get revenge. But now, after her day, she understood. And her hatred centered on Christina.

Stephen and Nelson — they were her life boats — her refuge. She wanted Nelson, but she would stay with Stephen if she had to. But Christina — Christina was everything she was not. Even as a chambermaid she had risen above her with her lifetime of pampering and fancy speech.

Rosey sat rocking in the darkness of the corner, terrified of the new direction her life had taken and livid that she could lose everything because of one person — the person who kept butting into her life, causing trouble, and then walking away.

She was only slightly better when she heard Stephen come back to her.

NELSON AND CHRISTINA

Nelson lay in bed, frustrated because he couldn't make himself calm down. It was as if the Bulldog's flight had loosed a torrent of prejudices, and at their base was his fear of inadequacy. Wingate Tire and Aviation was still surviving in a time when that alone was close to magnificent. Sales of tires had fallen off dramatically, and the aviation division was keeping alive with the production of the Home Racer, a design Nelson had purchased the rights to when he bought out a small factory years earlier. His firm had continually modified the aeroplane in an attempt to keep up with the advances in aeronautics, but nothing Wingate had done was striking enough to warrant notice in either the business or aviation community.

For Nelson it was like manufacturing Model T's at a time when even Henry himself had given up on them. He wanted his company to expand, to reflect his judgement and to demonstrate his might as an industrialist. They were building a lot of Home Racers, but the little aeroplane was still basically an old design in sticks and fabric.

Even though his firm was now making good headway establishing their airline subsidiary, it was slow going and there wasn't any glamour to reflect on Nelson.

And yet, he knew that since the Wingate fortune was now based on cash — government treasury notes and treasury bills, and not on industry, he was envied by almost everyone knowledgeable. Wingate Aviation's biggest profits came from interest — interest payed without fail, month after month after month.

Every time he thought it through, his frustrations boiled down to his absolute need to have a government contract to build advanced aeroplanes. He was desperate to come up with a design for a real aeroplane, not a toy, that he could mass produce. Nelson wanted assembly lines — long ones — and thousands upon thousands of workers producing Wingate aircraft.

And when he tossed about in his bed and analyzed it further, he took his logic to the extreme. Standing in Nelson's way, preventing him from his own vision of success, keeping him from truly shedding his father's lingering shadow, was the son of a chauffeur, Stephen Rheiner, and Boisvert Aviation.

He needed to know exactly what they were doing and the direction they intended to move. He would not build an aeroplane to have it eclipsed by a Boisvert design.

True, Rosey was trying to keep him apprized of what Stephen was working on, but her understanding of theory was so basic, and her drawings and explanations so crude, that so far, they were next to useless.

"But I'm helping you!" she had insisted after the Bulldog had rattled the manor. "Why can't you just take what I tell you and build a better aeroplane?" she had complained.

It was laughable to Nelson and that was exactly what he had done. Laughed at her.

"A child could tell me more about aircraft design than you've been telling me, Rosey! I need plans, I need prints, I need details, not stick drawings with misspellings and guesses explained with 'I think he said' and 'it might have been; I'm not sure!' I can guess Rosey, and I *pay* people a hell of a lot of money to come up with more than children's drawings!"

"Then do it yourself?" Rosey had responded angrily and then hissed, "You find out what Stephen's building — ." Nelson stopped her with the flat of his hand pressed against her mouth.

"Shut up! Just shut up!" he said and looked around as if he expected to find someone else in the room with them. "Christina's here, isn't she?"

Was she listening? Who knew? Was she aware that he was bedding Stephen Rheiner's wife? Certainly the other servants knew. Then he remembered the child and realized that it was all too compressed; too many of the wrong people were together at the wrong place at the wrong time! And when he thought of the likelihood that Rosey would harass Christina, he groaned audibly. It would not do — the entire situation just would not do! He had allowed his little game with the Van Luxall woman to blind him to the realities of his household. With the morning, changes would be made.

He rolled to his side and stared at the opaque windows.

Christina and Marilee walked together, Marilee telling how she had dropped a tray of glasses in the kitchen when the aeroplane had passed over the first time. "Good glasses, too!" she'd emphasized. She was mortified.

Just as she was describing the calamity, the housekeeper walked up to them. Marilee stopped mid-sentence.

"You're through working here," Mrs. Baker said without preamble, and stared at Christina.

The direction of the housekeeper's glance not withstanding, Marilee nearly fainted.

Christina responded, "I beg your pardon?" and then added, "Mam".

"Mister Wingate told me to tell you were through — he told me that this morning. So you're finished, isn't that clear enough?"

Marilee watched the two and wondered why they were discussing *her* problem — why the housekeeper was involving Christina. But gradually it sunk in that *Christina* was through. Christina was leaving. That was terrible news, too!

Christina didn't know what to say. This woman standing in front of her had gotten her fired. Rosey's mother had told Nelson something which had made him let her go. It was ludicrous — she couldn't even hold a job as a chambermaid.

The housekeeper watched in silence as long as she could. There was no way she wanted to tell the Van Luxall girl the rest of Nelson Wingate's message, but she knew she had to; there was no escaping it. She cleared her throat.

"You're to report to Wingate Aviation for lunch tomorrow. You and Mr. Wingate are to *dine* together." She pronounced 'dine' as if it meant playing in dog leavings.

Christina felt her heart restart.

Marilee looked from her new friend to the housekeeper. Although it didn't make any sense to her, she was thankful they weren't discussing something else — such as broken glasses, perhaps.

Christina arrived in the city at half past ten. She went to her hotel to change, and encountered the manager as she passed through the lobby. He saw her stained hands and reacted as if she'd been up to her elbows in some sort of filth, and Christina enjoyed his consternation.

She sat in Nelson's outer office and waited. His door was closed. At twelve fifteen it opened and Nelson breezed out, catching Christina and pulling her with him as he hastily departed.

"I'm really pressed for time, Christina; I'm sorry. I do want to have lunch with you, but I've got to get right back to work, after." He stopped himself and forced a slower pace. "How *are* you?" he asked as if he'd just noticed her. Before she could answer he saw her hands.

"Christina! I *am* sorry! It seemed like a grand joke at first — a playful payback." He nudged her side with his elbow and Christina got the impression it had all been carefully rehearsed. He went on, "But I don't have the time for it, and it was a bad idea, anyway." He continued in a rush of words, "I do still want you to put in some time on the production line. Tomorrow alright?. I think you'll get a better idea of what we do here. But you won't actually be *working*, Christina, not with your *hands*, I mean...."

Christina stopped him. "I want to, Nelson. I want to build aeroplanes. I want to touch things and bolt them together or whatever it is that you do — glue them, sew them, hammer them — whatever." She held up her hands. "It looks ridiculous, I know, but I really don't mind; I've never worked, Nelson — don't you see — we've never done anything but give orders and take money."

Nelson was very uncomfortable with her confessions.

"Yes, yes, Christina, I feel *very* guilty for saving the Wingate industries from ruin like so many other companies, and I'm absolutely *devastated* that we're sitting on more cash than we know what to do with, but let's not spend our lunch beating ourselves up too badly."

"Well, Nelson, that's all fine, but the point is, I want to work. If it means getting grease on me, fine."

Nelson indulged her. "I can't say that it has any appeal to me, Christina, but if that's what you want, we at Wingate will oblige. You'll be reporting to Sam Russell in hangar three. Tell him who you are." — Nelson smiled at that. — "He'll know who you are, of course; just tell him what you want to do."

Christina answered, but Nelson didn't hear her. He was trying to understand why Christina's beauty no longer affected him as it had before. He was neither incapacitated nor so awestruck that he was out of control. She was just as beautiful as ever, however; certainly the only woman who could look good with stained hands.

They dined, and it was more of a formality than anything social, Christina trying to piece together the last three days and Nelson wondering if she had learned anything at the manor. And all the while he looked her over. She would make a very presentable wife.

Christina reported to Sam Russell the next day, and she worked the line. She worked it for three months instead of one, and she was tempted to ask to stay another, but she knew Nelson wouldn't hear of it. She joined his staff then, and once more she lugged home boxes of figures and information.

Christina was now assistant to the production manager, and it wasn't long before he was taking her seriously. Not only did she do her office work well, she still continued to spend time at the production facilities, listening to the men and relaying their suggestions to Nelson's engineers. She was not the head of anything, but she forced herself into the heart of it all.

She had rented a room in the city and moved out of the hotel, managing at the last moment to scrape together enough money to leave the manager with a respectable tip.

Aviation was fascinating, but Christina immediately shared Nelson's disdain for the little aeroplane which was the still the backbone of the company; it was outdated and neither of them could believe people still bought the thing.

By midwinter, Wingate Aviation had four routes for their airline, and while business was deathly slow, it gave the company time to work through a series of blunders and miscalculations without a catastrophe. Mid-American Airways hopped back and forth across Ohio, Indiana, and Illinois, gaining experience and name recognition every day.

Christina continued working at the van of Wingate's efforts to design and build a pursuit aeroplane. It wasn't long before she learned that a major part of the firm's problem was Nelson's reluctance to build a prototype. No design was advanced enough, no aeroplane the sure thing that Nelson was looking for before he would commit the company name and resources to it.

"Can we get a contract with it?" and "Will it beat the Bulldog?" were the two most repeated and ill received questions through the winter. It was almost spring when Christina, backed by the design team and several vice-presidents, made a presentation and absolutely insisted that five of the crafts be built. "It's better than anything out there, Nelson," she had said evenly and firmly. "It's sound design, it's safety, and it should be fast as hell."

Nelson stared at the rendering of the aeroplane in Army Air Corps colors. Christina had insisted that the artist add to the background another seventy five of the planes flying in formation.

Nelson was about to speak, to ask the dread questions, when Christina once more took the floor. "Don't ask, Nelson; build."

And it was exactly the posture he needed to move him away from his paralysis. "How soon?" And then before anyone answered, he added, "I want it for the races in Cleveland. I've got to be seen at the National Air Races."

Christina answered, "If we started today, it would be impossible, Nelson. We wouldn't have enough time."

Nelson stood from his desk. His storm was coming.

Christina went on talking as if he were raptly attentive. "But we can't start today — because we started last month." She defied Nelson to challenge her. Only three other people in the room were aware of her bold move, and they were the lowliest of those gathered — the production men.

"We knew the refinements wouldn't alter the basic design so I authorized the airframes begun on five aeroplanes. If you'd care to see them, they're in hangar six."

That brought a laugh from nearly everyone, for hangar six was where the company stored seldom-used material. The joke at the aviation division was that if you didn't do your job well you'd end up in hangar six. In theory it was a crowded place. In reality it was where Christina had just risked being sent.

"Either way, that's where I'm headed," she said and laughed at her own grim joke.

Christina's mind had settled in with Wingate Aviation, but her heart was still sorting through the confusing flurry of speculation that had been dumped at her feet those days she had been at Fairelawn.

STEPHEN AND ROSEY AND NELSON

Stephen and Rosey settled into another truce. Stephen spent more time than ever at the airfield, and he hadn't the slightest inclination to ask Rosey where she spent hers. Things at Boisvert Aviation were up one day and then down the next as a flood of letters, requisitions, and redundant questions flowed from Washington. The first ten crafts were delivered after Stephen and Jim Schmidt put the plane through its paces for several senate committees and Army Air Corps representatives, and they now worked harder than ever to convince the appropriate powers to extend the order for another fifty.

In the meantime, the Army Air Corps was sending out mixed reviews of the Bulldog, for one aeroplane had already been lost in a landing accident. The pilot had miraculously escaped, and once Stephen learned of the circumstances involved, he was not particularly relieved to hear that the pilot was uninjured.

He had been extending the P-22 far beyond its design capabilities and then stupidly tried a tricky cross-wind landing with an exceptionally slow approach speed.

"The Bulldog's designed to fight and fly, not to do a coward's dance on landing," Stephen had muttered to anyone who would listen. There was an investigation and then another and another. Had the ill-fated pilot not been a congressman's son Stephen was sure the accident would have been chalked up to pilot error and then forgotten.

Further, Stephen's attempts to modify the craft to accept his retractable landing gear were running into problems at every turn.

And he, too, was preparing for the 1930 National Air Races in Cleveland. While it had still not been decided if he or Jim Schmidt, or both of them, would compete, the thought of hiring a hot-shot pilot to fly the Bulldog for them was never entertained.

"Can we do it?" he'd asked his friend, one day, and Smitty's reply hadn't been reassuring.

"We'll be up against the best and the fastest, Mr. Rheiner — planes we've never seen before and many we'll never see again. I'm afraid the Air Races are like gambling, only it's not just money, it's your reputation and your life at stake."

Stephen had known all along that Jim Schmidt was against the idea, but his objections were becoming more succinct.

"Well, then, dammit, Smitty, why are you even thinking of flying? I'll do it. I *want* to!"

"And for what reason?" Jim Schmidt had asked the boy. "Fame? It won't last. To prove the Bulldog? We know what it can do, and so does the Army — with the exception of one stupid and lucky pilot! I think you're risking too much for nothing."

But they continued with their preparations, stretching the limits of the powerplant and the wings with each race-induced modification.

"We've got to get the wheels up for the race," was Stephen's last requirement.

"She won't be as pretty," Jim Schmidt had countered, laughing quietly.

The wheel pants and the forward angled struts were the only awkward things about the plane, making the Bulldog look like it was skidding to a stop, its legs braced to the front.

Rosey was unraveled. She was unsure of where she stood with Nelson. Further, she was fearful that Stephen was fed up and could soon be willing to risk her telling all about Jacob Boisvert's death just to be rid of her. But she also understood that information was really significant only to Stephen and possibly Mrs. Boisvert, and so its value was quite limited.

She seldom went to the airfield anymore, although she did spend a lot of time looking at the plans Stephen left at the house. She still visited Fairelawn, but she was more circumspect when she did. No longer did she act as if she owned the manor. Her time with Nelson was now more sexual and less conversational. Undoubtably, he was using her; the balance now tipped to his advantage.

Rosey sensed that things were building, that Christina was closing in on her, that Stephen was at wit's end, and that even Nelson was on the verge of some sort of a decision regarding their future, and at the heart of it all were the upcoming National Air Races. It rankled her beyond words that a stupid contest would somehow determine her destiny, and the more she thought of it the more determined she became to be an active participant in its outcome.

Billy was, of course, oblivious to it all, bounced from knee to knee and home to home. His life was a succession of babysitters punctuated by frolicking visits by his father and disinterested hours with his mother.

And so fall passed to winter, and winter was giving way to spring, and Rosey had yet to discover the script for the part she was to play — until one morning an idea sprung whole into her thoughts. She was feeding Billy at the time, Stephen having left hours earlier, as usual.

She held a spoonful of food to the child's mouth.

"Open up, Billy; I think we can make your father very, very happy."

The baby clamped his mouth over the spoon and Rosey slid it out.

"So happy, I think maybe he'll ask us to live with him. Would you like that?"

Chance nudged a little of the child's food into his windpipe.

He gagged and spit, expelling his mouthful of cereal onto Rosey.

Rosey was at the offices of Wingate Tire and Aviation before noon and was lucky enough to catch Nelson in. She wore her best dress and had spent half of the morning on her hair, shining, soft curls like a cap on her head.

"Mr. Wingate told me to stop at his office; he wants to talk to me."

The receptionist eyed Rosey warily. "Did you make an appointment, Miss — I don't believe you told me your name — "

"Baker, Rosalind Baker, and he said to just stop by when I was in the city. And I'm there. I mean, *here*."

The woman left her desk and went to Nelson's door. She opened it just enough to pass through and then closed it quickly once she was inside.

"I suppose you think I've never *seen* him before," Rosey taunted quietly, and the other secretary in the room looked up from her work. Rosey smirked at her and then went back to examining her fingernails. "What do you think — he leaves here and climbs into a coffin until morning?"

The secretary laughed in spite of herself — the thought *had* crossed her mind. Nelson didn't enjoy a reputation as the easiest man in town to work for. She cut her laugh short when the receptionist came back out of Nelson's office.

"Mr. Wingate is *awfully* busy, Miss Baker."

Rosey prepared to storm through his door.

"He only has a minute to give you."

Rosey was by her and striding into Nelson's office, her curls bouncing with each step. "We'll see...." she said as she passed the startled receptionist.

Nelson sat behind his desk, expressionless. He had his hands folded together in front of him. His whole attitude exuded, 'This had better be good!'

Rosey stood, her upper thighs barely depressed against the lip of his desk. She allowed Nelson a moment to look her over, for she was learning to achieve some of the subterfuge she had seen wealthy women employ to look alluring.

"Nelson," she began at last. "I had an idea this morning, and I didn't know if I'd see you tonight. I think you'll like it."

He had his doubts, but he motioned with his hand toward one of the seats behind her. Rosey sat slowly, never taking her eyes off Nelson as she did.

"You want to hear it?" she asked.

Nelson gave her a half smile, still unwilling to commit himself to speech. It irritated Rosey and she became uncomfortable with his attitude. She pretended to look under his desk. "You have *Christina* Van *Luxall* under there doing some work for you or something?"

Nelson leaned onto his desk and spoke at last. "I don't approve of you interrupting my day, Rosey. I assume you really do have something to say — I'd appreciate it if you would save your humor for your husband and get on with it."

Rosey copied his tone and answered, "Well since I can't *tell* you enough about your precious *Bulldog* — my *husband's* aeroplane, that is — and since everything I draw for you is too simple, then why don't you and I just go out and *look* at the damned thing one night. We could start at Stephen's office and then go to the hangars. Unless the thought of it *frightens* you too much, Mr. Wingate."

Nelson didn't like the idea at first. In fact, it did frighten him, for all he could imagine was being cornered in a hangar by some foolish watchdog or accosted by a bread-line night watchman. But the more he thought of the Bulldog, and its expanding contract, the more he wished to see if he could discover where Boisvert Aviation was going with it. And if the offices at Boisvert were like his, there would be plans out in the open everywhere.

He looked at Rosey. She was still watching him closely. *And what of the complications with you my dear little Rosey?* he wondered. *You're so desperate to get me indebted to you, you poor child. You'd do anything to move into Fairelawn, wouldn't you?*

Rosey didn't like the way he was looking at her. "Well?" she challenged.

"I'll have to think about it," he said, even though he had made up his mind. "We'll talk about it later."

She stood and reached for Nelson's hand to shake it. "Do business with me, Mr. Wingate, and I'll make us both happy." He was more surprised by what she'd said than with the gesture.

"Possibly, child," he answered, "just possibly."

She turned then and walked away, but Nelson stopped her before she opened the door. "And Rosey, dear — don't *ever* come back to my office. I'll have your mother out on the street and you out of my life if you do anything so unimaginative again."

Rosey pulled the door open and left the room. She neither looked back nor answered. Nelson watched her go, following the movement of her hips as she walked past his receptionist and through the outer door.

In spite of it all, he did like her fire. *Damned shame she didn't come from money*, he thought and went back to his work.

Rosey tapped her foot as she waited for the elevator to reach her floor. She stared at the brass arrow as it crawled around the arc to 2 and then 3.

The doors opened and she was face to face with Christina.

Neither moved.

A man behind Christina squeezed past with an "Excuse me," and the elevator operator, sitting on a stool in the front corner, asked, "Something wrong, Miss Van Luxall? You did say 'three', didn't you?"

Rosey didn't like what she felt. Confronting Christina at Fairelawn, in a maid's uniform while *she* was dressed well was one thing, but Christina so obviously outclassed her now that she had to work very hard to bolster her bravado. She felt as if she had just been caught stealing a fork.

Christina stepped from the elevator and stood over Rosey, crowding her.

"Going down,?" Christina asked softly. "Or do you prefer the dumbwaiter — I believe there's one down the hall — for trash." And with her last comment and without waiting to see Rosey's reaction, Christina walked off, obviously headed for Nelson's office.

CHRISTINA

The evening after the encounter at the elevator, Christina decided she would move understanding the relationship between Nelson and Rosey from the back of her mind, to the absolute front.

She bathed, put on her bathrobe and then brewed and poured a huge cup of tea. Finally, she settled into the only comfortable chair in the room. She tucked her legs under her, reached over and turned the knob on the lamp beside her until only one of its four bulbs was lit, and then leaned her head back and stared at the ceiling.

Christina was going to approach the dilemma of Stephen and Rosey and Nelson with the same methodical logic that she had learned to bring to business, and that meant not only scraping past all the superfluous detail until she had the facts, it also meant starting at the beginning — the very beginning.

She set the saucer on her lap and lifted the cup from it, allowing the steam to wash over her face as she prepared to drink. She sipped slowly, taking herself back to The Chimneys and her youth.

Her youth — she was speaking of the passage of years, and it had seemed like a lifetime — her entire lifetime. And then Christina decided to push back further to the fall afternoon when Stephen and his father had come walking down the long driveway at The Chimneys; Phillip Rheiner taking long, carefree strides, his son bouncing playfully on his shoulders.

Christina remembered, and the years fell away and she was there with her sisters, playing on the Grand Lawn.

"Look there!" Abegaile shouted. "It's a man with a boy on his shoulders!" She turned to her sisters to see if they saw, too.

The girls were in front of the manor, playing clock golf, putting into the twelve buried cans surrounding the eccentric base. Christina bent over her ball, trying to concentrate on her second attempt at the fourth can. She stroked with a wooden putter nearly as tall as she and the ball rolled wide of its mark. "Darn!" she said and dropped her club as heavily as she dared. She looked down the road to see what her sister was making such a fuss about.

Little Stephen on his father's shoulders.

The girls giggled to each other. As the two approached, father and son probably, the girls giggled again and poked one another. Abegaile looked shyly from the side of her lowered head and spoke, barely moving her lips. "I bet they'll work here; Papa is still buying people."

Katherine laughed out loud. "Silly! People *work* for him. He pays them. He doesn't *buy* them!"

Christina took another drink of her tea. "Yes he does," she whispered to herself and went back to their encounter.

Stephen's father lowered him from his shoulders, removed his own hat and nudged Stephen to do the same. He then asked, from a respectable distance, "Excuse me, where would I find Mr. Van Lushall?"

Christina and Katherine looked at each other and giggled.

"Van *Luxall!* Van *Lux* all!" Christina said through her laugh, "He's our Papa and he's in the house. She pointed to a side entrance which lead directly to his office.

Abegaile whispered, "Van Lushall", and the three girls smiled and laughed.

Christina retrieved her putter and all three girls started maniacally hitting their golf balls back and forth, laughing and stealing glances at the young boy who now stood boldly watching them.

Stephen's father sank to his haunches and said to his son, wagging his finger in cadence with his speech, "Stand right here, and leave these girls alone, Stephen. I'll be back to get you in a little while." He walked to the door Christina had mentioned, his hat still in his hand. The door was opened, and he entered.

It would be another week before Mr. Van Luxall found a butler and a housekeeper to co-ordinate hiring the help.

As soon as his father was out of sight, Stephen jammed his hat back onto his head. He put his hands into the deep pockets of his baggy pants and nudged a pebble with his shoe.

The girls leaned on their putters and watched him.

"That fun?" Stephen finally asked, looking at Christina.

"It is," Katherine answered.

"Lots of fun," Christina reinforced.

Abegaile smiled at the boy.

They all watched each other a moment more.

"Don't look like it," Stephen said, probably in reaction to not being asked to join them.

And that was the beginning, Christina thought. She drank more of her tea and allowed her thoughts to leave Stephen and remember her sisters. "My God, I miss you," she whispered softly. "Katie, Abbie, I miss you so much!"

Christina put her cup down and closed her eyes. She cried silently and briefly, wiping the tears away from time to time.

"And Mama, where are you now, you poor woman? Are you happy, Mama? Are you happy at last?"

Christina took a deep breath, sniffling as she did. "That's enough!" she commanded herself. "When you're old and have nothing else to think of, you can do this to yourself, but not now."

"We grew up fast, Stephen," she said softly, forcing herself back to the boy. "We all grew up so fast!" Christina stared at the far wall of her room and saw Stephen running in the distance, laughing; for that was how she most often remembered him — full of life, taking each minute and each day as a fresh start, and running from place to place. For Stephen there was always too much to do and not enough time. As he got older he slowed some, but Christian decided it was because he had begun to notice things.

"Look-it here!" Stephen shouted to Abegaile and Katherine and Christina. "Look-it here! This frog's as big as my shoe!" he yelled and the girls ran over to the edge of the lagoon beneath the Octagonal Teahouse.

"I'm up here!" Stephen called until the girls finally realized he was high in the branches of a tree in the Maple Allee. "Eggs! Bird's eggs! There's a bunch of 'em in the nest!"

Always calling to them, always showing them things, teasing them, taking them places.

"There's a little pond back in the woods I bet you never saw! It's got a beaver dam and beavers, too, I bet!"

Christina found that she was smiling to herself as she remembered the three girls following Stephen everywhere they could, once they managed to escape the watchful eyes of the manor.

"And you grew up, too, Stephen," Christina said to her tea. "You grew up, too."

Stephen and the girls entered their early teens and the girls were constantly scandalizing each other with reports of his amorous adventures with the daughters of the help.

"He kissed Rita! I saw him kiss Rita!" Katherine proclaimed without prelude as she entered the room where Christina and Abegaile sat and played a game with cards. No one needed to be told who 'he' was. Only one boy mattered, even though there were always several about the grounds.

Christina thought of the boys who came to the manor to visit her and the twins — the boys who stepped down from long touring cars, holding their mother's or their nanny's hands. And not one of them had a spark of life. They were spoiled, they complained constantly about this scratch or that cut, and they bragged without end about what their fathers had done.

Nelson entered her thoughts, at his mother's side at first, haughty even then, but still the best of the lot. Christina and the girls had sometimes looked forward to his visits, for he was good-looking and interesting, and his appearances did break the monotony of their lessons. The girls knew he was their parents' version of an acceptable husband.

"Do you think one of us will marry Nelson?" Katherine had asked one morning as the girls sat in the Formal Garden and looked at picture books. Christina guessed they were about fifteen or sixteen at the time.

"I bet Christina does," Abegaile had answered shyly.

"Do you think *Stephen* will get married?" Katherine asked next.

Once more, it was Abegaile who answered, softly still, but with more hesitation and regret. "Stephen — will — marry — one of the girls from here," she said, and her sisters knew she meant that he would marry one of the help.

"You were right, Abbie," Christina whispered. "You were so right."

It was as if Christina had now reviewed all of the players sufficiently, for she moved her thoughts closer to the present. She didn't think of her sisters again, knowing that thinking of their deaths would hopelessly sadden and at the same time sidetrack her.

Rosey, Stephen, and Nelson. She repeated, their names an incantation to force her thoughts into an explanation of their actions since they'd grown up. *Rosey, Stephen, and Nelson.*

And then Christina stopped herself once more. She had wanted to explore her feelings for Stephen and she wasn't ready to bunch him with the others.

Do I love him? Was it all childish? She closed her eyes and remembered the night at the hidden garden and as she thought of it, there was nothing childish about it. It had been an answer to a dream she had never dared to have. It had been moments of happiness beyond her imagination, of love and trust, and of sharing.

Interrupted by the image of her father. Spoiled by him and taken away.

She started to think of the man but forced her mind back to Stephen and their relationship. She smiled to herself as she thought the word. *Relationship.* It had been so brief, could it truly have been as significant as she remembered? And had it been the same for him?

Christina knew she could only answer for herself and even that would be difficult.

And if he walked into this room right now and asked you to marry him, would you? If he wore the coarsest clothes and his language was halting and full of mistakes? Was it a boy you loved? Can he be a man for you, now?

At first Christina thought he could not. At first she believed that Stephen would have grown into someone she could not care for, but she did not delude herself for long. Stephen couldn't possibly mature into a man as refined as Nelson, and he would probably make many mistakes, but beneath it all she knew he would still be sensitive and honest and caring. He would still hold her carefully and listen to her and laugh with her, and he could not lose the ambition and the strength he brought to life.

No, he wouldn't be Nelson, and Christina was glad.

And what of Rosey? Stephen's wife. The mother of his child?

And with those thoughts Christina approached the questions she desperately wanted answered. *Would Stephen have married Rosey had she not been pregnant?* The answer was easy. *No.*

Did Rosey bear Stephen's child — or was it Nelson's? Christina only asked the question; she knew she could not know the answer.

If the child were Stephen's, what does that mean? Christina didn't like her answer. If Rosey had given Stephen a child, and he had married her because he was the father, then Stephen had inexorably slipped from her life and she could not imagine a way that things could be put to right again. If that were the case then the actions of the fates would have done more than separate them for a handful of years — their lives would have turned to paths which could never again converge except for the briefest moments.

If only Rosey knew the answer, then how could she force that information from her — provided Rosey knew. And how would she know if Rosey were telling the truth?

It was such a tangle to Christina, and so full of traps that she turned to Nelson in the hope that by exploring his relationship with Rosey she might find a clue. And then a new possibility hit her. *What if Nelson knew?* It was possible — under the right circumstances — that he could know who had helped to conceive the child. Of course, he could be more duplicitous than Rosey, and there was absolutely no reason for him to be honest with Christina. There could only be one answer from him. *No.*

And then something happened that Christina didn't expect. Her mind returned to Nelson and she thought of the things she had heard him say relative to Stephen and the Bulldog and Boisvert Aviation, and the more she thought of it the less well his hatred settled until she really questioned it, really explored why Nelson Wingate, still wealthy beyond imagination, could allow himself to be so centered on his hatred for a person like Stephen, regardless of the aviation industry and regardless of the contracts and the Air Races, and as she pursued her thoughts, the answer to all of Christina's questions became crystal clear.

In the end she didn't need Rosey or Nelson to answer her. In the end she knew that the child had to be Nelson's, and that both Rosey and Nelson knew it, and she also knew what Rosey could not — that the red haired girl had a stronger hold on Nelson than she imagined.

Christina felt a happiness which permeated her soul and allowed her love for Stephen, the love she had stupidly questioned earlier, to fill her body and consume her.

"Stephen," she whispered, "you play with people who think nothing of using or destroying you. You've stumbled into a game where everyone is armed but you."

Christina allowed herself to feel nothing but Stephen, and to think of nothing but love.

Later, before she rose and went to her bed, she made a promise to herself and to the life she was determined they would have at last.

"It's for me to bring us together, Stephen. It is for me to overcome both Nelson and Rosey, and I will."

ROSEY AND STEPHEN AND NELSON

Nelson waited a week before he approached Rosey to discuss her plan. He had decided to go with her to Boisvert Aviation, in the belief that he might find something, somewhere, which held the key to Stephen's downfall and the ultimate ascension of Wingate Aviation. His problem was timing, for the longer he waited, the better his chances were of knowing everything about Boisvert Aviation's plans. But the longer he waited, the less time he had for his own firm to either counter the Boisvert advances or possibly sabotage them.

He had not told Rosey of the latter, and he wasn't certain he ever would. If access to the Boisvert airfield were as easy as she intimated, Nelson suspected he would make more than one visit.

In the end, Nelson decided to wait until the second month before the races.

In the meantime, Rosey was beside herself with anticipation. Her greatest fear was not that they'd be caught, for she felt that if they were it would weld Nelson to her, their complicity an unbreakable bond. Her fear was that they would get there and there would be really nothing for him to learn, that the Bulldog was what *she* saw it as — an ugly but fast aeroplane.

A week before Rosey and Nelson were to go to the field, he had her carry out a subterfuge.

Rosey visited Stephen at Boisvert Aviation, walking with him as he passed in and out of various hangars, inspecting welds, offering suggestions, and keeping the pressure on an already overworked and exhausted production team. It had been decided that both Jim Schmidt and Stephen would fly in the air races, and therefore Boisvert Aviation was preparing *three* planes to compete — one for each of the pilots, and a back-up craft, and consequently, all of the problems were tripled.

"It seems like a waste of money," Rosey offered as they stood beneath one of the entries and Stephen watched the men working on the retractable landing gear and the wing profile modifications. The huge engine was off of the aeroplane, scattered in at least a thousand pieces on a series of work tables forming a semi-circle around the plane.

Stephen laughed at Rosey's comment and then looked at her warily.

"You sound like Smitty — you two aren't up to something are you?"

Rosey looked disgusted, and Stephen was sorry for his remark. He had meant it in jest but Rosey's response was too serious and too full of superiority to support his lighter mood.

"Can't you ever just take a joke, Rosey? Do you have to always make fun of somebody or act like they're so far beneath you?" He spoke quietly, afraid one of the workers might overhear him, but he was so angry he refused to wait until they were home.

"You're the one who brought up your holy, Mr. Schmidt, not me." And then Rosey lowered her voice too and brought her face close to Stephen's.

"He's not Jacob Boisvert, Stephen, and you can't make him take his place. Quit kidding yourself."

Stephen tilted his head back and let out a long sigh. He studied the roof of the hangar and asked himself again if it would ever end.

Rosey watched him and cursed herself. She hadn't intended to start a fight, that wasn't the idea at all, but she hated Stephen so much anymore, she could barely stand to be around him.

Finally, Stephen turned to her once more.

"Why don't you go home now, Rosey. I don't know why you wanted to come here in the first place if all you want to do is fight."

Rosey stared at him without speaking. Actually she had accomplished what she had intended and it didn't make any difference if she stayed any longer. She narrowed her eyes and then walked away from him and out the hangar door.

Two mechanics watched her go. They looked at Stephen and finally stole a glance at each other. Stephen Rheiner was a cracker-jack pilot, a brilliant designer, and a hell of a boss, but not one of them would trade places with him as long as it meant living with his shrew of a wife.

Stephen grimaced and then forced himself to think of little Billy.

That evening Rosey broke their dinner silence.

"You have to take me back to the field tonight."

She glared at Stephen, daring him to deny her.

"Why?" he said carefully, a forkful of food halfway to his mouth.

"I left my purse there somewhere — it's either in your office or one of the hangars."

Stephen almost asked her how she could forget her purse and not realize it until so much later, but he remembered their fight and let the question drop.

"I'll look for it in the morning."

"Like hell you will;" Rosey countered. "I don't trust one person out there. We'll get it tonight."

Stephen then thought of the prospect of Rosey accompanying him to the field the next day, and her plan to go to the field after dinner was a lot more appealing.

"Alright," be said, "but we're taking Billy — I was going to spend some time with him after dinner."

Rosey sneered at him. "How about *Smitty* and *Mrs. Boisvert?* Want to dig up anyone *else* to take with us?"

Even Rosey couldn't believe what she was saying. Her hatred was choking her beyond reason and she knew that if the Air Races had been any further into the future, she wouldn't have been able to wait.

Stephen pushed his chair back from the table and stood.

"Let's go — Billy can stay next door until we get back — I'll play with him tonight."

There was a light at the front door of Stephen's office which Rosey hadn't noticed before. She looked around as Stephen fumbled with his key. The door at each of the hangars was lighted, also.

They went into the building and Rosey pretended to look for her purse when in fact she was watching Stephen.

He went into his office and she heard him open a desk drawer. "You find it?" he called out to her.

"No," she answered simply and Stephen came out with a wad of keys on a ring.

He led her through the darkness to the hangars without another word. It wasn't until they were in the next to the last building that Rosey found what she was looking for.

"Here it is," she said, pulling her purse from behind a stack of wheels. She preceded Stephen out of the hangar and into the night. Stephen followed slowly, turning twice to see where she had retrieved her purse, and wondering how it had gotten there in the first place. He switched off the hangar lights and locked the door behind him.

They rode back to their home in silence.

"No guards, no watchmen, a few locks, and I know where he keeps the keys." Rosey spoke into the telephone and pictured Nelson sitting behind his desk. As the day approached he seemed to be distancing himself from her and Rosey felt that the opposite should have been the case.

"Good — and you're sure next Tuesday will be no problem?"

"I already told him I'm staying with my mother for a few days."

There was an extended silence and then Nelson repeated, simply, "Good."

Rosey waited for Nelson to speak again, and when he didn't, she slammed down her receiver.

He held the telephone away from him and looked at it and smiled.

"Oh, Rosey, I'm not sure I want to try to control your fire. I'm not sure at all." He put the receiver back on its cradle and patted his desk lightly with the flats of his hands. He looked back at the telephone and whispered, "And do you know, dearest Rosey, how easy it would be for those flames to consume you?" Nelson put his hands together, the fingertips touching, and examined the space between. "I think not, clever one."

Rosey went to Fairelawn Tuesday morning. Stephen was glad to have her gone. He took Billy with him to the airfield and had one of his secretaries watch him while he met with Jim Schmidt.

Stephen walked up behind him as he was bent over a set of plans, studying them intently. Stephen knew they were of the new retractable landing gear and he was anxious to learn how things were going.

"Well?" Stephen asked.

Jim didn't look up when he responded; instead, he lowered his head to his work. "Right here," he said, indicating a set lever, " I thought we might have a problem, and we do. Sometimes they just won't lock in the up position, and then sometimes they will, but they won't release to be lowered." He turned to Stephen. "There are so many factors working to force us away from a simple design and there are too many problems to overcome — vibration, severely limited space for the struts and wheels to tuck into — and at the same time we're paring away more and more of the strengthening members in the airframe. We're just inviting disaster, Mr. Rheiner. I still think we should scrap the idea of pulling up the wheels on the P-22 and make them an integral part of the design of our next craft."

Stephen had heard it all before, and while he agreed in principle, economics and political considerations kept him from going along with his friend.

He brought his head closer to the plans. "Can you see what's happening to keep it from operating properly?"

"Not really, I think we may have to take more skin off of the wings and the fuselage before we can be certain."

"Can't do it — we don't have time. Let's take a look. I'll meet you in the hangar."

Stephen left the drawing room and went back to his office to get his son.

"Come on, Billy. Let's go look at Daddy's toys."

The boy smiled at the word 'toys' and scooted off the lap of the woman who was holding him. He toddled across to his father. Stephen scooped him up, whirled him around once, and carried the boy out of his office.

"We'll be right back," he called to his secretaries. "We have a little work to do together." As he proceeded to the hangar where he was to meet Jim Schmidt, Stephen hefted Billy onto his shoulders.

They went to hangar three where they found Jim Schmidt waiting. One of the Bulldog prototypes was in the center. The aeroplane was an additional several feet higher than normal, for it was supported under its wings and tail section by sturdy wooden tripods. Almost comically, there was a section of thick rope looped several times from a tail brace on the Bulldog to a hefty timber joist at the side of the hangar. Stephen eyed the arrangement suspiciously as he approached.

"Looks like we're going to pull the hangar down on top of us!"

"Well, the whole place vibrates to beat the band, and the sound is deafening, but I don't know what else we can do unless you want to move the operation outside and lash her to a tree."

Stephen shook his head and then lowered himself to Billy's level. "Stay out of trouble for a few minutes; Daddy'll only be a minute." Then Stephen stood and called to one of the workers at a workbench at the side of the hangar. "Lank, keep an eye on Billy — don't let him fly off in anything, okay?"

The man smiled, gave Stephen a raised thumb, and called the boy over to him.

Jim Schmidt crawled under the prototype. Stephen followed. Unlike any of the other Bulldogs, this prototype was unique. First, they had lengthened the cockpit area and squeezed an extra seat behind the pilot. "Selling by inverting the stomach," Jim Schmidt called it, for the seat was used to take visiting brass from the Army Air Corps and influential politicians for hair-raising rides in the Bulldog. And it had worked.

Recently, the outboard and semi-rigid landing gear apparatus had been stripped away and various versions of retractable wheels and struts had been tried. The fourth attempt — the current attempt — seemed to have the most potential.

Stephen eyed the wheels now tucked into the underside of the wings. Little more than half of each of the wheels was actually within the wing.

"Damn them," Stephen said, indicating the protruding wheel bumps. "We need smaller tires that can take the beating they get on landing.

"Let's just call Wingate Tire and A. and have them whip us up a set."

The two men laughed briefly while Stephen raised his head until it was within inches of the underside of the wing. "Will they come down now?"

"Nope."

Stephen pounded on one of the wheels. "Can you see what's hanging up?"

"You try; I can't see it, Lefty can't see it, and Burns can't see it. We set up a light in the fuselage. Everything was working fine until we buttoned up the inspection panels. But nothing's hitting — I'd swear to it."

Stephen climbed into the cockpit head first and crawled and pulled himself past the rudder bar and the cables and wires until even his feet disappeared from sight.

Billy watched his father climb into the aeroplane — it looked like fun. Lank, the man taking care of him, had let the child escape from his line of sight and at the same time had become involved in a tricky part of the job he was doing. Billy toddled off toward his father's aeroplane.

The light that Jim Schmidt had mentioned was hot and bright and the sharp shadows it cast obscured what Stephen was trying to see. "Have you pulled the release?" he yelled out to Jim Schmidt.

"Three times — I'll try it again. I'll tell you when." He climbed up the ladder by the front cockpit and leaned into it until he felt the wheel-release handle. "You ready?"

Stephen wedged himself under a crossbar, his head painfully pressed against its sharp edge. He could just see the locking lever on the right strut.

Billy heard the men calling to each other. He wobbled by the right wing stanchion and continued under the wing. He laughed when he heard his father's muffled voice.

"Try it."

Jim Schmidt pulled the lever.

Nothing happened.

"Again," Stephen shouted.

Billy stopped and looked up at the huge black wheel over his head. He reached up to touch it.

Jim Schmidt pulled the lever.

Stephen strained to see what was moving. The lever still didn't budge.

"Again."

Jim Schmidt pulled the lever.

There was movement this time. The lever slid out of the way and both wheels arced heavily out from their pouches in the wings.

Billy looked over his head. The huge black wheel raced down toward him. Startled, he fell to a sitting position as the tire brushed within inches of his head and jolted into a locked, wheels-down position.

He pushed himself back up to his feet and touched the still vibrating tire with his finger tip.

Lank heard the landing gear of Bulldog snap down with a thud. In a panic, he realized he had lost track of Stephen's son. He saw him under the aeroplane and ran quickly and quietly to the boy. He whisked him back to his work station.

"You little devil — you're gonna get us both in trouble. Now stay put."

"Raise 'em!" Stephen called out.

"She'll be noisy as hell, boss," Jim Schmidt warned. He climbed into the front cockpit, his feet to the sides of where Stephen lay.

The gear was designed to be raised by hydraulic pressure generated by the engine when it was running.

"Wish to hell I'd the room to stop up my ears!" Stephen called back.

Jim Schmidt smiled and pulled two small strips of cloth from his shirt pocket and stuffed them into his.

"We're starting the engine!" he yelled to the others in the hangar.

Lank turned, located Billy and picked him up. "Gonna be real loud, young fella — cover yer ears like this."

Lank and Billy played the cover-your-ears game.

"CLEAR!"

The latest Bulldog engine came from the factory with an electrical starter. Everybody was in love with it.

The three other workmen in the hangar sauntered over to Lank and their boss's son.

"CLEAR!" one of them answered.

"CONTACT!"

Jim Schmidt engaged the starter and the massive propellor wheezed a quarter of a circle and then stopped. He tried again and this time the engine caught and started. The entire aeroplane immediately started to vibrate madly, magnifying the noise for Stephen and beating his head and body steadily.

Jim Schmidt gave the engine more throttle and both he and Stephen felt the aeroplane shift forward on its stanchions, straining at the rope which was keeping it from moving any farther forward.

One of the men by Billy and Lank ran over to swing open the hangar doors. The exhaust fumes were already noticeable.

The noise frightened the child and he struggled to get out of Lank's grasp, and as he did, he realized he didn't know where his father was.

Jim Schmidt engaged the wheels-up switch and the twin wheels began to rotate slowly toward the aeroplane.

Billy saw the movement and remembered his father's voice from inside the roaring machine. Lank had lowered himself to his haunches and had the child in front of him, his arms wrapped loosely around him.

Billy ducked under them and raced as fast as his tiny legs would carry him toward the aeroplane. Lank was looking up at the time and was in the process of shifting his weight to a different leg and didn't notice at first.

Jim Schmidt caught the movement out of the corner of his eye. He then realized that the child was heading toward the front of the aeroplane. He waved one arm wildly to attract Lank's attention. Lank saw him, saw the boy, and sprang after him. Simultaneously, Lank and one of the men started sawing at their throats.

Jim Schmidt frowned and then slammed his hand forward to the kill switch.

Lank knew he couldn't get to the child in time and he could see that he was heading edge-on for the propellor.

Billy stopped under the wing where the wheel was once more raised. Oddly, he put his hands to his ears just as Jim Schmidt shut the engine down. The man who had opened the hangar doors ran up to him, lifted him and jogged him back to Lank.

"What's the matter? Are the wheels secured? Why'd you shut down?" the voice inside the fuselage called.

Jim Schmidt felt Stephen edging back into the cockpit. The propeller was just stopping and one of the cylinders gave out a long 'shwoosh'. Jim Schmidt climbed out to give Stephen room to get out also.

"The wheels are up," he said calmly to his boss. "There's too damn much noise in here to think, so I shut her down. There's got to be a better way."

Later, when Stephen and Schmidt left the hangar, Stephen now carrying his son, he was startled at the dirty look Schmidt gave to Lank as they passed.

"Thanks, Lank," Stephen said to the man who was now staring sheepishly at his feet. Stephen looked at Jim Schmidt who simply shrugged his shoulders.

Jim Schmidt rolled over his boss's confusion.

"If God meant for us to raise landing gear, he'd have done the same for birds."

Even as Jim Schmidt spoke he realized his error.

"He did," Stephen answered.

"Well, you can bet he designed the gear first and the bird later!"

Stephen and Schmidt laughed and Billy enjoyed the view from his father's shoulders.

The sun set late and Rosey nervously paced Nelson's bedroom. He emerged from the bathroom and walked past her without speaking.

"How soon?" she asked.

"We'll leave in another hour. Don't be so anxious."

Later, Nelson asked, "And you're certain he doesn't go out there in the middle of the night to fondle his precious Bulldog?"

Rosey laughed bitterly. "Never."

"Quite embarrassing if he decides to tonight."

What Rosey had no way of knowing was that he frequently drove out to the airfield the nights she stayed at Fairelawn and Billy was at his unofficial nanny's.

Stephen was alone at their home. He sat at the kitchen table and studied the model he'd had made of the landing gear apparatus.

It was a warm summer evening but Nelson left up the top to his roadster. Rosey watched the headlights brighten the road ahead of them.

Stephen put the model down and walked out to their front porch. The lights were out in the other houses in his neighborhood. The night was noisy. Crickets rasped and two cats howled in the bushes beside the garage.

He looked up at the stars and thought about the Bulldog and then Christina. He'd overheard that she was working for Nelson Wingate now and the irony of it was bitter. Once more it appeared she had slipped from him. He expected to hear any day that they were getting married.

Wingate Tire and Aviation. He'd learned that they were fielding a racer too and that didn't surprise him in the least. He sensed Nelson's challenge and looked forward to the race. He wondered as he stood if he were more anxious to beat the man who had insulted him and Mr. Boisvert so many years ago, or the man who was now in control of Christina's life. He remembered angrily where Rosey was spending the night.

Nelson leafed through file after file in the outer office.

Requisition forms. Inventories. Orders.

He couldn't believe Rosey didn't know a damned thing other than the whereabouts of the keys.

He had placed a desk light on the file cabinet he was rifling.

"For God's sake, Rosey — where does he keep the plans?"

"How would I know — probably in Jim Schmidt's office," she answered angrily, trying to cover her fear. She barged into another office, this one much larger, with two drafting tables. There were technical drawings everywhere, including on the floor.

"Jesus Christ, why didn't you bring me here first?" Nelson whined. He walked quickly to each of the tables, leafing through oversized sheets of paper, shuffling them aside and studying what was in front of him. He looked up at the overhead light. He was angry that Rosey had turned it on but he refused to turn it off now and switch on one of the smaller lamps.

To hell with it.

The more he looked, the more interesting the drawings became.

"Retractable landing gear," he mumbled.

"I *told* you that," Rosey responded with her hands on her hips. "Weren't you *listening?*"

Nelson grabbed some blank paper and began sketching what he saw. Later he pulled out sheaves of drawings and explanations of engine modifications and then wing cutaways and profiles. Some of the plans he copied and some he rolled up to take with him.

When they left the office for the hangars, Nelson dropped a pile of papers and a thick roll of drawings through the open window and onto the front seat of his car.

Rosey kept looking over her shoulder and jumping with every sound.

They walked quickly through the first two hangars. At the third, Nelson couldn't get enough of the modified prototype. The landing gear was down and the underside of the fuselage had much of its covering removed. Nelson traced the hydraulic lines and gearing from the earlier drawings. "This has all been changed," he said to himself, realizing that the plans he'd seen earlier must have been preliminary.

Rosey crowded behind him. There were too many dark corners in the hangar and too many shadows. The only light was the small one which Nelson carried. As she hovered near Nelson she smelled his cologne. Before long she was not thinking of aeroplanes or Stephen or of the dark. She rested her hand lightly in Nelson's back and then began to move it slowly.

He didn't notice at first, but when he did he knew that fear was charging Rosey.

Stephen Rheiner's wife on Stephen Rheiner's aeroplane. The thought was irresistible.

He took her hand and walked her to the wooden ladder leading to the wing above them.

"On the wing," he said and she knew what he meant. She pulled her dress over her head and then took off her slip and her underclothes. She heard Nelson undoing his belt and then heard him unfasten his pants.

He switched off the light and guided Rosey up the ladder, holding the sides of her hips as she climbed. She moved onto the wing, feeling ahead of her with her hand, the thin, painted plywood cool beneath her. Nelson was beside her then and soon she was on her back.

A breeze rippled the corrugated roof of the hangar and Rosey felt the ribs of the aeroplane wing against her spine.

Stephen turned out the lights in the living room and closed the door behind him. He tossed the key to the old Battleship Roadster from hand to hand.

At first it wouldn't start, but then it did and he backed it out onto the street in front of their home. He thought of Billy asleep as he drove down the street.

Lank took another swallow of bootleg whiskey. He was still shaken from his day at the hangar and he was ashamed that he'd almost gotten Mr. Rheiner's son hurt. *Killed!* he thought and clumsily tipped the last of the burning liquid down his throat. He lined the little bottle up with the others. *Dammit, I got to do something to make up for it!*

It was as appealing to Rosey as it was to Nelson. *Fuck this aeroplane! Fuck this aeroplane!* she chanted silently in rhythm with his thrusts.

Lank stumbled down the stairs of his front porch to his old Model T. He leaned against the radiator and half-heartedly cranked the engine and then rested, nearly dozing when he did. He awoke with a start and finally succeeded in twirling the four cylinder to life.

He had no bands left in reverse, so he swung a wide loop in the back yard, awakening a dog, and weaved out his driveway, bumping down to the street, his mongrel nipping at the rear wheel for a quarter of a mile.

Stephen took the long way to the airfield, stopping once at an intersection which would have led him back through town. He had just jogged his car over the trolley tracks and remembered his ride from The Chimneys to the Boisvert airfield. He was sorely tempted to drive out to The Chimneys.

CHRISTINA

Christina surprised herself when she continued working for Nelson Wingate. Her first impulse had been to quit and go to Stephen, but she knew she really didn't have enough to bring to him yet, and so she decided to wait, certain that something would happen — an opportunity would present itself. And she was also certain that she wouldn't have to wait years.

Nelson had fallen in love with the new aircraft, and the powerplant was ready to be fitted onto at least one of them. The prototype was scheduled to fly in another month and while it was a very tight schedule, Christina was confident she and her crew would meet it.

I must be crazy, she thought every time she realized she was actually advancing Nelson's interests; but somehow she believed it would lead to his undoing and at the same time, she was anxious to prove herself; determined to accomplish what she had set out to do. *Everything* she had set out to do.

Twice she had nearly driven out to the Boisvert Aviation facilities. In fact, she had gotten so close once that she could see the hangars in the distance. "Oh, Stephen," she had murmured, "if you only knew what's going on around you."

She read that two more of her father's businesses had failed and that another was precariously close to shutting down, and she had been absolutely unmoved by the news, feeling neither happiness nor sadness, having so insulated herself that it was just another event. Her bank had never re-opened its doors, making it one of the six in the city which had failed immediately. Federal authorities were sifting through the incredible aftermath, but it appeared that the institution had not only made monumentally risky loans, all of which had defaulted, but it had skewed its own portfolio with absurdly aggressive and even leveraged stock positions so that in the end, it was a house of worthless paper.

Christina did decide that after the madness of the air races had passed, she would drive out to The Chimneys. If her father were there she would visit with him, if not, she would walk around the grounds once more. It was calling to her and she wasn't even sure she could wait that long.

STEPHEN AND ROSEY AND NELSON AND LANK

When Stephen pulled up to his office his lights momentarily flashed over the other vehicle. He reversed around so that they were once more on the side of the car. At first he couldn't place it, but once he did he looked around quickly. There were no lights except for those at the various doors.

He went into his office, moving quietly and carefully as he did, allowing the light outside of the door to illuminate his path. When he discovered his keys were missing he retraced his steps to his car. He stood at its side briefly, trying to decide where to go next. He stared at each of the hangars, and then instinctively walked toward hangar three. As he neared it he saw the door was ajar and a faint light he hadn't noticed earlier was just visible.

He stepped into the cavernous hangar and reached immediately for the light switch to his left. The hangar flooded with white light and Stephen shielded his eyes and looked around. At first he thought it was empty but then he saw the tipped ladder by the prototype, and in the shadow of the wing he made out the outline of a fallen figure.

Stephen walked to it slowly, looked behind him and to the side as he did. He had a feeling that there was at least one other person in the building with him and the body, and that that person was watching him.

He kneeled beside Clarence Lank. The man's head was to the side and it lay in a spreading pool. Stephen lowered his ear to Lank's chest and when he did he smelled the mixture of alcohol and blood. The man's heart was still but his body was not as cool as Stephen had expected.

He looked behind him and then searched the shadows in the hangar.

"What the hell were you doin' here?" Stephen asked the prone figure. He looked him over again and then thought back to when he had seen Smitty give Lank a dirty look as they were leaving the hangar.

"What's goin' on?" he asked and got back to his feet.

There were police and people from the newspaper. Stephen refused to allow the police to take the body to the morgue in the Black Maria that had just pulled into the hangar.

"He's a man, goddamn it;" he swore, "either get an ambulance out here and let him ride with dignity, or I'll take him myself."

One of the detectives who had roughly twisted Lank's head around to examine the wound at the back of his head looked up at Stephen.

"You Rheiner?"

Stephen nodded.

"You want to tell me what happened out here? I gotta tell you I can't prove it, but this don't look like no bump from a fall to me." He dropped Lank's head roughly to the floor and wiped his hands on a cloth he produced from his back pocket.

"This bird an 'alky'?"

Stephen didn't answer at first, then he said, "He drank some, sure, who doesn't?" He didn't know why he was lying; Lank was a good man but he lost a lot of time coming in late or not showing up at all. He'd tried going on the wagon several times, but he kept going back to it. Stephen and Jim Schmidt had just argued about it a few days earlier.

"He drinks again, send him down the road," Schmidt had insisted, but Stephen wouldn't do it.

"He'll kill himself if I do that, Smitty — where's your heart? Times are bad enough without causing more trouble."

"I've never seen a boozer that wasn't trouble," Jim Schmidt said and then refused to discuss it further.

"These keys belong to him?" the detective asked, indicating the clump of keys near where the body lay.

Stephen didn't have to look closely. "Yeh, sure."

"Why was this man here in the middle of the night? Why are you here in the middle of the night?" And then before Stephen could hope to answer either of the man's questions, he continued, the accusation thick, "Why were *you two* here in the middle of the night?"

"I come here any damn time I want, and Lank must have come in to do something he forgot."

Stephen and the detective locked eyes until one of the police told them an ambulance was on the way.

Rosey simmered. Nelson squeezed the steering wheel hard with both hands. Neither had spoken for the first several miles they drove through the darkness.

Nelson didn't know what to do next. Rosey had killed a man. And he had been there with her.

It was Rosey who first saw Lank's head rise above the wing as he climbed the ladder. He had stood beneath the wing for several minutes and listened, and then allowed his drunken wonder and curiosity to tempt him into taking a closer look. Rosey's head was to the side and not more than two feet away from the dark glassy eyes that swayed before her.

She had screamed at first but it had come at a time when Nelson mistook it for an indication of his prowess. Then Rosey had shoved him off of her.

"There! There! There's someone there!" She pointed as she insisted, and her finger surprised Lank. He shifted back too quickly and lost his balance and crashed to the floor. Nelson saw him just as he disappeared below the wing. He climbed down on a ladder near the cockpit and hastily put on his pants before he kneeled over the fallen man.

"He's just unconscious," he said to Rosey who was now down also and pulling on her own clothing. Nelson was trying to think of what to do next. He didn't know if the man had really seen him, or if there was someone with him, or if he had recognized Nelson's car, or what. He dressed quickly. Rosey was searching around beneath the aeroplane wing to be certain they didn't leave anything.

"I've got to see if he's alone," Nelson whispered and left Rosey. He checked outside, located Lank's car and then came to the hangar. He turned on the overhead lights as he entered. There beneath the Bulldog's wing he saw Rosey over the fallen man. She had twisted the body so that his face was on the hangar floor. Her right arm was raised and too late Nelson saw that she was wielding something that looked like an oversized wrench.

"ROSEY, STOP!" he called to her in unison with the blow.

She struck Lank with all of her strength.

The shock and the retreating life convulsed his body twice.

They were close to Fairelawn when Nelson spoke.

"My God, Rosey, I could have given him enough money to get out of town. He was a goddamned drunk. He wouldn't have caused any trouble — not if we payed him."

Although Nelson was speaking with all the conviction he could muster, he wasn't convinced of what he said.

Neither was Rosey.

"You make me sick," she hissed. "Just remember, *we* did it Nelson, it's just the same as if you'd hit him, too."

Nelson turned to her. There was really no way he could extricate himself and the thought made him ill.

Rosey shook her head. "'They'll think he got pie-eyed and fell. What are you worried about?" She was excited, still flushed from the sex and smugly triumphant.

"Jesus, Rosey, we have half of you husband's aeroplane plans right here with us!"

"So? They're what you want, aren't they? Make up your damned mind."

They didn't speak again until they pulled up behind Fairelawn. Rosey waited until Nelson had shut off the engine. The significance of the evening had truly settled in for both of them. Rosey had seen her chance and taken it.

"It's us now, Nelson. You got what you wanted and so have I. After the races — after enough time passes — I'm moving in, and so is our son."

Nelson's stomach was still churning. He couldn't believe what Rosey was saying, and then he did.

"I'm getting a divorce, Nelson. And we're getting married."

A damned aeroplane — this whole mess is over a goddamned aeroplane and a drunk!

Nelson intuitively knew that he couldn't fight Rosey — not now — not after what had happened. Of course, he could deny anything she said, and it would be her word against his, but he thought it through and knew that wouldn't work either.

Marry Rosey? Marry Rosey? And then he phrased it differently. *Take Stephen Rheiner's wife?* and when he thought of it that way, he believed perhaps he could, after all.

"We'll see, Rosey," he said as he gathered up the plans and led her into the manor, continually looking over his shoulder as he did.

CHRISTINA AND FRIENDS

The papers told the story on page eighteen. "Drunk Takes Last Dive On Bootleg Gin." And that was just about it.

While the incident didn't sound right to Stephen, he didn't know where to turn, but when Christina heard about it *she* couldn't turn away. It smelled of Rosey or Nelson and she couldn't force herself to think otherwise. How a drunk could have gotten into the middle of it she had no idea, but it sounded like he'd stumbled there.

Christina was still very much isolated in her life. She had already lost touch with Marilee, her friend at Fairelawn. Christina reviewed her last year and tried to discover someone she could turn to for help. When she finished she had decided on two persons, and one was Marilee. The other was a total stranger. She called him, introduced herself and simply said that she wished to meet him for a cup of coffee. He was busy, but a bachelor, and warily agreed. Her first inclination was to meet with the two of them immediately and simultaneously, but further thought convinced her that it would be wiser to stagger the meetings slightly.

Christina sat at the corner table of Larry's Brother's and looked up from her cup of tea to the entrance. Mostly couples came in, but the single men who were out eyed Christina and then checked around to see what their competition was. She ignored them all and waited. She felt certain she would know the man when he appeared.

When at last a tall, older gentleman in an expensive suit swept his eyes patiently across the room and then settled on Christina, she knew it was him. He walked confidently to her, extending his hand before he was close enough for her to take it. Christina smiled and held her own hand out to him.

"Christina Van Luxall," she offered, "thanks so much for coming out tonight."

"Miss Van Luxall," he smiled and said, "I've been anxious to meet you ever since you called." He thought a moment and then added, "Actually, I've heard enough about you through the years to have been more than curious a few times." And then, embarrassed with his omission, he amended, "Jim Schmidt, formerly of Wingate Tire and Aviation, currently of Boisvert Bulldog fame." He bowed low in the old world style, waving his hat with a flourish in front of him. He took a chair and then added, "My sympathy for the death of your father — he was a hell of a businessman."

Christina rocked. "I beg your pardon?" But as she said it she knew that it must be true and that she couldn't allow herself to even begin to absorb it.

Jim Schmidt realized what was happening and stumbled forward with an apology.

"I am truly sorry — I should have thought — I have a brother who works at the hospital."

Christina forced herself to speak. "No, my father and I haven't spoken for awhile. We were never close. I don't think anyone knows exactly how to get in touch with me, anyway. I'll see to the details in the morning. Please excuse me briefly."

She stood from the table and insisted her guest sit. Next, she signaled a waitress and when she arrived, passed her on to Jim Schmidt.

"Just a coffee," he said and watched Christina walk away from the table. In the seconds he had known her he was already moved and impressed. She was a tough one with a soft center, who was also prepared to control others. He wasn't so certain that Nelson Wingate had made out so badly when he'd traded him for this woman.

Christina pressed her hands onto the vanity and stared defiantly at herself in the mirror. "You won't cry. You won't cry." she challenged her image. She took a deep breath, filled her lungs and held it. Then when she let the air escape it was very, very slowly and toward the end Christina bit her lip and then said, cold and hard, "You listen to me, Christina Van Luxall — you will get through this meeting — you will get through this night — and you will survive. You're all that is left. You're it. You are alone. You will survive and then, when you're established — when this madness is behind you and you have what you want, you can let it take you. But not a second before."

As she spoke it was not in the abstract, for the 'it' she was referring to was the tidal wave of emotion she felt building in her upper chest and extending behind her and over her head. It was a mixture of hatred and love, and of loneliness and the knowledge of the futility of everything. It was still building and she knew that when she allowed it to fall on her — she could not keep it at bay forever — when she allowed it to swallow her — to take her — it was just possible that she wouldn't surface again.

Christina reached for the faucet handle. She grasped it with her right hand and stared into her own eyes. She twisted it then and when she did she was aware that she was attempting to rotate the handle clockwise, in counter-motion to the way it was intended to operate.

At first she brought just a little pressure to it but then she centered her resolve on that handle while she continued to stare at herself. She brought more and more pressure to bear until her fingers whitened and the butt of the handle pressed painfully into the palm of her hand. Harder and harder she torqued the lever and still she kept her face clear of emotion and her eyes defied her until there was a solid metallic snapping and the handle broke free in her hand, the brass stem sheered from its base.

She left the room then, the handle still in her hand and returned to the table where Jim Schmidt idly rotated his coffee cup in its saucer and watched her approach.

The woman who returned was the cut glass version of the one who had left and he was not so much impressed as he was in awe of the emotional strength which now sat opposite him.

"I need your help," she said simply, her voice level, and Jim Schmidt was prepared to do anything she asked.

And that's exactly what he said.

"Why?" she returned, "Why will you do anything I ask when you don't know me and you have no idea what's on my mind?" She sat in straight silence as she waited for him to explain.

He didn't hesitate.

"Miss Van Luxall, life is far too short and seldom more than mildly interesting. Recently I have been working with an extraordinary young man on a project that is far more successful than it has any right to be. We aren't building aeroplanes out there — we're building dreams, and if that isn't unusual enough, we're not building one man's dream, we're each building our own and it is the most incredible goddamned experience I've ever had in my life. It's like the awareness of what a man can do, of what I can do, has been awakened.

"These minutes I've spent with you have made me sure that there isn't just an extraordinary young man in this town. And so I'm being one hundred percent when I say, 'I'll do anything I can to help you.' Why wouldn't I? We both know you won't ask me to rob a bank — " he chuckled at that thought, " — they're all empty anyway! Seriously, Miss Van Luxall."

"Call me Christina, please."

But he couldn't.

"Seriously, Miss Van Luxall, I don't have a thing to fear and I have a feeling my life is going to take another step upward in both interest and education."

He stopped, took a long drink of coffee, and then asked, "What can I do for you?"

Christina looked at the man who had joined her and wished that he had been her father.

"Well," she began, "I have a dozen little stories to tell you, some of them very personal, some of them about business, and some of them nothing more than suspicions and unsubstantiated fears." She reached across the table and took his hand in both of hers. "I didn't intend to tell you much tonight — I had thought we could just talk about some of these things, but I really must tell you everything."

Christina stopped briefly, trying to put into words what she felt and what she should say next, and when she did speak at last, her words surprised her with their candor and the emotion behind them.

She had put the faucet handle on the table before she reached across. She looked at it and shook her head absently.

Jim Schmidt had been looking at it ever since she had lain it down. "You will be careful with my hand — " he said quietly.

Christina had been miles away. She blinked away her tears and then said, "I'm alone, Mr. Schmidt ... I've lost my natural family ...."

He squeezed her hand back and adopted a daughter before she said another word.

She told him everything, and he listened and came close to crying a few times himself, and then when the subject turned to Nelson Wingate and Stephen Rheiner and the child and Rosey, he was fascinated by the depth and breadth of the drama which seemed to be whirling about the two aircraft firms and this woman in front of him.

When at last she finished, running out of words and things to tell before she had expended her emotional need to confide in him, he sat back for a second and then leaned to her, now holding both her hands, "Christina Van Luxall, let me think of what you've told me. Let me allow it to become a part of me as it has become all of you, and then let's sit down again."

And just when he thought his evening of surprises was over, Marilee came through the café door and Christina introduced her and a new perspective was introduced along with a pleasant and trusting young servant girl.

STEPHEN AND ROSEY

Stephen was so depressed about the accident in hangar three that at first he didn't notice Rosey's new attitude. It was not so much a new attitude as it was an extreme exaggeration of her at her worst. She did nothing but berate Stephen, and did the opposite with Billy — she didn't pay any attention to him. During the same period Stephen was also oblivious to his son, and so the boy suffered.

Stephen was not sure of the accidental nature of Lank's death. But the suspicions he had he attributed to his own unwillingness to accept that another man had died at Boisvert Aviation. It tainted the aircraft, the business, the air races and the entire industry for him. Further, he believed that Jim Schmidt was somehow involved and that was something he didn't wish to confirm. Not only had he acted strangely toward Lank the day of the accident, he had acted peculiarly since. The man had changed and Stephen could think of no explanation. He had come to regard him as his only friend, but now Schmidt distanced himself. He was at the periphery watching and Stephen had the nagging suspicion that he was trying to find out what his employer knew.

Coincidental with his unease with Jim Schmidt, Stephen elevated the man in terms of his flying skills. Schmidt had located a flat stretch of land to the north with two trees at its extremities. Further, he had secured permission from the owners to turn the quiet countryside into a roaring hell. Stephen was not aware of the arrangement until Schmidt had instructed him that they would spend the next weeks practicing for the race.

The crews had come out to the airfield with the first light and had shattered the morning calm with the reverberations of one and then two snapping Bulldogs.

Jim Schmidt took off first, loafing aloft as he usually did, while Stephen, true to form, ripped into the sky angrily. They flew wing to wing until Jim Schmidt signaled Stephen to watch from aloft.

He veered off then, diving toward the field below. He leveled off and began a series of tighter and tighter circuits around the two trees he had chosen earlier. Faster and faster and ever lower he pushed the Bulldog, standing it on its side as it flew around the perimeter. Suddenly he shot back aloft and he was once more on Stephen's wing. He motioned the boy to follow him down and Stephen was immediately game.

They practiced through the early hours, Stephen in awe of the skill of Jim Schmidt, and Schmidt appreciative of the speed with which Stephen settled into the racing pace. They flew back to the airfield for a lunch set out by the crew. Jim Schmidt then outlined some of the maneuvers he wished to teach the boy.

"You're going to have other aeroplanes crawling all over you in the race, son; you'd better get used to being crowded. This afternoon I want you to concentrate on your speed and precision around those trees and try to do it without paying attention to me. Let me worry about us — you concentrate on those trees and the ground. We'll be going too damned fast for you to get out of my way. If we're in this damned race to win, then you'd better learn fast that that's how you fly — to win. From now on you worry about surviving when you drive your car. In the air I want to see the killer in you."

Stephen thought he was exaggerating until they were back at the practice field. He tried to take Jim Schmidt's advice, flying the course with determination, but the first time Jim Schmidt roared by, inches away and then cut in front of him, and he had to buck through Schmidt's prop wash, he thought he would need a change of pants when they landed — if they landed.

And it got worse. Jim Schmidt cut him off. Jim Schmidt swung wide toward him. Jim Schmidt cut his power at the most inopportune moments. Time after time Stephen lost his concentration and went flying off at a tangent, away from the two trees and the fields between, his heart thundering, the sweat pouring from him. But each time he had come back to the fight, trying to make the two trees and the distance between his reason for living. Gradually he came to trust that Jim Schmidt would not crash into him, that he was flying at the picnic, and that worked and he calmed down until he realized that in the race he would have no assurance that the other pilots weren't depending on *him* to get the hell out of *their* way.

Stephen wasn't sleeping well and as he lay in bed he allowed himself to count the number of nights Rosey was spending at Fairelawn. While he had no stomach for a confrontation before the races, he knew that after — if he managed to survive them — there would be some changes made.

He and Jim Schmidt practiced every day for two weeks. They had installed their retractable gear and so far they were working tolerably well. The increased performance and the sleek new lines of the Bulldog convinced Stephen that they had been worth the effort.

The race was eight days away.

Nelson interested both state senators in the accusation that the Boisvert Bulldog was unsafe and underpowered. An investigation was started and the Air Corps put a tentative hold on its final approval for fifty more of the aircraft.

But the recent word to Nelson had been disheartening.

"We can't do a damned thing, Nelson, my friend, without somebody sucking the propellers off those Bulldogs at the Air Races. You prove them slow and we can make a case for their being unreliable. Otherwise, thank you for your contributions, but it's out of our hands."

"Contributions, hell!" Nelson had warned. "You've got stock in Wingate; you've got a future with me!" but he knew they were hog-tied unless the Bulldog ran afoul at the races.

Christina Van Luxall's assurances aside, Nelson was not enthralled with the Wingate entries. The planes would probably be ready, and the pilots he'd hired were supposed to be among the best, but there just wasn't the excitement generated around the project that he had hoped for. It seemed that everything had hit a wall after the incident at Boisvert Aviation.

The incident was a running joke in his office and at the hangars, but it was forced and Nelson came to believe that his people were uncomfortable with both the accident and the need to make light of it. He also had the feeling everyone was watching him.

"Nelson!" Christina Van Luxall called from the end of the corridor. "Can I have a minute with you?"

She was using the same professional, cold, tone she had adopted lately and Nelson found it irritating beyond belief. He waited for her to walk to him and watched her closely as she did.

His latest torment was that he couldn't stop comparing her to Rosey, and in every detail Rosey was the loser.

"Yes?" he said tightly. "Another problem? Another delay?" he asked when both of them knew the project was going along more smoothly than either had expected.

"A detail — we need to schedule the installation of the newer powerplants and nobody is willing to interrupt the practice flights with your hot-shot pilots."

"Oh yes, well, you wouldn't understand the *flying*, aspect of it all, would you Christina — you really are quite earthbound these days, my dear." There was a hatred welling up between the two of them, an undisguised disgust which Nelson attributed to Christina's bitterness over the death of her father and the absolute shambles his fortunes had fallen into. 'Less than worthless' was the consensus regarding the silent factories and the lines of debtors he had left behind.

"Oh, yes; I don't think I ever got a chance to extend my condolences, Christina — your father was quite a character; I'm sure we'll all miss him terribly. I used to enjoy the old billiard room — but that's gone too, of course."

Christina barely heard him. All of her energy was concentrated on uncovering the clue — the chink in the armor — the tell-tale bit of evidence. She had settled into meeting weekly with Marilee and secretly with Jim Schmidt every few days. So far, neither had turned up anything.

The most consistent and newest bother Christina had these days was the plaintive urging by Paget et al that she come to their offices so they might discharge their fiduciary responsibilities. Christina had been brutal on the telephone.

"His fortune is gone, is it not?"

"Well, harrumph, well, yes, indeed, you might boil it down to such a simple, almost *vulgar* summary, Miss Van Luxall, but there are *details* you know — things that *must* be attended to."

"Unpaid fees, no doubt. Thirty days. I'll be in your office in thirty days; send me a letter regarding the time — I'll be there." With a quick "Thank you," she hung up.

She had demanded a private funeral in the shadow of the hulk that was The Chimneys. The Chimneys — she knew that what remained would be lost to her soon enough. *I can wait thirty days before I say goodbye,* she thought and forced her mind to other matters before reality embraced her.

"Yes, yes," Nelson was saying. "We'll do what you suggest, as usual."

She was lost for a moment and then collected her thoughts.

"Good."

She turned and was striding away from Nelson before he could add anything insulting.

Rosey gave Nelson his only respite. Had it not been for the madness of the upcoming air races, he might have been able to accept what the fates had dealt him. Rosey was no Christina Van Luxall, but she did clean up well, and she did warm his bed. And she was *still* Stephen Rheiner's wife.

An off-setting factor was that she now scared him half to death. He had never before encountered a ruthlessness which made his little games pale. Here was a woman who seized an opportunity — life and future consequences be damned. He had joked feebly with her once, that he would henceforth have all wrenches and similar blunt instruments packed, but her response had been a look that brought back images of her poised above that poor drunken fool, the weapon held high, and Nelson was at once sorry he had mentioned it.

And then, as the race day speeded toward them, Nelson reached a decision. He believed his days of controlling Rosey were fast disappearing and he determined to use her strength in a final challenge. He nurtured his courage for two days before he sat with her on the edge of his bed and used his most persuasive powers to lure her into one more act of violence.

Rosey had stared at him long after he had finished, and then slowly she had unbuttoned her blouse and undressed. And then, at the consummate moment she had whispered, "Give me a *real* challenge, you weak bastard," and that, had been that.

ROSEY AND NELSON AND THE BULLDOGS

Nelson studied the Bulldog's plans and searched for the perfect act of sabotage. When at last he found it he went to incredible extremes to make it clear and easy for Rosey. He constructed a miniature version of the aircraft, complete with written instructions, and for three evenings straight he drilled her on what to do and how to do it.

Twice he had taken her to the Wingate hangars late at night and had her crawl over his own aeroplanes as practice. She had been surprisingly clumsy at first, but eventually she learned to handle the required tools with relative ease.

Rosey had learned the two variations of the plan — disable the Bulldogs so they could not possibly enter the race, or disable the Bulldogs so they could not possibly *finish* the race. Rosey and Nelson each preferred a different plan. Rosey's only regret was that Christina Van Luxall would not be flying with Stephen.

Nelson prepared for the possibility that Rosey was discovered in the act.

Rosey prepared for the possibility that she was discovered in the act.

THE DAY BEFORE THE RACE

Day after day Marilee stole into Nelson's office at Fairelawn, risking dismissal, or worse, and each time she thought she would die from a weak heart at every sound she heard. It was, in the end, a nearly impossible task for her, for like Rosey trying to weasel information from Stephen, she didn't know what was important and what was not. Two days before the race she decided to check Nelson's bedroom, and it was there she found what Jim Schmidt suspected could turn out to be incriminating evidence.

Nelson missed what she had taken the very next day and fortunately his suspicions turned to Rosey. He confronted her and the tone of her denial frightened him more than the knowledge that his room had been violated.

She had listened to him obliquely accuse her and then blasted him back to the days when his father had lorded over him and he'd had to turn to the protective skirts of his mother; and while she was due to return soon from a trip abroad, her skirts would have afforded him no protection.

"You didn't lose it, you coward, and no one took it. Nelson Wingate, I know you, and I'll tell you this — you can't scare me, and if I ever think you can go behind my back to save your own skin, I'll come for you and it won't be with a wrench."

Both Nelson and Rosey stood in opposition, and while Rosey wondered how she could ever have loved the weakling before her, Nelson questioned how he had gotten himself so deeply into trouble. And all of it he blamed on his bad judgement regarding bedroom companions and the fact that the fates had created Stephen Rheiner and dumped him into Nelson's world.

Nelson wondered if Rosey were bluffing or if she really hadn't been the thief. He did recognize that he'd been foolish to expect her to crack under the feathery pressure he'd been able to bring to bear. With each new day he found that he was wielding less and less control.

He became unbearable at the office. Twice he almost fired key employees associated with the air races — and one time it had been Christina whom he attempted to bully.

She'd stopped him cold with, "I can get you a government contract; I can get you into the air races and I can be damned certain everyone who matters knows that Wingate Aviation is a contender. Or I can pack my desk. It doesn't really matter to me at this point, Nelson; I've proven myself. Are you that blind? Make up your mind and get off my back."

Nelson had hoped she would grovel or return to the attitude she'd had when he had first hired her, but it wasn't to be.

"I'm under a lot of pressure, Christina, alright? Let it drop."

The way she examined every inch of his face, somehow giving him the impression that she saw into him, into his mind, frightened him.

Crack, you worm, crack, she willed.

The racers were ready, the paint drying, the newest powerplants installed and tested. The pilots were as satisfied as Christina believed they were capable of admitting, and the race was nearly upon them, and still, she didn't have a thing to go on regarding the mysteries which were multiplying rather than being solved.

Jim Schmidt had been particularly cryptic the last time she'd spoken to him, and it was becoming obvious that Marilee was feeling more allegiance to him than she was to Christina. Additionally there was a rift between Stephen and Schmidt which was doubly aggravating when she learned Schmidt had discussed it thoroughly with Marilee before he mentioned it to her.

What the hell is going on? she asked herself hourly.

Most confusing for Christina was the latent desire for her aeroplanes to beat Stephen's. Of course she knew the Wingate Specials weren't hers like the Bulldogs were Stephen's, but she had run roughshod over the engineers, and she had moved Nelson off the dime to get them into production, and so she felt it was entirely reasonable for her to be possessive.

Jim Schmidt was looking forward to his next meeting with Marilee.

Stephen could tell that Schmidt's mind wasn't entirely on the race, and that confirmed his earlier suspicions that he had been involved with something with Lank. Further, Stephen had noticed that some of his plans were missing and he'd not liked Schmidt's reaction when he'd confronted him.

"Did you see them?" he'd repeated and Jim Schmidt had gotten that faraway look in his eyes that Stephen interpreted as guilt, when in fact it was Schmidt pulling away to ponder the loss's significance.

To make everything worse, Stephen's flying was off. He had learned to fly well, but he had not done it long enough or under life and death circumstances to allow him the narrow field of concentration necessary. At first he kept flashing back to finding Lank, but lately Mr. Boisvert's death had returned to haunt him.

Jim Schmidt had been particularly brutal after a near miss. They'd both landed the Bulldog's hot, and taxied them quickly back to the waiting crews, and there, in front of the others, Jim Schmidt had confronted his employer.

"Listen to me, son, and listen carefully — " He was poking his finger to within inches of Stephen's shocked face as he continued, "I'll race these goddamned aeroplanes because you asked me to, and it's my job. Those Bulldogs are ripping mad these days and I'll be damned if I have any more time to babysit you when we're up there. We'll be racing with professionals in just a few days — the best pilots in this country and a few other countries thrown in — but I've got to tell you something — either you get your mind on the goddamned race or park your damned Bulldog and stand in the crowd and watch."

Stephen had never seen Schmidt so mad, and that coupled with his last warning rattled him to the marrow of his bones.

"Concentrate, goddamn it, Stephen, or you're going to get us both killed!"

That evening, Jim Schmidt reviewed the day and knew that it had been a combination of the pre-race jitters and the events Christina Van Luxall had involved him in which had caused him to break. Still, he believed Stephen needed the talk and the warning; the boy just wasn't flying like he should — like he *had* to.

The night before the race Jim Schmidt and Marilee met.

"I'm sorry to do this to you, but you've got to put it back. Our best hope is that it hasn't been missed." He looked at the girl and was sorry to make her take another chance. "I'm sorry, Marilee; I wouldn't ask you to unless I thought it was absolutely necessary."

"But you haven't told Christina about it, have you?"

He knew her next question would be impossible to answer and so he saved her the trouble of asking.

"No, I haven't told her — and I don't know why. I don't think she can be of any help with this — and the fewer people we involve, the better."

It really had turned into a conspiracy between Marilee and Jim Schmidt, and both of them were glad.

But he couldn't help her when she was caught in Nelson's bedroom.

She'd sneaked in after her normal hours, moving as quietly and as quickly as she could, but no amount of stealth would have saved her. She was halfway across Nelson's room, the door to the hall closed, when it was abruptly opened, and the light switched on.

"What are you doing in here? What's that you're carrying?"

Marilee tried to swallow but felt her throat close dryly on itself and stick.

THE NIGHT BEFORE THE RACE

Christina couldn't sleep. The wall she'd built to hold back the memories of her sisters and her mother and her father was weakening and she didn't know how much longer she could keep it standing. Her father's death had been a tremendous shock and she hadn't yet allowed herself to truly assimilate the knowledge that she was now alone.

After the races, regardless of the outcome, she had to take some time off to purge herself emotionally. More and more frequently she thought of the little cabin on the lake and she longed for it. And she'd started tormenting herself with the thought of sharing it with Stephen. It would be a return to childhood for her — a return to that part of it which had been happy.

Nothing had come from her coalition with Marilee and Jim Schmidt. In fact, Marilee had missed their last meeting and Christina just didn't have the strength or the time to go looking for the girl.

At last Christina rose from her bed and brewed herself a cup of tea. Morning found her dozing fitfully in her chair, the tea cold and untouched.

Rosey drove away from Fairelawn alone. She had learned from Stephen that he and Jim Schmidt would not be flying to Cleveland until just before the races were to start. The Bulldogs were still in the hangars at Boisvert Aviation.

"You're not ready yet?" she taunted.

"Yes, Rosey, we're ready. There's not a damn thing to be done now — I sent everyone home to try and rest."

Rosey waited and then said, "Are you afraid?"

Stephen didn't hesitate to answer. "Yes, I'm afraid. Too many accidents happen in these races; I was probably wrong to ever involve the company in the first place." He was thinking of Jim Schmidt as he spoke.

Stephen thought a moment and then continued, glaring at his wife when he did, "After the races, after things settle down again, there are going to be some changes made. Everything's falling apart and we've been damned fools to ignore it." He waited for Rosey's reaction.

If anything helped determine Rosey's final course of action, it was that statement.

"*I'll* make the changes, Stephen Rheiner," she said bitterly as she drove through the night.

When she arrived at the airfield, the area around the hangars and Stephen's office was floodlit, overlapping circles of light bringing daylight to each entrance. Rosey slowed and then drove around behind hangar three. She parked the Buick so the front fender was below a window at the back. She had been at the hangar that day and unlocked a window in the bathroom.

Rosey climbed onto the fender, raised the window and wormed her way in, Nelson's drawings folded inside of her blouse, the few tools she'd practiced using in a purse she had slung around her neck.

Rosey wasn't afraid of Stephen's people finding her. It was Nelson and what he might try to do which concerned her. It would be just his level of courage to telephone someone that there was suspicious activity at the Boisvert field. Still, he would have to find a way to insure that she didn't implicate him. But then, Nelson wanted the Bulldogs disabled and so he would probably not be stupid enough to risk everything.

She nearly fell onto the floor as she climbed over the wash basin.

Rosey cracked the bathroom door. The inside of the hangar was brightly lighted. She looked as carefully as she could but didn't detect any movement. Stephen hadn't mentioned hiring a watchmen. Ever since she had moved to the Boisvert's with him, he had bragged that he was the field's first watchman and he'd be the last.

The three Bulldogs were staggered around the hangar floor. Even Rosey had to admit they looked fiercely beautiful. She went to the first, number 65 painted on its side. 64 and 66 were beyond it. There was a ladder by each of the cockpits.

Jim Schmidt checked his watch again. Marilee was late. Perhaps her meeting with Christina was taking longer than they'd expected. It irritated him. Christina Van Luxall insisted that the three of them meet in pairs, and while Schmidt enjoyed the time alone with each of the two women, it seemed so damned inefficient. He wished for the thousandth time that he were younger.

It was getting late and he of all people knew the importance of rest before pushing an aircraft to its limits. He looked at his watch again. He knew he didn't dare have any more coffee.

Under the right circumstances he would have looked forward to the race. He would never admit that to Stephen; already his adrenalin was pumping. But Stephen hadn't settled down yet. *I wish I were the damned boss,* he said to himself. *I'd ground that boy.* Even as he said it he knew that he wouldn't have. *There's always a first time, and Stephen has every right to be nervous and jumpy.* Jim Schmidt felt that once he was in the race, the boy would settle down. "He damned well better," he mumbled, and looked back at the door and then checked his watch again.

Another hour passed and Jim Schmidt knew he had to make a decision. He went to the pay telephone and started to call Christina but stopped himself. He tried Fairelawn but the switchboard was apparently shut down for the night. Everything was screwed up — he'd promised himself he'd go out to the field and look things over just one more time before he turned in, but now it was so damned late. He was tempted to sleep out there but he knew he would really feel bad in the morning if he did that.

"We're closing, Mack," a dim figure called to him.

He paid his bill and walked out into the night. "Where the hell *are* you, Marilee?" he asked out loud. He cursed himself for making her return to Nelson Wingate's room. "What the hell are we doing playing detective?"

He went to his car.

The lights from oncoming vehicles burned his eyes. "I'm just too damned tired," he said and turned toward his home.

The last thing he said before he fell asleep was, "You've got to be alright, Marilee; don't let me down."

Stephen had mixed emotions. He was glad that Rosey was driving to Cleveland with her mother. He didn't want her around, but he was also mad as hell that she was spending the night at Fairelawn.

He tossed around their double bed, finally throwing her pillow across the room.

"Damn!"

He got out of bed, put on his shoes and paced the bedroom, and then the living room. He went back to bed again. He forced his eyes closed and lay on his side. He turned onto his back and tried to keep his eyes shut.

He stared at the ceiling.

He got up and had a glass of milk and wondered how little Billy was doing. Rosey had taken him to Fairelawn. That was unusual. She usually left him behind every chance she could.

He went back to bed.

He must have dozed, for the next thing he knew a dog was barking in the neighbor's yard. He listened carefully and heard a bird calling to another.

He shaved and showered and then tried to force himself to eat but everything tasted flat, swelling in his mouth, difficult to swallow.

RACE DAY

Christina drove to Cleveland, turning down an invitation to fly in the company plane with Nelson. Once she hit the traffic heading for the grandstands, she wished she had, but she had a pass and more than a few times a policeman directed her around a log jam. By the time she got to the area where the Wingate Specials were parked, the morning was hot and she felt dusty and unclean.

All three crews waved to her as she strode over to them. The Specials were beautiful and she was proud of them.

There were aeroplanes circling overhead as thick as summer gnats, most of them private planes getting in the way of everyone else. But it wasn't difficult to tell the racers. They roared past, apparently making last minute tests, and then slid in fast for a landing, snorting and popping toward their respective pit areas. It was a din which Christina would have thought impossible. The air was thick with exhaust fumes, and clouds of dust rolled by from the cars parking in the adjacent fields.

Christina spent the morning and the early afternoon around the Wingate paddock area, talking with the crews and listening intently to the pilots who were to fly the Specials. But for as observant and pulled into the preparations as she felt she had been, she was surprised when several of the men from production kept on asking her the same question.

"How do the Specials look?"

"Do you like the paint job on the Specials?"

"Don't the Specials look great? Especially, number fifteen!"

"Nice paint job on the racers, eh?"

At last she decided there was something they wished her to see that she was missing and so she walked over to them, careful to stay out of the way of the ground crews. And when she finally saw she was moved to tears. Each of the Wingate aeroplanes was painted the same; bright red from the engine nacelle back to the cockpit where it was scalloped and bordered by the yellow after-half of the craft. And each was numbered, either fourteen, fifteen, or sixteen, with a large winged W painted under the number. The paint jobs were spotless, of course, and seemed to have at least two inches of gloss over the color, and while that was impressive, it was a name in script on the engine nacelle itself that finally caught her eye. There was her name written diagonally. Christina. On number fifteen.

She stared at it dumbly, unable to look at those who now surrounded her, and when she did they were all grins and lowered eyes. It was Nate Heinz who spoke for the workers.

"Miss Van Luxall, it's been our honor and pleasure to work on this project with you." He turned then and studied the racer behind him. "You started the biggest argument of all though, I have to tell you that. We wanted your name on the winner, and the question was, which of the three is gonna win this race — the fastest Special, the Special with the best pilot, or some combination. Those of us who said it was the Special that counted, won in the end. Fifteen can fly right out of her paint job if you let her. We built a tail wind into that plane, that's for sure!" He smiled as he spoke and looked repeatedly at her feet. When he stopped he shuffled around for a moment and then extended his hand. "We're damned proud, Miss Van Luxall!"

And then he excused himself for cursing and all of the others laughed.

"All you ever do is curse, Nate!" someone taunted.

"We want an apology from now on!" another shouted.

Christina waited until they quit teasing. "This is wonderful," she said, indicating not just fifteen, but all three Specials. "And working with you gentlemen has been the most rewarding experience I've ever had." She looked into the eyes of each of her admirers and concluded, "But I want to tell you something. While this race is important, it isn't what really matters to me, not who wins or loses, or what happens after. These last months have shown me what a group of dedicated and proud people can accomplish, and seeing you put these three aeroplanes together — being a part of the team that has made these possible, means more to me than crossing any finish line in the world. Thank you."

The men whooped and hollered and then someone led a "Hip — hip — hooray."

Even the mechanics nearly out of earshot sensed what was happening and joined in.

Both Bulldogs were idling impatiently, having been rolled out of the hangar and fueled and started, and Stephen and Jim Schmidt sat in their respective cockpits making last minute adjustments and scanning the jerking needles on the gauges arrayed in front of them. There was a skeleton crew at the Boisvert field, the majority having driven up to Cleveland the night before to set up the pit area.

Stephen set his feet on the rudder bar and look down at them briefly. What he saw held his attention briefly, but he decided it was water from the dew he'd accumulated on his boots. He wouldn't realize it was hydraulic fluid until later.

Jim Schmidt rolled out first, grabbing the air quickly and expertly, and then throttling back until Stephen was aloft also.

In an effort to help Stephen calm himself and feel better about his flying skills, Jim Schmidt had suggested their entrance to the skies over the air races should be dramatic. A mile from the field, the huge checkered pylons in sight, Jim Schmidt pushed his Bulldog into a gentle dive until he was skimming the treetops. Stephen followed.

The entire Boisvert crew in Cleveland slugged at the air with their fists in jubilant celebration when the two Bulldogs streaked by, Jim Schmidt in the lead and arrow straight and Stephen not ten feet behind and inverted. The two aeroplanes were impressive with their evil black paint, their thundering engines, and their sleek wheels-up profile.

It was a short show, for Jim Schmidt circled the field, pulled the lever and lowered his wheels. Stephen did the same. The planes were immediately refueled and the mechanics removed several engine panels and began the final fine-tuning. Jim Schmidt squeezed Stephen's shoulder.

"I've got a lot of old friends around here. I'll try to be back for the race."

He knew Stephen would want to be alone.

Stephen spoke briefly with the mechanics and was then assured by his secretaries that the Bulldogs were entered, accounted for, and all was set. He left the pit area, ostensibly to stretch his legs, but he walked unerring toward the Wingate contingent, their three Specials lined up and attracting quite a crowd. He stood at the perimeter, trying to catch a glimpse of her. He knew she was somewhere near — he could feel her. Again and again he craned his neck until he thought perhaps he had been wrong. It was as he looked one last time, his hands in his pockets, his neck high and his feet on tip-toe that he felt someone watching him. For an embarrassing second he feared Nelson Wingate was near and mocking his curiosity, but he remembered he had seen him earlier by the Specials, perfectly dressed and exuding the moneyed charm Stephen could never match.

Stephen turned, and there, not ten feet behind him, was Christina Van Luxall. He turned full to her and tried to pull his hands from his pockets, but they felt like lead, impossible to lift. He flushed, his skin prickling, the color hot on his face.

Christina was not without emotion either. She had been on the way to look at the Bulldogs — or so she had convinced herself. When she first saw Stephen her heart stopped and her stomach lightly lifted. He was not the handsome boy she remembered. He was a man now, fuller in the body and mature. His dark eyes and disheveled hair were perfect, an air of confidence beneath his surprise. She walked to him slowly, unaware of the people between them, unaware of the noise of the aeroplanes, oblivious to everything but Stephen Rheiner.

While it was Christina who was the first to close the distance between them, it was Stephen who spoke. "Christina," he pronounced carefully and then repeated, "Christina."

She was embarrassed and awkward, more the teen-aged girl than the assured woman, and she said, inanely, "I know — I just saw it written on the side of an aeroplane," and Stephen started, confused as to how she could know that he had penciled her name on the inside of his cockpit.

She reached out for his hands and Stephen finally succeeded in getting them out of his pockets, spilling their contents when he did. He looked to the ground and then to Christina and then back to the ground. He had never felt so stupid. He bent quickly and retrieved what he had dropped but didn't put it all back into his pockets. He held up an object for Christina to see.

"Do you remember Clarence?" he asked, more assured now that he had something to say, and more in love than ever because he was speaking of their past and of The Chimneys. "He gave me this — it's for good luck — and confidence, I guess."

Christina didn't look to his hand, instead she watched his eyes and looked at his face. "Have you had good luck, Stephen?"

He was uncomfortable with her question, her own life having been so riddled with tragedy. Instead of answering he tried to give the memento to her, but she refused.

"I'm alright, Stephen. You keep it for today."

He had almost summoned the courage to ask her if they could talk after the race or the next day or some time soon, when one of Stephen's crew ran up to him.

"Stephen — sir — Mr. Rheiner, we've been looking all over for you. There's a meeting for the pilots that's already started. You've got to go. Fast."

Christina took his hand. "Goodbye, Stephen. Be careful." She turned away from him quickly and whispered so softly she thought no one heard, "I love you."

Stephen stumbled away at a clumsy run. He couldn't believe what he'd just heard.

"Holy cow, are you late!" the man in coveralls admonished, pushing his employer ahead of him.

Nelson Wingate tried to keep his mind on the upcoming race and the attention his people were demanding. He couldn't understand why Rosey hadn't made an appearance. When the Bulldogs had flashed over the field in their ridiculous attempt at bravado he had waited with intense interest for them to drop their wheels for landing. When first the lead plane and then the other sprouted their awkward landing gear he was angered. He had wanted it to happen now, immediately, even though he knew the gear could cycle once, maybe even twice, if Rosey had done her job well. He searched the crowd for her. What the hell had happened?

Had he truly had control of her, he would have forbidden her to come anywhere near the races, but she was beyond his wishes. She had become more of a weapon than a woman or a companion. He scanned the empty faces of the people around him and wondered how he had allowed himself to become so colossally vulnerable.

Stephen attended the meeting and then found the restrooms. He went back to his plane and then back to the restroom.

Jim Schmidt watched him and smiled to himself. He knew the torment the boy was suffering. He, too, looked around him, hoping by some miracle Marilee would appear. It bothered him that he had put the race in front of being sure she hadn't gotten into trouble.

The doubts that Stephen was having about his flying skills, Jim Schmidt was having about his own priorities.

THE RACE

Stephen was certain he would throw up if something didn't happen soon to occupy his mind. His aeroplane vibrated noisily as the big engine whirled the metal propellor. The sun played on it. Jim Schmidt had edged his Bulldog a few feet ahead of Stephen's. He was slated to take-off first. Stephen looked around and then back toward the pit area. There was some sort of commotion.

Jim Schmidt pushed his throttle forward and the Bulldog, impatient from being leashed for too long, started its roll to the runway. Stephen hesitated and then followed. Jim Schmidt was flagged into the air. Stephen glanced back a last time. There were men in uniform talking to his ground crew. Someone pointed to the Bulldog. Army Air Corps? He couldn't tell. Then he was waved off. He slammed the throttle forward and rocketed ahead, his body pushed heavily into the back of the seat. The big Whirlwind roared. The tail lifted and he was off the ground. It had truly begun.

"Stop them! Stop them!" the woman and the girl shouted. The police were angrily trying to figure out how to handle the situation. It had been an incredible race to Cleveland. All of the telephone lines were jammed and so in the end the sprint had been inevitable, but now they were in a different city at a major event, trying to stop two aeroplanes from flying because of the accusations of two maids. The police longed for a few robbers to arrest as they fled a store.

Marilee looked around wildly for someone who could actually help. Jim Schmidt was in the air.

Christina — she had to find Christina.

She started shouting. "Find Christina Van Luxall! Find Miss Van Luxall!"

The police watched the two black aeroplanes sweep into the air and join the melee. At last their police uniforms had attracted the attention of a race official. He went into conference with them.

"Says who?"

"These girls — " one officer said, indicating Marilee and Claire Baker. "And there's another in the car. Mad as hell. Won't say a damn thing. This one says she's her mother — you figure it out." The two policemen had been swept away by the frantic urgency of Marilee and Rosey's mother, but as time passed and they found themselves in the position of actually supporting the accusations of the two maids, their resolve turned first to skepticism and then acute discomfort.

"Who the hell is Van Luxall?" one of the policemen asked. The other was watching the aeroplanes speeding overhead, trying to distance himself from what he had done. It wasn't going to look good on his record.

"She works at Wingate," Marilee insisted. "She's in charge of the Wingate aeroplanes or something."

As a group they moved toward the Wingate pit area. Nelson saw the police and then his housekeeper and someone he thought was one of his maids. His first impulse was to run. "Goddamn you, Rosalind Baker," he whispered under his breath and then sauntered toward the approaching group. He kept looking up to the sky as if that were where his real interest lay. But in reality, at that moment he couldn't have cared less if all three Specials turned into birds and flew away.

Stephen was not prepared for the madness he encountered. He knew he needed to but he couldn't keep his mind on his own race; there was just too much going on around him. He worried about the Bulldog, its engine, the other planes, the checkered pylons ahead and behind, the crowd below, and even if Christina were watching him. His mind wandered everywhere, as did his eyes. He studied his gauges in fits, judged his altitude and was even in the process of trying to ascertain the wind direction when a raucous blue fuselage filled the air directly in front of him. With its turbulence his plane bucked madly until the blue aeroplane pulled away. Stephen and the Bulldog roared off in an oblique, out of the path he had been flying. He wrestled his aeroplane back under control and reoriented himself. Badly shaken, his mind briefly cleared of everything but the airspace he occupied and the race itself, Stephen swore, "You son of a bitch!" and officially entered the competition. Angry and determined, he muscled back into the pack, nudging his throttle forward and concentrating until he finally caught the blue plane.

Once he was parallel, the other pilot looked surprised and then smug. He drifted dangerously close to Stephen. Wing tips nearly touched as they howled toward the approaching pylon. Stephen felt a wash of panic as he wondered if his antagonist would give him the room he needed to bank and turn, but then as quickly he dismissed his concern. "Fly your own damn race!" he shouted as much to himself as to his competitor and banked hard into his turn, the Bulldog growling and shuddering with the tremendous forces wrestling with it. The blue aeroplane banked also but was unable to turn as tightly as the Bulldog. Stephen was a plane length ahead as they pulled out. He continued his aggressive assault, consistently improving his own race and methodically catching each of the faster aeroplanes until immediately ahead of him was one of the few he actively sought. He recognized the big red and yellow racer for what it was, increased his throttle again and settled into pursuit of a Wingate Special. "Not today, you don't," Stephen muttered as he sawed back and forth behind the Special, looking for an opportunity to push the Bulldog still harder and fly past one of Nelson's best. But each time he attempted to move outside or inside of the Special its pilot seemed to have read Stephen's mind, for the red aeroplane anticipated his every move, blocking Stephen's ability to pass. Then, as they approached a marginally slower aircraft Stephen saw his chance. As the Wingate Special moved to the inside of the other aircraft, Stephen simultaneously jammed his throttle open and threw the Bulldog on its side, roaring between the two planes with inches to spare.

"One down," Stephen counted as he distanced their combined turbulence and righted the Bulldog, all the while marveling at the speed with which he had raced past the two.

His Boisvert Bulldog was clearly the superior craft. "Jacob, you are a genius," he muttered as he smiled grimly and set his sights on the pack of racers still in front of him. At full throttle the Bulldog made short work of half of them, and with each success the young man's confidence built as he realized it wasn't just the aeroplane that was his advantage. Both Jacob Boisvert and Jim Schmidt had helped bring out in him the skills of a gifted pilot and a ferocious racer. The thunderous sound pounded his sternum; the enveloping heat caressed him in his own sweat. Engine oil masked his face and streaked his goggles. Everything was one to immerse Stephen in the race. It was like nothing he had ever experienced and it was everything of which a man dreams: It was love, it was war, it was sex, it was children and he was in control of it all in a world wrought of machines and speed and power. Before the day was over he would acknowledge the second obsession in his life.

He raced on and on through the afternoon, banking neatly and then ripping into each straight away. Another turn, another pylon and there in front of him at last were the other two Wingate Specials, they obviously very much aware of his presence as they flew in tight formation, blocking the groove Stephen needed to fly through to keep his edge. They, too, jigged in front of him with each attempt he made to pass until Stephen almost flew through one of them, it being so bold in blocking that the young pilot had to ease back further on his throttle to keep the Bulldog from chewing into the red tail a few yards in front of him. For what seemed an eternity, he was trapped. Around and around the course they flew, Stephen's frustration growing with each lap as the two Wingate aeroplanes denied the youth any opportunity to use his superior speed and advance his position. Then, in the midst of the noise and turbulence and heady competition, Stephen felt his old boss settle into the cockpit with him. "Smarter," he whispered. "Fly smarter Stephen; we've built the Bulldogs and they're the best in the air, but now we need a pilot. A skillful pilot. A clever pilot."

With barely a moment's hesitation, Stephen pulled back on the stick, pegged his throttle and momentarily felt his airplane climb as if to go over the big red Special in front of him. Then as quickly he dove and roared under the right hand Special, it having drifted upward a few feet with his last maneuver. There was nothing but red and yellow above him and then blue sky as Stephen whooped and left the last Wingate Specials to dance in his prop wash.

Jim Schmidt was also flying through the competition. He and his Bulldog were one, and his world narrowed to the checkered pylon currently ahead of him. He swept past it, his arms heavy from the centrifugal force, and the Bulldog's engine howling. Some aeroplanes he edged past, others he passed so quickly it was actually frightening. He found his own groove and flew it, every move crystal clear and concise, the Bulldog strapped on and obeying cleanly. His race was not the same as Stephen's, for while the young pilot was in competition with every craft in front of him, Jim Schmidt ignored them. He wanted speed. The best speed, and the best path for the fastest circuit. Again. And again. And again.

In the course of the afternoon he too had passed the Wingate racers, maneuvering by one early on and then ripping through the others toward the end of the race. They were no different for him than trees beside the highway. Almost. Except for the smallest of smiles he allowed himself.

For much of the race he had been unaware of Stephen's progress, his time for babysitting long past. And then the boy was behind him and lap after lap they flew, first and second in the race. Until toward the end the fastest of the Wingate pilots managed to wring a sustained burst of extra horsepower from his screaming engine and pulled up beside Stephen. It was the same red craft the boy had flown under earlier in the race and so now as he looked across what he saw startled him into totally losing his concentration. There in bold script was the name, CHRISTINA.

And before he could completely digest what he saw, the Special was ahead of him and then slowing, but managing to skillfully keep Stephen from passing again.

"It's preposterous!" Nelson yelled. "You come here with these — these *women* — and interrupt me? You drag my *domestic staff* all the way to Cleveland because of some wild story?" He defied the police to explain themselves and they clearly believed they were in the wrong

"Well, there's another in the car," the one policeman offered apologetically, as if one more woman would shore up their crumbling case.

Nelson stared at his housekeeper and she withered. Marilee couldn't meet his eyes.

"I've other things on my mind, if you haven't noticed," Nelson spat and turned his back on the group. He raised his field glasses. The race was nearly over.

The police looked at one another.

"Let's get the other one," the taller policeman offered. "Yeh," his partner agreed, "let's."

Rosey seethed in the back of the police car. Handcuffed! She was handcuffed and locked in and the windows were rolled tight. *You'll pay, Nelson Wingate, you son of a bitch. You'll pay.*

That morning her mother who was absolutely screaming had dragged her from her bed. Then when Mary or what ever the hell her name was starting babbling about Nelson and Christina, she knew she'd been betrayed. *Does he think I'll keep my mouth shut?*

He'd been in it with the Van Luxall tramp all along. Rosey tried to decide when he had turned against her, and she was unable. Probably it was because of the drunk. He'd lost his nerve over a dead drunk and now he couldn't keep his mouth shut and let her take care of things. *Of all the stupid....*

Rosey thought she would pass out from the heat or explode from her anger.

At last, the police came back to her and roughly pulled her from the vehicle, their uncertainty manifesting itself in brute force.

Nelson frantically reviewed what was happening and he suspected they weren't aware of everything. There was a good chance they couldn't build a case as long as Rosey offered nothing. The way the police were talking it appeared she hadn't said much yet.

As soon as she was away from Nelson, Mrs. Baker regained her resolve and turned her thoughts angrily back to her daughter.

Rosey tried to walk in the middle of the group so her cuffed hands wouldn't be so visible — not that anyone was looking anywhere but up. There were scattered cheers.

Nelson saw Rosey. He tried to calm her with his eyes. He tried to force her to understand and remain silent. *Keep quiet, you ignorant tramp. Keep that big mouth of yours closed for once.*

Rosey watched him, saw him free and glaring at her and hated him.

Nelson didn't know what was happening when his housekeeper fell into step beside Rosey and whispered something into her ear. Whatever it was she said, it was gasoline on Rosey's fire. She leaped forward past the startled police as if she'd been pushed.

"*You* killed him, you bastard; you killed him with a wrench you were too stupid to get rid of and you blamed me! You forced me to do everything else and then you turned me out! And you denied your only son, you weak, simpering bastard!"

She whacked at him with her cuffs until the police gathered their wits and moved to restrain her.

"She's crazy! She's obviously insane!" Nelson shouted as he raised his hands in defense and backed away.

A small crowd had its attention pulled away from the race and was gathering. Christina fought through it. She had been standing away from the others, watching Stephen's plane in the sky above her, when Rosey's voice carried to her. She moved to within feet of the confrontation.

Rosey saw her and broke free again. She slammed into Christina, nearly knocking her down. "And you, you spoiled, rich bitch!" she swore and then hit her brutally, catching Christina on the side of her head with the edge of her metal cuffs. Christina reeled to the side. Nelson reacted as if he were being struck again. He turned away and hurried into the gathering crowd.

Fifty miles — the last seven laps.

It was over before Stephen realized it could be. His Bulldog had been flawless.

Jim Schmidt was still ahead of him, making a lazy curve over the countryside. The Wingate Special was to the right. Stephen steered to join Schmidt. He shook with residual adrenaline. His heart was still pounding, his mouth dry. They were first and third. They had proved everything they had set out to prove; there was no denying the strength of the Bulldog and the success of its design.

Jim Schmidt saw Stephen and throttled back further. They flew wing tip-to-wing tip, exchanging exhausted smiles and raised thumbs. Schmidt pointed down and Stephen nodded. There were still many planes left circling the course and so they were actually in no hurry to clear for a landing.

When the time came, Schmidt was the first to pull the handle to drop his gear. Stephen saw him lean forward and knew what he was about to do. He let his Bulldog slide farther off to the side so he could watch Schmidt's wheels drop. It was always fascinating in a comical sort of way.

But nothing happened.

Stephen saw Schmidt lean again and this time remain forward, his face uncomfortably close to the front of the canopy.

Nothing.

Schmidt looked at Stephen and it was the cool look of a professional.

He motioned for Stephen to drop his own gear, indicating he'd take care of himself. Stephen didn't want to touch his lever for two reasons: If he did and his gear dropped, the increased wind resistance would suck his plane backward away from his friend, and Stephen wanted to stay with him. But if his gear, too, refused to drop — well, it wasn't something he looked forward to knowing. Cruising beside Jim Schmidt had more appeal.

With the sight of Nelson so obviously fleeing, and her belief in his complicity with Christina, Rosey could stand no more. Her anger fell away, leaving a pitiful, defeated girl in its place. She dropped to her knees, at first wracked with uncontrolled sobbing, but as it abated she began to relate it all.

"I just wanted him to love me and so I went to him. And he did; he loved me. I know he did." She cried briefly and then continued. "We talked. We talked so much, about everything, and he listened to me. He wanted to hear me talk. And then the baby — Nelson's baby — spoiled it all and he sent me away. He denied our baby and he broke my heart."

She looked up at the circle of people around her — the police, Marilee, Christina, her mother. "I kept hoping he'd come back to me; but he never did and so I went back to him. At first I thought he'd changed — that we could have it like it was — but it wasn't the same anymore — I was wrong. He just wanted to use me. He made me do things. He made me bring him drawings of those stupid aeroplanes and he made me tell him what I knew about them — and then even that wasn't enough." As she delved deeper into her lie, the number of people Rosey could face as she spoke dwindled until all she could do was frown at Christina. "He made me go out to the aeroplanes that night and then when that drunk caught us, he killed him. Nelson killed him. 'DON'T!' I screamed, but it was too late, and he grabbed me and shook me hard and warned me that if I told anyone he'd be certain I went to jail." Rosey searched for a way to sound more pathetic. "And he said if I told a soul he'd say it was really me and they'd come and take my baby — they'd take little Billy away from me and put me in prison. And so I didn't tell anybody. But he kept wanting more and more. He made me do things to the aeroplanes — he made me. *He threatened me.* I didn't want to. But I had to." She looked up at the sky then and a bitter smile betrayed her.

Christina saw and grabbed Rosey. "What aeroplanes? What did you do?"

Rosey's smile broadened as her eyes narrowed. "What aeroplanes? Why, your precious Stephen and his precious Bulldogs," she hissed.

Christina backed out of the crowd and searched the sky. There were just a few aeroplanes left and it didn't take long to single out the two Bulldogs flying wing to wing. They seemed fine.

She ran back to Rosey. The police had just dragged her to her feet. "What did you do?" Christina demanded.

Rosey shocked her with a look of malevolence, and spat, "Are their wheels down, *Miss Van Luxall?* You tell me that!"

Christina didn't have to ask any more. *Of course they would be easy to disable, and a rank amateur could make it so they cycled at least once before they failed. But perhaps they would cycle twice!*

She looked back to the air.

Stephen pushed his goggles up and reached for his lever. He grasped it and pulled back slowly. Jim Schmidt watched.

Nothing happened.

Stephen smiled grimly at his friend but Schmidt motioned for him to try again.

Once more Stephen pulled back on the metal handle. There was a thump and his aeroplane dragged back away from Jim Schmidt's.

Schmidt chopped his power and then feathered the throttle until he was once more beside Stephen. He examined the landing gear — the partially extended landing gear. He motioned to Stephen that the wheels were barely halfway down and then flew his own aeroplane under Stephen's, studying the undercarriage. Then he came back to Stephen's side and started rocking his wings quickly, first one way, and then another.

Stephen could tell the wheels were not fully extended and he immediately understood Schmidt's suggestion — snap roll to force them the rest of the way down. The mechanism was such that once the wheels were unlocked and had been pumped part of the way it was possible for them to be lowered the rest of the way by sheer force.

Stephen snapped the Bulldog twice, first to the right and then to the left.

Schmidt saw the wheels move. He gestured for Stephen to be more aggressive.

Stephen violently flipped the Bulldog to one side and then another and with each movement, he felt a wheel lock down. Schmidt was ahead of him again but drifting back. He gave Stephen the thumbs up and the boy felt the tears blurring his eyes.

Schmidt saw him blinking and nothing in the world could have made him happier at that moment.

Except, perhaps, a pint of hydraulic fluid.

There followed an argument of gestures, with Stephen and Schmidt both insisting the other go down first. Schmidt wanted the boy down so he could concentrate on his crash landing, while Stephen wanted to follow Schmidt and attempt to land close to where the other Bulldog came to rest.

Schmidt suspected Stephen's plan and was also aware of the danger.

He was about to insist again, when he heard the big Whirlwind cough. They'd been flying without regard for their fuel, and Schmidt had just had his decision made for him. He looked down at the field and then husbanded his altitude as best he could, the engine now running erratically. He saw an open area beyond the grandstands that he thought he could reach. As he made his decision his engine coughed one last time, backfired a black cloud and then died, the propeller wind milling briefly.

Stephen nodded and forced a smile to Schmidt and then slowed his aeroplane.

There was a price for the Bulldog's ability to fly fast: It was designed to be pulled violently through the air on its stubby wings by a huge engine. And if that engine stopped the game was changed; it did not glide well. At all. In fact, it showed a propensity to fall from the air with alarming rapidity. Jacob Boisvert used to joke that his aeroplane's huge radial engine should be left at full throttle for at least a half an hour after landing, just in case. So Schmidt's unpowered Bulldog dropped toward the ground like a rock. He used his last airworthiness to pull the nose up. The plane slammed onto the soft grass and bounced high. Schmidt fought to keep the nose up but there was no response in the controls.

Stephen landed "hot" and chopped his power, the stricken Bulldog off to the left and less than a hundred yards in front of him. Schmidt's Bulldog came down again, its lower cylinders plowing through the grass, leaving a deep brown trough as it slid. Stephen's plane cut the distance between the two quickly.

Stop! Stop! Stop! Stephen willed the other plane. If only Schmidt's plane would stop before it dug in so far that it flipped over. And over.

Stephen was not the only one hoping.

Then the Bulldog started to veer to the right and Stephen saw that if it continued they would be on a collision course. "DAMN!" he swore, desperate for the other aeroplane to get out of his way, but fearing that it would not. He had been foolish to follow Schmidt so closely.

The Bulldog started to dig its nose deeper and then it began to arc into the air, the tail slowly rising to flip the aeroplane over onto its cockpit.

It was all happening directly in front of Stephen, now less than fifty yards away.

Stephen had no choice. He jammed the throttle forward and pulled back on the stick. But he didn't have enough speed. The Bulldog couldn't fly again. It was not possible.

"Oh please, baby," Stephen crooned and patted the side of the Bulldog where he had written Christina's name, and before the breath of the last syllable left his lips the Bulldog grabbed the air, however briefly.

Schmidt's mind was on his tilting aircraft when Stephen thundered over, one of his wheels smashing through the tail behind him. "DAMMIT, BOY!" he yelled and then his Bulldog fell back and to the side, Stephen's plane having arrested its movement before it flipped onto its back — and Schmidt's head.

Schmidt tore the canopy open and was out before the Bulldog quit rocking. "Sorry kid," he amended as he jumped down and ran stiffly away from the broken wreck. He had seen more than one empty gas tank explode. The vapors were volatile killers. "One cup of vaporized gasoline," he remembered his friend, Jacob Boisvert, chanting, "packs the punch of five sticks of TNT!"

Stephen had no time to think of Schmidt. His Bulldog, after its impossible leap over the other aeroplane, was running out of field fast. There were trees ahead and coincidental with that realization his engine sputtered and died. He was rolling too fast.

Instinctively, he reached again for the landing gear lever and pulled it back and the Bulldog started to settle. First the underside of the aeroplane dragged, then the engine nacelle tore away and flew over Stephen's head, and then both blades of the propeller bent flush with the sides of the aeroplane.

Stephen's Bulldog left its own trail of torn-up sod, and it ended less than twenty feet from the first tree.

Stephen sat back into his seat. He had no way of hearing Schmidt running across the field yelling, "GET OUT, BOY! GET THE HELL OUT!"

The crowd was moving like a giant wave toward the site of the two downed planes. Christina and Marilee had jumped in with the crew in a Model T they used to drag the Specials in and out of hangars. They wove through the crowd, quickly outdistancing those on foot, and kept pace with the fire engine and the ambulance which blared beside them on the right and left.

By the time Schmidt got onto Stephen's wing the boy had the cockpit open and was stupidly checking his gauges. "GET OUT! GET OUT!" Schmidt shouted and tugged at him.

The two cleared the wing and ran together across the field and away from the Bulldog; Stephen at last understanding and now helping the exhausted Schmidt.

There was a ridiculously minor pop from Stephen's Bulldog and a few flames snaked up its side, but the fire crew was on it and had them doused immediately.

Stephen and Schmidt stopped to watch, their arms on the other's shoulder, their goggles pushed up revealing two raccoon-like oil darkened faces. "Kind of a let down," Schmidt managed, still wheezing, and Stephen laughed, a little at first, but when Schmidt joined they were nearly drunk with relief.

Then Stephen felt another set of arms around him and he was pulled away from his friend. Christina held him, and she started to cry, but Stephen and Schmidt's laughter was still in her mind and she pushed him to arms' length and smiled.

"I love you, Stephen," she said at last and then embraced him again.

He swept her up then, holding her to him, unaware of where she'd come from or where she'd been; simply reacting to what he'd heard her say.

CHRISTINA AND STEPHEN

The sun was setting and Christina lay in Stephen's arms, half the quilts already a ragged pile on the floor, the others mounded heavily on them. Winter had arrived early. They had come to the cabin a week ago and intended to stay at least one more.

The sun came through the window and warmed Christina's face as the room cooled. It would be another in a succession of nights of alternately sleeping, talking and then losing themselves in one another. Stephen was nearly asleep already. Christina idly traced the lines of his face and softly asked, "Did you really think of me *every* day?"

Stephen stirred slightly. A hint of a smile came to him. "Every day. Every single day."

"You couldn't have every day," she taunted quietly. As she had a thousand times before. It was her touchstone, her way of erasing the intervening years, the heartaches and the pain during their separation. She watched the sky darken further and they both became young once more, young, and at The Chimneys, and innocent, and just falling into love.

Stephen yawned. He raised himself to one elbow and looked out the window and into the twilight. "Do you think we'll ever sleep an entire night?" He then looked at Christina, who was now watching him as he spoke. "I was awake a lot of nights at The Chimneys. I used to lay in bed and think of you asleep in your fine room. I used to think of somehow sneaking in and looking at you when you were asleep. I would just look at you and it was wonderful."

"I thought of you, too, Stephen;" Christina interrupted, "of all the times I saw you that day, what you said, what you wore. How you walked."

Christina saddened then, as Stephen knew she would. She became quiet.

"I miss them, too," he whispered, and they both knew he was speaking of her sisters. He leaned to her and kissed her cheek gently. "I think of them with you. Laughing. Whispering secrets to you. You three were so happy. I used to tell my Pop that you three were the happiest, luckiest people I knew."

Christina closed her eyes and returned to her sisters and their short life together. "Sometimes we were, Stephen, but many times we were on the same lifeboat together, sad, and wishing things were different: that our brother had lived; that Mama was happy; that Papa loved us. I hope they're all happy now."

They lay for a moment in silence.

"I bet the girls are," Stephen added at last. "I can't see your parents happy or laughing, or anything like that, but I'm sure Abbie and Katey are."

It was soothing to Christina for Stephen to speak so familiarly of her sisters. He thought of them as his own and she knew he loved and missed them.

They lay quietly, the night descending upon them, each lost in their own memories.

Christina tucked deeply into the bends and nooks Stephen made as he lay on his side. She held him to her and smelled his neck and felt his strength. He was the first to fall asleep again, his breathing deep and regular. Christina drifted through their past. She was saddened, but not as before. It was no longer a weight dragging her to the depths of a bottomless sea. The last months had been full of discoveries and surprises. They had Billy with them and Christina knew she would come to love him as her own, just as she knew, instinctively, that she would love his sister — or his brother, whichever it was going to be — nothing was certain yet.

One of the biggest surprises had been the long-delayed meeting with her father's solicitors and it had begun as uncomfortably as she thought it would. She was working at Boisvert by then and impatient to get that part of her life behind her.

Christina still wore the role of a career woman as easily as she did her tailored clothes, and so when she strode into the staid and over-important law offices with the self possessed air of a de Lempicka portrait, every man present was threatened and intent on reestablishing his dominance. Paget was gone, but some of the other faces she recognized. Arlen Guthrie attempted to control the meeting from the outset. "Miss Van Luxall — oh yes, Mrs. *Rheiner*, yes, yes. Well, it was ..." he hesitated.

Christina had no patience.

"You needn't bother me with the details. My father's money is gone — how much do I owe you?"

The old man in rich and ancient pinstripes, obviously piqued, "harumphed," and made a show of forcing her to wait for him to continue. He dug out an antique pocket watch, stared at it and then reluctantly resumed speaking. "Well, yes, your father's estate is in shambles as you've surmised." He went on to tell her the details: the failed companies, the foreclosures, the pending auction of The Chimneys. It seemed to take hours and in fact, it did.

At last the man behind the big desk stopped; the papers he had read stacked tall and neat to his left. "There is still the matter of your account, Miss — Mrs. — "

Christina waved off his attempt to remember who she was.

"Indeed," he continued, and then he stopped and grinned. It was devilish, and worn by a man in his early 60's, it pared ten years from him — perhaps more. He began again with a wholly different tone. "*I* always enjoyed your father, Mrs. Rheiner, and I know I was one of the few who did — if you'll excuse me that comment. He was tough and he was smart and even at the end he had a way of seeing just a little beyond what the rest of us were stumbling toward. I know about the check he gave you, Mrs. Rheiner (he smiled to himself at his continuing success with her name), and he and I had a laugh or two at your expense when things began to fall apart."

He reached to a side drawer and opened it and pulled out several brown legal folders, each larger than the last.

"Yes, we laughed, and he — he was a big man, big to me at least — he towered over me after we'd had our last laugh, so to speak, and then he threatened me, Mrs. Rheiner. Your father actually threatened me. Physically.

"He told me that I was to gather every government obligation he had and transfer them to our custody, and to hold them in your name. The threat, you see, was that I'd better find six million dollars worth of them."

He smiled at Christina's confusion.

"At that juncture it wasn't impossible — things were heading downhill fast but your father had more money than anyone in this town ever dreamed. His challenge was for us to do it, and as he put it, 'To not tell another damned soul about it or he'd sure as hell jam his foot down on whoever did.'

"That was during one of his more lucid moments."

Mr. Guthrie tilted his tall leather chair back, so absorbed was he in what he said that he came close to being casual. "I discouraged him — I can tell you that. He had no obligation to do it — no legal obligation — the original check he gave you was offered in good faith drawn against what were at the time, good funds, and well, frankly, it seemed a bit extravagant for the services rendered. You see, he needed that money — desperately toward the end. I believe he could have used those funds to have saved at least half of the businesses he eventually lost."

And then Guthrie became more serious, tipping forward to his desk and lowering his voice. "I can't tell you, in the end, after it all settled out, if that act killed him or prolonged his life." He slowly slid the envelopes across the desk to Christina.

When the meeting was completed, he waited until the others left, and then moved to her side. "I told you I liked your father, Mrs. Rheiner, and that was a bit understated. I truly cared for him, more than anyone knew, and I pitied him. This town has not seen a more brilliant mind and probably never will." He paused then and Christina could see he was struggling with what he was about to say. He drew himself up as they walked to the door, and concluded, "I wish I could tell you he made his gesture to you from love, but I cannot with an easy conscience do that. I don't believe he knew the word or understood the emotion. Something was missing from the man, Mrs. Rheiner; something that drew me inexplicably to him.

"He was a man with one purpose in his life. I never knew him to do anything that would not advance his fortune. He destroyed many people on his way up. Ruined them. Smashed them and never gave them another thought. He wanted an empire. He needed an empire. And then in the end, when every decision he made was paramount to preserving all that he had built, he did the one thing I am at a loss to explain."

They stopped at the door and Christina held his eyes, hoping for one more sentence. At last the old man opened his mouth as if to speak, thought better of it, took a step back, turned, and reentered the gloomy sanctuary of his office without another word.

And so she was once again a wealthy woman. And if she chose, a powerful one. Stephen was not yet fully aware of her financial position or the extent of her growth as a woman and a person with whom to be reckoned. There was the arrangement with Nelson relative to Wingate Aviation to which he was not privy. He did know she had used a trust account to rescue The Chimneys from the auction block and he could tell she was struggling with a series of important choices, but he was embarrassed to ask of the details. Instead he buried himself in the logistics of the Army Air Corps contract that Jim Schmidt kept assuring him they could handle.

The closest he'd come so far to understanding her resolve had been in the first weeks after the race when the newspapers and the town were abuzz with the scandals involving the National Air Races, Nelson, Rosey, the murder, and little Billy. Rosey was being held and Nelson was fighting mightily to extricate himself from her expanding accusations. Nelson's denials — denials buttressed by plenty of money, the "old boy network" and a prejudice against giving credence to a domestic's testimony — appeared to be winning over the right people. And even though the reading public was entranced by Rosey's stories; titillated, fascinated, enthralled and then thrilled by the details she kept supplying the press: the secret encounters, Nelson's sexual proclivities, and his overwhelming need to crush the Boisvert Aviation Company, that same reading public knew the ways of the world;

knew that in the end, Nelson would buy his way out of trouble and Rosey, pathetic Rosey, would stay in jail.

But that was not to be. Christina and Stephen had been discussing the scandal and the impending trial over lunch. Stephen was disgusted with the ease it appeared Nelson was distancing himself from the affair and lamented, "He's guilty as sin. Everybody knows it. How can those people just ignore it?" It was, of course, a rhetorical question for Stephen knew that Nelson was using his political and financial power to its fullest extent. But something in the way Stephen phrased his anger seemed to awaken a dormant thought in Christina. She placed the newspaper she'd been reading back onto the table and looked directly at and then through Stephen.

"I think you're right, Stephen; he's 'guilty as sin', and there's a good chance he will walk away from it. But perhaps. . ."

Later that day Stephen came in on a telephone conversation Christina was having with Arlen Guthrie. "Then do it," was all he heard her say. And before the week was out the press was reporting that perhaps Nelson Wingate was involved after all; that the girl's stories might indeed have been closer to the truth than first thought. It was as things began to head south for the Wingate fortunes that Christina engineered a series of meetings with Nelson. Meetings where she suggested that should he be "inconvenienced" as she referred to it, someone he trusted should be guiding his company.

"I know Wingate Aviation and I know you, Nelson. I'm the best you dare hope for. Sign the papers and concentrate on your legal problems. I'll do the rest." When he whined that there was an enormous conflict of interest because of her involvement with Boisvert Aviation, she simply responded, "Then don't sign them. The next best thing to a fast 'yes' is a fast 'no', Nelson. Please don't waste my time; I'm surprised you have so much to spare."

That came to be the side of Christina that Stephen respected and feared — not in the sense that he felt it could be turned against him, more that he saw some of her father in her. But in the end he knew that a woman of her intelligence who had been through all she'd experienced would have some hard edges and some scars. He chose to ignore the edges and attempt to be a balm for her wounds.

Christina lay and thought of these and other things until at last, she too fell asleep. Together, she and Stephen held one another and slumbered into the night.

Well past midnight, Stephen awoke from his dream with a start. Rosey was chasing him through The Chimneys and he could not escape. She found him every time he tried to hide from her until she finally cornered him in the hidden garden. Christina's statue was there, whole and standing, and he had finally gone to it, trying to keep it between Rosey and himself. "You can't hide, you can't hide," Rosey kept chanting to him, and then she grew a death's head and reached with huge arms around the statue. Stephen called out from his sleep. He sat up, his heart pounding, his body clammy.

Apparently his voice had not carried out of his dream, for Christina lay asleep beside him, her features as serene and calming as Rosey's had been demented. The fire in the fireplace was nearly out, the room cold and unforgiving. Stephen swung his feet from the bed, pulled on a heavy flannel shirt and then went to the wood stacked beside the stone fireplace. It wasn't long before he had coaxed the embers back to flames, the dry wood he'd added now popping and burning hard. At last he sat on the floor before it, his knees drawn to his chest, his chin resting on them.

Rosey. No matter how hard he tried, he could not hate her for what she'd done and neither could he drive her from his mind. She haunted him daily, her defeated life weighing heavily on him, their failed marriage an open wound.

Stephen let the heat from the fire bathe him as he remembered his first visit to her in jail. It was worse than he could ever have thought, she a hull of the girl he'd teased and romped with at The Chimneys, her skin sallow, all signs of her spirit gone along with her anger. She denied nothing; she admitted nothing; merely stared at him as he asked her what she wished for him to do.

"I love our Billy," he said finally, unable to distance himself emotionally from his son. "I'm divorcing you and I'm taking him with me. I know what you're telling everyone about his father, but it doesn't matter to me. I love him and he doesn't need to be hurt by this mess you've created."

Rosey looked long at Stephen and said the only word she was to direct to him. Calmly and vacantly she looked into his eyes and for a second he could see the old Rosey hiding in their depths. "Good," was all she whispered, that word carrying to him without emotion; not with rancor nor relief nor sadness. "Good," was all she said and Stephen had no more questions for her. They sat in silence for another half an hour until at last Rosey stood and walked over to the matron who waited in the corner.

Stephen heard the heavy door unlocked and heard his wife shuffle from the room and down the long corridor and out of his life.

The fire popped and an ember landed before him. Little blue flames surrounded it briefly and then it merely glowed and smoked, finally cooling on the cold stone hearth. Her heard Christina sigh in her sleep and he looked over his shoulder to his wife in their bed.

The end.

Printed in the United States
6254